SERVANT AND MISTRESS

T0272920

Servant and Mistress

THAMES RIVER PRESS
An imprint of Wimbledon Publishing Company Limited (WPC)
Another imprint of WPC is Anthem Press (www.anthempress.com)
First published in the United Kingdom in 2013 by
THAMES RIVER PRESS
75–76 Blackfriars Road
London SE1 8HA

www.thamesriverpress.com

A CIP record for this book is available from the British Library.

ISBN 978-0-85728-134-0

This title is also available as an eBook

SERVANT AND MISTRESS

LUCINDA RHYS-EVANS

THAMES RIVER PRESS

Prologue

What you are about to read is a true story based on the journals and jottings of the writer and academic Stephen Mason, whose ten erotic tales – published alongside this volume under the title *The Servant and Mistress Stories* – have achieved some notoriety.

Stephen's sister, a friend of one of my university colleagues, contacted me and gave me the material. As a key relative, she had been required to go to Hong Kong to identify her brother's body and sort out his affairs. In the course of clearing his Mid Levels apartment, she had discovered a box marked 'Confidential.' When, three months later and back in England, she opened it, she was so upset by what she found inside, she taped the box up again and sent it to me.

She remembered her brother as a kind, witty and sensible man, and did not want to read anything that might destroy that memory. However, as she knew I was interested in male sexuality and familiar with Hong Kong – and was aware that, in life, Stephen had always wanted to help others – she felt I might be able to make productive use of the material. Her only condition was that all names be changed.

As author, I have tried to stay in the background, letting the journals and jottings tell their own tale. At times, I have used direct quotations, and, at others, reconstructed events and thought processes and put them in the third person. I have made full use of email exchanges stored on a computer disc found in Stephen's box and have filled in gaps in the narrative, particularly in the last chapters, as a result of my own research.

The ten short stories are available in a separate volume that can be read before or after finishing this volume – or indeed in parallel with it. In essence, they tell the same tale in parable form: the tale of a person seeking the ultimate sexual and, perhaps, in a perverse way, ultimate romantic experience – a person progressing, or regressing, inexorably towards his death.

Lucinda Rhys–Evans

PART ONE
THE CELLAR DOOR

According to a journal found after his death in Macau in July 2001 – a journal that will be quoted from extensively in this reconstruction of his last months – it was just before Christmas 2000 that Stephen Mason began his search for a female partner to experiment with sexually.

On December 10th, he sent off a personal advertisement, along with a cheque for HK$120, to *Hong Kong Magazine*, a weekly what's-on guide for the city. On December 18th, under the heading 'Men seeking Women,' the magazine published the following text, having first checked with Stephen that the wording was correct:

> British writer and academic (50) – tall, slim, healthy and successful – wishes to explore his submissive side. He seeks a woman (35–50), who enjoys dominant role-playing, with whom he can share fantasies and form a mutually stimulating friendship. She has imagination and intelligence, speaks and reads English well and likes acting. Letter (+ photograph?) appreciated. Confidentiality respected.

The first reply Stephen received was from a policewoman named Angel. She was Chinese and aged forty. He met her for a drink in a Wanchai bar just two days after the advertisement appeared. She wore a red blouse, black leather miniskirt and knee-high black leather boots. Stephen, in a handwritten jotting later that evening, hoped she might be the 'right sort of woman.' She was not attractive in a conventional way and tended to mumble, but he could imagine her ordering him to do things that might disgust and excite him at the same time, so he agreed to meet her again, two days later, for dinner.

They met near the MTR station in Causeway Bay. He arrived by taxi and found her, as agreed, standing by the main entrance to Sogo department store. He was disappointed to discover she had exchanged her leather skirt and knee-length boots for a turquoise dress with matching stole and strapped high heels, but he put on a brave face and led the way towards the harbour. He was wearing black jeans, a black T-shirt and a dark grey corduroy jacket, a sombre contrast to the cockatoo cocktail dress of his date.

"I like your shoes," he said, lying.

"Thank you," she said, tottering along beside him as they headed north on an overcrowded, neon-lit street towards the harbour. "I got them in a sale."

"Not so easy to walk in as boots," he added with a smile.

"No," she replied with a giggle. "They're not."

They ate at the Excelsior Hotel in a Thai restaurant on the first floor. Stephen had to move tables twice to escape the air-con. The blue baseball cap, used to protect his close-cropped balding head from the icy winds of Hong Kong's over-cooled interiors, had been left at home. He felt it might affect his image as a prospective player.

Angel seemed unaffected by the relocations and consumed rice, lobster, udon noodles, garupa and various types of choi in quick succession, and again in parallel. She claimed to have been on a diet since the Mid-Autumn Festival, but judging from her – for a Chinese woman – full figure it must have been a chocolate and dim sum diet. After the last noodle had disappeared between her bright red lips, Stephen began the audition.

"Are you a plainclothes cop?"

It had occurred to him that the Hong Kong vice squad might be following up his ad, undercover. They had recently arrested two ex-pat civil servants at a leatherwear party in Lan Kwai Fong. Maybe, as a well-paid expatriate reader in creative writing at the prestigious Hong Kong Institute for the Arts, he was next.

"No," Angel said, as the waiter topped up their cups with over-brewed jasmine tea. "I'm a superintendent and wear a full uniform – even in the office."

"What's it like?"

"White blouse with epaulettes. Blue knee-length skirt, and boots."

"Smart," he said, seeing a chance of turning conversation in the desired direction.

"Do you like uniforms?" she asked with a grin.

"I might do. I don't really know."

He felt himself blushing. He should ask whether she wore stockings and what colour her police-issue panties were. He should show his hand and take a risk. But it was his first outing, and the only role he knew was that of the polite dinner companion, the conventional new man looking for a long-term partner in a non-predatory manner.

"Do you wear a gun, too?" he asked instead.

"Only if I'm on the street. On patrol."

He nodded.

"And handcuffs," she added, with what he thought was a suggestive smile.

"Oh, yes?" he chuckled, again missing his cue.

"Want to tie me up sometime?" would, perhaps, have been the experienced player's line. Or not? Perhaps the process was subtler than he realised. Perhaps there was some code between submissives and dominants, like that between gay men, a code to let each other know you were of the same persuasion – and available.

"How'd you like my ad?" he asked in a casual tone.

"Which was yours?"

His heart sank. She did not even know which advertisement he had placed.

"You answer a lot?"

"Quite a few. Don't you?"

"No," he replied, "only one up to now. And that was three years ago."

She laughed. He blushed again.

"This is the first time I've advertised," he continued, trying to stay calm.

"A man who doesn't play around. I like that."

His heart sank. Maybe his plan was a mistake. The meal would cost a bomb and he would have to pay; the Chinese did not go Dutch. He moved to wind up the audition.

"I'll get the …" he began, but she interrupted him.

"So what does your ad say?"

"What does it say?" he repeated.

She nodded and he decided to give her one more chance. He scanned her face, and settled on the crooked full-lipped mouth. He imagined it far above him, at the far end of long leather boots, blue starched skirt and crisp white blouse with epaulettes. He heard red-lipstick lips ordering him to put his hands up, saw police-trained fingers cuffing them together. She might still do. Perhaps the police force made sadists out of all its members. Perhaps she gained genuine pleasure from controlling other people.

"Well?" she asked, leaning forward until the stole dropped off her shoulders.

"Oh, something about me wanting to explore my submissive side," he said.

She looked at her plate, toyed with a remaining fish fin and glanced up again.

"What does submissive mean?"

The expression on her face was not that of a self-assured police superintendent used to wielding a whip; more that of an ugly duckling trying to curry favour.

"The opposite to dominant," he said.

He wanted to snap at her, he wanted to break down and cry. But he didn't. He kept his usual polite tone of voice. It wasn't her fault for not understanding. It was his fault for assuming she would speak perfect English as his recent Chinese partner, Su-yin, had. Hong Kong people spoke Cantonese as their mother tongue, not English. English was used for getting by abroad, talking to Filipino maids and – in emergency, when the home-grown men had all found second wives in China – for landing a rich expatriate husband.

"I like a man to be dominant," she said. "Someone who can take control."

When he got home that night, Stephen found a message from Angel on his answer machine. She said how much she had enjoyed the evening, and asked him to ring her back – she was already in bed and feeling lonely.

Stephen ignored the message and vowed to make a new start on the investigation after Christmas, when, he hoped, further responses to his advertisement would arrive in the post. And next time round, he would use his skills as a writer to describe what it was he wanted. He would put his fantasy down on paper and make it available to his potential partner – for information, or even enactment – so that there could be no confusion about the meaning of 'submissive' and 'dominant,' or the type of relationship he desired.

2

Before the Internet took off, people answered personal ads, such as those in *HK Magazine*, either by phoning a number, punching in an identity code and leaving a message or by writing a letter that was then forwarded by the magazine to the advertiser.

On 5th January, Stephen received a buff-coloured envelope with one letter inside. He was not optimistic. Since meeting Angel, he had received only two phone messages and no letters. The callers – one from Thailand and one from mainland China – spoke minimal English. The Thai woman repeated her one phrase, "Me young and beautiful," and the Chinese woman from Guangdong just laughed. The laugh was promising, but when pressed she laughed again and said, "Me no speak English." Stephen wondered how they read the ads. Perhaps there was an agency selling translations, or perhaps they were prostitutes put up to it by their pimps.

But the new letter was different. Typed on the centre of a blank sheet of A4 paper was a simple message: "Hi, I am a Chinese woman of forty-six who enjoys being dominant. I am happy to help you explore your submissive side. Please ring me on 9254 7592." That was all. Stephen felt a chill run down his spine, and a twinge of anxiety knot his stomach. This was the real thing, the first letter to respond directly to the key part of the advertisement, to the part that made it different.

★

I rang that evening at eight. Her voice was husky, flat and bored sounding, her English good, with a slight American twang. Educated woman in need of a thrill, I decided. Sure she'd meet me, she said. She was working late at the office right now – a firm of lawyers in Central – but she could make it in an hour. And yes, the Excelsior in Causeway Bay would be fine – she knew it well.

I showered, shaved, trimmed protruding nose hairs and, this time, donned black Versace jeans and a matching black D&G shirt, open at the neck. No need for a jacket; that was too conventional, too academic.

By eight-forty five, I was sitting in the hotel lobby surrounded by Japanese businessmen dressed in matching suits and ties. At eight fifty-five, my date entered through the revolving door. It had to be her. Apart from uniformed airline staff and the occasional *gweipo*, there were no other women in sight.

She came across and held out a hand.

"Stephen?"

"Sure," I said, standing up and shaking the proffered hand. "Nice to meet you…"

"Christine. Need a drink."

"Sure," I repeated, tuning in to her American intonation, and following her to the bar.

She picked a table in the smoking section, well away from the window, and ordered a pink gin. I ordered a Heineken. She was not a tall woman – maybe five foot five – but had on high heels, which brought her up to around five nine. She was dressed in a smart charcoal-grey suit with waisted jacket, and mid-thigh skirt. Her sparsely made-up face was lived-in with narrow lips, hollowed cheeks, black bags under the eyes and an age line or two across the brow. Her body was in good condition with a firm, rounded behind unusual on a Chinese woman.

As we waited for the drinks, her dark Asian eyes examined me without a hint of shyness or sentimentality.

"So?" she said. "What's your plan?"

My plan? No small talk, no finding out what I do or where I'm from? Just – what's my plan?

"What do you mean?" I said, smiling my new man smile, playing for time.

"How do you plan to go about exploring your submissive side?"

No smile on her part, just an enquiring gaze at the man sitting opposite.

"You sound like a lawyer," I said, retreating into calm conversational waters despite her willingness to put to sea.

"I'm a paralegal, not a lawyer. Only *gweilos* get to be lawyers in our firm. The white guys."

"Sure. I know what *gweilos* are."

Was this her motive? Resentment at privileged western men hiding behind their occidental glass ceiling, a desire to break the glass and steal their trousers?

"All white and all guys," she repeated, lighting up a Camel cigarette. "Work me to the bone, too. Most nights I'm not through till nine."

"Wow!"

She pocketed her lighter and blasted a plume of blue smoke into the already smoky air of the low-lit bar.

"Yeah. They'd fuck up without me." A hint of a smile, tinged with bitterness, flickered on her narrow lips and disappeared again. "Still, I didn't come here to talk shop. What's your plan?"

She wasn't letting me off the hook. She was forcing me on to the stage in a badly lit cellar frequented by unconventional types with unconventional tastes. She wouldn't be interested in, or impressed by, my straight theatre record or my monogamous credentials.

"I don't know exactly."

I hesitated, and was glad to see the waiter approach with our drinks. I watched him pour my beer, and when he had gone, I raised my glass to Christine.

"Cheers!"

She nodded curtly and took a slug of gin. I sank half the Heineken and felt Dutch courage fill my veins.

"Do you have things you enjoy doing?" I asked. "That you'd like to try out?"

She shrugged her shoulders and took a drag on the Camel.

"You're the investigator," she said, exhaling. "I'm the one who's going to help."

"Of course," I said, trying not to slip back into my Hugh Grant persona. "Sure."

I took a second sip of beer and a handful of peanuts. She crossed her legs and I caught a flash of stocking and suspender.

"You wear stockings?" I asked, without thinking.

"Yeah. Any objections?"

"No. Not at all." I felt my cheeks redden. "Very few women do these days."

"Well, I do. Makes me feel different from the pricks upstairs."

"Great. I like stockings. I find them sexy."

No smile. Not even a nod of acknowledgement. Her face remained expressionless, inscrutable, hard and hungry – hungry for sex, or hungry for revenge, or some harsh mixture of the two. I felt scared. If I represented the white men she so resented, where would she draw the line between pain and pleasure?

"Do you enjoy being dominant?" I asked. "Physically, I mean."

"Depends," she said. "Wouldn't want to damage a guy. But having one at my mercy. Yeah, that turns me on. Yeah."

I felt relieved, my confidence returned.

"Shall I write a story?"

"What for?"

"For us to act out?"

For the first time, she smiled – a lecherous smile, a greedy smile.

"Sure. You're the writer," she said, stubbing out her cigarette. "Go ahead. Don't give me too many lines though."

"I'll do it tomorrow and give it to you on Thursday. OK?"

"That's quick, or is it already written?"

"No, it'll be a new story – for you, for us. And if you like it, we can do a performance at the weekend."

She nodded, unabashed by the directness of my proposal. I emptied my beer glass. I had done it. I had broken the new man's well-behaved mould. I was up and running.

"We shouldn't know too much about each other," I continued, stumbling over my words. "When we act it out, I mean. We'll play the parts as if we're strangers."

She nodded again, following my logic.

"We'll meet a couple of days before. I'll give you the story and that's it. No drink. No talk. And then, if you have questions – or want to change or add bits – you can ring me before the performance day. But I think we should do it as soon as possible."

"Sure," she said. "Why not?"

She seemed unfazed by my sudden stream of confidence. Maybe dominant women liked their submissive partners to be the planners. It suited me. I was in control of my own submission. I was writing the script, I was casting, I was directing. It was the ideal way of approaching things first time around.

★

Stephen's excitement grew over the next few days. He wrote a story called *The Dinner Invitation* and revised it several times. He met Christine in Admiralty MTR station and handed her the typed pages in a white envelope. "See you Sunday" were the only words exchanged, and then her high heels clicked off to the ticket barrier. He watched her swaying hips disappear into the crowd, and felt faint: a real life paralegal dissolving into a figment of his imagination, his words about to enter her and reappear as flesh.

At this point, some of you may wish to read the story Stephen gave Christine – the first of ten tales he wrote before his death that are now compiled in a companion volume to this entitled *The Servant and Mistress Stories*. If you read it now, you will, in one way, experience the same feeling of crossing the line between fiction and reality that Stephen did. But with an important difference: you will play out both the story, and Stephen's description of its re-enactment, in your head. It is up to you. Read it before, read it afterwards or read it – along with the other stories – when you have finished this, the main tale. The written word has always been in the reader's control, and though writers may prefer their work to be read from start to finish, some people cannot resist reading the last page first. They have to know what happens in order to be able to enjoy the story. Then everything is a question of how and why the end is reached, not of what that end will be. In this book, you already know Stephen will die, and you read on to find out the reasons for this tragedy. Whether you read the story written for Christine now, later or never will not affect that process – nor, unfortunately, change its writer's fate.

★

On Sunday, after breakfast, I reread the story and rehearsed it in detail. I set the table, put the footstool in place and checked the props and my costume. Then I stood on the stool and did a trial removal of my lower clothes. I became so excited I could not subdue my erection, even to urinate: the thought that we would soon act out the words I had written, without any further social interaction, transformed me into an overexcited child.

After the rehearsal, I went shopping for a new dress shirt. Outside it was cool and sunny, with low humidity in the mid-sixties. I walked down the hill to Stubbs Road and caught a number six bus into town. Sitting at the front of the upper deck, watching the Sunday crowds form on Queen's Road East, I felt like a teenager preparing for his first date. The date on which he knows he will kiss, or be kissed, for the first time.

At Pacific Place, I descended from the bus and entered the shopping centre. I ascended an escalator to Lane Crawford's, the top people's store that dominates the northern front of the mall, and ran straight into the stench of its cosmetics department. Counter girls in house livery and *maquillage du jour* stared at me, hoping I was there to buy a New Year's gift for my *tai-tai* or mother. I ignored them and walked on through Furnishings, Bedlinen, Glassware and Haberdashery to Gentlemen's Clothing.

An attendant in a funeral-parlour suit approached me.

"Sir?" he inquired, Chinese male imitating English butler, a legacy of empire.

"I'm after a dress shirt," I said.

"And the occasion, sir?" he oiled.

I imagined rows of middle-aged Caucasian men ordering dress shirts for sexual charades, and Slimeball knowing their answers would be a lie.

"A dinner party."

"A dinner party. Nothing too showy then, sir?"

"No. Pleats rather than frills I think. And not too modern."

I cheered the departure of the British in 1997, but could still play the colonial.

"Just a minute, sir. Please take a seat."

I sat and felt momentarily depressed – teenage-kisser on a first date replaced by middle-aged man past his sell-by date. Was I bravely pushing back a border to discover new territory, or merely grubbing around in the wasteland of a deep frozen adolescence?

By midday, I was back at my flat with a new dress shirt laid out, lines learnt and the requisite crudités prepared. An hour later the doorbell rang. I opened it. Christine stood on the threshold wearing a casual blouse and trousers, and carrying a small Louis Vuitton case. We had agreed to change into costume after she arrived, as, in the story, she was the hostess and I the guest. Once dressed, we would stay in role until the action was complete.

"Am I early?" she asked.

"No," I replied. "Dead on time. Please come in."

She entered and I closed the door behind her. She stood, case in hand, without speaking. I again noticed the firm lines of her body.

"Do you want something to drink?" I asked. "Before you change?"

She shook her head.

"Nervous?" I added.

Again she shook her head.

"No, not nervous. Just trying to remember my lines."

I laughed and told her not to worry about lines, as long as the main events and conclusion of the story were included. We stood in silence for a moment, then I showed her into the spare bedroom, closed the door and went to change myself.

Ten minutes later I heard her enter the living room and pour a drink. This was my cue. I left the safety of my bedroom and knocked on the imaginary door of her imaginary penthouse in Old Peak Road.

"Come in," she said, her voice in character no different from her voice in real life.

My first disappointment, the realization that what I had imagined in fiction might not be what I got in the flesh, was her dress.

Instead of the fifties-style, full-skirted, satin cocktail dress described in the story, she had chosen a tight fitting sleeveless black number, with a low back and a hem set two inches above the knee. I was immaculate in dinner jacket, black bow tie, dress shirt and cummerbund. Just what the script demanded.

"You're looking smart," she said, improvising as suggested.

"Thank you," I replied.

I have acted on stage before and am not scared of an audience, but as Angel, the name I had given Christine's character in the story, sat down on one of the two leather sofas and asked me, in line with the script, to pour myself a whisky, I realised my actor's state of preparedness was the opposite to the relaxed and receptive state of a reader.

Readers, sitting in bed or on the sofa, are not subject to the physical and psychological pressures of the situation they are reading about. The scene is recreated in their minds, insulating them from direct involvement at the same time as keeping them, like a good conductor of electricity, at the centre of the action. It is virtual reality at its best. But the reality I found myself in, as Christine and I began to act out the story that I had written and she had read, was not virtual and not imagined. Nor, though we had both agreed not to step out of role except in emergency, was it real. It was a theatrical pretence held together, not by the presence of an audience, but by the mutual agreement of two performers, two virtual strangers. The idea was to have fun, but, as I sipped whisky and chitchatted about life in London with my make-believe hostess, I was not. And as our story progressed, as we moved from conventional chit-chat on the sofa to titillation at the table, as the moment approached when she would – as she must, if she was to stay in character – force me to expose the 'little difference' that makes the male actor in pornography unable to pretend, so the gap between me and my performance, between my real feelings and my acted feelings, widened until it was unbridgeable.

Following the footstool episode that had so excited my imagination earlier, I felt nothing for most of the rest of the performance, but, like a good 'trooper,' I kept going. After making me eat her underwear, she changed the script and made me lick cream off her nipples. She was doing better than me. She was enjoying herself. I could smell and taste her excitement, despite the sickly sweetness of Mr Whippy, and I did my best to match her enthusiasm. The show must go on. But only in the last scene, with Christine, as per script, demanding that I masturbate myself in front of her, did I manage to bring character, actor, self and imagination together for the short time it took me to come.

Afterwards, as I lay on the floor, wet with fluids from her and me, I felt I had entered myself in the wrong race and fallen at the first fence, or chosen the wrong jockey.

"Did you enjoy it?" she mumbled, half-opening her eyes.

"Sort of," I lied. "Not sure I'm a masochist though."

"My fault," she said. "I kept getting lines mixed up. And the order of events."

"Yes," I said, standing up to pull on my underpants. "Easier for me. Fewer lines!"

"Be better second time round," she said, reaching for her dress. "More relaxed."

Second time round? I wasn't sure.

I wanted to forget the whole episode and return to my role as a conventional serial-monogamist, who charms the pants off sexually conventional women in a sexually conventional manner. The perverse and persistent will o' the wisp that, since my breakup with Su-yin, had emerged so forcefully from my unconscious would have to wait.

3

But, a week later, Stephen had recovered from his session with Christine and was ready to try again. He told himself it had been a first attempt, a first experiment, and that it did not prove, one way or another, whether he was a fringe player at heart. The important thing was that he had taken the plunge. He had moved from theoretical research in his mind to field study in the flesh. And now he was ready to dive in again. In fact, he was impatient to do so because, looking back at his first swim, he felt the same sense of excitement and arousal he had experienced when looking forward to it. He had suffered stage fright, been too self-conscious – as he sometimes was at the start of conventional sexual encounters – and now he was keen to repeat the experience with someone new.

So when – after a weekend spent walking on Lantau with his work colleague Connor – a second buff-coloured envelope from *Hong Kong Magazine* dropped into his mailbox, he tore it open with renewed zeal. Inside he found a smaller, chocolate-coloured envelope with a copy of his advertisement pasted on the back. Inside that, a white card folded in two. Inside the card, glued to the top left hand corner, a two-millimetre strip of photograph cut from the centre of a larger picture. Part of a woman's face and body could be discerned, but the figure was in shadow and remained opaque. On the right hand side, a short text had been printed: 'Dear British Writer, Feeling nervous to write to you. I don't know much about my English. But my imagination and creativity is brilliant. If you are nice to me, I will be much nicer to you. I am Asian, middle of 30s, healthy and hope to hear from you: aiaiaiai32@hotmail.com.'

He sent a mail from his computer at work and received a reply from a Japanese woman of 36 named Aioko. Her English was seductive in its playful misuse of language, juxtaposition of unrelated items and creation of non-existent composite words. She said she was a dog lover but not interested in rugby, a cat lover but not interested in fortune telling. She enjoyed steak and kidney pie but did not think cranberry sauce suitable for turkeys. The originality of her wording made Stephen reply instantly and, in one mail, he told this stranger more about himself than he had told Christine in an entire evening.

★

On Friday, after work, I walked across Harcourt Gardens in the chill air of a dank January twilight, descended into the underpass that led to Pacific Place and took a lift to the Marriott Hotel – a grander location with more sense of place than the Excelsior in Causeway Bay. I entered the lobby area and sat down on the largest of the leather sofas.

There were several women waiting, all in their thirties and all Asian.

Despite our mail exchanges, Aioko had said little about her looks, and the snippet of photograph was too opaque to be of use. She would be wearing a blue skirt and white blouse, she had said in her morning mail, and I must approach her as she would be too nervous to approach me. In a further mail, just before the meeting, she wrote: 'My Aioko Japan office-worker heart beats fast at thought of meeting British successful writer.' I did not reply, but sensed there was going to be something different about this, my first Japanese woman, something I had not come across before in other women – or men.

Two of the females had on blue skirts and white blouses. I opted for the more conventionally attractive of the two, seated directly across from me. Her face was round and lightly made-up, her figure pleasantly full. Her white blouse was plain, and her skirt tight to the knee. I leant across and coughed. The woman glanced at me and turned away.

"Excuse me?" I said. "Are you by any chance Aioko?"

"No, I am not," she replied, picking up the magazine on her knee.

I stared over at the other woman, a diminutive figure with a small, angular, mouse-like face and a frail looking body. Only the calves, rising out of a pair of sensible black shoes, showed any sign of robustness. My eyes caught hers and she gave a nod and a wisp of a smile. I stood up and walked over to where she was sitting.

"I know you choose her," she said, the look of a hurt child filling her face.

"Aioko?" I said with relief.

She nodded, rose to her feet and bowed.

She was tiny, five foot at the most, with no flesh to speak of apart from the powerful calves now supporting her minimal frame. Her face was heavy with makeup, and, as she smiled, I noticed her teeth were stained brown in places.

"Disappointed?"

"Not at all," I lied. "She was the nearest. That's why I tried her first."

"Ooooh," said Aioko, with a long drawn-out, upward-ascending sound. "I see."

I felt a shiver slither down my spine.

The long drawn out 'Oh!' was pure Japanese in sound, range and style; a distinctive intonation that struck a chord somewhere in my brain — a distant echo of Kurosawa films, watched at school in the chemistry lab to the accompaniment of a rattling projector. This sound, along with her angular face and Japanese office-worker's uniform — she worked as a secretary for Toshiba — made her immediately exotic and mysterious to me.

"A drink?" I suggested, holding my arm out towards the bar.

"Yes, please," she said, with a kind of half-giggle.

"After you."

She giggled again, hunched her shoulders up towards her chin and set off down the steps to the lounge bar. We picked a low coffee table in a far-flung corner and sat down opposite each other on two upholstered armchairs in salmon pink. She gazed across at me, cocked her head to one side and giggled again.

"Oh dear," she said. "Very nervous."

"No need," I said, trying to put her at ease with an avuncular smile.

She shivered and nodded.

"Perhaps wine will help. You drink wine?"

"No," I said. "But I'll have a beer to keep you company."

"May I order a bottle?" she whispered, leaning forward and screwing up her mouth like a child on the wangle with dad.

"Yes, of course," I replied.

I knew Japanese women, like Hong Kong women, expected men to pay. But that was all right. I had gone Dutch enough in my life, and something about her made me feel protective.

"I like wine," she said, picking up a pistachio from the silver bowl on the table in front of us and peeling off the husk.

"You drink a lot?"

She nodded again.

"I've had a difficult year."

"Oh," I said, in a non-committal manner.

I felt protective towards her, but did not want to become a father confessor straight off, if at all. I was too good at that – that was the stuff of the conventional long-term primary relationship I aimed to steer clear off this time around.

"Mmmm," she murmured, with her upward ascending tone, this one starting even deeper in her throat and ascending to the very top of her head. "Mmmm. I've been a little crazy. *Baka*, we say in Japanese."

She nodded again, more to herself than to me, and tears filled her eyes.

My defences – my intention of remaining a hard-nosed, fringe investigator in search of new thrills – were swept away by the forlorn little face in front of me.

I leant across and put a hand on her shoulder.

"Do you want to talk about it?"

She shook her head and pursed her lips to hold back the tears.

"I don't mind," I continued. "I'm a good listener."

"Thank you, British successful writer," she said, smiling through her tears. "But I think English will be too bad. And we only just meet. And…"

A second wave of tears welled up, hovered in her eyes, lost their equilibrium as she blinked and rolled down her cheek. I offered her a paper napkin.

"Please."

"You're a very kind writer," she whispered, wiping the tears from her cheek, and then added. "As well as successful."

"I'm not so successful," I laughed, with a deprecatory gesture. "A few scripts here and there. The odd short story and academic paper."

"More successful than me, I think."

She screwed up her face and stared down at her lap.

We sat in silence for a moment, and then the bottle of wine and an ice cold Beck's arrived. I waved the waiter away and poured her a glass of the house red.

"Drink this."

I handed her the glass, picked up the beer – which had been decanted into a tall tumbler with Heineken stamped on the side – and watched as her thin lips sipped the wine, still trembling as they did so. Her eyes were red from crying and she continued to keep her gaze averted from mine.

But, after a few sips, she revived, blew her nose – discreetly, in a Japanese way – and began to talk.

"I'm a married woman. Confidentiality is important. That's why I answered *your* ad, 'Confidentiality respected' you wrote. I wouldn't want people to know I meet you."

I nodded, but refrained from pointing out that this was our first meeting and that there was no guarantee we would meet again. And it was, in every way, a first meeting. Despite our detailed mail exchanges, we were strangers in the flesh.

"I don't live with my husband," she continued, taking a clean napkin and wiping the corner of her eyes with care, to avoid smudging the mascara. "But am still married, and people know I'm married, and for a Japanese lady that's…"

"Your husband is Japanese?" I interrupted.

"Not this one. First husband Japanese. This husband Hong Konger. Chinese."

And her story did not get any simpler. But when I had pieced it together, from her fragmented and impressionistic English, it ran something like this:

She had come to Hong Kong twelve years ago with her first husband, a – in her words – "boring Japanese businessman husband," and spent the first six years attending tea parties for other wives of boring Japanese businessmen husbands. She herself had been bored to tears – "bored boring Japanese businessman wife" – and had eventually asked husband number one for a divorce. He had agreed and returned to Japan. There had been no children. She had survived on her own for a while, landed the job at Toshiba and then met her current husband – "good friend Hong Kong Chinese man."

Well, used to be good friend. After five years of marriage, things had gone wrong there too. One evening, nine months ago, they had a row about something she had cooked – or hadn't cooked – and, after that, he refused to speak to her for six months.

"Even if I speak to him," she said, on the brink of tears again. "He refuses to answer. Just looks the other way."

"Very cruel," I said, waving to the waiter to bring another beer.

"Made me *baka*, crazy," she continued, filling up her glass for the third time and wiping a lone tear from her left eye with a nail-varnished little finger.

"I should think so."

She had survived, she said, by going to the cinema – "every evening six weeks, sometimes same film four times" – and visiting friends. Then, one Saturday morning, when she could no longer tolerate the silence of exile in Coventry – or its Sino-Japanese equivalent – she packed a case and boarded a ferry to the island of Cheung Chau. She found herself a cheap apartment, commuted to work each day by boat and, at weekends, began her first artistic endeavour – decorating mirrors with shells from a nearby beach.

"I used to be designer. In Japan. Before first marriage."

"That's where the creativity and imagination come in."

"Yes," she said. "Both husbands do not like me doing art work. So, I do not do. Or, maybe, I cannot do – if they are there. Living alone, it returns – slowly. The art."

She sounded like me. The artist, who cannot live 'with or without' someone, the person who needs to be alone to create, yet hankers for the warmth and security of love.

"And now you live apart, do you talk to your husband? Your second husband?"

She nodded.

"We meet once or twice a month. He seems happier. Mmm."

A long, reflective, ascending tone – starting with a frown and ending with a smile.

"Perhaps you should divorce him."

"No," she said firmly. "He's my husband."

"You did it before."

"This is different"

She did not elaborate, and I did not probe. I was suffering from information overload and beginning to doubt whether Aioko, as potential investigative assistant to my personal investigation, was worth pursuing.

Then I remembered her note: 'If you are nice to me, I will be much nicer to you.'

What would 'nicer' mean? I was curious. I was also a kind-hearted man, used to helping those in trouble, so I decided to stay and be nice to her, at least until she had finished her bottle of wine.

"You mean you've not met anyone else?"

Her eyes flashed at me with something approaching anger then softened.

"Of course. The writer. Sees everything."

"So you have?"

An even more complex story began, involving a group of Japanese friends – mostly female – who had treated her as the 'servant girl,' as the 'good sort' good for a laugh, the party organizer with the extra dollars and a shoulder to cry on. She organized the outings, booked the restaurants, paid the lion's share and took the rap for failed activities. She was the group's mascot and scapegoat. Though less robust of constitution than her peers, she was expected to keep up with them. Drink enormous amounts, go to bars four nights a week and party on the beach at weekends: a manic – and for her masochistic – social whirl that drove her more *baka* than the silence of hubby. In particular, the group leader made her mad. She was a sadistic woman who took pleasure in loading Aioko's shoulders with alternate sacks of praise and pressure, and using the 'little one' as confidante or whipping girl dependant on mood and time of the month.

Then one day last November, on a Saturday night after a drunken party, Aioko stole the group leader's lover.

"The leader wasn't married?" I asked.

"Yes, leader had husband, but leader had extra boyfriend too. Aioko steals boyfriend. Then Aioko has boyfriend and husband! *Totemo baka ne?*"

She burst out laughing and took a swig of wine.

Keeping up with the group's bacchanalian habits could not have been that difficult for her. Alcohol was a familiar fuel and the more she drank, the more her eccentric English suffered. But with me filling in the gaps and providing subtitles, a picture emerged of a woman caught at the centre of a complex web. The leader's stolen boyfriend – a married American living in Europe and occasionally visiting Hong Kong on business – had, after defecting from the leader and bringing new light into the 'little one's' dark, silent life, himself been unfaithful to Aioko. When he came to Hong Kong she met him in his hotel, and, on his last visit, she had found a blonde hair on the bed. She questioned him about it, but he dismissed her suspicions, saying it must belong to one of the maids. But all maids were Chinese or Filipino. She knew that. So he was lying.

The wine was finished. Her depression and tears returned. It was time to go.

"I'm sorry," she sobbed. "You won't want to see *baka* Japanese lady again."

And, probably, I should not, though somehow I think I will. Aioko-san. It sounds so different. She sounds and looks so different – her way of talking, her Japanese mannerisms, her sudden changes of mood. I am intrigued by her otherness, by her imagination and creativity, by her complexity. Complex and creative women in difficult situations have never put me off. I see them as a challenge, as people to be helped. I must be careful, of course. I must keep my distance, and not forget the main aim – a Japanese angle on the investigation. And, maybe, that is all she wants from me – an English adventure to ease her pain. We will see.

4

The next day Stephen received an email from Aioko.

In it, she thanked him for listening to her story and asked whether he would like to meet again. He replied that, as he had to move out of his Mid Levels flat for a couple of days while a new parquet floor was laid, he would contact her next week when he returned from the hotel his landlord had agreed to pay for as temporary accommodation.

He pressed the send button, expecting no further contact until after the weekend. But, thirty minutes later, when he returned to his email account to send a memo to the Institute's personnel office, there was another message from aiaiaiai36@hotmail.com: 'Wow, Stephen-san! Successful British writer so successful landlord pays for hotel! Can I visit you there on Friday after work – definitely not in crying mode? Aioko.'

He should have said no and, if it had been a letter or a message on his voicemail, he would have done so after a minute's reflection. But personal emailing was a new game for Stephen. He read the message and then, without thinking, pressed the reply button and wrote: 'If you visit successful British writer in hotel, you must be wearing Japanese office worker's uniform as before (along with best silk panties!) and be prepared to play a game. Understand if you'd rather wait for next drink!'

He read it through, chuckled to himself and pressed the send button.

Five minutes later a mail arrived to say the Japanese office worker would be there at seven. Successful British writer must let her know the hotel's name and remember to 'bring bottle of wine and beer, to avoid expense of mini-bar.' Stephen did some quick thinking, but his thoughts did not include turning down the offer. He was on a roll, and rolling too fast to spot pitfalls in his path. He debated using one of the two stories he had written since meeting Christine – the first inspired by an attractively severe Indian woman in the Institute's personnel department, the second by his Filipino cleaner – but, in the end, decided to improvise. Aioko, he sensed, had a vivid imagination and would prefer spontaneity to a pre-scripted plot.

★

I checked in at lunchtime – room 1705, double bed, beige carpet, dark wood furniture and large television. My landlord was prepared to pay HK$1000 a night and I had chosen the Renaissance Harbour View Hotel in Wanchai. It was near work, offered an off-season deal and was big enough to be discreet. After a room service lunch of tuna salad, I returned to the Institute and sent a mail to Aioko. I addressed her as 'Japanese Office Worker' and said I expected her at seven o'clock, dressed as requested. I gave her the hotel name and my room number and signed myself, 'Successful British Boss.'

After work, I returned to the hotel, showered and put on a T-shirt and jeans. By seven o'clock I was relaxed and ready to go. Being away from home and having no lines to learn increased the erotic charge and decreased the tension I had felt with Christine.

I heard a knock, crossed the room, opened the door and found Aioko standing at attention in a white blouse, blue skirt and high heels – her lips lipstick-red, her eyes dark with mascara and no hint of the melancholy features I had seen at the Marriott.

"Japanese Office Worker reporting for duty," she said, with her trademark hunching of the shoulders and half-giggle. "May I come in?"

"Of course," I replied. "Make yourself at home."

She marched in, unpacked her overnight bag, inspected and made use of the bathroom, fetched me a beer from the fridge and then handed me the bottle of wine together with a corkscrew provided by the hotel.

"Please! British successful boss task, I think."

I pulled the cork and poured her a glass. She produced two packets of prawn potato crisps, and emptied the contents into a bowl.

"There! Office worker's task done! Cheers! *Kanpai*!"

She raised her glass. I opened my beer can and toasted her. I was not a drinker, but Aioko gave me little choice.

"I thought we might order a room service meal, before…"

"We play the game you mentioned in your mail?"

"Yes. Eat first, then game."

"Ooh, how exciting!" she exclaimed, hunching her shoulders and giggling.

With repetition, giggle and hunch took on an artificial, almost manic air, though not enough to disturb. Some form of Japanese flirtation no doubt and, like all flirtation, performed to conceal deeper feelings.

I watched her sip the wine and wondered what I had let myself in for.

"I think you like me like this?" she said, aware of my eyes on her body.

She crossed her legs and fluttered her eyelashes. Her navy blue, single-pleat office skirt rode up her thigh and, again, I noticed the firmness of her calves.

"Yes! Just how a Japanese office worker should be!"

Aioko hunched and giggled and took another sip of wine.

"Shall we eat?" I asked.

"Yes, please."

We ordered a mountain of food – soup noodles, pizza, chicken, salad and rice –and when we had finished, Aioko cleared the dishes and handed me a second can of beer.

"What are the rules, Writer-san?" she asked, her face glowing. "Of your game."

"Simple," I replied. "Once we start, you are the boss. You can ask me to do anything for, to or with you – or with myself – apart from kissing and intercourse."

"Intercourse?" she inquired.

"Penetration. My thing inside your thing."

"*Wakarimashita*. Understood."

"But anything else."

"Wow! *Baka no saka desu ne?*"

"I beg your pardon?"

"'Baka' means 'crazy,' 'saka' means 'writer.'"

"You don't want to play?"

"*Mochiron* – of course. I'm 'baka' too, remember?"

I nodded. A couple of 'crazies' in a hotel room – office worker and boss about to swap roles, with no guarantee of the outcome.

"Good. From now until midnight you are the boss."

I glanced at my watch. The second hand was approaching nine o'clock. I waited for it to reach the top, waited for it to cover the '12' and then looked up.

"Go!"

Aioko stopped smiling and observed me. Perhaps wondering if I meant what I had said, perhaps getting into role.

She sat in silence for a while and then spoke.

"Fetch me clean glass for my wine. Quick!"

I fetched a glass and placed it on the table. I was about to pour the wine, when she raised a hand to stop me, held up the glass and inspected it.

"Not clean. Please wash!"

I did as she asked. She accepted the clean glass, gulped down the wine I had poured and told me to run a bath.

When I returned, she was on the bed. She had removed her blouse and skirt and now wore only a white bra and pink satin panties. She arched her bottom towards me.

"You like?"

"Very much."

"Not too small?"

"Small but powerful."

It was small but shapely and, encased in satin, delicate as a piece of porcelain.

"A power bottom," she giggled, and then resumed her stern tone. "Kiss it!"

I walked across to the bed, knelt down and kissed the taut satin.

"Mmm!" she sighed.

I kissed again, feeling my body respond to this mild humiliation.

"That's enough!" she snapped. "Check bath!"

I went to the bathroom.

"Lots of bubbles and hot!" she called. "Japanese lady like hot bath."

I reduced the flow of cold, added bath oil and tried to stop thinking. Relax and enjoy, let the mind go. She's in charge – don't think, just obey.

"Come here!"

I returned to the bedroom.

"Kiss my bottom again!"

I bent and kissed the soft satin. Again, I felt excitement mount.

"Enough!" she snapped. "Carry me to bathroom and put me in bath."

She saw the concern on my face, but offered no sympathy.

She arched her bottom, slipped off her panties and removed her bra. Her pubic mound was shaved and smooth – her breasts small with sharp, dark-coloured nipples.

"Before you pick me up," she said, "remove clothes."

I chuckled to myself. This was like one of my stories.

I removed my shirt, slipped off my socks, unbuckled my belt and stepped out of the black jeans, but did not remove my underpants. I preferred to keep my outward indicator of arousal under wraps, not because I was ashamed, but because women often assumed that an indicator not standing at twelve o'clock was a sign of failure on their part, a sign that the man was not aroused.

"Come here," she commanded.

I stood before her. She rolled the underpants down to my knees and watched as the second hand made it to three o'clock. And then sank back to four.

"Carry me!" she hissed, unconcerned by the clock's performance.

I would have preferred to kiss her bottom again, but if a man says to a woman: you may do anything you please, she will do just that – please herself. This was the paradox of my investigation. If the woman enjoyed being dominant, it might be in a way that left me cold. If she was pretending to enjoy, in order to please me, she was no different from the paid prostitute. I wanted the woman to enjoy herself, at the same time as reaching a new level of pleasure myself. Was I asking too much? Were there such women? Women who enjoyed bossing men, women who took pleasure in humiliating them? And if there were, were they what I wanted? Or did I just want alternative sex, an alternative to the intercourse I now found so boring and boorish?

Head buzzing, I lifted Aioko, carried her to the bathroom and lowered her into the bath. I felt a twinge in my back and winced. She seemed unaware of my difficulty and lay back with her hair spread out across the rear rim of the bath.

"Writer-san more strong than I think. Mm! Perhaps real man after all!"

She glanced at my second hand to see what time it was. I wanted her to reach out and pull it up to twelve o'clock. I wanted her to squeeze my nipples. I wanted to be in the bath, her hand between my legs, fondling me.

The second hand moved in time with my imagination, and she took the credit.

"You like Aioko-san in bath, yes?"

I nodded.

"Good. Please wash her. Every bit."

I washed her breasts and shoulders, her back and stomach, and then she rolled over and I soaped her well-muscled calves and porcelain behind. I put my fingers gently between her legs and felt her wetness mix with the soap and water on my hand. She closed her eyes and moaned, squeezed her thighs together and let me play with her.

"Not yet!" she snapped after a while. "Fetch me wine!"

I did as she asked and placed a new glass of wine on the edge of the bath.

"Now go. I want to be alone."

She was playing the game for real, enjoying the exercise of power, but, for me, having no control was not what I had imagined. I lay down on the bed, tail between my legs – a dog dismissed by its mistress. I debated getting dressed and sneaking out of the hotel, then decided against it. I must persist with each separate investigation – learn from each experience, without losing heart.

I did not have to see this Japanese woman again; there would be other letters.

"Want to get out. Towel, please."

Aioko's high-pitched voice disturbed my reverie.

I rolled off the bed, went to the bathroom, unfolded a white towel and held it up for Aioko. She stepped out of the bath and I wrapped her up in the soft cotton, patting her dry from top to bottom. She curled up in my arms and put her thumb in her mouth.

"Little tiny Aioko," she whispered, half in a dream.

Suddenly I felt close to this fragile figure and, disregarding the rules I had set for the game, I bent to kiss her lips. But, as I did so, big, demanding Aioko returned.

"Carry me to bed!" she commanded.

I took a deep breath, bent my knees and lifted her body into my arms. Her head rested on my shoulder and I smelt wine on her breath. I laid her on the bed – stomach down as requested – and watched as she put her head on the clean white pillow and closed her eyes. Maybe she would sleep. Maybe that was the best way to end the game.

I crept towards the bathroom to clean my teeth, but was summoned back.

"Power bottom needs massage!"

I returned and stroked her behind, letting my fingers run up and down its crease.

"Mmmm!" she moaned. "British successful writer's hands very soft!"

"Good," I whispered. "Relax and go to sleep."

"*Nani*?" she exclaimed, spitting out the Japanese word for 'what.' "Game not finished, Writer-san! Game not finished!"

I glanced at the time. She was right. Eleven o'clock. One hour to go.

She rolled over and pointed at her nipples.

"With mouth."

I sucked her right nipple, then her left one. She made no attempt to touch me, but lay with her hands by her side, eyes closed. I brushed my lips down across her stomach to the shaven mound between her legs.

"Oh no!" she cried, spreading her legs wider.

I continued, letting my tongue and forefinger explore the opening.

"Oh no, oh no," she cried, pushing my head between her thighs. "More. More!"

I licked harder. My finger slipped inside, pressed up against the wall of her vagina and slid in and out. She was very wet.

"Oh no," she repeated. "Harder. More."

My tongue was tired, but she kept my head clamped between her thighs.

"Oh no," she yelled again, and this time added: "It's no good! Oh no!"

She pushed my head away and started to play with herself, her fingers gouging into her hole and flailing back and forth.

"That's it," I encouraged. "Come for me."

"I want to, I want to," she screamed. "But no good!"

I put one hand on her breast and slid the other down to help her efforts. But she had both hands at work, with no room for mine.

"It's no good! No good! Ohhh!"

With a loud ascending tone, she arched her back off the bed, pulled and squeezed her clitoris with one hand, and jammed the fingers of the other through her legs and up her vagina from behind. She was forcing herself, hurting herself. Was it the only way she knew to reach an orgasm? I wanted to stop her. Tell her to be gentle, to come in her own good time, or not at all. No one was compelling her. She was the boss, not me.

She collapsed back on the bed, buried her head in a pillow and burst into tears. Her shoulders shook and shuddered with frustration.

"It's no good. It's no good. It's no good," she kept repeating.

I tried to comfort her but she pushed me away. I retreated to an armchair and watched her frame wrack itself with sobs. Was this how all evenings ended with Aioko – in tears? Was it the wine? Or me? Or something I brought out in her? No, I had not known her long enough for that. It must be a pattern, triggered by her troubles of the past year, or further back. Not my business, not part of my investigation.

Her sobbing subsided and she lay still. I crept to the bathroom, cleaned my teeth, then slipped under the sheet beside her and curled up, my face towards hers.

Her eyes opened and she grinned.

"Still the boss," she hissed. "One half-hour more. On your back, Writer-san!"

No. I did not want anymore. It was past bedtime. My body was sore, my mind sated. But I had to obey, or call the game off. And that would upset her more. She wanted to please me, though she was in no fit state to do so. I had not pleased her, she had not pleased herself; pleasing me was her last chance of a successful conclusion to the game.

I rolled on to my back. Her hand grabbed my penis and yanked it up and down. When the flesh refused to respond, she grabbed my balls and squeezed them. Still nothing. She wanted instant response. I was a slow-riser, in need of coaxing.

She rolled over and started laughing, the hollow laughter of a drunk person.

"What you like, Writer-san? What you like?"

"My nipples are quite sensitive," I said. "For a man."

"Ooohhhh!"

And with her longest ascending tone to date, Aioko launched herself on my small pink protuberances.

She squeezed and pinched the right one until it was sore, and then, seeing that this produced a positive reaction below, leant down and bit the left one, hard. My penis and body jumped upwards in an involuntary spasm of pain.

"You like that. Me, Japanese fencer! Very tough!"

She bent down and bit the left nipple again, so hard this time that I yelped and rolled away. I put my fingers up to where her teeth had been. Blood oozed and tears pricked my eyes. This was crazy. Not what I was after.

I turned back and found Aioko snoring beside me. The game was over.

5

I did not sleep well that night. My head was thick with thoughts and emotions. I hovered between two courses of action: waking Aioko and kissing her full on the mouth – it was strange to have done so much and not to have kissed – or packing my bag and leaving. In the end, I stayed. But my confused state was exacerbated by the room's location, beneath the hotel laundry. A dull thumping drummed into my brain. And when that stopped, Aioko's snoring started. Later, she cried out in her sleep, waking once with tears pouring down her cheeks. I wiped them away and curled my arm around her shoulders. She nestled up, like a child seeking comfort from a nightmare.

The grey of morning crept into the room. A foghorn penetrated the net curtains, and the mist of my mind. My eyes flickered. I was in a plane, in a snowstorm, and the pilot had asked me to take control. I was flying through the storm, landing in my mother's bedroom. She was asleep. I was creeping into bed beside her, cuddling up as close as I dared, frightened she would wake.

A foghorn sounded again, its tone deep and dark. I opened my eyes and gazed at the sleeping form beside me. Without makeup, in the cold light of day, Aioko was another person. No longer the *baka* office worker with manic smile and over-bright eyes, now a mature woman of thirty-six with grey hairs breaking through and worries lining the forehead of a serious face; a face which seemed softer than that of the Japanese fencer who had almost bitten off my nipple – a vulnerable face, in need of protection and care.

I bent and kissed her brow. She opened her eyes and stared at me in confusion. Then she smiled, a half-smile, and rolled on to her side away from me.

"Did my sneezing disturb you?" she said.

"Your sneezing?"

"Yes, I sneeze in my sleep. My husband complains."

"Your snore? Is that what you mean?"

She laughed, a grown-up laugh, not the giggle that went with the shoulder hunch.

"'Snore'? It's called 'snore,' what I do? Husband and I speak Japanese. I never learn English word."

"'Sneeze' is when you go 'Atishoo!'"

"A tissue?"

She laughed again

"Something like that."

"You can remember Aioko as the girl who sneezed in the night."

"Yes."

I climbed out of bed and drew back the net curtains. A cruise liner loomed in the mist outside the window, a Star Ferry weighed anchor at the Wanchai terminal below. I wanted to be on it, a commuter with a job in a bank or a shop or a restaurant, an everyday person with no compulsion to think things through and work things out. I wanted to be swallowed up by the mist and tucked into ordinary life; on a ship, a train or a plane – going somewhere, anywhere, my destination pre-ordained, not open to question.

I walked across the anonymous room.

The air smelt of cleaning fluid and air freshener, the thick-pile carpet tickled my feet. By the door, I put on a pair of complementary slippers and switched on the kettle.

"Tea?" I called

"Mm! No milk, no sugar. *Arigato*."

I made two cups and set them down either side of the bed. Aioko sat up and leant forward. I propped up the pillows behind her. She sank back into the soft white wall, her fragile face wiser than the night before, the playful child grown old. I climbed in beside her, and we sat sipping tea like a married couple.

"First man I know to drink tea in bed. First man to bring me tea in bed," she murmured.

"Early morning tea is an important ritual for me."

"Like Japanese tea ceremony – only in bed," she observed.

"Yes. When I was small, my mother let me join her in bed and share her morning cup. When I was older, she would bring one to my room."

"Nice mother."

"Not always, but she taught me the importance of early morning tea."

"Oooh."

A quiet, relaxed ascending tone, like the cooing of a wood-pigeon in the coolness of an English summer morning

"And ever since I have made it myself, almost every day of my life."

"Never someone else make for you?" she inquired sleepily.

"No. It helps me get up. The first getting-up is to make tea. I know I will return to bed, so it makes it easier. And then, when I have to rise in earnest, I am refreshed by the tea and ready to go."

"Ooooh." Coo.

"It's an in-between place, an in-between time. A haven from the day ahead, a time to reflect on what's to come."

Silence again. The laundry vibrated above our heads and a kestrel, down from the Peak to catch breakfast, floated past the window, gliding on the humid harbour air.

"And digest what's gone before," I added

She nodded. Her head sank in thought, eyes closed, brow furrowed.

I sipped my tea.

Then she leant forward, put her cup down on the bedside table and turned to me.

"Writer-san?"

"Yes?"

"Before I go, I want to come."

"I'm sorry? I don't understand."

"You know," she pointed between her legs. "Down below."

"But…"

"And then that's it. We never see each other again. OK?"

"But…" I began again.

"Please, Writer-san. It's important to me. Please?"

We were no longer bound by the rules of the game, but saying no to heartfelt requests was impossible for me. Her expression was not flirtatious – there was no giggle; just a request from a serious-faced woman with no makeup and worry lines on her brow.

"But why?"

"I can't say. I want to come for you. Then I go. Meeting a success."

I thought for a moment, and then put down my teacup.

"You really want me to…?"

"Together. You start. I finish. That way best, I think."

The kestrel swept past again, this time swooping in search of prey. I was jealous. In my next life, I would be a bird. Birds do not indulge in oral sex, too painful with those pointed beaks.

But humans can and do, and my human bondage that morning meant slipping below the sheet to Aioko's mound, opening sealed lips and licking a sleepy clitoris awake. She moaned and writhed in a languid manner. Perhaps the self-inflicted violence of the previous night had been an attempt to break through the alcohol. Now she enjoyed herself in a sensuous way, and I went about my work with care – not rushing the pace or forcing the issue.

But as juices flowed and mixed with the taste of tea on my tongue, her movements became more jagged. My head was buffeted between her thighs, making it hard to keep my mouth in place. Muscled calves curled and uncurled around my torso, heels dug into my back. Then a tiny hand crept down and moved aside my lips.

"Your fingers inside. Me outside," she ordered. "Quick"

I inserted my forefinger and middle finger and slid them up and down against the front wall of her vagina. Her fingers squished, squashed and squeezed the long-suffering clitoris. Suddenly she threw back the sheet, arched her back and pelvis into the air – almost breaking my fingers in the process – and came with a cry of anguish.

"Oh no! *Iku*! *Iku*! Oh no!"

She collapsed back on the bed sobbing, and covered her face with a pillow. I remained frozen between her legs. I wanted to hug and kiss her. To say, "It's over now!" as if she had undergone some ordeal. Her hold on my head slackened. I eased myself up the bed and tried to lift the pillow. Her grip on it tightened. I rearranged the remaining pillows and returned to sipping tea.

After a minute or two, she climbed out of bed, showered and put on a grey T-shirt and jeans. She passed on makeup, packed her toothbrush and office uniform into her bag and said she must go. She gave me a bow, but no kiss – not even on the cheek.

When I said I could accompany her to the ferry terminal, she declined the offer. We should not be seen leaving the hotel together, she said. She bowed again and left.

As the door closed, I jumped out of bed and ran to open it, but stopped, my forefinger on the handle.

What did I have to say? Why would I call her back?

Five minutes later, the phone rang. My heart beat harder. Was it her? Had she changed her mind? Did she want me to come down and wave goodbye as she sailed away?

It was Aioko, but the voice was flat and tired, ordinary and worn to match the jeans and T-shirt. She had left her earrings by the bed. Could I leave them in an envelope at reception? She would pick them up another time. Just write 'Aioko' on the front. I said I would bring them down now. No, she said, she was at the ferry terminal and did not want to walk back. I could bring them there, I said. No, she said. She would pick them up another day. And with that, she cut the line.

I crossed to the window and stared down at the terminal below. I watched until the next ferry arrived, trying to distinguish Aioko in the waiting crowd. I watched as passengers boarded, but could not spot her. I watched as the ageing green and white push-me pull-you boat sailed away into the mist. Then, as it disappeared beneath the bird-like curves of the Convention Centre roof, I waved.

I felt empty, drained, and miserable. My nipple throbbed – her presence sore beneath the skin.

6

After work, on the Friday following my night with Auoko, I went to pick up my sister, Irene, from Chep Lak Kok airport. She was passing through Hong Kong on her way to Australia. She had organized a trekking holiday in the Blue Mountains with some distant cousins, but wanted to break her journey for one night to 'catch a glimpse of her dear brother.' She is five years older than me, married with two grown-up children and lives in Edinburgh. Her husband is a professor of Celtic archaeology and never travels. She does 'community chores' on a voluntary basis and is active in local politics. As a child, I looked up to her and she was always the boss. I ran errands for her, accepted the roles she allocated in games and Christmas charades, and suffered in silence when she presented me as an amusing diversion for her visiting girlfriends. When she left home to go to university, and I had Mother to myself – at least in the school holidays – we became good friends. She thinks Mother made us compete for affection and that was why we were never close as children. I suspect it had more to do with age, and the fact that I was a bookworm and she was a girl guide.

But I always enjoy seeing her, and, when she emerged from the customs hall, a warm breath of normality blew into my investigator's soul. Her familiar weather-beaten face and sensible clothes reminded me that I was not alone in the world, and that – despite the obsessive nature of my investigation – I was not mad. I treated her to a taxi home, HK$300 door to door. A waste of good money, Irene said, but she was clearly touched by the gesture. She was jetlagged and, at fifty-five, in need of restorative sleep. So, after a toast and soup snack, she went straight to bed with a promise to 'catch up' in the morning.

The next day we made our ritual trek to Stanley Market on the south side of Hong Kong Island. She had visited me four times and always insisted on making this trip. She liked the views, she said. So, as usual, we took a number 61 bus over the top of the island. She marvelled at the panoramic vistas, and, as on her previous two visits, bemoaned the tourists in Stanley. I, as before, reminded her she was one.

"No, I'm family of a resident, Stephen. That's different."

Her heart was socialist, but she had a fine nose for social difference.

We squeezed into the packed alleyways of the tiny street market and flowed with the crowd in and out of clothes shops, bric-a-brac stores, picture stalls and shoe shops. German voices, French voices, American voices and mainland Putonghua voices swirled around us. Package tourists, regardless of their origin, were herded into coaches and driven across the island – through Aberdeen tunnel, not over the scenic top – to spend their dollars, francs, deutschmarks and renminbis in Stanley's covered market. Mongkok and Wanchai offered better bargains, but this was the place in the guidebooks, so this is where the tourists came.

Irene bought a sensible size rucksack in black for her Blue Mountain hike in Australia and a Tommy Hilfiger sweatshirt apiece for son and daughter. They took after their mother – uncomplicated pleasant beings into physical activity, good food and good company. They lived in London and worked in the City, one as a broker and one as a banker. Both were happily married, and sometimes I wondered where my introspective, investigative side came from. Even my own son, Tom, was more like Irene than me.

"Tom's doing well for himself," Irene said, on the way back.

We were seated at the front of the top deck of a bus, climbing up Repulse Bay Road from Deep Water Bay. Aberdeen and the South Island coastline were spread out below us, sparkling in the bright spring sunshine.

"Yes. Living in Leeds still, I gather. Running his restaurant."

"Chain of restaurants. Pops up and sees me in Edinburgh now and then."

"With his wife?"

"Cheryl. If she has the time, but she's a busy girl these days."

"Solicitor, isn't she?"

"Barrister, Stephen. Much more impressive."

I smiled and stared out of the window. There it was again, our mother's nose for social ranking.

"Tom says he might come out this summer," I said, watching a distant cable car at Ocean Park sway its way across a hillside. "But he said that last year and never did."

"Maybe you should go back?"

"No. I'll wait till my contract's finished."

"That's another two years, isn't it?"

I nodded, my eyes still glued to the window. I had decided not to visit Europe this time round. I had done so twice a year on my first tour of duty, and, each trip, found it harder to fly back to the humid heat of Hong Kong. I was a northern European through and through, and found the sub-tropical climate and environment of South East Asia – even in its post-British colonial form – alien and alienating. This time, I had decided to regard Hong Kong as a prison, the Institute as my cell and the contract a sentence to be served without parole. That way I killed two birds with one stone: I broke the unsettling pattern of boarding school attendance imposed on me from the age of eight, and I had more time to concentrate on myself and my investigation.

"Don't you miss each other, you and Tom?" Irene asked, after a pause to admire the view now receding behind us.

"I can't speak for him, but I feel fine."

"I'd find it strange. Not seeing my child for so long."

The bus crested the hill and began to roll downwards towards the cricket club and the first Happy Valley high rises. In the distance, Kowloon's hills, free from their usual winter smog, shone out sharp and bright in doctored postcard green.

"He's grown up, Irene. Maybe we've let each other go. Still close in spirit, but free to go our own ways. I saw him every holiday – and several weekends in between – until he was seventeen. We're not strangers."

"Yes, but…"

"We're good friends. Not close in the way you are with yours."

Irene nodded. My relationship with Tom made her sad, I knew. When he was younger, she was always inviting us to Edinburgh. So he could get to know her children better, so she could bond him into the family tree – or the family sheep pen, as I called it. I accepted her invitations at the start, until Tom was ten. Then I went to Holland to take up an academic post for five years and our families drifted apart. Now Tom had renewed the contact, at least with Irene, and saw her more than me. It made me feel a failure, not as a father, but as an innovator. I wanted to liberate my son from family ties. He might not be introspective like me, but I had hoped to make him an independent soul more interested in future friends than old familiar faces. I was bad at roots. Irene kept them watered.

"And his mum? Are you two still in touch?"

I shook my head and pressed the bell.

Our stop was next and Tom's mother stayed tucked away in my mind, resting in peace as she had done since our breakup after Tom's birth. She had wanted a child and I had given her one. I attended the birth, cut the umbilical cord on the midwife's insistence and never for one moment regretted my son's arrival. I loved him then with all my heart, and have done ever since. His mother and I kept in touch to talk Tom business until he was eighteen, and made sure he never suffered administratively. I stayed with the two of them for the first six months of his life and then cared for Tom, by myself, every other weekend, until he was six. When I took up a teaching post in Amsterdam, Tom flew out once a month with a luggage tag around his neck and an airhostess to deliver him into my safekeeping. I do miss him; at least I miss the child he used to be, but his mum I never miss. I believe she and I were destined to make Tom, but that was all. God moves in mysterious ways and that was one of them. He had not made a mistake.

Irene dropped the subject over lunch, and then went for a nap. But later, as we sipped afternoon tea in the Mandarin Hotel on Des Voeux Road, her bags already checked-in at Central Terminal, she returned to the topic of children.

"Ever thought of having another one?" she said, cutting a king-size scone in two and spreading a thick wedge of Devonshire cream on both halves.

"Another what?" I asked.

I was watching a Japanese airhostess in a pale blue JAL uniform. She was sitting with an American man in one of the window seats across the gangway from our table. He was drinking beer. She was drinking wine. She had leant forward across the table between them, as the Mandarin's voluminous armchairs were too far apart for real intimacy. I could tell she was Japanese. She had the same angular features as Aioko and, through the mumble and murmur and teacup clatter, I could hear the odd word of Japanese. I had bought myself a teach-yourself book and tape set and was already on lesson three. "*Sumimasen,*" I heard her say, and warmth welled up in my stomach. I wanted to be the American man. No, I wanted Irene to be Aioko. I wanted my Japanese fencer sitting across from me now, wearing her white office blouse and navy blue skirt and smiling her mystery smile. It would feel so right. We would belong together.

"Another child," Irene replied.

"No. One's enough. Done that, been there."

"Well, another mum at least," Irene continued, with a laugh.

She was in dangerous waters, navigating a safe passage with humour.

"No point having another mum, if she's not going to be one."

"You know what I mean, Stephen."

And I did. But I wanted to concentrate on the Japanese fantasy and sip my Lapsang Souchong tea, not confront the reality of my relationship situation. I was happy for Irene to natter about her children, or our cousins in Australia, or whatever else came into her mind. That gave me a sense of normality, of belonging in a non-claustrophobic sort of way. But Irene probing into my personal life required attention. I had to be on guard.

"That nice Chinese woman, Su-yin," she continued, using our mother's turn of phrase, "is she still around?"

Su-yin had accompanied me back to Europe once, and met selected friends and relations in Holland and England. She had gone down well with Irene.

"A sensible sort of woman, I thought. Past child-bearing age, too, I'd have said."

"Irene! You're sounding like Mother," I countered with a good-humoured chuckle, trying to close the subject.

"You should have someone, Stephen. You're getting on."

"I'm getting on fine, Irene. Honestly. Su-yin's a good friend, but we're not partners anymore. That's all."

"Shame," Irene sighed, mounding her last dollop of cream onto a morsel of scone. "But, apart from Tom's mum, you've never stayed long in one port-of-call, have you?"

"You sound like an ageing ex-pat," I laughed.

"What do you mean?" said Irene.

"Brits who've been in Hong Kong more than twenty years speak like characters in a fifties film. Terry Thomas's, I call them. 'Totally weird' is Tom's phrase."

"I see," said Irene, taking a bite of scone and munching in silence for a while.

I returned to the airhostess, and snippets of Japanese floated past my ear. But not for long; a sip of tea to settle the scone and Irene was back on the warpath.

"I think you should find yourself a nice, sensible woman and stop playing hard to get. Soon they won't want you anymore. Had you thought of that?"

It had crossed my mind, but in Hong Kong I still had a few years to go.

"There is a Japanese woman," I said, after a long pause to observe the airhostess stand, bow to her companion and depart.

"Oh dear," exclaimed Irene. "Japanese? Is that a good idea?"

"Irene!" I said, pushing my chair back. "Time to put you on a plane."

Later, at Hong Kong Station, waiting for the next airport train to arrive, I asked her a question that surfaced in my mind for no particular reason.

"You remember Sally?"

"Your 'nanny'? Of course I do."

"Did she have a boyfriend?"

46

"Not that I ever met. But then she was *your* nanny. I'd gone to boarding school."

"Village girl of eighteen. There must have been a village beau who fancied her?"

A sign flashed up: 'Next train in six minutes.' Irene glanced at her watch. She liked to be well on time.

"Yes. But now I come to think of it, Mother thought she was a lesbo."

"Gay? Sally?"

"Yes. Towards the end, Mother and I had some good chats about old times."

"Who was the girlfriend?" I said, my curiosity kindled.

"Oh, I don't know. Mother thought it was that Duffin girl."

"Muriel Duffin? The builder's daughter?"

"Yes. Wore too much makeup. Do you remember her?"

Muriel Duffin, *femme fatale* of the village. Dark-haired, narrow hipped and a red-painted mouth half-open. I had a crush on her from the age of ten. She was in her twenties then, but for me, secluded for much of the year in a boy's boarding school and surrounded by women who looked like horses and smelt of gin, she was a mysterious, exciting figure. In the holidays, I used to watch her from my bedroom window, as she tapped her way up the village street in high heels and a pencil skirt. Once, she glanced up and gave me her crooked smile and a wink. She was a 'bad girl,' my mother said, always out with a different man. And, now it seemed, with women too.

"I do. How funny. What made Mother suspicious?"

"Well, when Sally was sorting apples from the orchard – storing them for winter, you know – Muriel used to come and help."

"Sounds innocent enough."

"Yes and no. Do you remember where the apples were stored?"

I thought back, and nodded.

"In the cellar."

"Exactly. And once or twice, when mother returned from shopping in York, she found Sally and Muriel down there. With the door locked!"

"Wow. And where was I?"

"Probably down there, too! Sally wouldn't have wanted Mother coming in and finding you bawling your head off, would she?"

"No."

At that moment, the train came in. Picking up her shoulder bag, Irene hugged me and ran towards the ticket barrier. I waved and blew a kiss.

I had enjoyed seeing her, but family members can be dangerous. They have access to files long since closed and forgotten. Neither Muriel nor Sally triggered bad memories, but that night their ghostly forms haunted my mind and would not go away. Muriel tapping up the street in her heels, and Sally, in her workaday stockings and suspender belt, pulling back the bedclothes to smack me for some petty crime. Nothing X-rated, but, when I tried to imagine the two of them in the cellar, my mind went blank and the phantoms faded into fog – unusual for a man with such a Rabelaisian mind.

7

Despite his misgivings that she had forgotten him, Aioko called the evening Irene left.

Stephen picked up the receiver and a tiny voice said, "*Moshi moshi!* Aioko *desu!*" He smiled. The Japanese language appealed to him, particularly this telephone greeting. "*Moshi moshi!* Stephen *desu!*" he answered. There was silence, then a long ascending "Oooh!" followed by a compliment: "Successful British Writer-san soon write in Japanese *desune*?" It was sarcastic in tone, but he did not care. This was the first time she had phoned him since that morning at the hotel, and her voice sounded as intriguing down the line as it did in real life. She was in hibernation, she said, but would like to meet for a short drink, the next evening.

He agreed without hesitation and, at six, was sitting on the largest of the black leather sofas in the lobby of the Marriott. When Aioko arrived, they did not kiss – their two faces had still made no contact – but exchanged bows and walked to a corner table in the lounge bar. Aioko was her old office-girl self with red lips, white blouse and blue skirt. Stephen felt alive in her presence, fascinated by her ability to be such different people at different times – not just in appearance, but in behaviour too. They ordered beers and sat and smiled at each other, seeing who could eat the most complimentary pumpkin seeds before the drinks arrived. When they did, Aioko took a sip or two from the tall Heineken glass, and the playful smile fell from her face. She had a favour to ask. She would like him to take her out for a meal on Tuesday next week. By then her hibernation would be ended and she needed his support. A routine cervical smear had shown up an anomaly and the result of a second, more complex test was due on Wednesday. Stephen wondered why she needed to see him the night before, and not the night after, but remained silent. He was happy to be of service, and agreed to book a table somewhere.

She thanked him and her smile returned.

At eight, after two beers apiece, she rose to leave. When hibernating, she explained, she had to be indoors by nine. A strange kind of hibernation, Stephen commented, and she laughed her high-pitched laugh and agreed – very strange! But he must get used to it. Hibernation happened every two months.

Fine by me, he said, I like a woman who needs time on her own.

She giggled and departed. He watched her trot off across the lobby, turn, wave and disappear into a lift. After the doors had closed, he let her image hang in his mind. He had no choice: the objective investigator already in thrall to his third specimen.

★

The day before her hospital visit, I took Aioko out for a meal as agreed.

I chose Dan Ryan's in Pacific Place, a Chicago-style grill serving American-sized portions at reasonable prices. Su-yin had introduced me to the place soon after I met her, and, on his one and only visit to Hong Kong in 1998, Tom had chosen to eat there twice. Aioko knew and liked it, too. It served a mega-house salad with all her favourite vegetables, and her favourite Budweiser beer on tap.

We met at six and sat for a while in the dimly lit bar next to the restaurant area sipping Buds. I needed to be trained as a proper beer drinker, she said, like all the other pot-bellied, glassy-eyed ex-pats on the barstools beside us. I could not imagine myself as fat and pot-bellied, I retorted, and she laughed her high-pitched laugh.

"Of course. 'British Writer – tall, slim healthy and successful.'"

She knew the advertisement off by heart.

After twenty minutes, we were shown to a booth with high-backed, dark-wood benches and a dark brown table. The space afforded privacy and Aioko detailed her recent medical history.

This was one long list of woes: mixed-up files, interminable waits in drab hospital waiting rooms, unsympathetic doctors and finally the news that she would have to come back again this week to hear the result of the most recent test.

"But why see me tonight, Aioko-san?" I asked, when she had finished her tale. "Wouldn't it be better on Friday? Then we could have celebrated, or commiserated."

Aioko nodded and flashed an empty smile. She was halfway through her salad. Suddenly, she pushed it aside and stood up.

"Ladies room. *Sumimasen!*"

She beetled off, sturdy calves propelling her at speed between the crowded tables. She was gone for ten minutes. I finished my tuna steak, ordered another beer for Aioko and a mineral water for myself.

When she returned, her eyes were red.

"What's the matter?" I said, handing her the fresh glass of Budweiser.

"Oh, Writer-san," she sobbed. "I'm so frightened."

"Of what?"

She shook her head and did not reply. She seemed fragile, vulnerable. I wanted to jump up and join her on the other side of the table. Cuddle her in my arms and tell her not to worry. But something held me back.

"Of what they say tomorrow," she said eventually. "At the hospital."

"You think it might be serious?"

She nodded, her lips turned downwards to block a sob. I reached across the table and took her hand. Tiny fingers folded into my palm. They were trembling.

"It might be nothing," I said. "So-called anomalies are often harmless."

She bit her lip and shook her head.

"Not mine. Not mine."

This time the sob broke through. She withdrew her fingers, dropped her head to the table and buried her face in her hands. Her shoulders heaved in one last attempt at self-control. Then she burst into tears and cried her heart out, like a child.

"Poor Aioko-san," I said. "You're really upset."

I glanced around. No one was watching. And, even if they had been, it would not have mattered. I leant forward and stroked her hair.

"Tell you what," I whispered. "Why don't you stay at my place tonight?"

She raised her head, and gazed at me with bloodshot eyes.

"Are you sure?"

I nodded.

"Why not? You won't feel so alone. I can help see off the demons."

She took my free hand in hers, sandwiching it between two tiny palms.

"Oh, Writer-san. You're a kind man," she said. "Very kind man."

Was I? Or was I just keen to continue our physical investigation? I smiled at her. At that moment, my feelings had little to do with sex. The thought of tucking her up in bed and kissing her goodnight was foremost in my mind. She made me feel protective. She made me want to care for her. I wanted her to smile back and be happy again

"Shall we go?"

"When I finish beer," she said. "If I am to die, I will die drunk."

I laughed, and held up my water to clink with her bottle.

"*Kanpai!*" she cried, her office-worker self reappearing like a phoenix.

"And," I said, "here's the bonus deal: if you turn out to be very ill, I will take you to Tahiti – if you turn out to be quite ill, I will take you to Hawaii."

"And if not ill at all?" she cried with glee.

"I will take you to Macau, to recover from the thought that you might have been."

"Will you, Writer-san? Will you really take me to Hawaii?"

"Of course, I am a man of my word."

And, at that moment, my affection surged like a Waikiki breaker and I rode the surf of emotion far into the future, imagining myself at her service forever: Aioko always ill, but never dying – Aioko always in need of me, and me always there. And gazing into her eyes, I thought I saw my feeling reflected, though it might have been the beer.

By the time we reached my flat, she was quite recovered and rushed from room to room like a child in a new home, squealing with delight, her ascending 'Ooohs!' and 'Aaahs!' increasing in range and volume with each new discovery.

"Oh, Writer-san, this is perfect! Writerworld, I shall call it. Aioko's private place to escape and recover."

A woman making possessive remarks about my home normally set off alarm bells, but with Aioko I was just happy she liked it. I started to draw the curtains.

"Leave them open, Writer-san. Let's lie here and look at the sky."

And before I could respond, she had removed all her clothes and collapsed on my sheepskin rug in front of the window.

"Mm! Rug feels nice. I have sheepskin at home. I lie naked on that, too."

"Shall I take my clothes off?" I asked.

"Of course!" she cried. "Naked Office Worker lies on floor for naked Writer."

I removed my clothes and knelt down beside her. She rotated her hips, pursed her lips and half-closed her eyes. I took this as a sign, and bent to kiss her, warmth and excitement flowing through my body. But as my mouth approached hers, she averted her lips. I tried again. This time she let my lips touch hers, but her mouth did not open.

"No kissing, Writer-san," she hissed. "Writer's rules. Remember?"

"But…" I began.

She put a finger to my mouth, and hunched her shoulders.

"Writer-san *totemo* confused *ne*?" she giggled.

She seemed to enjoy my discomfort. I shook my head, excitement ebbing away.

"Not at all," I lied. "It's just that, well, I feel close to you tonight."

She giggled again, and put her hand between her legs.

"Writer-san want to be close here?"

I hesitated, not sure whether, without a kiss, I was ready to do what I imagined she wanted me to do. Seeing my hesitation, she rolled onto her stomach, drew her knees up under her chest, pushed her arms out along the rug, buried her face in the wool and arched her bottom high into the air, until it was pointing directly at me. I felt my penis grow again and positioned myself behind her until its tip touched her vagina and began to ease into her body, my male lust tempered by tenderness.

"Too slow," she yelled. "Harder, harder!"

I pushed forward, but the lack of closeness, the lack of a kiss, the lack of emotion from Aioko's side offended my – or my penis's – sensibilities and the erection subsided.

"Oh, no!" she cried again, her fingers moving in to stimulate herself.

I withdrew my penis and put my mouth to her lower lips. Her fingers pushed back and forth against my tongue and, after a minute, she came, emitting a cry of pain before collapsing with her back to me. I lay down and held her, hoping she would touch me, too, or turn to kiss my lips. But she made no move to do so and was soon fast asleep, knocked out by the wine, the beer and the fear of what her result might reveal.

For a moment I wondered if she was disappointed. Perhaps she had wanted me to ride her like a stallion, thoughts of love subsumed in lust. Or had she been too far gone to care? I picked her up, carried her to bed and climbed in beside her. Servant Stephen and Mistress Aioko, asleep in each other's arms, dreaming of Hawaii, Tahiti and beyond.

8

She rang on Wednesday evening to say the hospital test had turned out negative. There was still one other anomaly to check, but it was not, as far as the doctors could tell, life threatening or in need of immediate treatment. She had rung me first, she explained, because I had been so kind and concerned. I was glad she had, I said. I had been worried and ready to order up tickets for Tahiti.

"And now?" she laughed.

"Well," I replied, "not quite nothing, but not quite anything leaves you somewhere between Hawaii and Macau."

"Hong Kong!" she giggled.

She was sounding much better.

"Or Japan," I said. "We'll have to see. Meanwhile, enjoy your new-found health."

"Thank you, Writer-san," she whispered, and then in a tiny child's voice added the Japanese word for 'goodnight,' "*Oyasumi nasai.*"

"*Oyasumi nasai,*" I replied, my chest filling with warmth.

On Friday evening, she came to dinner. She arrived from work with a bag of Japanese 'surprises' bought during her lunch hour. I was to make salad while she prepared delicacies for a Japanese buffet. But we ended up doing each other's work. I diced cloves of garlic for the 'non-traditional' miso soup, and she sliced organic carrots for my mega-salad. A bottle of red wine was opened and the kitchen buzzed with culinary activity. She had exchanged her office uniform for a flower-patterned shift. This, she announced, she would keep at Writerworld, along with a spare set of office clothes, in case there were any more 'Tuesdays pretending to be Fridays' – a reference to our meal at Dan Ryan's. But after her third glass of wine, she removed the shift and continued slicing in pink panties and no bra. Every now and then she would hunch her shoulders, giggle and offer me a nipple to suck, seasoned with a clove of freshly cut garlic.

"Mmm!" she sighed, as I sucked away for the third or fourth time and she poured herself a fifth glass of wine. "I love raw *ninniku*. Do you?"

"On your nipple, yes!" I replied, returning to my chopping board.

"Or my bottom," she giggled.

"*Ninniku no oshiri*," I said, showing off my Japanese.

"Oh, Writer-san!" she squealed with glee. "You've learnt word for bottom in Japanese. Where did you learn? From second naughty Japanese office worker?"

"No, no. From dictionary. *Ninniku* – garlic, *Oshiri* – buttocks!"

"Oooh!"

A record-breaking, full-octave ascending tone, followed by a removal of the pink panties and a descent to the kitchen floor. I watched in amazement as she stretched out on the cold black marble tiles, spread her legs apart and pouted at me.

"Bet never kissed naked Japanese woman on kitchen floor before. *Ne*?"

"*Ie. Zenzen shimashita*," I said, struggling with my Japanese and my belt buckle at the same time. I did not want to be on the kitchen floor but had no choice.

"You know Japanese word for this?" she said, pointing between her legs.

"No. Not in dictionary."

"Ah! But you look, Writer-san. You look!"

I nodded and, still in my underpants, knelt between her thighs. The marble felt cold to my bony knees, and would deep-freeze more sensitive parts.

"*Ninniku! Ninniku!*" she shrieked, reaching up her hand to the work surface for another clove of garlic.

She crushed it between her fingers and smeared her two nipples.

"*Ninniku no chikubi wa desu ka! Tabete o kudasai!*"

I looked blank, not sure what was expected of me.

"Garlic – what do you call these?" she held up her nipples.

"Nipples."

"Garlic nipples! Eat please!" she giggled. "*Tabete o kudasai!* Office worker commands."

I bent down and sucked her two erect nipples.

"Mmm! *Oshiri. Chikubi.* Writer-san want to learn word for this?"

Again she pointed between her legs. I straightened up. My back was hurting. Was I too old for this? Crouching semi-naked on a cold kitchen floor above a naked woman? She placed a finger on her clitoris and slid it back and forth, with less violence than usual.

"Want to know word, Writer-san?" she repeated.

"Maybe later," I said. "Let's eat first."

"*Hai*! Eat first" she said, jamming the remaining sliver of garlic into her vagina and pulling my head down between her legs.

"*Ninniku no omanko!* Garlic cunt! *Tabete o kudasai!*"

And so, once again, I was eating, sucking and licking between Aioko's legs, this time garlic flavoured *omanko*. And she was sighing and writhing, this time on a cold marble floor. And, as before, she made no effort to touch me, apart from brushing her hand across my underpants to check the effect of her garlic cunt. Moderate to strong, but not gale force. I was hungry for food, not sex.

She slipped from beneath me and stood up.

"*Sumimasen*! Writer-san needs Aioko *no* miso soup *ne*?"

I glanced up from my position on all fours and nodded. She ruffled my hair and wiggled her pubic mound against my nose.

"Finish *omanko* meal later. *Omanko no* pudding *desune.*"

She laughed at her own joke then rushed to the stove to check the rattling pots and pans. She lifted the lid of one at the back and gave a shriek of horror.

"Oh no! Aioko burn Writer-san's best pan!"

"Oh dear," I said. "Japanese lesson on kitchen floor, burnt rice on kitchen stove."

"No problem!" Aioko cried, separating the good from the burnt grains. "I make rice tea from black bits. Like Aioko's mum. *Totemo oishii!*"

"She burns pans too?" I asked, transfixed by the sight of a naked woman dashing about my kitchen with pans and bowls and boiling water.

"More wine, *Niban*!" she said, ignoring my question and holding out her glass.

"Yes, *Ichiban*!" I obeyed.

She was Number One, *Ichiban*; I was Number Two, *Niban* – happy to follow orders. And, as the alcohol penetrated deeper into her mind and body, Aioko mellowed but did not cry. Perhaps the Japanese specialities neutralised the depressive effect of Bordeaux red. We drank miso soup, ate homemade sushi and nibbled sour plum rice dumplings, or *onigiri*, off the end of chopsticks. Then, when the salad bowl was empty and the last *ninniku* clove inside Aioko's stomach, we sipped burnt rice tea.

And as we sipped, Aioko talked. She sat in her shift, back against the floor-to-ceiling window of the living room, her thin body framed by the night sky and the gaudy lights of Hong Kong's high-rise jungle. I sat on the sofa and listened. The sketch she had made, on that first evening in the Marriott, was given colour and perspective. The setting and history of her complex world became clearer, though its characters stayed vague. Aioko allotted them codenames, not because she didn't trust me, she said, but because, in Hong Kong, you never knew when you might come across someone from someone else's life. If you didn't know their real name, you wouldn't know who they were – even if you did meet them – and the temptation to exchange gossip or 'tell tales,' as she put it, would be minimised. This seemed an excessive precaution, but she said she had suffered a great deal from people 'telling tales' about her – as Aioko – so pseudonyms must be used.

First of all, there were the 'Lantau's' – a Japanese couple from the island of the same name. They headed up the informal social club to which Aioko had belonged. The female of the couple had been Aioko's best friend, the woman whose lover Aioko had now stolen. This lover, codenamed 'Superman,' flew in from abroad, like his namesake, to save – or service – his women in Hong Kong. Or his *woman*. Aioko said he was no longer 'lover of Lantau lady, only of Aioko.' She had insisted on that and Superman had agreed.

One wife and one lover was enough. She went on to describe how other characters – Sai Kung, Snobby, Ms Sony and her husband – fitted in and how she had dumped them all except for Superman and husband. And now even Superman was in question, she added, fixing me with a stare and hunching her shoulders.

My ears pricked up. The husband seemed harmless – impecunious, prone to silence, no longer a lover for his wife – but Superman posed a threat. Even the codename turned my stomach: the active sexual partner, the real man – the performer against whom I would be measured. Supposing he was a traditional American stud who fucked like a stallion when confronted with a naked female bottom pointed in his direction? Supposing he was one of those muscle-bound gymnasts from the movies? Supposing he *was* Superman? I would be lost before I began – unless being fucked from behind like a mare in heat was not what Aioko wanted; unless she had developed a liking for non-stud like sexual behaviour; unless, and this was what made my ears prick up, she was happy for the stud to vanish from the stage.

"Why is 'Superman' in question?" I asked, trying not to sound too curious. "Because of the blonde hair on the bed?"

"Partly. Mm."

"And what else?"

"Did not ring me up after hospital appointment. Still no call!"

"Oh," I said, repressing a surge of smugness. "Maybe he's too busy."

"If too busy for Aioko, not good for Aioko."

I nodded and wondered why I was so keen for this man, who I had never met and knew nothing about, to be badmouthed and dumped. Was I jealous? And, if so, why? I was investigating alternatives and Aioko was my co-investigator. If she had another lover who was conventional and dominant in bed, and she liked that too, what was the problem? Hadn't I foresworn monogamy, hadn't I set my heart on finding an alternative form of sexual activity to pumping a pecker in and out like an aerobics instructor? What was going on? Why was this man looming like a demon over my shoulder, mocking my submissive self and waving his giant erection in my face?

"Why don't you just ditch him?" I said, without thinking.

"Ditch him?" she said, her eyes taking on a hard, playful look.

"Tell him to disappear. Why not?"

"Mm…" she murmured, considering the question. "Maybe. Maybe not."

And then, fixing her enigmatic, red-lipstick smile in place, she crawled across the room to where I was sitting on the sofa, climbed up, placed her feet either side of my thighs and pulled up her shift.

"*Omanko no* pudding time," she giggled, hunching her shoulders. "Hungry?"

Again I wanted to take her in my arms and kiss her on the real lips, on the red-mouth lips. But, instead, and for the third time in our short relationship, our two sets of hands and my one set of lips and dutiful tongue combined to give Aioko an orgasm. And, as before, once her cries of anguished pleasure ceased, I carried her to bed and she slept, leaving me untouched.

But I did not feel alone.

I trusted that a time would come when she would touch me too.

9

And it did, sooner than he had hoped. The day after Aioko and Stephen's naked chef meal, the Chinese celebrated Ching Ming, a festival when families visited the graves of ancestors to burn fake money and air tickets, and anything else they thought might be of use in the mirror world of the dead. It was believed that when an object disappeared in flames, its incinerated atoms were reconstituted on the 'other side,' in a world where technology, tourism and inflation all kept pace with the land of the living.

Aioko spent the day with her Chinese husband's family, burning, eating and playing Mahjong. Stephen went to his office and sent the following mail:

> *Ohayo gozaimasu* Aioko-san,
>
> At lunchtime, I sat in the hairdressers being given a soft number three by the attractive Chinese boy, who cuts my hair. 'Soft' means he uses scissors instead of electric shears. He takes great care, snipping individually the blades of thinning grass that make up my lawn. I am surprised he lavishes so much attention on such an ageing head, but grateful. It soothes my brain and settles my soul. Today, as I sat and he snipped, a soft snow of downy white fluff floated past my eyes and I saw an image of myself in Hokkaido, in winter, holding hands with you.

Aioko was touched by his description of Hokkaido snow and said she looked forward to holding hands again on the Tuesday after Ching Ming.

On that day she visited Writerworld, and servant and mistress again cooked dinner. She drank less and did not lie naked on the kitchen floor, though still burnt the pan and munched raw *ninniku*. After the meal, they sat on the sofa gazing down at the brightly lit football fields of Happy Valley, and this time he told her more about his life and, in particular, about his son, Tom. When she heard Tom was taller than Stephen, she nicknamed him the Tall Prince.

They went to bed early, and Aioko came with less assistance than usual from her own hands. Afterwards, Stephen lay with his arm around her, her head nestling on his left shoulder, her free hand resting on his chest.

She stroked the hairs and touched the nipples with a forefinger. He shivered.

"Nipples still sore from Fencer's mouth?" she murmured.

"No. Quite healed. They like your gentle touch."

"Mmm!"

The familiar ascending tone increased their sensitivity, like some snake charmer's pipe. Her thumb and forefinger gently squeezed, first the left and then the right one. Stephen slid his hand under the bedclothes and felt for his penis. It was already half-erect. His nipples were a reliable source of arousal, often better than the snake itself. He held the snakehead in his palm, and, when Aioko saw what he was doing, she threw back the duvet to watch. Perhaps she had wanted him to do this before, but not dared ask. Perhaps she was hoping the snake would grow big enough to slip inside her. But she had come, and it was Stephen's turn. She sat up to free her other hand and knelt beside him. Both nipples were stroked and squeezed, and sometimes even licked and sucked, but never bitten. He felt tenderness and lust fuse and flow around his body. She watched his hand at work below and seemed to time her touch to his. He wanted to kiss her, but, when her gaze caught his, there was just a twinkle in her eye, no look of love or longing.

"*Binkan na chikubi desune?*" she hissed, moving her tongue across his right nipple. "Writer-san has *totemo* sensitive nipples."

"*Hai. Hai!*" he gasped.

Her eyes moved down his body, her fingers moved faster, his penis grew longer and firmer. At the last minute, he took her left

62

hand and folded it around the enflamed head. Seconds later he ejaculated, with a short sob of pleasure. The first blob of semen reached his left nipple. The rest landed on his stomach and trickled into his navel.

"Mm! *Takusan* Writer cream *desu ne!*" she cried, jumping off the bed and running to the bathroom to wash her hands.

Stephen lay back – content but unsatisfied. Not because he had come outside of her, but because she had not kissed him.

When she returned, Aioko handed Stephen some tissue and climbed into bed.

"Writer-san take shower now?"

"Do I have to?" he said. "I'd rather kiss and cuddle."

She giggled and pushed him up.

"Japanese very clean people. *Showa sugu o kudasai*! Please take shower!"

He obeyed, and went to stand under the hot jet of water she had turned on for him.

Was this what life with Aioko-san would be like, he wondered: him playing with her, her playing with herself – her playing with him, him playing with himself? He smiled and watched his wasted seed disappear into oblivion. He could live with that, as long as Aioko could, too. And the kissing? That would come in time. There was no rush.

★

Now, I am truly content.

Last night, Aioko and I celebrated her thirty-seventh birthday at the Peak Café surrounded by loud-mouthed expatriates and defiant Chinese. We were in our element, commenting on the diners. Was she a mistress? Was he a lover? Why were Americans so loud and boring? Was the Japanese wife's bottom as fine as Aioko's and was the Japanese husband, being so kind and solicitous to his wife in public, a beast and buttock beater at home? By the end of the meal, we were, in our estimation, the only two with credibility and Aioko, flushed from a bottle of wine, was ready to 'get her clothes off.'

She swayed out of the restaurant and headed for a bus. That way, she said, we could enjoy the views and save money. The roller coaster route, with its precipitous drops to Aberdeen and sheer wooded hillsides above Wanchai, was a risky option after food, but I went along with the whim. We found a bus, climbed to the top deck and settled on the front seat. We held hands, but did no more. Japanese etiquette and Aioko's married status won out over Bordeaux and Bohemian credentials. The bus swayed down the road, picking up speed as the gradient increased. It lurched round bends, threatening to crash through frail barriers on to the rocks below, and, when the camber subsided, tilted sharply to one side, its centre of gravity within a whisker of shifting from here to eternity.

Aioko's head rested on my shoulder.

"Oh, Writer-san. Even if we crash, I do not care."

"Why's that?" I asked, as the bus swerved to avoid a truck and hit a branch.

"Because it feels so right. Here with you."

I stared out at the lights of Wanchai below. I did not share her romantic acceptance of death, but, at that moment, I made a vow to be everything for her: her friend, her partner and her muse – her real lover, as well as her investigative lover. I wanted to do more than share cream tea and lie naked on the kitchen floor; I wanted to be Superman, too, and take her in the way supermen did when they flew in and whisked her off to a hotel. A tall order, but as the bus hurtled down towards the sea, I was convinced that to conquer her heart I must also conquer her body in a conventional way.

In normal circumstances, such pressure to perform might have led to impotence, but her profession of contentment at being with me – in life or death – acted as an aphrodisiac. Despite my desire to investigate alternatives, I was a man who needed emotional warmth from the woman's side – a sense of being loved – as well as touch and titillation for the eye. So when we reached home, I was ready to consummate at last.

"Carry me to bed, Writer-san," ordered naked Aioko, from the living room floor.

I undressed and bent to kiss her mouth. She let me do so for the first time – briefly, but it was enough. Her lips opened and my tongue found hers. It was a powerful connection, perhaps because we had waited so long, perhaps because mouths are the most intimate part of our bodies; the part that speaks and talks and cries and laughs, as well as kisses – the part that is of a higher order than those lower, so-called private parts.

I carried her to bed with ease. No pain or cracking in the back.

We kissed and stroked and my body came alive. She played with herself and then, sensing the hardness of my body, removed her lips from mine, knelt on the bed and arched her bottom in the air. I knelt behind her, helped her fingers with my own and then slipped inside. I felt her warmth surround me for the first time. I pushed in as deep as I could go, and then withdrew, until my tip was almost out. She moaned. Her hands worked faster. I drove in again and she buried her face in a pillow, squeezing the pink teapot spout and rotating her buttocks. I gazed down at the body beneath me. I did not find it sexy – it was too bony, too angular – but that did not matter tonight. I was fuelling my member with love, not lust – riding on my feelings.

Sometime later, Aioko came with a cry of pain and pleasure, and as her vagina contracted around my manhood, it made me the hardest man of all. I was happy, she was happy, and as I thrust in and out in triumph, my mind and body soared into space, high on their success at playing Superman. And when I came inside her, juddering in spasms before collapsing on her back, I knew it was enough. I had performed. I had fulfilled my part as a normal lover, as a normal man, and flushed the leader's former lover from Aioko's body and soul.

"Have you finished?" she asked.

"Mmm!" I acknowledged, snuggling up for post-coital closeness.

"Quick, under shower," she said, extricating herself from my body. "Come on!"

I shook my head, chuckled and rolled off the bed to join her in the bathroom. Adam had entered Eve, and Eden was in sight.

10

Next morning, as they ate a breakfast of muesli, rice and oatcakes, Aioko invited Stephen to visit her 'hideaway' in Cheung Chau.

"I want to show you my artwork," she said.

"I'd like to see it," he replied.

"You are first person," she added, spreading organic plum jam on to an oatcake.

"To visit your home?"

"No. You are second to visit home. Husband is first. You are first to see artwork."

"I'm honoured," he said, chopping apple into his pre-soaked bowl of muesli, savouring the fact that Superman had never been a guest.

"Husband not interested in art," she concluded, wiping her hands on a piece of kitchen towel. "He thinks I waste my time."

He repressed a grin of triumph.

Last night had achieved three goals. Superman sidelined, an invitation to her home and a favourable comparison with hubby. Perhaps Aioko now saw the advantages of having her men rolled into one – of excluding previous players from the stage.

★

Today, I took a taxi to the Outlying Islands Ferry Terminal in Central and boarded a slow boat to Cheung Chau. No air conditioning, apart from in an ice-cold compartment on the top deck. I sat below, letting the damp April wind blow over my face.

The boat chugged its way passed Kennedy Town, Eastern District and Stonecutter's Island, crossed a short expanse of open sea dotted with moored container ships, left Peng Chau to starboard, rounded a rocky headland and pulled into the tiny harbour of Cheung Chau.

Aioko was waiting on the dockside. She seemed nervous.

"We must walk separately to my flat," she said. "Me first, you follow."

"Why?" I asked.

"Chinese neighbours cannot see married woman receive male visitor," she hissed.

"But how do they know you're married?" I said, confused by Aioko-the-artist's caution and conservatism.

"Husband has made visit, remember? He is Chinese, introduced himself to neighbours. Everyone knows I am the wife."

"And can't the wife have male friends?" I persisted.

Aioko shook her head and scampered off along a crowded seafront street. I counted to five and followed. Overflowing seafood restaurants jostled for space with clothes shops and bric-a-brac stalls selling everything from baseball caps to painted seashells. People in weekend mood dawdled along, paying little attention to where they were going and bumping into each other with regularity. But it was Saturday and there were no frayed tempers, just a smile, a step to the side and a muttered '*Mgoi sai!*'

As requested, I kept my distance from 'the wife,' and several times lost sight of her tiny frame as it darted in and out of the crowds.

After five minutes, she reached an alleyway that led off to the right, away from the harbour. She turned and beckoned, and then disappeared. The alleyway was dark and narrow, with cramped rows of three storey houses rising up on either side. I peered down it, and, at first, could not see Aioko. Then, as my eyes shook off the brightness of the sun and accustomed themselves to the gloom, I made her out at the far end, pointing to a house with a faded green door. She glanced to left and right and entered the building.

I ambled down the alleyway, trying to look inconspicuous. When I reached the door, I found it ajar. I stepped inside and heard a hiss from the stairway ascending into darkness above my head. Craning my neck and straining my eyes, I made out a hand beckoning me up to the first floor. I climbed the stairs and, at the top, was grabbed by the hand and pulled into one of the flats.

"Shoes off, please!" she whispered. "And keep voice down."

"Yes, madam!" I whispered back, a broad grin on my face.

I removed my shoes, stood up and took stock of my surroundings. I was in a small living room, with a tiny table for eating to one side and an alcove with a raised, cushion-covered platform for sitting or lying on at the far end. Off the living room were a small kitchen and bathroom, and a cupboard of a bedroom with a bed frame fitted to the three inside walls – a design that made entering the room and climbing into bed one and the same action.

"This is Aioko's little home!" Aioko whispered, with a note of pride in her voice. "I found it all by myself. Not a palace like Writerworld, but it is mine."

"It's great," I said. "The perfect artist's hideaway."

Part of me was jealous. The place had a simple, cosy feel and made my own flat – with its four rooms, IKEA beds, leather sofas and glass-topped dining table – seem bourgeois and conventional. Aioko's 'little home' felt and looked like it belonged to an artist; mine could have been the home of any professional person – creative or not.

"This is some of my work," said Aioko, indicating a row of small, rectangular, unframed mirrors decorated with tiny, whole seashells and cut fragments of larger shells.

They were laid out on the only table in the room, as if waiting to be graded by an examiner at college. I bent to inspect them and Aioko watched with bated breath. Each mirror had its own unique pattern of shells carefully glued in place around the outer edge, and each group of shells had its own individual, translucent hue ranging from coral pink to pure white. The shells had been collected with care and an eye for aesthetic appeal. They were not the sort of bombastic, giant-sized shells sold in seaside gift shops, but tiny jewels of the ocean, each with its own sea-washed shape and colour. I went back and forth along the row, and finally picked out a mirror with a simple pattern of miniscule purplish kauri shells and triangular slithers of silvery razor shell.

"I like this one," I said, holding it up.

"Why?" she asked, flattered by my interest.

"I like its simplicity," I replied "The symmetry of the pattern and the clean-cut lines of the shell fragments."

She nodded with satisfaction at my comment.

"You like order and symmetry, don't you?" I continued

"Yes," she laughed. "In my art, order – in my mind, chaos. In my home, order – in my life, chaos."

I avoided the larger topic contained in her response and stayed with the frames.

"Have you showed them to anyone else?"

She shook her head.

"You should. Maybe try and sell some."

"Too artistic, I think," she murmured. "Shell work in shops all bright and shiny. From factory, no individual touch. People call this art, I think."

I noticed the repeated use of 'I think' and remembered, from my last lesson on tape, that the Japanese often qualified what they said with '*to omoimasu.*' In fact, if quoting the opinion or desire of a third person, they were grammatically obliged to do so. This rule was posited on the premise that you could only surmise what someone thought or wanted, and could not say for certain. A respectful approach to other people's minds, though it might, I suppose, sometimes signify an unwillingness to accept other people's needs and wishes.

"Art or not, they'd sell," I said, and then added, "I think."

"Maybe," she said, a little mournfully. "But I prefer exhibition in gallery."

"Yes," I nodded. "Somewhere like the Fringe. You know that?"

"*Hai*," she replied with a smile. "Very artist place *desu ne.*"

"Yes. Though a gallery might regard the mirrors more as craftwork than artwork."

"And you?"

Her face stared up at me intently.

It was a new face. Not the office worker, not the early morning muted person, not the naked tea server drunk upon the kitchen floor. A serious face, not a game-playing or flirtatious face: an involved and committed face, not a melancholy or tear-stained child's face. I inspected the mirror I was holding more closely. The kauri shells had been positioned in such a way that their tiny, vagina-like lips together formed an almost imperceptible oval shape in counterpoint to the rectangular piece of glass. The outer rim, between the pattern of shells and the edge of the mirror, had been washed with a matt white watercolour to offset and absorb the translucent glow of the shells.

"It's more than just craft," I concluded, after a minute's silence.

"You really think so?"

The little girl face returned. The eyes sparkled.

"I really think so."

Aioko threw her arms round my neck and kissed me, and then withdrew as a shadow of doubt crossed her brow.

"You only say so because it is made by me?"

I shook my head.

"It's nothing to do with Aioko-san, friend of Writer-san. Everything to do with Aioko-san the artist."

She hugged me again and then, taking the mirror from my hand, went into the tiny kitchen.

I followed her and watched as she wrapped it up in the same chocolate-brown paper used to make the envelope for her response to my advertisement.

"What are you doing?"

"This is your favourite?"

I glanced back along the row of mirrors and nodded.

"So, I give you as gift."

"But the collection…"

"Aioko mirror must leave home. Show itself to world, allow world to see itself."

She finished her wrapping and held out the parcel to me with both hands. She then made a low bow.

"Please accept, Writer-san, this gift from artist Aioko."

"I am most honoured," I said, bowing in return. "Thank you."

Some may laugh at the way Japanese people bow so much – I have now discovered that even the weather forecasters and newscasters on television do it – but I like the custom. The bow shows respect, humility and recognition of another's presence, whilst preserving the integrity of an individual's physical space – unlike the hearty American handshake, or Russian bear hug. It does not crowd the mind with unnecessary words and excessive fulsomeness. It is an understatement, leaving room for the recipient to interpret and appreciate the gesture, as he or she will. Of course, like 'You're welcome' or 'Have a nice day,' it has probably been devalued in everyday Japanese usage. But, at such a moment as the one described above, its minimalism seemed mature, its formality loaded with a delicate emotional overtone far in advance of our occidental overkill. 'Less is more,' they say in relation to many forms of artistic expression and the same might be said, in certain situations, of physical contact between humans.

Later, Aioko prepared a picnic lunch of sour plum rice balls, avocado *onigiri*, raw carrots and hardboiled eggs. She packed it all into a small, old-fashioned wicker basket, which in turn was fitted into a large striped shopping bag. Beer was taken from the fridge and put in my rucksack. Then, after leaving the flat thirty seconds apart to fool the nosy neighbours, we walked to the ferry terminal and took a small boat to the much larger island of Lantau. In Mui Wo, where the boat docked, we climbed on to a single-decker bus with hard seats, no air-conditioning and a morose driver. It was full of picnickers like us, and the only free space was right at the back, squeezed between boy scouts on a hiking tour. When the engine finally rattled into life, the bus crawled up hill and down dale along the southern side of the island, until it reached a long expanse of sandy beach. This, Aioko explained, was where she found her shells. I was impressed. I had assumed she bought them from a shop in Cheung Chau. I told her this and she laughed. Shop-bought shells were too big, too shiny. They were treated with a chemical to enhance colouring, and no longer possessed the translucence and natural sheen of the original. Size and hue were critical for Aioko, so she sought her shells on the seashore.

Alighting from the bus, we walked down a track between fields of maize and rice and along the white sandy beach until we found a spot to ourselves. I sunk the handle of my outsize parasol, carried at all times to protect my balding head from the sun, into the sand and Aioko spread a tartan travelling rug on the shaded ground beneath.

Her smaller red umbrella, nicknamed Akaioko because *akai* means red in Japanese, was positioned to protect the food.

When everything was in place, we sat down and ate and drank until the last *onigiri* and the last drop of beer were gone. Then we lay beside each other and dozed. I felt at one with myself and the world. I did not need to hold Aioko's hand. Just lying there, I felt closer to my artist friend than I ever had before, and, perhaps, on that afternoon, she felt as close to me.

11

The Monday after their picnic was May 1st, reinstated as a holiday after Hong Kong's return to China. The following day, Tuesday May 2nd, was Buddha's birthday. Two days off for people of all persuasions to enjoy with a clean conscience and a full wallet.

On Monday, Stephen went for a walk with his Institute colleague Connor, and on Tuesday stayed at home writing. Returning to work on Wednesday, he found the following email from Aioko – he did not have an Internet connection at home.

Writer-san,
    Can I meet you this evening after work, if you are not busy?
I want to talk with you for an hour or so.
    Aioko

★

Despite a previous engagement, I agreed to meet, and, at six o'clock, found Aioko seated at our usual table in the Marriott bar. Beyond the floor-to-ceiling window, which flanked the leather armchairs, the night lights of Hong Kong flickered on one by one and a cruise ship hooted as it pulled away from the dock in Tsim Sha Tsui. Aioko was wearing her office uniform of white blouse and blue skirt, and had a red chiffon scarf around her neck. She had ordered wine for herself and a Beck's beer for me. She smiled, a red-lipstick smile, and hunched her shoulders into her neck as she had done on our first meeting. I now recognized this as a sign of nervousness.

I sat down and smiled a cautious smile.

She repeated her smile and shoulder hunch, and giggled.

"Our private place, yes?"

I nodded, and took a handful of pumpkin seeds from the dish on the table.

"And Writer-san has cancelled all important meetings to see me *ne*?"

I nodded again, and sipped my beer.

"You must like me very much, I think."

"Well," I said with a grin, "if a cocktail party at the French Consulate in celebration of Le French May Cultural Festival counts as important, then, yes, I do."

"You cancelled that?!" she exclaimed.

I nodded.

"Mm!" she intoned in her ascending manner. "Aioko very important, I think."

She giggled again and took a large swig of wine.

"So, what did you want to talk about?" I asked, as casually as possible.

"In a minute, Writer-san, in a minute. First we enjoy drinks. *Kanpai!*"

She raised her glass. I shrugged my shoulders and raised my glass, too.

"*Kanpai*, Aioko-san!"

Something about her demeanour was out of kilter. She was playing with me, as she often did, enjoying the game and parading her power. Yet she was also nervous, on edge. Should I have dropped everything on her account? Was getting drunk and proving her power the only agenda? Le French May was not the most important event in Hong Kong's cultural calendar, but there were useful contacts at the consulate and my absence would be noted.

"Writer-san," she said suddenly. "The bad news will come on Tuesday."

"I beg your pardon?"

"Tuesday next week, I hibernate," she continued

"That's not bad news."

"But you cannot see me when in hibernation," she persisted, giving me another bright lipstick smile.

"Aioko," I said, "I respect your right to time by yourself. Whenever you want it. You know that."

The smile broadened and the shoulders hunched higher than usual. She emptied her wineglass and signalled to the waiter to bring another one.

"But I won't be by myself, Writer-san!" she cried, almost in triumph.

A wave of nausea welled up in my stomach as my mind grasped what she was talking about, what she might be talking about. She saw the upset hit my eyes and giggled again.

"Bad news *desu ne*? Bad news for Writer-san *ne*?"

"Aioko," I said, losing patience, "just tell me what you're trying to say and stop faffing around."

"'Faffing?'"

I was getting angry and upset at the same time. I emptied my beer glass. The waiter arrived with Aioko's refill. I ordered a second bottle of Beck's. I wanted to regain control of my feelings. I did not want to make a bad impression. I needed to put my hopes for her and me on ice, play the role of an experienced man of the world. Not let her see I was so affected by news that had not even been announced.

"Who are you going to see, Aioko?" I asked.

"Superman," she said, in an innocent tone that cut through me like a knife.

"Superman?" I queried, still pretending not to understand.

"The American man from Europe, the blonde-hair-on-the-bed man. He rang last night. He arrives in Hong Kong next Tuesday. Then I hibernate."

"To hibernate means to be by yourself. Doesn't it?"

She laughed, and then realising my question was serious, stared at me in disbelief.

"Hibernation is when he visits, Writer-san. You know that?"

"I most certainly do not," I replied, with the righteousness of a man who is telling the truth, the whole truth and nothing but the truth. "I have always assumed hibernation meant you needed time to yourself. That is what the word means."

"Oh, Writer-san! Writer-san!" she wailed. "Now you will be hurt and not like me!"

I ignored the diversion and persevered with my fact-finding mission.

"You want to see him?" I asked, unable to mask the note of desperation in my voice.

"I must," she said, lowering her eyes into the wineglass, and trying to lose herself in the dark red liquid.

"Why?"

"Because if I don't, he won't ask me again."

She swirled the wine round in her glass and kept staring at it.

"Maybe, that's a good thing," I said softly, sensing a chink in her armour.

"For you!"

She grinned again, her eyes glancing up, full of playful reproach.

But I was not in playful mode, and even if I had been, this was a game I was ill equipped to play. My mind and body were being inundated with a potent brew of 100% proof jealousy – bitter tasting sexual jealousy of the most primitive male sort. I wanted to see off the competition, the opposition, before it set foot near my property. My man of the world dissolved into a jilted teenager, the nerd pushed aside by the blonde beefcake, the creep who has sand kicked in his face.

"No. Not for me, for you," I said, stiffening my upper lip. "But it's your choice, not mine."

I sat back and stared at her, trying to make her choose me there and then, willing her to banish this other man from her mind once and for all, before the poison of his presence – impending and actual – seeped into the pristine arteries of our relationship.

"And I choose him," she said, twisting the lipstick on her mouth into the stubborn stance of a child. "For the time he is here. Then I see Writer-san again."

I shrugged my shoulders and felt tears well up in my eyes. I fought them back, excused myself and went to the washroom.

I snapped at the white-coated attendant, who tried to press the soap dispenser for me and hand me a towel to dry my hands. These shadowy figures who prowl outside the cubicles and turn on helpful running water annoy and unsettle me at the best of times, and tonight they seemed to be intruding not only on the privacy of my urination, but also on my sudden and very private grief. Public toilets, even in hotels, should be a sanctuary, a temporary separation from the world, not a place where greasy-haired grovelers seek to earn a dollar from the penny you have spent. These soft-soled shufflers inhabit Asia more than Europe and America, and Su-yin said I was unfair to be so hard. They were only doing their job, she said, and I should let them. But tonight, I moved to another basin, rejecting the one he had prepared for me, and grabbed my own towel from his pile, casting it angrily into the wicker laundry basket by the door, 'Mind your own business,' I felt like shouting. 'Not mine!'

But when I reached our table in the corner, I found the sad-eyed keeper of the toilets had served his purpose after all. My burst of aggression, at his expense, had burnt off the toxic brew of jealousy. I was calmer, more dispassionate.

I sat down and smiled at Aioko.

"That's better!"

"Writer-san still angry?"

She had dropped her sadistic, playful manner and now regarded me with the eyes of a penitent child.

"No, of course not. See the guy. See how you feel. Then we'll move on."

"Thank you, Writer-san."

"No need for thanks," I chuckled. "After all, you met him before me."

"Yes," she whispered, almost to herself. "But I think I like you more."

She held out a hand and I took it. A tear rolled down her cheek and I squeezed her fingers. I was glad I had recovered, glad I could give her space to express what she felt, whether heartfelt or not. I had so nearly stormed out and left her in the arms of Superman, and yet now she was confirming I meant something to her, perhaps already more than he did. Jealousy was premature and immature.

★

Or so he thought. But that night, in the cold hour before dawn, he awoke and was no longer in control. His mind and body filled with foreboding. He lay awake fighting off feelings, pushing them into his stomach where they lay dormant, but not defeated, whilst his mind searched for a solution. His first recourse was to words, the balm of the writer. Put it on paper and it would not seem so bad. On paper, it could be read by her – she could see the suffering, share the pain and understand how much she meant to him. But did Aioko want to see the pain her Writer-san was going through, let alone share it? Did she not prefer to have her men separate and silent – at least, on the emotional front? She was looking for surface sunshine, not deep-sea storms. Pain was not in the package for her. That was his side of things. Part of him knew this, knew he should protect her and keep his emotions hidden. But, in the end, he could not.

Dear Aioko-san,

    I have had a bad night. This is my own fault for not being able to put things in perspective. But I feel I should not hide what happened, should not grin and bear it. That way leads to false masks and hidden resentment, not something that belongs between us. My unsettled state of mind is a result of your revelation in the bar last night, and has to do with your married American lover from Europe. I do not want to be a vehicle for revenge – a retaliation for the blonde hair you found on your bed and nothing more – nor just a British writer 'on the side' to an existing American 'on the side,' a secondary extramarital affair to the primary extramarital affair. I am sure you don't see it like that, but that is how it feels. It IS good I know about his visit, it IS good that I now know 'hibernation' is not always hibernation to allow self-recovery, but sometimes (always?) seeing that other man. It is good to know, but I must protect myself from the pain knowledge brings, pain made worse by misunderstanding. In March you said: 'When he next visits I will hibernate.' I thought you meant: 'I will not be available to see him, now I've met you.' Arrogant of me to draw such a conclusion. Oh, Aioko-san, I feel so much for you and you must do what you want when you want. I am not a controlling man, but cannot hide my pain. So let's keep physical closeness and further meetings and mailings for when he's been and gone. It will help me and, meanwhile, I will keep our kisses and touching, coming and going, Adam in Eve, and cream for your tea stored until you 'return.'

Stephen

12

If Stephen had kept to his plan, and Aioko had allowed and encouraged him to do so, they might both have kept on an even keel. But there was an addictive element to the bond between them, formed and fuelled by their daily mail exchanges. Apart from considered pieces like the one above, mails were often sent without thought, and read without the writer's presence to nuance content through speech, or help interpret – through body language and, if need be, body contact – what lay between the lines.

Aioko's first reply on Thursday upped the emotional ante a notch, and gave Stephen hope that the sensitive insights of a writer might prevail over the imagined brawn of a superman. Whether she was playing, concerned or just confused is hard to tell:

Dear Stephen,

I am sorry my poor English hurt you. Yes, all of what you said is right. I am stupid lady. I never doubt you will understand my 'hibernation.' You are so unlucky to have met me. I am wrong. I did the wrong thing. I can accept any punishments, so I agree to your suggestions about not touching and not meeting. It is so painful to read your mail. Because I like you so much and you are getting to be my most important person, that's true. I know it's difficult for you to believe anything that I say, but please… I am sorry. I cannot go on. If there is any chance, could I visit Writerworld for a 'last meal' next week, before I go into hibernation?

Aioko

Stephen's resolve to remain apart from Aioko until Superman had been and gone collapsed.

Ohayo gozaimasu Aioko-san,
    Rules are there to be broken. You are welcome on Monday. I will cook sole fish with *takusan ninniku* and buy a new bottle of wine. Monday is Friday *desu ne*!

So, with the visit of her American friend only two days away, Aioko once again climbed on a number six bus and made her way to Writerworld. Again, she and Stephen kissed politely at the door, and again, after she had changed into her floral pattern dress, she helped him cut vegetables for the salad. They talked about 'after' – though the visit was never mentioned – about 'later on in the summer.' How they would go for more picnics, take a ferry to Macau and stay at the Westin Resort Hotel. How they would walk across Hac Sa beach in the moonlight to Fernando's Portuguese restaurant and order his tomato salad soaked in olive oil, and a piled-high plate of garlic prawns. How they would drink Portuguese beer straight from the bottle, and how, if they still had room, they would order freshly grilled sardines with boiled potatoes and maybe even chicken and more beer. How they would walk back hand in hand, beside the softly breaking sea, and maybe stop to sit on the black sand and stare up at the stars, which, unlike in neon-lit Hong Kong, shone bright and clear in the night sky above Hac Sa beach.

    That is what they would do 'after.' Now they took the food to the table, ate the sole, sipped their drinks with surface chatter, and then carried the dirty dishes through to the kitchen. She washed, dressed in his blue butcher's apron, and he dried. When the last saucepan had been scoured back to silver, and the last plate stored in its designated cupboard, they sat on the sofa holding hands and staring out at the lights of Hong Kong.

    Stephen relaxed. A quiet confidence flowed into his body. He wanted Aioko to take an image of a strong and caring conventional lover with her into the void of the visit. This, he had decided whilst cooking, would be a better image than either 'abstainer' or 'cream tea party man.' He had shown his conventional credentials once, now competition was at the door and it was time to show them again. He wanted the memory of Adam in Eve to be fresh in her mind, fresh enough to exclude, by its very potency and intensity, the entrance of any other Adam into Eve.

So, later, as they lay under the sheets together, he put a hand across and stroked Aioko's flat stomach. She moaned and asked if this was another rule 'there to be broken.' Did she want him to break it? he whispered. *Tabun*, she replied in Japanese, 'Perhaps.' He let his hand play across her nipples, and then back across her stomach and down to the curls of her freshly grown pubic hair. Her own fingers followed his, and together the two sets played a dance around her lower lips until they were wet.

He wanted her to reach out and help his tree grow, but he knew she preferred to touch herself and that he must function on his own. That was how it was for Superman too, and if Superman had no need of help then nor did he. She parted her legs and pulled him on top of her body. He bent to kiss her mouth — to power his desire with emotion — but she shook her head and covered her face with a pillow. She liked her sex separate from intimacy, raw like sashimi. She liked the male to perform its act of coition in a hard anonymous way, without a face or name. Then she could wash away the evidence and return to her civilized Japanese self, outwardly so respectful of another's body space.

At least that was how it seemed to Stephen, left alone above her faceless frame. Her hand was quickening and she was arching up in expectation of his entrance, the inner stimulation required for her climax. But his hardness, nurtured slowly from the quiet bubble of confidence while cooking, began to soften, and as it softened, the spectre of Superman returned. Returned with such a force that Stephen almost cried out in pain. He was being laughed at, scorned and ridiculed: 'Yours is so soft and little, how could it ever be of use to man or beast, let alone a full-grown woman? Prove your virility? Implant a potent padlock in her mind and cunt to keep my penis out? Don't make me laugh. I'm so big and so automatic in my hardness that you can never compete. Lust not love, that's what she wants and that's what I give. You're just a phallic failure. So fuck off!'

With crazy voices screaming in his head, Stephen crouched over Aioko's body. Why had he embarked on this mission to prove his potency? Why had he not let sleeping dogs lie, if all they did when woken was turn tail and run? Now he was trapped. He wanted to switch off, rewind and re-instate his rule. No intimacy until a week on Wednesday. He wanted to regain the high ground, where grunting, rutting supermen could not touch him and the ring of celibacy protected him from scorn.

But Aioko was up and running, and he had wound her up, so now he must help her reach the end. He lowered his lips to her clitoris and inserted a finger inside her vagina, a bony substitute for the blood-engorged knob of flesh she was expecting. She groaned in frustration, let him help for a while and then removed his finger and lips and, with her right hand rubbing outside and her left hand within, climaxed on her own.

She left the bed and went to the bathroom. She showed no sign of disappointment, and when her ablutions were complete, she called Stephen in to share her shower.

But what was there to wash away, he wondered, as hot water bounced off his cold skin. No sticky residue of love, apart from on two fingertips, and a basin would suffice for that. Taking a shower after failing seemed fraudulent. And what memory would now be locked inside her head? What longing for a real man would grow as *he* approached?

When Aioko returned to the bedroom, leaving him alone to waste water, he was overwhelmed. He knelt in the bath, buried his head in his hands and cried – softly at first and then louder and louder. He wanted Aioko to hear, to come and comfort, to swear her love and renounce all supermen, to say their touch meant nothing in comparison with his.

She came, but not to console. She yanked back the shower curtain and stared down at his crouched, naked body. She reached across and turned off the shower tap

"*Nani! Nani!*" she whined like a child, upset because Daddy is no longer behaving in the expected adult manner. "*Nan desu ka.* What is it? *Nani, nani, nani!*"

"I don't know," he moaned. "I feel so frightened, so alone."

"Not my fault, not my fault!" she shouted.

"No, not your fault," he sobbed. "My fault."

"You try to make me feel bad!" she hissed. "About my friend."

"No," he said. "I make myself feel bad, you are not to blame."

"No!" she screamed. "Aioko not to blame! Not Aioko fault!"

He wept again. She stamped her foot, pulled the shower curtain shut, ran out of the bathroom and slammed the door behind her.

Ten minutes later, when he climbed into bed, she was curled up in a ball, snoring.

The next morning, they breakfasted in silence and he again resolved not to see her until the storm had passed. But Aioko, on arrival at work, felt bad, in need of reassurance.

Writer-san,

Aioko is worried about you. I know you are crying now – crying, crying and crying for *baka* Aioko! Because *Baka* Queen IS *baka*. So crazy, she doesn't have any words for you, the King Shark Fighter. Sorry! I don't know what I should do.

Aioko, Queen of Aiokolando

This short message opened a floodgate in Stephen, and though his reply was hard to digest for someone with limited English, and, perhaps, not the best way to mend bridges, there is no doubting its sincerity, just as there is no doubting the stranglehold Aioko now had over him. He was in submission to her whims – whether she intended to be whimsical or not – in a way that was more painful than any smack or bitten nipple.

Dear Aioko-san,

Like a cloud approaching the sun, your visitor darkens the brightness of the light that shines when I am with you. I turn the other way, towards the still blue horizon, but know the dark cloud will come. Its looming mass cramps my body, numbs my mind, although I do my best to be the person that I am. It mocks my search for pleasure, its shadow stopping me from entering you. It sucks away the urges that are mine as man, it says: 'She is mine, she likes the storm more than the sun. Run and hide, gentle man, while I let loose the force of nature. You can't compete!' And so you are drawn from me, enveloped in the darkness and I must wait until the storm is passed, prevented by the rain from reaching you. I hide in the woods, hoping that afterwards the sun will shine as brightly as before. Hoping the cloud will not hover on the horizon, keeping us from contentment, from feeling the heat in heart and body that is ours. Hoping you will not be lost to me; that I will not stay hidden in the wood, too frightened to return. Hoping I will free myself to be fierce storm as well as gentle sun when weathervanes revolve.

    Stephen

If now, finally, Aioko had left him alone, Stephen's wound might have healed without the bloodletting that was to follow. But that same day, she mailed back to say how much she liked her Writer-san and how she understood his pain, and his need to be alone. And then, on Wednesday, just before she went to meet the American, she sent another brief note: 'I'm not excited to meet him today, like I used to be. Just confused. Don't know how I will feel tomorrow, day after tomorrow, but if King allows I want to come back to Writerworld!' Stephen, blind to anything but his need for Aioko, misread or misinterpreted this as a request from her to visit him on Friday – the 'day after tomorrow' – only two days into her hibernation. He was overjoyed. He mailed back: 'Most welcome to come!' She pointed out the misinterpretation, but did agree to meet him for a drink on Friday. A dangerous consolation clutched at by Stephen, who was now in a bad way.

    On Wednesday night, the night of the American's arrival in Hong Kong, he suffered an attack of extreme anguish. He awoke in the dark and imagined Aioko 'giving herself up to the force of the storm.' He wanted to ring, to share the storm if only by proxy. He wanted to talk to her as she lay beneath her American cloud, to hear her say she preferred his sun to the rain now entering her body. He had never experienced such derangement, such despair.

At five thirty on Thursday morning, he rose with the first streaks of dawn and poured the bitter anguish on to paper in one of the most macabre of his short stories, *The Burning Cockpit*. Then, later, responding to Aioko's offer of a drink, he poured out more pain to her. He was desperate to break the other man's grasp, determined to win Aioko by the sheer force of his suffering.

Dear Aioko,
    Of course I would love a drink with you tomorrow – IF you will come back with me afterwards. I did not sleep more than an hour last night, thinking about you and where you were. Of course not ringing, I'm not a fool. I didn't cry, I just felt pain and numbness – heart hurting, stomach frozen, awake and thinking and feeling. So, in the darkest hours of tonight reach out your hands and hold me, wherever you are. Aioko, I kiss you. I miss you.
    Stephen, the Sharkfighting King

Aioko did not reply that day. Stephen waited and waited, not daring to write again. He spent a second sleepless night imagining the worst, imagining aerobics beyond imagination. Then, at 5.30 p.m. on Friday, when he was almost beside himself with despair, fingers sore from checking emails at work, a six-word message arrived from aiaiaiai36: 'Still want to meet at six?' it read. 'Yes,' he replied, in a calm virtual voice. 'Still want to see you.'

13

I set off early from work to reserve our favourite corner seat at the Marriott. I was nervous, unsure whether she was meeting me because she wanted to, or because I had forced her to. Had I stayed a minute longer at my desk, I would have found a second mail from her to put my mind at rest: 'I will run to Marriott after work,' it said. 'Want to get there earlier than you.'

But I was there first, and, when she found me sitting in the bar, she broke her rule and kissed me on the cheek. Then she sat down, smiled her lipstick smile and leant across to squeeze my hand. I grasped my beer and drank down half the glass. I felt the smile was false, a smile of pity, not affection. I imagined her waking up that morning in some hotel where blonde-haired chambermaids are hired. I saw her kiss the Yankee cloud goodbye, saw his shadow cover her, heard her sigh as lips met lips. Tears welled up in my eyes.

"Thanks for coming," I said, biting down on my own lip. "Wine?"

"Oh, no!" she hissed. "You said no tears if we met."

"I know. I'll be all right."

I took a tissue from my pocket and blew my nose.

"See? Just fine," I laughed. "And how are you?"

"Confused. Very confused."

"Because of me?"

"Yes, because of you. Because of him." She grabbed a handful of peanuts and held them tightly in her palm. "But let's not talk of that"

I nodded, and felt tears well up again. I swallowed and smiled.

"Shall I order a wine, or do you want to go straight back?"

"To where?" she asked.

"To Writerworld. Where else?" I said, watching as she let the peanuts trickle from her hand into an ashtray.

"I go to Aiokolando tonight," she said, after a moment's silence. Her face took on a cool, almost cold expression.

"But you promised…" I stammered.

"No promise," she said calmly, with a flash of smile that contained neither pity nor affection. "*You* said I must."

"I said: 'I would love a drink with you – if you will come back with me.'"

"You said that. I said 'drink,' Writer-san. I never agreed to come back!"

"But…"

"You misunderstood I would come and stay today. I cleared up misunderstanding. Said I would meet for drink. Then I go home. *Wakarimasu ka?*"

She smiled her defensive smile, hunched her shoulders high and giggled. Then she picked up a single peanut and put it in her mouth and giggled again. I was losing control. She had enticed me here under false pretences, to play with me, to torment me with the presence of her friend. I could not sit and drink beer, talk of this but not of that and then let her go – to him, or to her home, or worst of all to her home with him.

"Please, Aioko!" I said, begging for the first time. "Please!"

She shook her head and smiled again. Always the smile. So cruel to smile at a time like this, to smile the same smile that she smiled when she lay on the kitchen floor, or stretched out naked on my woollen rug. I felt pathetic. I was grovelling, but beyond caring. I was in pain, and wanted her to ease it.

"Please," I said once more, letting the tears roll down my cheeks.

"No! You cannot cry here," she hissed. "Not in public place."

"I need you, Aioko. Just tonight. Please." I was begging again. "Just for a meal, and then we'll see."

"all right," she muttered through gritted teeth. Other drinkers were now aware of my tears. "But no staying."

"Thank you," I mumbled, wiping my eyes with a napkin from the table. "I've bought the food. Aioko's favourite! Miso soup from City-Super…"

But she did not hear me. She grabbed her bag.

"Come on! Let's go," she hissed. "And, please, no crying. Japanese woman cannot be seen with crying man."

I nodded and stood up. She trotted off in front of me and I followed, head bowed, like a child who has got its way, but knows there will be a price to pay.

We did not talk much in the taxi, though I took her hand and she let me hold it. She stared out of the window at the rain and the bleary neon signs on Queen's Road East, and avoided my eyes. Half way up Stubbs Road, near Shiu Fai Terrace, we came to a halt behind a number fifteen bus. Slope repair on the high, almost vertical rocks that climbed up to the right. Workmen had blocked off half the road and a dark-skinned woman with cloth wrapped round her head sat next to the bus with her board set to 'Stop!'

I stared down to my left.

Rows of gravestones perched one above the other, dripping with water, balanced for eternity on the steep descent that dropped to Happy Valley racecourse far below.

"I wonder if they watch the horses?" I said, my voice almost back to normal.

"*Nani*?" she said, without turning from her misted window.

"The dead souls. I wonder if they bet on the horses."

"*Wakarimasen*," she sighed. "I don't understand."

"Doesn't matter. It was a joke."

She removed her hand from mine to wipe away the condensation that had formed on her side of the car.

"English jokes sometimes hard to understand," she said. "Like English writer's words. Too difficult for Japanese lady."

"Yes," I nodded, and for the first time added. "Sorry."

And then the woman with the cloth round her head switched the sign to 'Go.' The taxi driver jolted into first gear. The number fifteen bus, bound for the Peak with a full load of tourists, belched a black cloud of diesel fumes and lurched forward. And Aioko and I again sat in silence, separated by our selves.

When we reached the flat, Aioko recovered her poise. I felt the vice of anguish loosen. We were at home in this space, at home with the surroundings, at home with each other. I hung up my umbrella and we busied ourselves with cooking. Aioko declined wine, and said she would prefer mineral water. I made no comment. Now that she was with me, in my home, the thought of her in bed with him lost its power. She was in my presence, there was nothing to imagine, no horrors to be conjured up, no other reality to impinge on mine. I was almost content, safe in the eye of a storm that had raged for more than a week. I watched her toss the salad. Her face seemed worn and tired. She had been through the mill, too. She glanced up and caught my eye. I smiled and she smiled back, and, for the first time that evening, I believed the message on her lips.

We ate at the table and talked about her boss. He had been recalled to Japan at short notice and she wondered if this was a bad sign, a first indication that Toshiba might be reducing its workforce in Hong Kong. More likely to do with him, I said, dissatisfaction with his performance, disappointing sales figures, that sort of thing. She hoped he would not leave. He often played golf and 'visited clients,' leaving her free to daydream, sleep or email. She did not want a busybody boss who peered over her shoulder and gave her tasks from dawn till dusk.

"Do you email a lot?" I asked.

She nodded, and added some soy sauce to her organic miso soup. It had been recommended as a prostate protector by my Australian naturopath and was MSG free.

"With two girlfriends in Tokyo. We mail every day."

"What about?"

"Office gossip. Friend gossip. One comes to Hong Kong next weekend. We plan what to do on her visit. Make lists."

"Has she been here before?" I asked, wondering whether Aioko would invite me to meet the friend, and whether I was a topic of their gossip.

"No. First time."

I nodded and helped myself to more soup.

"*Oiishi desu ka*, Writer-san," she said, helping herself to some more too.

"Mm! *Totemo oiishi desu ne*," I enthused. "Delicious!"

After supper we washed up as usual. Then she said she must go. My heart sank and my stomach froze. Without her there, the nightmares would return.

"Why not stay?" I said calmly. "It's nine o'clock already."

She hesitated, and took out her ferry timetable.

"Just to sleep, of course," I added. "I can use the small room if you like."

Her finger moved down the page. Then she folded up the orange and green First Ferry leaflet, and returned it to her purse.

"Ferry at ten o'clock. I take that."

"Are you sure?" I said.

She nodded and smiled her defensive smile – same formation of the lips as any other smile – but pushing me away, not drawing me in.

"Well," I continued, "we have half an hour. Let's sit down."

She glanced at me with a mixture of suspicion and anxiety in her eyes, then walked across to the sofa, smoothed her blue-pleated skirt against the underside of her thighs, and lowered herself on to the dark green leather. She had not changed out of her office clothes. In fact, for the first time, she had not removed one article of clothing, only her shoes. The floral patterned slip was still in its cupboard and would not be worn tonight. Her body was dressed for flight, not fun, and her mind was on its way home – or on its way to him.

My mind worked overtime. How could I make her stay? I did not want to cause another scene, but what rational argument could I use? Rain with a light wind from the south was forecast. No reason for the ferry to be suspended. No typhoon in sight.

I joined her on the sofa, and we sat in silence. I leant my head against the high-backed headrest and closed my eyes. She sat upright, on the edge of her seat, and flicked through a magazine from the coffee table. No physical contact, together but apart. Then, without warning and without looking up, she broached the subject of her own accord.

"Writer-san wants Queen to stay, *desune*."

I opened my eyes and nodded, relief coursing round my body.

"But Queen cannot stay tonight," she added, still turning the pages of her magazine.

She glanced up and flashed an ice-cold smile, a glint of satisfaction in her eyes.

"Why?" I asked.

"Queen needs to be alone. To hibernate." She paused and searched my face. "That makes you sad *ne*?"

"Yes," I said.

She turned back to her magazine.

Why did she play with me like this? Did she enjoy it? Did she enjoy proving her power? Gain pleasure from making me confess my need? Revel in rejecting it? And why use the word 'hibernate'? Was she hinting she would go to him? Tonight? I put my hand out and touched her knee. She did not respond.

"King needs Queen. If she goes, he will cry."

"Not my fault," she hissed. "Not my fault, if King cries."

"No, not Queen's fault, but Queen can stop the tears," I said, still in control, sensing she might relent.

Suddenly, she threw the magazine to the floor and stood up.

"Not my fault! Not my fault!" she cried, her voice now high-pitched and whiny. "And King must let me go."

"To him?" I snapped.

"No! No! No! To my home. That is only place I feel safe. I do not want to be here."

I fell silent, frozen inside. What we had built up was tumbling down. The poison in my veins had spread to hers. Writerworld, my home, the place she called her heaven, was now a hell she wanted to escape from. And I, the understanding, gentle Englishman who helped her deal with life, who let her come and go at will was now a prison guard. She did not understand my needs, did not want to understand them. She needed me to care for her when no one else was there, but did not want to cope with me when I was on my knees. Or, so it seemed, as desperation tipped the scales of my mind.

She grabbed her bag and headed to the door. She opened it, and then turned to me.

"And if I want to see him, I will. You cannot stop me, Writer-san! And if it makes you cry, I'm sorry, but it's not my fault. It's not my fault. Goodbye."

I jumped up, ran to the door and slammed it shut before she could leave. I was no longer in control.

"Please, Aioko-san. Please stay. Just tonight!"

I was behaving badly, but did not care. I could not let her out of my sight.

"No, Writer-san! No! Please let me go."

I was blocking the door, blocking her path. My rational mind was numbed by a need that seemed so much more urgent than her need to be alone. I had to make her understand, I had to make her stay. I dropped to my knees and buried my head in her skirt. I felt like a child. I was a child. And being a child again hurt and humiliated me.

"Please, Aioko-san," I sobbed. "Please stay and hold me tight."

She started to push my head away, but then relented and stroked my hair instead, as if I were a dog. I wrapped my arms around her legs and let the tears flow. I cried, she stroked. And slowly this small sign from her, this small repeated gesture of concern and affection, calmed me down. I released her and shuffled away from the door, still on my knees. I covered my face in my hands and lowered my head to the hard wooden floor. I was still sobbing, but she was free to go. I could not stop her, must not stop her. I knew that. I heard the door open, and close again.

But no footsteps tapped across the marble tiles towards the lift. There was silence, apart from the distant rumble of traffic and the ticking of a clock by the television. I lifted my head and looked round. She was still standing by the door, shaking like a leaf.

I stood up and took her in my arms.

"I'm sorry," I said.

She nodded, and then let me lead her to the bedroom and put her to bed. I hung her office clothes on a hanger and put them in the wardrobe, next to the unused slip. I undressed, climbed in beside her and snuggled up to her still-trembling body. I rested my face on her shoulder and felt tears roll from her cheek onto mine.

"Not my fault!" she whispered, and then fell fast asleep.

★

The next morning she was up early.

She had not slept well and was keen to be on her way. She seemed ill at ease and fragile, yawning and shivering at the same time. Stephen offered to accompany her to the Outlying Islands ferry terminal. She probably thought he was checking up on her, making sure she did not return to Superman's hotel, but she let him come and seemed in some ways glad to have him by her side. And when they parted on the dock, she turned and waved before she disappeared inside the boat.

Stephen walked towards his work, and, on the way, rested on a waterfront bench near the PLA Barracks. Aioko's ferry was visible from where he sat. It was an old one with a funnel, not a new catamaran with sleek lines and no character. He sat and waited as the hooters sounded, moorings were slipped and the boat headed off on its lopsided way to Cheung Chau. He wanted to be on it with her; he found it hard to be apart. But, as he watched and raised his hand to wave, he felt released from the pain of jealousy.

Back at his office, he wrote a poem for her to read on Monday.

AIOKO-SAN
Forgive me please, Aioko-san
For being such a jealous man
For asking you to stay with me
When it was clear you had to be
In your queendom, in your home
Secure and safe, but quite alone
Thank you, though, Aioko-san
For helping out a jealous man
For staying wakeful by his side
And drying tears that he had cried
In future, Queen can always say
Dear King, tonight I will not stay
We live and learn, Aioko-san
And now I'm not a jealous man

Aioko reacted with scepticism and despair. A weekend shuttling between Stephen and the American had left her confused.

Dear Stephen,

I'm not sure if you really change your feeling for me. I guess you still want to cry. My feeling? I don't like anybody and hate myself. Want to be in Aiokolando, alone. I don't know who I am, where I am, why I'm doing this or doing that. Why? Why? Why?

Aioko

But despair – genuine or not – was bait bound to keep Stephen on line, just as optimism and contrition from his side was enough to keep her hooked. She needed her problems to be centre stage, not his. He was servant. She was mistress. So, for the next forty-eight hours, she sent him more and more desperate mails, culminating in one at 5.15 on Tuesday that read: 'I'm sick. I can't think anything, can't do anything. I'm crazy, very, very sick.' Stephen replied at once: 'Do you need help? In words? In person? Just let me know, don't try and crawl through the tunnel alone. I'm here till 5.45.' She mailed at five forty-five on the dot. He must meet her immediately in a bar in Two Exchange Square, an office building not far from the Outlying Islands Ferry Terminal. She would be waiting. He read the message, cancelled a meeting with staff and jumped in a taxi.

The bar was a dark place with dim-lit cubbyholes designed for high-flying couples and incognito businessmen, cramped and murky like Aioko's mood. He wandered back and forth in the gloom and then saw a small figure peer out of a booth at the back. It was her, his Queen. They stayed for two hours, while she talked and he listened. She talked about her confusion, but did not mention the American friend. She talked about her second husband and how she did not know if she could live with him again. She talked about her mother and her artwork. She talked about a father who had ignored his daughter's creativity, chased other women and made the mother ill, leaving Aioko all alone to fend for house and home. She told of how he climbed into her bed when her mother was away and touched her, and how she bit his hand and screamed. Of how he beat her mother and begged his daughter for forgiveness. She talked of her first husband's lack of imagination, his temper if food was not on time. Of his inability to have sex, unless she was tied up tight with rope, her mouth sealed with tape. She talked about Japan, about her problems, about her life, and did not once ask Stephen how he felt.

But Stephen did not mind, and did not interrupt or cry.

She said that Stephen now knew more about her than any other person in the world, and that she relied on him to help her sort things out. He was thrilled to have such trust and confidence put in him and offered to help in any way he could. And when she said she wanted to go home, he did not protest or demand she stay with him. He walked her to the ferry and, for a moment at the gate, they held hands and stared into each other's eyes. And then she scurried off to catch her boat: a tired, crazy dormouse in the dusk.

14

And so the second part of their relationship began.

Stephen saw two paths ahead and hoped to be able to walk them both with Aioko. On the first path, the original investigation would continue – through her. He would experiment with all forms of sexual contact other than intercourse and there would be no more competition with the cloud. If it should hang over Hong Kong again, he would regard it as a primitive throwback, an unsophisticated phenomenon that amused Aioko on a lower plain than her relationship with him. On the second path, a lasting bond would be formed, positing an eventual outcome of intercourse within a monogamous relationship.

The contradictions would be reconciled by path one merging into path two, the fringe production moving to the main stage. Stephen was a believer in dialectics and this was, for him, a dialectical process as inevitable as the ultimate defeat of the bourgeoisie by the working class. A step he should have recognized and taken long ago. Thesis: someone into unconventional sex. Antithesis: conventional monogamy. Synthesis: unconventional sex within a conventional relationship. Not a very original piece of Hegelian logic, or even a new idea, but one Stephen had failed to recognize as the best possible solution for his serial monogamist tendencies. Conventional relationships failed because his enthusiasm for intercourse waned within eighteen months, and disappeared soon after. The partner protested, familiarity prevented introduction of an alternative approach and they parted. But if intercourse were no longer a prerequisite, no longer a measure of success and viability, if both partners accepted other forms of physical contact as proof of potency, then the sell-by date might be extended, or even made to last forever.

Of course, love and affection were needed, that was inherent in the antithesis, but these elements were present with Aioko, alongside a predilection for off-centre sex. At least, that was how Stephen saw things. Whether Aioko, with her limited English and non-dialectical approach to life, had any inkling of what his mind was up to seems doubtful. She was interested in fancies and feelings, not worked-out paths and plans. She was happy to perform on any stage with Stephen, as long as he provided creature comforts, artistic appreciation and a shoulder to cry on.

And yet progress down path two was faster than path one – at least initially.

Stephen decided it was time to present Aioko to a wider public. Up until now, it had always been the two of them alone. No friends on whom to project a joint image, no relations to reflect back familial approval. Some couples would have withered and died without outside confirmation, without an opportunity to show off the added value of their togetherness. Stephen and Aioko had not missed the audience, but now, Stephen decided, it was time to raise the curtain. The third parties would come from his side, because Aioko was a married woman with a respectable image. She could not introduce Stephen to her circle as anything but a passing friend, and if she did that, she said, other Japanese women, with better bottoms than hers, would pounce on such an eligible Englishman. So, it was Stephen who set about gathering an audience for their coming out.

By chance, son Tom and sister Irene were both passing through Hong Kong at the end of May. By chance, or by intent: they had a good relationship and had probably planned the visits to coincide. Irene was returning from Australia and Tom was on his way to New Zealand. He ran a chain of restaurants in the north of England under the name Tom's Fodder: informal eating houses where people could bring their own food and have it cooked, by an expert chef, in any way they chose. A strange idea, but it had proved successful, and now a company down under was showing interest. Both sister and son were suitable people for Aioko to meet and suitable foils for her varied and variable public personae. Neither of them was prejudiced, both of them were good at talking to strangers and putting people at ease, and both were discreet when it came to probing into the whys and wherefores of Stephen's women. They had given up trying to give advice – apart from the general admonishment on Irene's part that he 'must settle down sometime.'

To this familial mix Stephen added a dash of outside blood in the form of his Australian work colleague and good friend Connor. Aioko was nervous. She worried Connor might know her Japanese friends. Stephen said this was unlikely. Connor mixed with British and Australian ex-pats and was too drunk on social occasions to remember anyone the next day, let alone a week later. Stephen wanted him to dilute the family mix, provide Aioko with a drinking partner – Irene was a teetotaller, Tom into dope – and offer an Antipodean angle for Tom's research.

Tom was flying in on Friday afternoon and Irene on Saturday morning, so Stephen planned the meal for Saturday evening. Tom would be twenty-four hours into the new time zone, jetlag from Australia was minimal, and Connor was due back from a student tour of Thailand that day. After briefly considering the idea of cooking a meal in Writerworld, Stephen decided to eat out. He chose a restaurant in Repulse Bay, a settlement of up-market high rise blocks set around a sandy inlet on the south coast of Hong Kong Island. The restaurant, Spices, occupied one end of the lower ground floor of the old Repulse Bay hotel and had a large outside eating area. Stephen preferred a light sea breeze to the ice-cold air-con of dining rooms, and knew that the buffet offered a wide enough variety of East Asian dishes to suit all tastes. Aioko, excited by the idea of discovering a new 'rich people's restaurant,' approved the choice and Stephen booked a table for eight o'clock.

*

Aioko was waiting for us when we stepped out of the taxi. She had not dared sit down before the 'family' arrived. She bowed to Irene and Tom, and Tom said '*Konban wa*' with such a winning smile that Aioko decided she would sit next to him.

"The son of Stephen speaks Japanese," she said with her best lipstick smile, patting the chair beside her. "He sits next to me."

"A bit," Tom laughed, sitting down at the round wooden table next to Aioko. "Japanese for businessmen. I learnt it at college."

I watched him and smiled. He was a good-looking man with broad shoulders, a narrow waist and long, athletic legs; his fine brown hair, cropped to a number three level, accentuated his heavy-set eyebrows and the long eyelashes inherited from me. As a teenager, he had smoked and drunk, but still worked out twice a week. As an adult, he only smoked the occasional joint and – along with his wife – went to the gym every day. Yesterday, at the airport, he had hugged me with affection, stooping as he did so, making me feel old and frail in his strong, masculine arms. Later I had crept into his bedroom and gazed down at the sleeping man who was my son: mouth open, arm behind head, one leg outside the covers – exactly the position he had always assumed as a little boy.

Now, settled in his seat next to Aioko, the grown-up Tom turned and bowed to his Japanese neighbour.

"*Dozo yoroshiku!*" he said, his accent more Leeds than Tokyo. "'Pleased to meet you', *desu ne?*"

"So!" cooed Aioko, with a long rising tone. "I think son speak more Japanese than father *desu ne.*"

We all laughed, and Aioko winked at me. Her eyes were bright and alive.

"So, where do you come from in Japan?" asked Irene, in her 'interested' voice, a voice cultivated at Edinburgh dinner parties to keep the conversation flowing and guests at their ease. "I've been there once, a long time ago."

"Near Mount Fuji," said Aioko, flashing a smile at my son. "Mother has small house just to north of Mount Fuji."

"What a beautiful setting," said Irene. "I took a tour there. A day trip from Tokyo, by coach."

"Oh, yes," Aioko nodded, "many tourists. Our house just behind tourist hotel where buses stop."

"Perhaps I saw it without knowing," laughed Irene.

"Easy to remember," continued Aioko. "Hotel, then lake, then Fuji in background – usually first stop for Fuji tour buses. Best photograph place for Fuji."

"Really, how fascinating," said Irene, turning to incorporate me into the conversation. "You've been to Japan, haven't you, Stephen?"

"Just once," I said, wondering why Aioko had never told me where her mother lived. Perhaps I had never asked. "I went to Mount Fuji, too. I remember the hotel."

Aioko giggled, and seemed to backtrack from her earlier statement.

"Oh, there are many hotels. I do not think you saw one near mother's house."

I wanted to ask her for a more detailed description, but the sharp tone in her voice and a flash of anger in her eyes made me hesitate.

"Perhaps Tom could open restaurants in Japan," said Irene, changing the subject.

Her social antennae had sensed the tension and it was Tom's turn to be brought back into the conversation. The topic was a goldmine and we all listened to Tom's explanation of how a new market should be approached.

Ten minutes later Connor arrived, apologizing for his lateness in a bluff Australian way and smelling of cheap aftershave – a gift, he later told me, from a 'dab-handed' girl in Bangkok. Introductions were made, and, after a brief assessment of Connor's potential, I saw Aioko opt for my son as her partner. He was by far the younger of the two and by far the better looking. Connor's face had spent too much pre-factor-thirty time in the outback and been further distressed, if not quite destroyed, by alcohol.

Aioko had already started flirting with Tom, and Tom seemed happy to play along. They were now discussing the possibility of karaoke in Tom's Fodder outlets. Connor clapped me on the back, ordered another bottle of wine and was soon in conversation with Irene. A village in the Blue Mountains, where he stayed as a child, had been her base for hiking. Perfect. I was happy to sit back, observe and listen. I was the host who had brought these people together, the creator of the performance, and just as the playwright does not need to star in his own play, so I, on this occasion, did not need, or even want, to be the centre of attention. Occasionally a question would be thrown in my direction – about writing, or family, or both – and I would answer, toss in an anecdote or two and then throw the ball back on the table and withdraw to the sidelines. Every now and then someone went to fetch more food from the buffet, alone or with a partner, and conversation would switch to a more general topic, such as climate or fashion or food.

In this way, after two hours of chomping and chatting, most of us were full to bursting. Only Connor – not one to worry about his waistline – continued to commute back and forth.

"I just love this coconut pudding," he said, returning with his third plateful of sweetmeats. "Try a bit, Irene," he added, offering my sister a mouthful.

"Mm, yummy," enthused Irene. "Condensed milk, that's what does it."

"Condensed milk," echoed Connor, jamming the rest of the pudding into his mouth and washing it down with red wine. "That takes me back."

And they were off again, reminiscing about childhood sweets and treats, and the relative merits of Lyons and Walls ice cream. The topic of conversation between Aioko and Tom moved on to babies, and the best age to have them.

"You're not too old," I heard Tom say.

"No? I can still have a baby?" she smiled, as her eye caught mine and winked again. "A little tiny Aioko?"

"Why not?" said Tom, wiping his mouth with a napkin and turning in my direction. "How old was Mum, Dad? When she had me?"

"Thirty," I replied.

"That's very young," exclaimed Aioko. "I am old woman."

"Nonsense!" retorted Tom.

"What do you think, Writer-san," – she was now drunk enough to use our private name for me in public – "can I still have baby?"

"Of course," I said, smiling at her warmly and wishing I could take her in my arms and kiss her there and then. "Of course, you can. And a very fine child it would be."

At that moment, Tom stood up to go to the washroom, leaving an empty space between Aioko and me. Aioko leant across and whispered in my ear.

"Oh, I do want baby after seeing handsome, handsome son. Little tiny baby with tiny power bottom like Aioko."

I chuckled and squeezed her hand. She kissed me on the cheek and sat back in her seat with tears in her eyes.

At ten o'clock, with the last drop of wine drunk, and the last crumb of coconut pudding scraped from Connor's plate, we stood up to go. Connor had to dash. He was due to meet a friend in a Lan Kwai Fong bar. He jumped – or fell – into a taxi, blew us kisses and was gone. He had suggested sharing the cab, but Irene wanted to take the bus back over the top, as we had in March, and view the lights of Hong Kong from the upper deck. Tom, wilting from jetlag and wine, said he would join her.

"What do you want to do, Aioko?" I asked.

She hesitated, and the ever-watchful Irene jumped in.

"Why don't you two go for a walk, Stephen? On the beach or something. It's such a lovely night. We can let ourselves in and make the cocoa, can't we, Tom?"

Tom nodded and yawned. Aioko giggled. She had drunk a great deal of wine and was still making eyes at Tom, but he was passed noticing and ready for bed.

"Big shister shays you must take me on beach, Writer-shan," she whispered for all to hear, the slur in her voice more noticeable than it had been at the table.

I nodded and laughed.

"Fine by me, if you want to go."

"Mm," she said, beaming at Tom. "Hard to say goodbye to handsome son, but, yes, I'd like that."

So, after much bowing and nodding and see-you-again-sooning, we left Tom and Irene at the bus stop and headed down the steps to Repulse Bay beach. It was a warm evening, but not too hot. The humidity was low for Hong Kong, around sixty-five per cent, and there was a fresh breeze blowing in off the South China Sea. Aioko put her arm round my waist for support, as we negotiated the steep steps one by one. This was the first time she had shown physical intimacy toward me in public, and when we reached the bottom, she slipped her hand in mine and squeezed it.

"Writer-san very lucky. Very, very lucky," she said, almost to herself.

"Why, Aioko-san?" I asked, squeezing her hand in return,

"Such a beautiful son. Aioko very jealous."

I nodded. I was glad she liked him. Glad and proud.

"He's a good lad. Doing all right for himself, too."

"Very lucky," Aioko repeated, and bending down she slipped off her high heel shoes and stepped on to the soft powdery sand.

It looked more like snow in the moonlight, and as we walked across it hand in hand towards the glinting sea, I again imagined us in Hokkaido in northern Japan, in winter. Both older, her hair grey and my head bald, but hand in hand; still happy, though many years had passed.

When we were almost at the water's edge, and could hear the lapping of the wavelets as they broke against the shore, I stopped and faced her. Behind us, the lights of Repulse Bay shone into the night sky; in front of us, the sea stretched away into darkness.

"Shall we sit down?" I whispered.

She nodded and, finding a dry spot, we lowered ourselves onto the sand. We sat for a while in silence, hand in hand, staring out to sea, listening to the waves. Then she turned towards me, took my face in her hands and – for only the second time since I had met her – kissed me on the mouth in a normal way.

Her lips opened against my already-open lips and the wetness of her tongue touched mine. Softness and warmth coursed round my body, as they had done once before, on a garden path in England, when a blonde-haired girl in riding clothes, two years my senior and taller by a hand, had taken me outside and kissed me on the mouth.

My first kiss, Aioko's kiss now, indescribably soft with no hardness in the loins to mar the moment; just a feeling of belonging and a gentleness of touching that spoke of a time before birth, that seemed to remove the physical burden of my body. I let her kiss me, and she let me kiss her, and so we must have sat on the soft receiving sand for ten minutes or more. No caressing, no teenage fumbling, no compulsion to conform, no wish or need to progress beyond this moment. Our most articulate and yet most intimate parts fused as one; spared from the need to speak, seeking solace and finding it, as they did so long ago around a mother's breast. Simple solace, requiring no thought or explanation, an endless flowing to and fro, from me to her, from her to me, in time with the waves, in time with the wind, in time with our souls. It was the new beginning I had hoped for, and, at that moment, I could not have cared what stage we were on – fringe, main, or the final stage of life. If we had died there and then, I would not have been concerned, because I believe we would have passed into death without noticing. Returned in peace to the womb and water from where we came, returned to where the kissing never stops.

But suddenly, Aioko broke away, glanced at her watch – a watch that Superman had given her, a watch that had caused me so much pain before – and jumped up.

"Writer-san, I must go," she hissed. "Last ferry in half an hour."

"Of course," I said, coming back to earth and standing up. "We'll take a taxi."

"No, no" she cried. "You go home, see your guests. I'll be all right."

I bent to kiss her again, but she was already scurrying away across the sand, like some insect scared by a flash of self-consciousness that does not belong to its species.

"Come on, Writer-san!" she called. "Come on!"

And I obeyed.

Perhaps it had only been the wine in her mixing with the dream in me – though somehow it felt like more. But, whatever it was, I slept that night like a baby in paradise; quite alone, yet quite content, surrounded by a warm sea of endless hope.

15

On Sunday morning, Tom stayed in bed whilst Irene and I went for a walk in Tai Tam Country Park.

We set out from Parkview and headed downhill towards the twin reservoirs, an uninterrupted view of green hillsides and blue sea stretching out before us.

"Seems a nice girl," Irene said, after walking in silence for a while.

We had exhausted scenery, weather and work, and now, I sensed, Irene felt it was a good moment to broach what was, from her point of view, the main topic of the walk.

"But she's married, you say?" she added.

"Yes. To a second husband," I replied.

"Oh dear. Can't keep 'em?"

"Or they can't keep her," I laughed, but added no further information.

I did not want to divulge secrets about Aioko to my sister. I trusted Irene and knew there was no one of importance she could tell, but was afraid of her using the information to construct a case for or against the relationship.

"She reminded me of Mother," Irene continued. "Not physically, of course, Mother was a big woman, but her mode of behaviour – her way of presenting herself in public. Very similar."

"How do you mean?" I asked, uneasy about the comparison to our mother.

"Well," said Irene, after a moment's thought. "She's a play-actor isn't she? Enjoys an audience. Not in such a loud way as Mother, but still with the same wiles."

"Wiles?"

"Oh, you know. A smile here, a giggle there, a raising of the eyebrows – drawing attention to herself."

"Sounds as if you didn't like her much," I observed dryly. Irene could be tactless in her comments. I did not want her to put a foot in it and end up in an argument.

"No, I did. It's just… Well, she's a bit of a flirt, isn't she?"

I laughed.

"You were jealous. Because she was getting on so well with Tom."

"Perhaps," acknowledged Irene with a nod. "I used to be jealous of Mother, too. When she flirted with my boyfriends. And with you."

"With me?" I exclaimed in surprise. "Mother flirted with me?"

"Oh, yes. When you were a teenager. Especially when you brought a girlfriend home. Then she would go all out to keep your attention on Mum, and not on the girl. And, even if there was no girlfriend, she didn't want you talking to me. You were her boy, and she made sure you danced to her tune."

I chuckled again.

"You should have been the writer, Irene, not me. I thought the world just passed you by. Now it seems you were busy observing the minutiae of family life."

"I was learning," said Irene, stopping and turning to admire the view. "Learning not to be like Mother. After Father died, I decided I wanted to be like him. Cheerful, outgoing, saying what I meant and not playing games."

"You've succeeded there," I said, stopping too, and wondering whether her statement meant that I had ended up like Mother. "With yourself and with your children."

"I hope so."

I sat down on a rocky outcropping.

We had crossed the Upper Tai Tam reservoir dam, turned left and were now halfway up the long tree covered ascent to Mount Parker. A break in the woods afforded us a glimpse of the landscape below and it was a good place to rest. The day had heated up and my upper body was soaked in sweat. I pulled a bottle of Evian from my rucksack and handed it to Irene. She took a swig and returned it to me. I drank a quarter of the large litre flask and returned it to my pack. Beneath us, the water of the two reservoirs shone like polished green glass, not a ripple to be seen, just the shimmer of an embryonic heat haze resting on the surface as the sun began its daily process of evaporation.

There had been a reservoir near our childhood house, a cold grey stretch of water where my nanny Sally used to take me in a pushchair. She met a friend there, who arrived on a horse, riding bareback, with just a rope halter for control. The friend would jump off and tie the halter to a rusting, wrought iron seat that overlooked the water. Then she and Sally would sit and chat, sometimes for an hour or more, whilst I was left to sleep. Once, I remember, they picked buttercups from a meadow by the water and shone them under each other's cheeks, to see if they liked butter. When they were done, the friend lent down and held the yellow-leafed wildflower under my chin, and tickled me with it. I put up a hand to make her stop, but she threw the flower away and tickled me with her fingers. Around the neck at first, and then all over. I didn't like it, twisting and turning under the restraining straps of the pushchair, squirming this way and that to avoid my tormentor. Sally laughed, but then, when I began to cry, she pulled her friend away and came to comfort me. She kissed me on the head, undid the straps and, lifting me out of the chair, carried me to the seat and sat me on her knee. When that happened, her friend climbed on the horse and galloped away. Jealous, too, perhaps.

"What was that friend of Sally's called?" I mused out loud. "The one you mentioned last time? Suspected lesbo."

"Muriel. Muriel Duffin. Why?"

We had been sitting in silence, enjoying the view. I was amazed at the clarity of the memory brought to mind by the water below. It had appeared from nowhere and did not belong to my standard list of childhood memories, often fixed in place by photographs.

"I was recalling how Sally used to meet her – by the reservoir. Me in the pushchair, Sally and Muriel on the seat."

"Yes, they were good friends," said Irene. "She came to a bad end though."

"Who, Sally?" I asked, a note of alarm in my voice.

"No, no. Muriel. Got mixed up with some Hell's Angel from Doncaster. You were away at school by then."

"I thought she was a lesbian?"

Irene laughed, though there was a note of sadness in her laughter.

"I think, to coin a phrase, she'd have 'done it with anything' given half a chance – man, woman or beast. She was a strange one, that Muriel. Anyway, we'd better get moving. I promised Tom we'd be back for lunch."

Irene wanted to change the subject, I could tell. I had touched on some unwelcome memory that, in her case, was better left alone. But I was curious about the 'bad end' Muriel had come to. I remembered seeing her once, dressed from top to toe in black leather astride the back of a motorbike, parading herself – and what I now realized must have been her long-haired Angel – outside the village pub on a cool summer evening. I was home from boarding school for half-term, full of frustrated teenage desires, and the image of that woman in leather – who I would not then have recognized as my pushchair tormentor – stayed in my mind for several months, fuelling fantasy after fantasy between the rough cotton sheets of my dormitory bed.

"So what happened?" I asked.

"To Muriel?"

"Yes."

"She was killed in a motorcycle accident. Overtaking a truck on the blind crest of a hill. You know, that stretch of the A64 near Castle Howard, not far from our village. An accident black-spot till they built the dual carriageway."

"Was she killed outright?"

Irene nodded.

"So they said. The bike hit a tractor head on. No helmets in those days, but even if there had been…"

Her voice tailed off. She stood up, stretched and set off at a brisk pace. I followed, hard put to keep up. The hill was steep, but nothing compared to the mountains Irene climbed in Scotland, or the Alpine peaks she had scaled – some with two children in tow – when younger. She was an outdoor girl, always had been.

"Did you know Muriel?" I asked, out of breath from the effort of keeping up. "I mean to talk to."

Irene shook her head and quickened her pace.

"Not really. We had a 'contretemps' once, that's all."

"A 'contretemps'?"

That was a Mother word; a euphemism for a serious event that was best dealt with by being treated as not serious – as a mere 'contretemps.'

"What happened?" I persisted.

"I'd rather not talk about it, Stephen. It was a long time ago."

My curiosity was kindled into a blaze, but, with an effort, and out of respect for my sister's sensibilities, I remained silent. She was not easily put out, and if she preferred to let sleeping dogs lie, so would I.

Then, at the top of the hill, where the road divides – with one half climbing on up to the summit of Mount Parker and the other plunging down to Quarry Bay – she changed her mind. We were sitting at a picnic table overlooking the valley below, drinking water, sharing a banana and getting our breath back. The last part of the climb had been hard work and we had walked in silence, concentrating our efforts on the ascent.

"Very briefly, this is what happened," she said, when her half of the banana was finished and the skin had been lobbed into a nearby litterbin.

"You don't have to tell me," I said. The subject had not been mentioned for half an hour, but I knew what she was referring to.

"I know. I've never told a soul, but now I will. And because you're my brother, I know it will go no further. 'Cross your heart and hope to die,' etc."

I made the childhood sign of secrecy above my heart, and she began her tale.

"During school holidays, when I was eleven or twelve, I used to go down to the stable yard at the back of the house and read in the loft above the saddle room. It was a quiet spot away from you and Mother. You were six at the time and always nagging me to play. I was growing up fast and no longer interested in childish games. Sally would tell you not to pester me, but you still persisted, so the loft was my secret hideaway. It could only be reached by a ladder from the saddle room and was forbidden territory for you. Climbing up a ladder was considered unsafe for a six-year-old, and, as the ladder could be pulled up once inside the loft, it was a retreat from all comers."

"I remember that," I said. "I used to go up there, too, when I was older."

"Well, one Saturday afternoon, I was reading in the loft, sitting with the hay loading door ajar to let in light, when I heard a noise. I turned around and saw Muriel standing behind me in the shadows. I can remember exactly how she looked. She was wearing a worn pair of jodhpurs, mud-spattered brown jodhpur-boots, a beige windcheater open to the waist, and a white blouse with the top two buttons undone so that the upper half of her large breasts were visible. Her black hair was tied back in a ponytail and she was carrying a riding switch. I asked her what she was doing there, and she said she often came up after exercising the horse. When Father died, Mother used to hire her on and off to exercise our one remaining horse, Nelly. I had not yet developed my interest in horses – that had been Father's thing – but Mother refused to sell, saying Father would have wanted us to keep Nelly until she died. Sally had suggested Muriel, I suppose, and that was why she was there that day, in the loft with me. I said I was reading and did not want to be disturbed. She laughed and hit the side of her boot with the switch. She called me a bookworm and asked why I wasn't interested in anything else. 'Like what?' I retorted and she said – quite bluntly – 'Like sex, for instance.' To be honest, I'd hardly heard the word at that age; boarding school girls lead a cloistered life and, in the fifties, there was not the exposure to the subject – on television or in magazines – that there is today. But I had heard the phrase 'the opposite sex' used by Mother, so, not wishing to admit my ignorance, I told Sally I wasn't interested in the 'opposite sex.' 'Don't have to be boys,' she persisted, 'girls can do it with girls too, you know.' I didn't know what she meant, so just shrugged my shoulders and went back to reading. 'I thought all you boarding school girls did it,' she said, her tone jeering now, 'but maybe you're too young.' I buried myself deeper in my book and tried to ignore her.

But she came and stood above me, and, when I glanced up, I saw that she was undoing the side-buttons of her jodhpurs. I asked what she was doing and she said she'd show me hers if I'd show her mine. 'My what?' I asked, in all innocence, as I really didn't know what she was on about. 'Your fanny, dumbo. Your wee hole, the thing between your legs.' I felt myself going bright red, and, for the first time, felt scared. 'Go away,' I said, 'or I'll tell my mother.' 'Please yourself, Miss Prim,' she said, doing her buttons up again, 'but you're missing something very nice.' And then curiosity got the better of me, or, perhaps, I felt a sudden surge of confidence: I was, after all, the lady and she the village girl, a more important distinction than age. 'All right,' I said, 'but it'll have to be quick.' 'You first,' she said, 'here, I'll help you.' And, before I knew what was happening, she had bent down, stood me up, pulled up my dress and lowered my knickers. She told me to hold the dress up under my armpits. As she inspected me, I felt myself go beetroot from top to toe, but she just laughed and said something about a 'sweet little 'airless 'ole.' Then she lowered her jodhpurs and underpants, and I stared in amazement at her dark mass of pubic hair. I had never seen hair down there before and didn't even know it existed. And, for a while after, I assumed only village girls were like that. I couldn't imagine Mother having a great big bush between her legs. I was shocked, but also curious. She wanted me to touch it, but I refused. I said I'd rather just look. Then she put a finger between my legs, quite gently, and kissed me on the mouth. I froze at first, then struggled and broke free. I was ashamed because it did feel nice, but also wrong and, anyway, she smelt of Nelly, all horse dung and sweat. She grabbed me again and tried to push my face between her legs, but this time I pinched her hard behind the knee and she yelped and let me go. I made a run for the ladder, but she caught me again. I let her kiss me, but kept my hands between my legs. 'Next time I'll touch down there then,' she whispered in my ear, as we heard voices approaching in the stable yard, 'and not a word to your mum, all right?' I nodded. I would have been much too ashamed to say anything to anyone and never have until today – although I'm no longer ashamed. And there never was a next time. A week after the 'contretemps,' Nelly died and there was no reason for Muriel to be on our property anymore. She used to beckon to me in the village street sometimes, and part of me wanted to go and see what would happen if she touched some more. But most of me was too frightened and, believe it or not, I was something of a snob at that age and didn't like to be seen mixing with village girls. So that's it. That's the story of Muriel and me."

Irene's face lit up with relief when she had finished, and I smiled at her.

"Not too painful?" I asked softly.

"Not with you. No," she replied with a laugh. "In fact, I feel better for the telling." She paused, gazed out across the valley and then added, "Sometimes I wonder, though."

"Wonder what?"

"Wonder what would have happened – if I'd let her go 'all the way.'"

"What do you mean?" I said.

"Well, maybe I'd have grown up preferring the touch of my own sex."

"Become a lesbian, you mean?"

"Possibly."

I shook my head.

"I don't think sexuality is formed by a one-off event like that."

Irene nodded and screwed the top back on the now-empty Evian bottle. The sun emerged from behind a cloud and the landscape lit up in greens and blues and browns. A group of schoolgirls in their white uniforms ran past our table laughing and shouting in Cantonese. I watched them collapse on the grass, and then sit up straight as teacher approached. I wondered what children were doing in uniform on a Sunday and then remembered the countless Sunday schools introduced by the British to rid its subject people of superstition. A complex mixture of inheritance, environment and history shaped us, not single events. Irene was living proof of that. For some, the loft experience might have been traumatic – for my sister, just a part of growing up. I watched her pack the empty bottle back in the rucksack, ready for disposal at the next recycling bin.

"I think children get over things more easily than we imagine," I added as an afterthought.

"Yes. But in a strange sort of way I fell in love with Muriel, and stayed in love with her for a year or two. Not just in awe, in love. Maybe everyone falls in love with their first real kisser."

"Maybe," I agreed, thinking of my own older girl in riding clothes.

"I was quite upset when she was killed."

"How old were you then?"

"Twenty-two, last year at university."

"Did you go to the funeral?"

"No." Irene shook her head. "Mother told me about the accident, when I came home after graduation. By then Muriel had been dead and buried for two months."

I nodded, amazed at the complexity and secrecy of people's personal history and the scars and rainbows it left in its wake. I thought I knew my sister as well as anyone, but, in the end, I realized, as we strode off down the hill to Quarry Bay, we really only know ourselves — and even then through a glass, very darkly.

16

On Monday, Tom flew on to New Zealand and Irene back to Britain.

The two of them had cooked a meal for Stephen on Sunday evening – spaghetti bolognese from Tom and a salade niçoise from Irene. Afterwards they played Monopoly, with Tom owning most of the board by the end of the game. Stephen skipped work on Monday and took his guests shopping in Tsim Sha Tsui. He led them up Nathan Road's Golden Mile, across Kowloon Park to Canton Road and back through Ocean Terminal to the Star Ferry. On the way, they bought discreet designer clothes for Irene, electronic gizmos for Tom, books for Stephen and a watch of dubious origin for Tom's wife Cheryl. They ate a late lunch buffet in the Hong Kong Hotel and returned home. Newspapers and snoozing for an hour or two, a bowl of soup at seven, then, as the departure times of the flights were close, a joint trek to the airport. After fond farewells, sister and son disappeared through the barrier leaving Stephen alone, unaware, as the image of departing smiles and waving hands faded from his retina, that he had seen them for the last time.

When he reached home, the flat felt empty. He would have liked someone to be there, to keep him company, to share the sadness he felt whenever his son left. He would liked to have had a partner waiting for him – like Irene did, like Tom did: someone who belonged with him, someone who did not need to return to a life elsewhere, someone for whom the centre of life was Stephen. He would have liked Aioko to be there. Her Saturday night kiss was fresh in his mind and he was keen to progress down the second path of real intimacy, bond himself to her and her to him. The first path, the original investigation into his submissive side, no longer seemed important.

They met for a drink on Tuesday, but she did not stay the night at Writerworld. She was busy with new artwork and wanted to complete it while still in the mood. Perhaps she was testing Stephen, checking whether he would be upset. He was not. They bowed goodbye in the Marriott lobby without tears or melancholy, agreeing to spend Saturday night and the whole of Sunday together.

On Saturday morning, Stephen bought tickets for the musical *Miss Saigon*, and beforehand they ate a meal at the Peninsula. Aioko had seen the show in Japan, but was so touched by the meal and theatre tickets that she broke her rule and kissed Stephen at table, calling him the most 'considerate, kind and generous man' she had ever known. They enjoyed *Miss Saigon* – a no-expenses-spared production in the Grand Theatre of the Cultural Centre – and let its emotive music, tear-jerking storyline and melodramatic climax wash over them in hi-tech waves of sound and light without resistance. Stephen, seeing it for the first time, was impressed by its criticism of French and American colonialism – sharp, despite the sugar coating. Aioko, uninterested in politics, marvelled at the set and costumes and wished she had followed a career in stage design.

After the show, they took a Star Ferry back. They sat hand in hand, letting the warm May wind caress their faces and watching the neon skyline of Hong Kong Island – bright and clear against the dark hills behind – draw nearer. They slept in each other's arms without any sexual contact, lying in green grass by the side of the second path.

The next morning they ate a breakfast of muesli, fruit, oatcakes and jam, read the *South China Morning Post* and then walked along the full length of Bowen Road and on down through Hong Kong Park to Pacific Place. They had lunch – *tempura no teishoku* – in a small Japanese restaurant in Queensway Plaza above Admiralty MTR, and afterwards took a number six bus back to Writerworld. They were both sleepy, from the walk and from the effects of a small decanter of *sake* Aioko had ordered with the meal. Stephen had never tried *sake*, despite his one visit to Japan with Su–yin, and

Aioko said he must. He liked its smooth taste, and refused to believe it was a strong brew. But by the time they reached Writerworld, he was half-asleep.

Aioko led him to bed, laid him down, undressed him – apart from his underpants – and then crawled in beside him. As he dozed off, he heard her voice, as if from a great distance. She was telling him that he was too good for her, that she was a bad girl, that he would be hurt again and again by her, and that she was no good. She was a lady lost in limbo – a word Stephen had taught her at lunch to describe her unresolved situation – a lady lost in limbo with no way out. He heard the distant voice, but at the same time felt her head nestle into his shoulder and her tiny fingers rest upon his stomach.

When he awoke, he felt more alive and refreshed than he ever had in his entire life. He lay gazing at Aioko breathing softly beside him, mouth open, brow furrowed. She opened her eyes and smiled. The furrows smoothed and the eyes lit up, she slid across, put her arm around his chest and held him tight. When she was asleep once more, he removed the arm and crept out of bed. He sat in his study and wrote a poem, the most heartfelt, touching poem he had ever written for anyone.

BAD GIRL
I sleep so deep
I know the sleep is healing
I sleep so deep
I know my inner feeling
Must be right

Bad girl softly sneezing
By my side
Gentle breathing easing
With a sigh
Her bare arm like a child's
Round me tight.

She dreams of her own badness
Of 'baka' queen and sadness

But who she is her dreams do not reveal
She flutters like an insect
As I touch her resting neck
And then settles with my shoulder
As a shield.

'Bad girl bad for you', she said
But would I want to be instead
With someone else on Sunday
Sleeping here
No way, no doubts, my head is clear
My soul at peace when bad girl's near
There's nowhere else
And no one else like her

So small and fragile bad girl is
In need of love and care
A look of sadness in her eyes
That's like a baby's stare
Take care of me she seems to say
But when you try she turns away
And cries 'I'm bad, you must not stay!'
And yet I'm here beside her deep in sleep.

A girl whose badness comes and goes
Whose feelings, break and ebb and flow
Who wants to love and be admired
Crazy today, tomorrow tired
A girl who's yet to meet her grown-up self
And me the shore on which she breaks
A life-worn beach prepared to take
Her bad girl ways and good girl woes
Her warmth that cools, and doubts that grow
A kingdom she is conquering by stealth

He did not show the poem to Aioko. Perhaps he felt it was too personal, too revealing of his feelings for her. And if, that afternoon, he had, it would probably not have received the response he hoped for.

As it was, when she woke a second time, Aioko called him to the bed and told him she was so full of energy she wanted to go home and work on her mirrors. Did Stephen mind? Of course not, he replied, though his heart sank. He had prepared miso soup and was looking forward to a second night by her side, but he said nothing.

Well then, she'd be off.

In a flash she was showered, dressed and at the door, hunching her shoulders, giggling and saying goodbye all at once. Should he accompany her to the ferry? No, she said, she'd rather go alone. Fine, he said with a smile, and let her leave without a fight.

He trusted her now and was happy, as the poem suggests, to accept her as a whole – her mood changes, her need to be alone, her craziness. He trusted her because he assumed that his feelings, though still unspoken, were reciprocated. An assumption that, on Tuesday, led him to turn his back on the cellar door, step back on to the main stage and declare – albeit in an oblique manner – where, for him, the second path was heading.

This is what he sent, in an attachment to a mail confirming their date on Friday:

LOST IN LIMBO

This morning, I went to the hairdresser and sat under Hokkaido snow for a second time. Snip, snip, went the scissors, as the soft white fluff floated down before my eyes. Perhaps I would see Aioko again, standing in a winter scene – a frown upon her face, because it is cold and she wants to be in Hawaii or Tahiti. But all I saw were the mists that surround people who are in limbo. Sometimes bright, white mist with sunlight breaking through and images beginning to emerge. Sometimes dark, dank wetness with no light to penetrate the swirling uncertainty of what is to come. Perhaps, that is why we stay in limbo. We are frightened of what might be lurking in the mist, wary of the warmth that might welcome us there. Snip. Snip. I hope the removal of fluff from my head will shed some light, will melt the mist, but all I see is Aioko on a beach in Lantau, under Akaioko's cousin, the big red sun umbrella. Waiting. Waiting for the future to reveal itself. Leaning across to kiss me. Her lips warm and soft. Lips in limbo, on leave from real life.

When I was leaving the hairdresser, I passed a Japanese mother with two children – one a toddler, the other a baby. The mother was trying to make the baby go to sleep, encouraging the older girl to hoodwink her little sister into night time slumber. '*Oyasumi nasai*,' said the mother. '*Oyasumi nasai*,' said the sister, with an additional prod at the babies arm. '*Oyasumi nasai*,' they said together and the baby, sensing perhaps that this was all a game, smiled and closed its eyes. And then, for a moment, the limbo-enclosing mist that had remained with me cleared. In the clearing, I saw an image: a Japanese girl of sixteen arm-in-arm with my son, now forty. Of course, I thought: little Aioko with the tiny, tiny bottom who is to be his new young wife. But my son, somehow reading my thoughts, shook his head and laughed: 'Don't be daft, Dad! She's not my wife. She's my sister.'

It must have taken Aioko some time to unravel the full meaning of Stephen's message, and there was no response until the following morning. It revealed little:

I finished your green shampoo on Sunday, washing *baka* Queen's hair. I buy you new bottle and give it to you in Marriott tonight, Wednesday. 6 p.m. Usual table.

17

I was surprised at the suggestion. Aioko had said she wanted to concentrate on her artwork until the end of the week and our next official date was on Friday. But her wish was my command, and I thought no more about it.

I cancelled a planned meeting at the Goethe Institute and arrived at the Marriott five minutes early. Our usual corner table was occupied, so I sat at one further down the bar, next to an unopened grand piano. Not as private, but still with a view of the harbour, now darkening as twilight turned to dusk. At six, Aioko tripped in wearing her blue skirt and white blouse and carrying a big black shoulder bag. She sat down, and when the waiter arrived, ordered beer instead of wine. I followed suit.

"I thought you wanted to work on your mirrors," I said, after we had greeted each other, exchanged office news and taken a sip or two of beer.

"Yes. I do. Just one drink and then I must go," she replied.

"Oh," I said, unable to disguise my disappointment.

I had cancelled a meeting and come running, assuming there was something on her mind, something important to discuss. She smiled, a warm version of her lipstick smile, and put out a hand. I hesitated, but then took it and forgave her. I had vowed to accept the bad girl with her badness still intact. I swallowed my disappointment and bathed in her smile.

"And here's present for you," she said, reaching into her black bag. "For Writerworld – and almost bald writer," she added with a giggle.

She handed me a Watson's plastic carrier bag. I reached inside and pulled out a jumbo-sized bottle of my usual green shampoo.

Aioko washed her hair each visit, and a bottle that used to last me months now disappeared in weeks.

"Japanese lady's hair use too much of Writer-san shampoo."

"Yes," I laughed. "But I don't mind. I like her hair."

"Now, she use no more," Aioko added, ignoring my complement. "Not good for Writer-san."

I laughed again and took a sip of beer.

"Don't be silly, Aioko-san. Of course you can use my shampoo."

"Look on back of bottle," she said, her voice sounding tense for the first time that evening.

I turned the bottle round, and saw a thick black line drawn across the back with an indelible pen. The line was almost at the bottom of the bottle.

"Writer-san not to see me, until shampoo reaches line. No cheating."

I stared at the black line, and then at her, and then back at the line. I was so shocked by what she seemed to be saying that at first I could not speak.

"*Wakarimasu ka*, Writer-san?" she said, this time with the most false smile I had ever seen on her lips "*Wakarimasu ka*? Aioko hibernating. Again."

"Again? So soon?" was all I could bring myself to say.

She nodded. I sat in silence, fighting back the tears. I bit my lip, swallowed hard, took a sip of beer and found my tongue.

"This is absurd, Aioko. It would take me months to reach that line."

"*So desu ne*," she nodded, with the plastic smile still in place. "*Mochiron* – very long time. But Aioko in long hibernation."

"With him?"

"With him, with me, with husband, with lot of people, but not with you!"

She recited the list almost in triumph, as if she had rehearsed it. I felt anger rise up and replace the urge to cry. I picked up the shampoo and thrust it at her.

"No thanks, Aioko. I don't want to play this game. Not this one."

"You don't want to see me again?" she said, hunching her shoulders and pouting like a little girl offended

"Of course I do," I said sharply. "And I will. On Friday night, as planned."

Aioko giggled, took the bottle from my outstretched hand and fingered the black line.

"Writer-san cannot use enough shampoo by day after tomorrow, I think."

"Writer-san bloody can," I said, grabbing back the bottle.

She flinched and raised her arms protectively in front of her chest. She thought I was going to hit her, but words and weeping are my only form of attack.

"I'll flush it down the toilet, right here in the Marriott restroom," I muttered, rising from my seat.

"Writer-san angry *desu ne*?" she whimpered, still acting the frightened child.

"Yes, angry."

"But Writer-san promised. Never be angry again. Let Queen do what she want."

"Within reason," I said, sinking back into my seat.

"But Queen not reasonable, Queen bad girl. Probably very bad girl."

I sat staring at her. She seemed so fragile, so vulnerable, so lost in limbo.

I felt my anger evaporate, turn to pity and then dissolve into the affection I could not help but feel for her – even when she was sending me away, even when she was being the very baddest of bad girls

"You're so crazy, Aioko."

"*Baka! Baka! Totemo baka!*" she cried, tears rolling down her cheeks.

"But why, Aioko-san?" I asked softly. "Why send me away?"

"I need time," she sobbed. "To think, to work things out."

"Such a long time?"

"Yes."

"No meal on Friday?"

"No," she said, wiping her cheek with a napkin. "Friday will make more bad memories. Like last time."

"He is coming then?"

"Maybe."

"So soon? But…" I paused, then, after a moment's silence, added, "You got my mail. The limbo one?"

She nodded

"You understood it? The baby?"

She nodded again, and then glanced up at me through her tears.

"Bad girl not good for you."

"Why not? I can cope," I grinned.

"Please go, Writer-san," she cried. "Please. And take the bottle."

She picked up the shampoo and held it out, her hand shaking under the weight.

"Take it, please! And go!"

I grabbed the bottle, stood up and walked out of the bar without turning.

I took the lift down to the third floor and exited through the glass doors into Pacific Place. I was barely aware of my surroundings, of the rich people's designer shops flashing past me on both sides, of the too-white, whitened *tai-tais* dawdling along the walkway towards me like demented divas in a daydream. It all seemed unreal, unfamiliar, a nightmare, a place to escape from now she had banished me from the Garden of Eden.

I walked on and out of the shopping mall, up the moving staircase and into the hot humid air of Hong Kong Park. Past tourists taking pointless photographs, past couples holding hands or more, past sleeping tropical birds in their wire mesh prison. I walked on up to Kennedy Road, on up to McDonald Road, on and up to Bowen Road – lungs bursting, sweat pouring, mind reeling. Five hundred feet above sea level and I still could not understand. I could not understand why she wanted to see her American friend again. I could not understand why she did not want to see me – and for so long. I could not understand why she ditched me when he called, every time. I could not understand why she had to be so cruel. I could not understand it all along Bowen Road – past late night doggie-walkers, past desk-bound evening joggers, past men who looked like me with balding heads and empty eyes. I could not understand it when, after forty-five minutes of climbing and walking in sweltering heat, I stopped at the junction with Stubbs

Road and stared down at the racecourse: Wednesday night, race night – horses coming round the last bend, jockey with gold cap out in front, one in black closing fast…

But the horses disappeared, the grandstand blocked my view, the outcome not revealed, and all I could do was turn and stumble the last hundred yards to my flat. I could not understand why he was back so soon. She said he came every two months, now he was back after two weeks. I could not understand, but I had to try.

★

When he reached home, he rang Aioko, but hung up before she could answer. Dripping with sweat, he lay down on his bed, the same bed he had shared with her a few days earlier.

He lay and shivered and stared at the white stucco ceiling.

He could think of nothing but her, and refused to accept he might not see her again. He was in denial. She had played games like this before. She was testing him, seeing how much he cared for her, how far he would go to keep her, to please her. Well, the truth was, he would go a long way. He would walk to the ends of the earth for her, because, at the moment, little else mattered.

Next day, his resolve hardened by the tossing and turning of a sleepless night, he mailed Aioko from work, pretending nothing had happened. He sent a light-hearted poem celebrating their togetherness, a reflection of their bond seen through the eyes of a waiter at the Marriott hotel, an attempt to put the previous evening's unpleasant scene in context and erase the blot of a green shampoo bottle on their favourite meeting place. There was no other message.

He would have done better, perhaps, to send the Bad Girl poem. An honest confession of love, with considerable insight into the complexity of the person he now loved, or hoped to be allowed to love. As it was, his attempt at denying the situation through a hastily written piece of sentimental verse produced only a sharp, unsentimental response with no ambivalence: 'Please don't mail, please don't call. I will contact you when I think level has reached line.'

Stephen was disappointed, but his resolve unshaken by this cold confirmation of the shampoo edict.

She was taking time out to reflect on the situation, he reasoned; thinking about his limbo story and its implicit offer of a long-term relationship with children; asking the American man to come back earlier than usual in order to announce the end of their two monthly trysts. He, Stephen, would wait for a while and give her room to reflect. If, after that, she was still silent, still holding to the ridiculous black line, he would contact her again. He held his breath, cleared his mind and tried to concentrate on work.

But a week later, on Thursday, he decided a 'while' had already passed, and that – afraid to lose face by doing it herself – Aioko was now waiting for him to break open the edict and save her from her own resolution.

Dear Queen,

I do respect your period of reflection, but am concerned that silence on all fronts between us for too long might not be a good thing. Silence is often more destructive than words, whatever the topic, and produces much deeper and harsher memories than talk. Communication is important and openness central to our friendship. You know almost everything about me, and I about you. Secrets are unnecessary. We've done our crying over secrets. Maybe, you really are thinking about your relationship with me. Maybe, you are working out something with your husband. Maybe, your American friend IS here, and you think I'll be upset. I won't, even if I know. I understand you better now. I've cried my tears for bad girl's badness. So please remember: unexplained silence is a killer. Knowing why there is silence, and what I am waiting for, is easier. *Wakarimasu ka?*

Writer-in-waiting

There was no reply. He waited one more day, and then left a voicemail message asking her to ring back and confirm she was 'all right.' She never did. By the weekend, he was trying her mobile every hour, blocking the display of his number when he called.

On Sunday, anonymous corporate voices in Putonghua, Cantonese and English replaced her voice message: 'This phone is currently switched off. Please try again later.'

He walked into work and mailed her his Bad Girl poem, better late than never. Then he sat for two hours, alone in his office, staring at the screen, waiting for a reply.

None came.

By Sunday evening, he was desperate and rang Connor. No reply: 'On dance tour in Europe, back in two weeks.' He debated ringing Su-yin in Beijing, or going to a bar in Wanchai and talking to a stranger, but in the end felt too upset to do anything. He lay on his bed sweating, imagining her with *him*, haunted by the image of himself without her. At nine, he went to sleep, exhausted and in tears. Another day wasted, another day gone.

18

On Monday, after a fretful night, I awoke and remembered that Aioko had once given me her Toshiba visiting card. I jumped out of bed and ran into the living room. I flipped open my wallet, pulled out a bunch of name cards from a pocket behind the loose change pouch and spread them out on the glass-topped coffee table. Academics, government officials, consuls from various countries, Su-yin, Connor, my son Tom... And there it was: Harada Aioko, Electronic Goods, Senior Officer – English on one side, Japanese on the other.

I clenched my fist in triumph and glanced at the clock above the television. Eight forty, twenty minutes before she reached work. She had never missed a day at the office, she once told me, never been off sick or played truant. She was an honourable and dedicated Japanese office worker worthy of her Senior Officer title, even if that name was no more than a face-saving euphemism for secretary.

I went to the kitchen, put on the kettle, took my pre-soaked muesli out of the fridge and chopped in some apple. Even at times like this, I kept to my rituals. I grabbed my blue Ikea teacup from the draining board, ripped open a sachet of organic breakfast tea and placed it in the cup. I glanced at the kitchen clock. Eight forty-five, fifteen minutes to go. The kettle boiled and I filled the cup. I let it stand for two minutes and then added a dash of organic soya milk. I was a health-food marketer's dream, triggered into instant consumption by the word 'organic.' I went through to the living room and sat at the glass-topped dining table. I would not check the time until I had finished my muesli. I munched and crunched and then checked. It was eight fifty. Ten minutes to go.

I took my tea to the leather sofa nearest the window, sat down and stared out at the racecourse and football grounds below. Cars and buses streamed out of Aberdeen tunnel, bearing suited commuters – male and female, young and old – to their offices in North Point, Causeway Bay, Wanchai and Central. From my vantage point, far above, the vehicles looked like toys, ready to be picked up and packed away in a box till their owner felt like playing with them again.

I closed my eyes.

I was tired, but also on edge, and wanted to compose myself before ringing Aioko at her office. I was sure she would be there and did not want to put a foot wrong once I had her on the line. She had told me never to ring Toshiba, so I must first apologize and then have some good reason for ringing.

I ran through the options. Not heard from you for two weeks and am worried? Pathetic: she had told me not to call her. Going away for a while and wanted to let you know in case you tried to contact me? No good: could tell her that by mail. Try again. Am very ill, can't go to work, no Internet at home, your mobile switched off. Possible: but why call her? Why not my secretary or a friend or a doctor? Try again.

I took a sip of tea, sat back and waited for my brain to wave.

Thirty seconds later, it did.

Aioko had been due to visit the hospital on the Friday after our cancelled meal, the Friday just gone, to have her blood count checked – a follow-up to the 'not serious anomaly.' Bingo! I called you over the weekend, got no reply; was worried you might be in hospital, so rang the office to find out. Yes: that was it. Convincing because – now I had remembered her appointment – my concern was real and, if she were ill and lying in a ward somewhere, email was not a viable alternative.

I glanced at the clock: 9.01. She was never late. I picked up her card from the glass table, went to the phone and dialled the direct number printed beneath her name.

The phone rang three times and was picked up.

"*Wai*?" a voice said in Cantonese. It could have been Aioko's.

I took a deep breath and hesitated.

"*Moshi, moshi?*" The voice spoke again, this time in Japanese. It sounded even more like Aioko.

I was still silent and the voice tried English.

"Hello? This is Toshiba office Hong Kong."

"Hello?" I said, my voice, despite all the preparation, tense and high-pitched. "Is that Aioko?"

"*Sumimasen?* Excuse me?"

"Ms Harada Aioko. Harada-san."

"*Harada san Nihon e ikimashita. Yasumi desu. Dare desu ka.*"

It still sounded like Aioko. Had she recognized my voice? Was she speaking Japanese to put me off?

"*Nihongo wa hanashimasen,*" I stammered. "*Igirisu-jin desu.* Do…"

"*E sumimasen,*" the voice said. "Thought you Japanese. Sorry. You look for Harada-san?"

"Yes. Harada-san. Aioko."

"*Wakarimashita.* Harada-san in Japan. Return in two weeks."

"Oh, thank you," I said.

"Goodbye, thank you," the voice said.

"Excuse me? Is she there on business?"

There was a silence. I assumed the receiver had been replaced and began to replace mine. Then the same voice came back on the line, almost in a whisper.

"You Aioko *no tomodachi*? Aioko friend?"

"Yes."

"Not business?"

"No."

"*Yasumi desu.* Holiday. To see mother."

There was a pause.

"When did she leave?" I asked.

"Saturday *to omoimasu,*" said the Aioko-soundalike.

"Right. Thank you. *Arigato.*"

"You are welcome," the voice said, "*Domo arigato.*"

"Yes, *domo arigato.* Goodbye. *Sayonara.*"

"*Sayonara. Domo arigato gozaimashita…*"

I put the receiver down. Japanese signing-off rituals could last forever.

I sat back on the sofa. Aioko was in Japan? Visiting her mother? Then why had she not told me? Why all this talk of hibernation and needing to be alone? But it rang true. Her phone had been switched off since Saturday and she was unlikely to lie to her employers. They might need to contact her. Then a horrible thought struck me. Suppose she had gone to Japan with the American? Or gone to Japan to meet the American, with her mother as an excuse for the trip to colleagues at work? My mind whirled. I had so often dreamt of visiting Japan with Aioko, of travelling on the bullet train to Hokkaido, of meeting her mother, of becoming part of a Japanese family and learning to speak the language properly. The thought of him acting out my dream was too much to bear.

I stood up and felt dizzy. A plane passed overhead. The traffic rumbled below.

I rotated my neck and felt the cerebral smog lift, the dark clouds of imagination retreat. It was ten past nine. I should be at work. I dialled my office and said I was sick. Food poisoning? Yes. Seafood? Yes, seafood with friends on Cheung Chau. Hope you are better soon. Yes, just cancel my appointments. A crazy plan was forming, and the practical side of me needed peace and quiet to make it a sane, viable plan that could be sold to the world without adverse consequences for me.

Several phone calls later, the crazy-to-sane conversion was complete. I would fly to Japan on Wednesday. How I was to find Aioko I had no idea, but at least I would be in the same country. I had asked a colleague at Nihon University in Tokyo to fax a letter to my office inviting me to guest lecture as an emergency replacement. The Japanese colleague's name was Taka Iimura and I had met him at a conference in Beijing. We had shared a room and, one night, sneaked off and got drunk in a yuppie bar with communist characteristics. Well, Taka got drunk. He was due to give a talk the next day on 'Japanese Animation: The Educational Front,' and was feeling nervous. Alcohol followed by a prostitute was, according to him, the Japanese cure for (male) nerves. But as he was gay, and homosexuality was forbidden in the People's Republic, he decided to double the dose of alcohol. By midnight he was incapable of standing, and when I got him into a taxi, he kept trying to kiss me. Back at the room, he made it over the threshold, but missed the bed by a few feet, hit the floor and threw up. I dragged him to the bathroom, dumped him in the bath and organized a housekeeping team to clear up. I paid the tips, got him undressed, showered and into bed, and set his alarm for eight. The next morning, he was eternally grateful and promised to return the favour anytime, anywhere.

Now, I was calling it in.

I received approval for the trip and, for the next forty-eight hours, my energy level was high, despite, or perhaps because of, the complete insanity of the plan. Here I was, a fifty-year old academic – supposedly in the middle of a controlled investigation into my sexual predilections in a non-monogamous context – beetling off to Japan like a love-crazed teenager cum jealous husband. But my emotions were driving me, not my reason, and giving me the green light to cast aside common sense. They were also giving me the strength to ignore my fear of flying, a phobia that had dogged me since I was twenty, and on Wednesday morning I boarded a JAL 747 for Tokyo without a moment's hesitation.

I arrived at Naruda at 2 p.m. and passed through immigration without incident. Then, in the crowded arrivals hall, surrounded by fast-moving strangers all confident of their purpose and place in life, I succumbed to a momentary attack of sanity. Would it not be better to return home on the next flight, before I made a complete fool of myself?

Probably, but such reasoning went against the emotional current that had swept me through the air, and the idea of boarding a plane again filled me with the usual terror.

I took a deep breath, made my way outside and climbed on a bus headed for Shinjuku. The hotel I had booked was the same one used with Su-yin on my Christmas visit to Japan two years ago and I hoped it would give me a sense of familiarity in unfamiliar surroundings. It also claimed to be part of the Marriott chain and I imagined entering the bar and finding Aioko seated in a corner seat, eagerly awaiting me as she had so often in Hong Kong.

Two hours later, after a tortuous journey across Tokyo on traffic-saturated, double-decker, high-rise highways, the bus drew up outside a thirty-storey building one block away from the neon-lit alleys, dubious clubs and schoolgirl 'whores' for which the area was famous. Shinjuku: the place where people came after work to unwind, where students came to get drunk and laid, and where tourists, like me, came to see and hear if all the things they had read about were true.

But this time I was not a tourist, and I needed to make a plan.

My room was on the twenty-seventh floor and faced west with a panoramic view of the Tokyo suburbs and a distant range of mountains. An appropriate view, I thought, a good omen. My only chance of finding Aioko lay in that direction. The information she had imparted at dinner in Repulse Bay was my sole clue to her whereabouts. Her mother lived in the shadow of Mount Fuji near a lakeside hotel where tourist buses stopped. That was all I had to go on. Su-yin and I had taken such a bus on my last visit, and I had to assume the same tour was still on offer. If not, I was stuck.

I unpacked, stretched out on the bed and rang down to reception.

"*Konban wa*," a voice said.

"*Konban wa.* You speak English?"

"Of course, sir. How can I help?"

"Do you still do day trips to Mount Fuji?"

"Yes, sir. We do five different itineraries. One of six hours, two of eight hours, one of ten hours and one of twelve hours."

"Wow, that's quite a choice," I said, laughing to cover my disappointment. There had been one tour last time, not five. How would I know which to choose?

"Do you have details of the routes? I want the one that goes to a hotel near a lake with Mount Fuji in the background."

She laughed – in a friendly manner, not to mock me.

"Many hotels near lakes with Fuji in background, sir. Perhaps best if you come down and check map of tour route."

"Will you be there in half an hour?"

I felt it was important to talk to her – as if she were the only one who could help.

"Yes, sir. But anyone at reception…"

"And your name is?" I interrupted

"Aioko, sir."

That settled it. I showered, put on fresh underwear, a clean shirt and jeans and headed down to the main lobby. I asked for Aioko and a male receptionist said she was busy. Could he deal with my enquiry? I shook my head and said I would wait. I wanted to talk to her in person. He gave me an ingratiating smile, perhaps a Japanese version of the Western wink, and turned to the next customer. I leant against the counter and tried to work out which of the half dozen, black-suited females was Aioko. I picked a woman with shortcut, henna-dyed hair, onyx earrings and glasses. She did not resemble my Aioko, but looked the most knowledgeable of the bunch. She was trying to help two geriatric Americans, who were being difficult and refusing to accept her explanations.

At last they shuffled off, shaking their heads and snapping at each other. I waited to see if their helper would come my way. The man with the ingratiating smile whispered in her ear and nodded in my direction. I had picked the right one.

"Yes, sir," she said, approaching me with an all-purpose smile in place, ready to face the challenge of another foreign guest. "My name is Aioko. How can I help?"

I returned the smile. I wanted her to know I was different to the geriatrics.

"Room 2010. Mr Mason. I spoke to you about tours to Mount Fuji."

"The man looking for lake with view?" she asked, a twinkle in her eye.

"That's me," I said.

I explained how I had been in the hotel two years ago at Christmas, how I had taken a tour and how I wanted to repeat the experience 'for sentimental reasons.'

"I understand, sir," she said with a bow. "Please wait, while I check records."

She returned in less than a minute.

"Tour, two years ago, is same as ten-hour tour now," she announced.

"It still stops at a hotel by a lake, in the shadow of Mount Fuji?" I asked.

"First stop, sir, with lunch in hotel optional extra."

"That's it," I exclaimed. "I remember now. We opted out of lunch and ate a can of tuna in the car park. Hardly Christmas dinner, but we'd eaten too much the night before."

I chuckled, remembering our search for a can opener in the hotel kitchen. Aioko waited to see if I had more to add, her smile straining at the edges. Reminiscing was not her business. I stared at the brochure she had brought. There was the lake and the hotel.

"You're a genius, Aioko," I beamed. "Spot on."

"I book you on it for tomorrow, sir?" she enquired, unimpressed by my use of her first name and keen for a swift and successful conclusion to our conversation.

"Yes. Please do."

I was entered in the computer and equipped with brochure and boarding card.

"The bus leaves at 8.30 a.m., sir. Shall I order an alarm call?"

"Yes," I nodded. "Thanks. 7.30 should do."

"Thank you, sir," she replied. "Anything else I can help you with?"

"No. That's it," I said, shaking my head.

I wished she could come with me and hold my hand – just until her namesake was found. But she was ready to close.

"Have a pleasant evening, sir."

Plan in place, I wandered out of the hotel and into the mayhem of Shinjuku station at rush hour – waves of people pouring in from all directions, countless commuters crisscrossing with practiced dexterity. I joined a diagonal wave and rode it across the concourse to a map of the metro system. I stopped and stared at it. A young man beside me smiled and asked in English if he could help. Japanese people are polite and friendly to strangers, unlike their Hong Kong counterparts. I thanked him in Japanese and said I was just looking, no particular destination in mind. He bowed, joined a passing wave and disappeared into the crowd. I could live here, I thought, as I turned from the metro map, swam through the sea of bodies, joined an upward bound escalator and emerged outside.

I was at the end of a neon-lit alley leading into the club district. Ahead of me, a group of over made-up schoolgirls – straight from the classroom in rolled down white ankle socks, plaid skirts and white blouses – headed, giggling, into the lion's den. Whether for business or pleasure, it was difficult to tell. At the alley's entrance, middle-aged men eyed up the new arrivals, checking their potential as pocket money earners. But the girls ignored the smiles on watery lips, the bowing of balding heads and surreptitious signalling of bony hands. They giggled, held on to each other and passed on by. Just looking, I decided, not looking for trouble; an assertion of their power over, rather than under, men. I debated following these feral darers into the den, using them as a kind of tour guide to the intricacy of Japan's sexual mores, but suddenly my spirits sank.

Here I was watching schoolgirls and fantasizing about living in Japan, when I knew for a fact Aioko would never live in her country of birth. These middle-aged men were members of the club she had run away from. They had wives at home sipping tea and preparing miso soup, daughters waiting to be groped. Aioko had been there, done that. Now she was a free agent, beholden to no man. So what was I doing here trying to catch her? I turned from the neon lights and hurried back towards my hotel. I would have an early night and hope my spirits had recovered by morning. Once my intellect got its foot in the door, I was lost. The emotional certainty of my feelings for Aioko – and the need for her to know about that certainty – were the driving force behind my trip, the reason I was here, scurrying through Shinjuku like a rat out of hell. I did not want to put her in a cage, or treat her like a schoolgirl. I wanted to fly alongside her – to Hokkaido, to Hawaii, to Tahiti. I wanted our souls to bond, as they had on my bed two Sundays ago.

19

Next morning, I awoke refreshed – my spirits restored, my emotions back at the helm – and, by nine o'clock, I was travelling at speed through Tokyo's western suburbs.

The coach was not full. Apart from myself, I counted fifteen others. A handful of Americans, including the grumpy geriatrics, two Australian couples travelling as a team, a sprinkling of Hong Kong Chinese and a loan nun from Mexico. The tour guide was a young man, eager to please. He wore a maroon blazer and company tie with loose cotton trousers in a light shade of grey. His English was good, though over enunciated. He kept us informed, but did not have the avuncular air that had endeared me to the tour guide two years ago. That guide had been an elderly Japanese man in an outdated sports jacket, who dispensed anecdotes in a warm, heavily accented voice; our current guide kept his comments to a minimum.

After a further hour's drive on a four-lane freeway, past ripening slopes of tea interspersed with dense woodland and rocky outcroppings, we pulled into a service area. I relieved myself and headed for the green tea dispenser. I had learnt on my trip with Su-yin that Japanese motorway service stations offered free tea as a contribution to public health. Cone-shaped paper cups stacked next to a vending machine that dispensed a pre-set amount of the free-radical eradicating liquid. I filled my cup and wandered back outside to breathe in the mountain air. By the entrance door, I checked our whereabouts on a map. Mount Fuji on the left, our service station a little to the right and a high barrier of hills between the two. The freeway wound along a volcanic valley before emerging by a lake to the north of Fuji. That must be the lake, I decided. I peered closer to see if the hotel was marked. It was, together with a built up area climbing the side of a hill. I crossed my fingers: please let Aioko and her mother be in one of the houses there. Please.

"Wagons rolling!" a voice shouted behind me.

I turned to see the male American geriatric waving in my direction. I drained my tea and ran across to the coach.

"Don't wanna get stranded in strange territory, son."

I smiled, drawing a veil of English reserve across my eyes. Despite the illusion of closeness his mode of address gave, I did not intend to become his intimate. Americans often assumed they had a right to your company and I wanted to protect my privacy. I boarded the bus, found my place and glued my face to the window. He shuffled by and sank into the seat behind.

"Couldn't get you a burger, hon – only had that raw fish muck."

"They'd better do a steak lunch," the wife muttered.

"Goddamn better do."

Two hours later, our coach pulled into the car park of the hotel, a modern concrete affair with three stories and a flat roof. It was half past twelve. There was a scheduled stop of two hours for lunch, photography, strolling and any comfort activities not completed at the service station. I climbed out and took my bearings. The lake was directly in front of the hotel and behind the lake, rising up towards the sky, was the smooth conical form of Mount Fuji bathed in the bright light of a midday sun. The perfect picture, and my fellow passengers – unable to believe, or use, their eyes – clicked away to make it real. Behind the hotel, a tree-covered hill climbed up towards a rocky ridge; at the foot of the hill stood the cluster of houses on which my hopes were pinned.

The maroon-jacketed guide approached me holding a pen and clipboard.

"Excuse me, sir," he said, bowing with his head. "Are you booked for lunch?"

"No," I replied. "I'm going for a walk."

"Bus leave at 2.30, sir. Back by 2.15, please."

He bowed again and walked away.

"And if I'm not?" I called after him. "What happens?"

He turned and grinned, thinking perhaps I was making an English joke.

"Then you stuck here, sir."

"Could I rejoin the tour tomorrow?" I asked.

Sensing this was a serious enquiry, he retraced his steps and pulled out a mobile phone from his inside pocket. He pressed several keys, waited a few seconds, read something off the display screen and then jotted down a figure on the clipboard.

"Tomorrow's coach almost full. But, if you pay another 5000 yen, I can…"

"I'll try and be on time," I interrupted. "If I'm not, don't worry."

And with that I strode off towards the lake.

Perhaps my guide thought I was going to drown myself in its steel-grey waters, or that I was a *harakiri* case intent on starving to death in the wooded foothills of Mount Fuji like those life-weary Japanese, who leave their bodies on the sacred ground for a walker to stumble over while their spirits rise to eternal rest on the snow-capped summit.

Whatever the reason for his concern, he was not going to let me go.

"Excuse me, sir," he called, hurrying after me. "If not coming back, I need to know. Otherwise, bus must wait extra half hour. Then passengers very upset."

Yes, I thought, especially the geriatrics. They would lash out at him with the backs of their tongues and pester receptionist Aioko afterwards. I stopped and turned.

"If I'm not back by 2.15, cross me off the list," I said. "And if you want me to sign something absolving you of responsibility, I will."

"But what will you do?" the guide asked, a tone of concern in his voice.

"That is my business," I replied. "Maybe I'll jump in the lake and drown, maybe I won't. Depends how I feel after my walk."

The guide looked alarmed and then grinned again.

"You make joke, yes?"

I nodded.

"Very good," he said, laughing too loudly and reaching inside his pocket again.

Perhaps tour guides were given training on how to deal with the English sense of humour, on how to cope with the English predilection for saying the opposite of what was meant. Even Aioko had been confused. One day I had remarked, tongue in cheek, 'Great weather for a picnic.' She had cried, 'But it's raining!' My subsequent explanation of irony and English humour had been thorough, but she still got caught out.

"Just sign here, sir," the guide said, handing me a closely printed sheet of paper. "If you return on time, I destroy. If not, nobody worry and I keep my job."

I signed the form and handed it back.

"Thank you, sir." He returned the phone and form to his inside pocket and bowed again. "Goodbye, sir. I hope you enjoy your drowning."

He grinned, waiting for my laughter at his use of English humour. I thought of trying to explain why his remark was not funny, but let it pass. I had wasted enough time. I chuckled politely and hoped he would not try out his comic skills on the two Americans. Despite sharing a language with the English, Americans do not understand ironic humour, even when used correctly. The guide's version would be a disaster.

I waved goodbye and set off through the hotel gates. I followed the shore of the lake for a few hundred yards and then turned to the right and began to climb up a narrow road towards the cluster of houses. I walked for five minutes and was approaching the first house – a small, whitewashed affair with a steep, sloping, red-tiled alpine roof – when a familiar figure emerged from its front door and walked briskly away up the village street. A weight lifted from my shoulders, a grin spread across my face. I could not believe my luck. It was Aioko. Of that, there was no doubt.

I paused. Should I shout out and run after her? Or wait in front of the house and give her time to see and register my presence when she returned? Or, perhaps, knock on the door of the house, make acquaintance with the mother and be there when Aioko entered? She would be shocked whatever I did, but shocked and angry or shocked and glad to see me? I had no idea. My emotions longed for the latter. My intellect feared the former. I felt my feet go cold, despite the summer heat. Perhaps I should return to the hotel, have lunch and disappear, leaving her unaware of my visit.

She was almost out of sight now, striding up the steep street. She had reached the last of the red-roofed houses and would soon be in the wood. Was she going for a walk? Following some childhood route to the rocky ridge above the village? Would that not be the best place to talk to her? To explain what I felt, to try and make her understand why I had come, why I had had to come, why her silence had become impossible for me to tolerate, impossible and incomprehensible? I glanced back down at the hotel with the bus in front; at the lake with an inverted version of Mount Fuji reflected on its surface; and then up at the mountain itself silhouetted against the summer sky, towering above the surrounding countryside, dominating the landscape majestically like the god it was. I stood and stared, seeking an answer in its perfect form, as many had before me.

The next thing I knew, someone was tapping me on the shoulder.

"What are you doing here, Writer-san?"

I turned. Aioko, unmade up and wearing the jeans and T-shirt she had worn that first hotel morning, was standing in front of me smiling the softest smile I had ever seen.

"You're not angry?" was all I could say.

She shook her head, took my arm and turned me round to face Mount Fuji again.

"Not angry, Writer-san. Just sad. Very sad."

"Why sad?" I asked.

"Because of you, my Writer-san," she whispered, squeezing my arm in hers.

"Because of me?"

She nodded.

"You come all this way, spend all this money, waste all this time just to see a bad girl. That makes me sad."

"It's not a waste."

She smiled and squeezed my hand.

"Perhaps not for you," she murmured.

"Aren't you glad to see me?" I asked, shading my eyes to gauge her expression.

"Always glad to see you. When time is right."

"And now?"

"Now? Now, Writer-san must go home."

She raised a finger to my face and wiped away a tear. Then she took my hand and began to lead me down the hill, away from her house. I glanced back. Why not take me to the village, to the secret ridge? I did not want to leave. I did not want to go home. I felt at home here, in the shadow of the mountain, in the shade of the hill, on the other side of the world from my own childhood. Through the looking glass and safe from who I was.

"I can't meet your mother?"

She shook her head and smiled.

"I am married Japanese lady, remember?"

I nodded, allowing myself to be led down the hill like a child.

Suddenly, a cold stab of jealousy pierced my stomach.

"Is there another visitor there?" I asked, stopping and staring back up at the house.

Aioko reached across and wiped the sweat from my brow.

"No, Writer-san, just my mother."

We walked on down the hill, hand in hand, in silence, and when we reached the main road, she held out an envelope.

"I went up the village to post this," she said. "But when I reached the post box, I decided not to. I thought: I will talk to Writer-san when I return to Hong Kong. Then, on way back to mother's house, I saw you standing there, staring at our mountain and I felt so sad, so sad. Perhaps, if you had surprised me, knocked on our front door and told my mother who you were, perhaps then I would have been angry. Shouted at you to go away, refused to talk to you. But, as it was, I saw you standing quite still, quite alone. I thought you would turn before I reached you. It takes five minutes to walk down the village street. But you did not turn, and I took that as a sign. A sign I should not be angry."

"Oh, Aioko!" I said, tears rolling down my cheeks.

"So, when you are safely home – back in Hong Kong, back in Writerworld, back in familiar space – read this letter. Not before. Not in Tokyo hotel, not on plane, but at home, with memories of us. *Wakarimasu ka.*"

I hesitated then took the letter and nodded.

"Will you have lunch with me?" I asked.

She shook her head.

"Better not."

"But I will see you again? In Hong Kong?"

"In time."

She smiled, glanced from left to right to check no one was watching and then, standing on tiptoe, reached up with her lips and kissed me on the cheek.

"Now, you must go, Writer-san. Your bus will leave soon. Goodbye."

I held out my arms to hug her, to keep her beside me.

But she was gone, like a grasshopper, running back up the narrow road to her village, scampering up the hill as she must have done many times before when a child – after saying goodbye to her father, after fishing in the lake, after walking in the moonlight with a village boy. I watched her go, and, like that boy, knew I could not follow.

I walked back to the hotel and sat on a bench. My heart was dammed, the flow of emotions blocked, my feelings turned back on themselves like a rerouted river – my mind frozen, numb to the core, not yet ready or willing to deal with the consequences.

20

At 2.25, the guide came and told me it was time to go.

He said he was glad to see that I had not drowned myself. I did not smile. I climbed on the bus, slumped into my seat and stared out of the window as we pulled away from the hotel, leaving Aioko's home behind. We stopped at the foot of Mount Fuji, but I did not have the energy to get out and touch the sacred soil. I felt the mountain had betrayed me, misled me, led me up the garden path and left me in the lurch. I stared at the dense birch woods, next to our parking place. These were the woods that the *harakiri* crowd frequented, the lost souls for whom life had lost its meaning. If I had not felt so tired, so incapable of action of any sort, I might have joined them. I wrapped my windcheater more tightly round my chest. The air-conditioning was on too high, blowing at me from all directions like some bitter winter wind.

I half-closed my eyes and felt the bus move off. Past Shinto shrines, tea fields and more shrines, up to a lake cradled in the crater of an extinct volcano. Here I was forced to leave the bus. We had to take a boat across the lake, to be met by a different bus on the other side. I refused a 'Welcome aboard!' drink offered by the guide and stood on the upper deck, quite alone, staring at the water below. Up here the sun had disappeared and everything was grey – the lake, the walls of the crater, even the boat itself. On the other side, in the new bus, I found a seat less plagued by wind, and, curling up with my head against the window, I went to sleep lulled by the monotonous voice of our guide and the hum of a Mitsubishi diesel engine.

When I awoke, we were in the outer suburbs of Tokyo. I was covered in sweat and shivering. I pulled a sleeveless pullover from my rucksack and put it on. I still felt cold. I had a chill, from the air-conditioning, or from the flight the day before. It had been cold on the plane, too. I shivered again and the image of flying, of being trapped in a tin box hurtling through the sky at five hundred miles an hour, flashed through my mind. I felt faint and clutched at the seat in front of me.

How was I going to board a plane if I could not even stand the thought of flying, if even the imagined sensation of flight fuelled my fever? Now there was no positive emotion to tranquillise the phobia, only the realization – the slow, cold, rational realization – that she might not love me after all. I had come to Japan to see her, to confirm my love for her and hers for me. But I would return empty handed: with nothing to help me on the plane, nothing to fly home for, nothing to keep me in the air, nothing to stop the plane from falling into the black wetness of a shark-infested South China Sea.

I closed my eyes again, but the bus had stopped. The other passengers were leaving.

"Bye, son," the geriatric shouted, as he passed my seat.

I waved my hand, tried to stand and failed. I took a deep breath and tried again.

"You all right, sir?"

It was the guide. He had been standing by the exit door receiving tips from the passengers, and I was the only one left in the bus.

"Fine," I nodded. "Bit of a chill from the air-con. *Kaze da to omoimasu.*"

He held out a hand to help me up, and then guided me along the gangway and down the steps. I reached in my pocket for some money, to thank him for his concern, for the words of tour-guide wisdom that I had slept through. But he raised his hand.

"Please, sir," he grinned. "You teach me English humour. Very grateful."

"You're welcome," I said, using an American phrase that never normally crossed my lips.

"Now, you go and kill yourself in hot bath!"

"Very good," I said. "Very good English humour."

I shook his hand, staggered towards the hotel entrance and swayed through the revolving door into the lobby. I just made it to the lift, slumped on to the floor as it shot up twenty-seven floors and then half-walked, half-crawled, along an over-cool corridor to my room. I was dead-beat and running a fever. I collapsed on the bed and went to sleep.

When I awoke, it was three in the morning and still dark outside.

I heard a rumbling sound and the distant wail of a siren. I froze. I was on the twenty-seventh floor of a hotel in Tokyo, and an earthquake was about to happen.

I climbed out of bed, still shivering, and sat on the toilet to urinate. I was too weak to stand. I felt my brow. It was hot and my throat was sore. I climbed back into bed, but the bedclothes were soaked in sweat. I pulled off the top sheet and threw it across the room. The rumbling grew louder. A second siren pierced the night. Then I remembered. This hotel had rubber springs to cushion the effect of quaking earth. Su-yin and I had inspected them, last time, to put my mind at rest. I closed my eyes and tried to fall asleep.

But thoughts, manic repetitive thoughts, kept catching me in mid-fall. I had to get back to Hong Kong, but could not fly. I could not fly, but had to get back. How else? By boat? Did anyone travel by boat these days? And how long would it take? Perhaps I could ask Aioko to come with me, and wipe my fevered brow as I sailed across the Sea of Japan. But Aioko was fast asleep beneath Mount Fuji, protected from my fever by the sacred snow that never melted on its peak. I had no means of calling her. But the other Aioko could help, the Aioko downstairs. She received guests, soothed brows and solved problems – any problems, all the problems there were to be solved. Aioko, with the hennaed hair and onyx earrings, could tap me back to Hong Kong on her Toshiba keyboard. She would help, in the morning. The world would look different through her glasses. And, at last, I fell through the thoughts and into the dreams beneath.

"Is Aioko available?" I asked.

It was eight forty-five and I was sitting in bed, sipping a hot lemon drink made from a sachet I had found in the inside pocket of my sponge bag. The sachet was passed its sell-by date, but I needed something. My head was aching, my throat still sore and, according to the thermometer I carried with me, I was running a temperature of 38.4 C.

"Aioko on duty in ten minutes, sir. Can I help?"

"No," I said, stifling a cough. "Ask her to ring me, please."

Ten minutes later she rang.

"Aioko?" I gasped.

"Yes, sir?"

"It's me. Mr Mason. 2010"

"Oh, yes. Lake-with-view-of-Mount-Fuji man. You enjoy tour?"

"Yes," I said, and then broke into a fit of coughing.

"You all right, sir?" she asked, a note of professional concern in her voice.

"Yes," I spluttered. "Well, no. I have a cold. *Kaze da to omoimasu.*"

"Shall I send up medicine, sir?" she continued, ignoring my phrasebook Japanese.

"No. Well, yes – all right." I blew my nose and tried to concentrate. "Aioko, I need your help."

"Of course, Mr Mason, that is why I am here – to help you."

I was not being such a simple customer as last time. She was taking cover behind defensive phrases. "How can I be of assistance?"

"I want you to book me a ticket back to Hong Kong."

"Yes, sir. No problem. Departing at what time, sir?"

"By boat, Aioko. By any boat that gets me there."

"By boat?"

I heard her laugh and say something to a colleague, then she came back on the line.

"We have no information on boats, sir. Perhaps you could…"

"Please, Aioko," I said, coughing again. "It's very important. Boat to China will do. And then train. I just don't want to fly."

"I see."

She again conferred with someone. I crossed my free set of fingers.

"Can I call you back, sir?"

I nodded, and let the receiver drop into its rest. I was exhausted. The brief conversation had drained me. I lay back on the pillow and fell asleep.

I dreamt of a plane crash, though I was not in the plane. It was the plane I should have been on, but had missed because the coach to the airport had gone via Mount Fuji and the guide had talked too long. Aioko, who was a combination of the two Aioko's, said I could stay with her as long as I did not mind earthquakes. She put me to bed, in the attic of her mother's house beneath the red tiles, and I fell asleep. When I awoke, Aioko was my sister Irene and I was in the loft above the stables of my mother's house. Irene, aged eighteen, was showing me her pubic hair and trying to push my face between her legs. 'Lick!' she kept saying, 'Lick!' But when I looked up it was Muriel, with nanny Sally sucking her friend's breast and spanking my bottom at the same time.

I cried out in pain and the phone rang.

"You are lucky, sir," Aioko's voice said.

"Lucky?" I murmured, still half in the loft.

"We find boat from Kobe to Shanghai with one space left."

"One space?" I wheezed, not sounding very grateful for my receptionist's achievement. "I have to share a cabin?"

"No, sir. Space left is Captain's Suite – bedroom, living room, shower."

"Expensive?"

"No, sir. About same as economy to Hong Kong, but with train fare from Shanghai on top. You arrange train in Shanghai hotel. That hotel we can also book."

I thought of the return airline ticket in my jacket pocket, of the long journey home by boat and train, of my current state of health. And then thought of the plane, of being five miles high, of the millimetres of metal between me and a freefall back to Mother Earth.

"I'll take it," I said, feeling that surge of utter relief all aerophobics experience when a planned flight is cancelled, postponed or avoided. "You're an angel, Aioko. Angels can fly, but sometimes I can't. Thank you."

"Thank you, sir," she said. "I'll make the arrangements. Boat leaves tomorrow at midday and arrives in Shanghai two days later. I book you on *shinkasen* from Tokyo to Kobe leaving Central Station at 8 a.m."

148

"*Shinkasen?*" I queried.

"The bullet train, sir. Two hours to Kobe. Very fast and never leaves ground."

She laughed, and I imagined her onyx earrings shaking, her hennaed hair falling across her brow and her keyboard fingers sweeping it deftly back into place.

"Good. I'll pay for the tickets with my bill. See you tomorrow."

I put the receiver down and grinned. Then I remembered she would not be on duty when I left for the station. Should I dial up to say goodbye? No, I was just another client, no one special for her, an unusual case successfully solved. File closed.

Like it was for my Aioko-san? Had she closed my file too or left it open on her desk? My head was clearing and I was sweating less. Perhaps I should read the letter. Perhaps it would say, 'Be patient, dear Writer-san!' Perhaps I had been right all along and her time alone was time to think things through, to think things through in my favour. Keeping me from meeting her mother was not a sign of rejection, sending me back to Hong Kong did not mean banishment from her life. There had been no anger at my unexpected appearance, and she had kissed me on the cheek before running off.

I reached for the thermometer and put it under my arm. As I waited for the beep-beep to indicate digital registration of my maximum temperature, I relaxed and felt some of the emotional optimism that had driven me to Japan in the first place. Not enough to push me on a plane and regret booking a four-day sea and land journey, but enough to buoy up my hopes and keep them from wandering lost in the woods beneath Mount Fuji.

The next morning, Taka, my official host from Nihon University, took me to the station. I was still running a temperature and not fit to travel. But the boat only departed once a week, and I could not be away from work too long without causing comment.

I had called Taka the previous afternoon to confess the truth about my trip. I needed to confide in someone, and he seemed a suitable candidate. He was almost a stranger, uninvolved in my everyday life and not in a position to gossip. He was Japanese, with an insider's insight into Aioko's behaviour, and a gay man, with an outsider's angle on me.

When he heard I was ill, he told me not to talk on the phone and said he would come over after work. He arrived at six, loaded with alternative cold remedies. He raided the mini-bar for scotch and mixed it with the fresh lemon, ginger, garlic and seaweed he had brought. The scotch not used for medicinal purposes went down his throat along with two cans of beer, a mini-decanter of herb-infused *sake* and a half-bottle of red wine.

And whilst he drank, he listened, making only occasional comment. When I dozed off, at the midpoint of my story, he went to the shops for fruit, flowers and a packet of Japanese commercial cold remedies. He was behaving as if I were his oldest friend and it touched me. I did not mention the original advertisement, or my initial motivation for meeting Aioko, but did explain Aioko's complicated triangle with her husband, the American friend and me.

When I had finished, Taka made me drink a cup of ginger tea – this time laced with vodka – and suggested I doze, while he considered my situation and formulated advice.

When I awoke, it was dark, and Taka was snoring on the sofa. He had not thrown up this time, and finding a set of earplugs in the drawer by my bed, I jammed them in and fell asleep again.

Next morning, Taka was up first, unaffected by his consumption of the entire mini-bar. He insisted on packing my case and taking the train with me to Kobe. Otherwise, he said, wagging his finger, I would not find the boat and end up in an Osaka hospital. I protested that for him to go all that way and back was mad, and what about his work. He said I was his work for the day. And, tomorrow, he would fax my Institute in Hong Kong to announce I was staying on for extra seminars. I could have hugged him, but did not want to pass on my cold. He was returning my favour in Beijing with interest, and covering the mini-bar felt like a very small deposit on the amount I owed.

In the taxi to the station, he said he had slept on my story and formed an opinion. Aioko sounded like a typical Japanese woman. She enjoyed playing games, and was also a stickler for propriety. She seemed confused, at the moment, but might end up opting for her writer and making him her third husband, if that was what he wanted. On the other hand, the game playing might win out over her real feelings. Many Japanese women had been taught to repress their deeper emotions and play act in the surface world in order to survive. Taka advised me to keep my distance as requested and leave the ball in her court. I did not tell him about the letter. I feared he would make me open it, and I did not want to share that moment of truth with him. I felt confident the letter would give a positive twist to the story, but wanted to read it by myself, at a suitable moment.

I slept all the way from Tokyo to Osaka lulled by the silent smoothness of our early morning *shinkasen*, the original high-speed train. In Osaka, I felt feverish and would have been lost without Taka's help. He found a taxi driver prepared to take us to Kobe – Osaka's twin city on the far side of the harbour – and told me to go back to sleep. It would take us half an hour to reach the departure dock.

When I came to, the taxi was motionless and its driver in tears.

"What's the matter?" I asked, happy to stay curled up in my corner of the back seat and let Taka run my life.

"It's about face," Taka replied with a wink.

So few people took the slow boat to China, the taxi driver did not know where to go. But he had not admitted this to Taka at the start of the journey, and was now lost. He was crying, bowing and apologizing all at once, whilst Taka offered soothing words and leafed through an Osaka street atlas. After five minutes of penance and a phone call to the docks, we were on our way.

On arrival, the driver refused to accept any fare and offered me one thousand yen as a 'token of apology.' I declined the note, held out in both hands with head bowed, and, as the taxi and its penitent driver drove off, Taka explained the importance of professional honour in Japan and the impossibility of admitting failure.

"Like me with Aioko," I joked.

"If you fail, you will admit it," said Taka, putting his arm round my shoulders. "But, for the moment, have faith in your goal and let her come to you."

We drank a last cup of tea, and said goodbye at the customs desk. He made me promise to mail him the end of the 'story.' I said

I would and thanked him for his help. He laughed. He had done nothing compared with my services for him in Beijing. We hugged, despite my cold, and waved once more.

Then I was ushered through to a waiting room, where I sat shivering and sweating until the time for embarkation came. I just made it up the gangplank and on to the small sturdy boat that would be my home for the next two days. A tall Chinese cabin steward, in navy blue, met me and showed me to my suite. It was at the front of the ship, beneath the captain's bridge. My steward opened the door, smiled and led the way inside. A small living room with front facing window gave on to a bedroom with double bed and side facing window. Both were old-fashioned in appearance, with dark wood panelling and faded Chinese patterns, but warm and welcoming compared to the cramped confines of an airliner's interior. There was a small kitchen area with a kettle – a shower room, and even a television. There was also a brochure with information about the boat, the cabin, the food and the route, in either Japanese or Chinese. I asked the steward for tea, and so was his reply. I was in a no-English zone and my croaky, cold-ridden voice could rest.

When the steward had left, I took off my jeans and shirt and put the letter from Aioko on the bedside cabinet. I then collapsed diagonally across the double bunk.

I wanted to watch the shores of Japan disappear, to have Aioko in mind as I sailed away from her country of birth. But I was too exhausted, and, within minutes, fell fast asleep, the letter unopened and my mind once more in the land of make-believe.

Dear Writer-san,

Thank you for your poem about 'Bad Girl.' It is very touching poem, I think, and probably very true poem too. I read in Internet Café in Tokyo, yesterday, when I go to meet girlfriend Minako-san for *tempura no teishoku*. I stay with mother in country and feel peaceful. Nobody else, just her and me. I do not know what to say to you, but you say silence is more painful than words. Maybe, you will not agree when you read these words I write now. Oh, Writer-san, I do not want to hurt you, but I am afraid I may do so. Hurt you two times. I do not love you, Writer-san. I can never marry you and have baby Aioko-san as sister for your son. Your Limbo story made me cry, but it is a story and I, Aioko, cannot be in it. I am married to second husband. Here the sun shines and Mount Fuji is very beautiful. I walk in the woods above village and feel myself again. I see who I am. I see what I want. You are good man, Writer-san, kind man, caring man. I am bad girl with bad ways. Husband is kind man, too, when he opens mouth. But I need bad man sometimes. Bad man excites me more than good man. Why, I do not know. You try to be bad man, but you are too nice. I do not understand games you want to play in bed, on floor of Writerworld. You are not like other men. You are *baka na saka*, crazy writer. I am no longer excited by you, you are not excited by me, I do not make you wild, you do not desire me, you do not lose control, you do not overpower me – like he does. Perhaps it is way we start in hotel. Perhaps it is how you are with all women. You will cry when you read this, be very hurt, but he is what bad girl needs. I will want to see him every time he comes and you will want to stop me. We can be friends, Writer-san – *Tomodachi desu ne*. I like to talk, to eat – to drink with you. But I cannot be wife, cannot be lover for you. *Sumimasen*.

Bad Girl

PART TWO
THE CELLAR

21

At what point Stephen read Aioko's handwritten letter is not certain, though it must have been after writing about his journey to Japan.

In that detailed description, reprinted above, he is still full of optimism and hope, determined to believe all will turn out well. Perhaps he wrote up the journey during his boat trip and then, as a reward for putting down in words what he had just experienced, read the letter. He may still have been at large on the Yellow Sea, or entering the Yangtze River's long and sinewy delta, where ochre-coloured silt from far inland gives the sea its name. Or, recovered from his fever, he put down his pen and went on to the wind-blown deck to read the letter, just as the small but sturdy ship rounded the last bend into Shanghai and the well-preserved and imposing nineteenth-century skyline of the Bund came into view in all its colonial glory. Or perhaps it was later in the Shanghai Shangri La Hotel – lying alone in yet another double bed, sipping yet another cup of complementary tea – when he opened the crumpled envelope. Or was it on the last stage of his journey, in the overnight train to Hong Kong, bouncing back and forth in his Soft Sleeper compartment, single occupation only, listening to the noises of the night as they flashed past his window and echoed down the corridor outside his door?

Wherever it was, at some point on that long and tortuous journey, he read the devastating news. Because when he stepped out of the train in Hung Hom station, he was a defeated man, barely able to hail a taxi and crawl inside. He rang in sick to work and remained in bed for ten days. Bronchitis was the official diagnosis, brought on by his travels and failure to nurse the Mount Fuji fever. But, in truth, his soul was sicker than his body – sick with unrequited love and jealousy. Connor and the departmental secretary shopped for him and made sure he did not starve, and the rest of the time he slept a dark, dreamless sleep knowing the cure for his sickness was unobtainable.

And then, when sleep no longer came, he lay under his beige-patterned duvet shivering, coughing and tormenting himself. He imagined the American with her, over her, under her, around her and in her – here, there and everywhere. He imagined how things might have been different, how things could have been different, how he might have seen off the Superman she now needed more than him. He flailed himself with the 'ifs' of recent history: if only he had opted for normal sex that first night in the hotel, if only he had not forbidden kissing on the mouth, if only he had allowed intimacy to develop in a natural and normal way. If only – everything would have been all right. And when the flailing stopped, he cold-showered himself with the realization that such a rewrite of his relationship was pure fantasy. He had been investigating, in search of something new and different. Without the investigation, he would not have met the object of his desire and despair, and without ruling out such Superman set pieces as kissing on the mouth and copulation, there would have been no newness to investigate. The most classic *pas de deux* in the repertoire could not have won over Aioko, or sated his curiosity – that was the truth. She was after revenge and adventure, not a replacement, and he was after the key to his condition, intent on descending the stairs and delving into darkness, discovering why penetration no longer appealed and why he longed for more – searching for the secret that would reunite his mind and body and weld him to the world.

Later, when the bronchitis had abated and he was up to jotting down notes, he compared the impact of Aioko's letter to 'having a cellar door slammed in my face and locked' – presumably with him on the inside. He had seen her as his salvation, the person who could play cellar games but prevent him from descending into the cellar itself, the person to bring his fringe production to the main stage and anchor his errant needs to a stable base. And, had she been a different kind of woman, had she had complementary physical needs to Stephen's, she might have been the one to round the circle and keep her Writer-san from disappearing into darkness. But she would have had to be a very different person. A real bad girl, not a girl who played at being bad by sleeping with an American salesman and hiding her misdeeds from a husband on the edge of catatonia. That was conventional badness, or barely bad at all, not the kind of badness that fed on pain and power and the suffering of a man forced to submit to the whims of a perverted female mind. She had done her best on the emotional level. She knew how to cause pain in the heart, how to play games with people's feelings, how to seek and hold attention and play a fish on her line. But there was no parallel interest in the physical field. No delight in the submission of her prey, no desire to play games with its body. And, as the letter showed, she was now finished with emotional toying, too.

So, as the days went by and his health returned, Stephen decided to revert to his investigation. He had put his heart on his sleeve and exposed his emotions too early in the game – not the actions of a scientist. Aioko's rejection had left a wound and embracing the darkness of his submissive side would, he decided, be the best balm. He still thought of her, but did not try to contact her. Instead, he wrote a story called *She and Me* to answer a nagging investigator's doubt. Were there any women who enjoyed dominating and humiliating men? Or were they all figments of the male imagination, paid-for appeasements for the guilt men felt at dominating women in other ways? The story diverted him for a while, but being a figment of his imagination offered little insight into the real world and was no substitute for further field study in the flesh. For Stephen, primary relationships had been a prison to escape from – perhaps because he couldn't accept that it was life itself, rather than his relationships, that formed the prison's walls – and this time he determined there would be no return to the security of cell and cellmate, no pandering to the investigator's soft side and no relapse into premature romance.

His first print advertisement had produced only a modest response. Now he placed a profile on the *South China Morning Post* website. He initially drafted a humorous text – 'Creative man investigating the Marks in his make-up seeks woman with a genuine Spencer side to undertake M&S shopping spree for mutual pleasure.' – but did not submit it. He feared too few people would understand his inversion of S&M, despite the presence of two Marks and Spencer's stores in Hong Kong, and switched to a more poetic style: 'Meek male Moon seeks female Sun to heat up his soul and bring colour to his cheeks.' This he posted, and, in an expanded description of 'person sought,' stressed – as he had in his *Hong Kong Magazine* advertisement – the importance of imagination.

After a week of waiting, he received a first response by email. A woman with the codename Camellia wrote saying that she had been attracted by the sun and moon metaphor. This sounded hopeful, but initial exchanges were mundane. She was a Hong Kong Chinese woman, aged forty-one, unmarried and working as a sales manager in an electronics firm. Stephen did not, as many men do, immediately state that he was after sex, and sex of a certain kind. Rather, he played the understanding 'listener,' commenting on her emails in an informed and involved manner.

And he was not entirely playacting. He may have imagined himself as a tough fringe investigator plumbing the depths of perversity, but his innate good manners and genuine interest in other people meant he came across as the educated and sincere man a large part of him really was. Like many older people, and people new to the net, he did not have the cavalier approach of younger and more jaded users, and did not even bother to change his name. The only misinformation he gave Camellia concerned his place of work and his single status: he said he worked at City University instead of the Arts Institute and admitted to an ongoing relationship with a woman – a half-untruth, as Aioko lived on in his heart. Luckily Camellia did want sex, and, luckily, she raised the topic first. Otherwise, Stephen might have stayed polite to the end and closed the exchange assuming she was a knowledgeable woman in search of a friend and nothing more.

In the second week of exchanging emails, Camellia curtailed a response to a comment he had made about social democracy developing in urban China, and wrote:

> Let's change the subject now. I want to tell my story and hear your opinion as to whether I'm a decadent person. Right

now, I feel like one! But if I tell you, perhaps I will never meet you – I might be too embarrassed! Well, here goes… I have only slept with one man once, and that was three months ago in March. I had never had sex before that. A woman loses her virginity at forty-one with someone she didn't love and had only just met – can you believe that? And even this one time, I did not mean to have sex. It was because the man licked my ears. A new experience, and I was aroused. In fact, I liked it more than having him inside me. Afterwards, I longed for more, but he never called. I met him through this site and am ashamed to tell you that no one had ever approached or dated me before in my life. I don't know why. I am normal, not ugly and have an easygoing personality. So I blame destiny, I am destined to be a loner all my life. But, as a New Year's resolution, I decided that, even if I were partner-less, I would indulge myself in sexual pleasure. Because I had never experienced it – and still haven't really. I did not enjoy my first time, apart from the ear licking, perhaps because I was unskilled and too passive. Maybe that is why he did not return for more. What do you think, Stephen? Should I stop being a slut now? I imagine that sex without emotions cannot reach the level of sex with emotions, but what can I do? I'll never have sex with emotions, because no one loves me. I do not regret what I have done, but am scared of becoming a decadent person with no morals at all. I have never told this to anyone in the world – not even my first-time man. But I'm feeling better, now it is off my chest. I trust and respect you, because of your sincere and genuine letter-writing. Sorry for being so frank. I hope you do not feel offended. Please tell me what to do… Cheers,

Desperate Camellia.

Stephen was wary. He imagined a desperate woman, eager to grab and keep the first available man, a woman whose desperation might make her dangerous. But after rereading her other emails, with their sane and educated comments, he changed his mind. He decided that she was, like him, an intelligent person trying to experience a part of life that had passed her by. She was also an almost clean sheet, but not young and immature as most clean sheets were supposed to be. He felt intrigued by her case and saw its potential for advancing his own investigation.

Dear Desperate Camellia,

No need to be desperate, but maybe a little cautious. I was surprised to hear your story, but not shocked. First of all, you are not decadent and not a slut, and telling me what you have need not embarrass you and need not preclude us meeting, if we both want to – though we may not. I have long ago learnt that the world is made up of human beings with different experiences of life. I am glad your first taste of sex was not all bad, but maybe you should have spent more time just kissing and playing – 'making out,' as teenagers call it in America – rather than going straight to intercourse, which, at the best of times, can be boring.

Perhaps you need a sexual mentor, and are not yet ready for a full-blooded penetrative love partner. Seriously! Someone who can gently demonstrate what sex is all about, without engaging in intercourse and without the complication of an emotional involvement. Worrying whether the other person found you 'OK' in bed and where it was all leading would undermine the learning process, whereas a mentor would be there to teach and nothing more. Someone with whom you can touch and stroke, who can show you what men like and help you discover what you like. Fun and excitement, and basic to advanced 'education,' in a friendly – but not over-emotional – safe-sex training context! Liberating your mind and body in an unfamiliar area.

I doubt whether you are doomed forever to be without a partner, and a little 'learning' from someone who is NOT a potential partner would give you physical confidence if Mr Right did turn up. This is what many young men do with older women, and it makes them more considerate as lovers and more appreciative of the potential of sex. So, if you are keen (desperate!) to find out what sex can offer, I am prepared to share my knowledge – as a mentor. Don't laugh! I am not married though am involved in a relationship, and could NOT develop one with you. But non-penetrative sex with other people is allowed for my partner and I – provided it does not go on too long.

So, in the same way that I was not thrown off-balance by your confession (though surprised), I hope you will not be shocked by my offer, but receive it in good faith and accept or reject it as you see fit. Your trust and respect in me is not misplaced, and I shall continue to be honest and open in my written responses. And, whatever happens, do not despair, Camellia. Life is full of pleasant surprises, and it is NEVER too late to learn new ways and experience new things.

Stephen

Camellia replied the next day thanking him for his concern, further analysing her only sexual experience and ending up by accepting his offer. She addressed him this time as 'Dear Lecturer Stephen.'

…You have brought out the main issue – what I need is a sexual mentor. I don't know anything about men. What is this creature, what do they think, what are their likes and dislikes? Masculinity, together with the mechanics of sex, are the new subjects I need to learn about. I must thank you for your kind and friendly offer, which I am interested in. Maybe, you can give Camellia a more positive and sensible approach to these matters. The only problem is that I feel embarrassed to meet you face to face. Also, I feel strange at the idea of having physical contact (I know – no penetrative sex, for sure) with someone I respect. So, I'm interested, but a bit scared… I hope I don't look like a weird person to you.

Student Camellia

This time, Stephen was quick to respond, sketching out his proposed curriculum and reassuring her that touching between respectful friends was quite acceptable and not something she had to feel nervous about.

Dear Student Camellia,

Thanks for your mail. I'm glad you're interested in my 'offer.' Maybe it would be fun to progress from topic to topic using a three-year BA format spread over three sessions – i.e. one session equals one year. As you are a mature student, we do not want to take too long over your tertiary sex education! Something like this:

Year 1.

Semester 1: Theory – Masculinity and Femininity: What men and women want (*Lust and Love*, *Romance and Pornography*, *Sex and Sensuality*, etc.)

Semester 2: Practice – Kissing & body stroking with clothes on.

Year 2.

Semester 1: Undressing and More Intimate Touching (*Oral Sex or Not*)

Semester 2: Helping Her Come, Helping Him Come (*Orgasm: Theory and Practice*)

Year 3.

Semester 1: Theory – Intercourse and Positions (*Poverty of Penetration*)

Semester 2: Sexual Fantasy and the Games People Play (*S&M, B&D, Fetishism*)

(*Ten credit units per semester. Retakes possible, if course is failed. Electives, for more in depth study, available.*)

Imagination and fantasy play an important role in sex, so note down any fantasies you have for discussion, comment and possible practice in Year Three. You do not need to feel nervous about touching someone you respect.

I respect you, too, and, in my opinion, touching with mutual respect (if not deep emotion) is 'moral' and rewarding. Also, you are an apprentice, so shout out when you need to – 'Do that again!' 'Can I try this?' – or have a fit of the giggles! I suggest we meet for a drink first, to ensure you feel secure about me, and then hold the session at your place straight afterwards. I do not think you are weird, merely someone who missed the boat on sex and would like to make up for lost time. I have never met anyone in that position, and hope I am not being over ambitious in trying to help.

Stephen signed himself 'Lecturer Stephen,' and then changed it to 'Lecherer Stephen.' The new word better suited his role, he said, though the official English word was 'lecher' not 'lecherer.' She checked the meaning of lecher in her dictionary, and from this point on they addressed each other as 'Student' and 'Lecherer' in their mails.

Camellia set up a meeting for the following Wednesday, at 3.30 p.m. in the coffee shop of the Park Lane Hotel in Causeway Bay. In pre-meeting correspondence, she told him her real name was Amy. She would, however, prefer him to call her Camellia. She said she had never developed fantasies because there was little practical experience to build on. Her only (unimagined) images of sex were from kissing and modest erotic activity in movies – especially French art films of the fifties. She had never watched pornography or seen a pornographic magazine. She was, Stephen realized, more of a blank sheet than a contemporary teenage virgin. Today's sixteen-year-old was exposed to images of sex in all its forms via the Internet. Camellia was the Victorian maiden spinster; the eldest daughter locked up in the East Wing, with only suitable novels for company, waiting for a nefarious Lothario to whisk her off and ravish her unsoiled body.

When the day of their meeting arrived, Stephen sent a mail describing how he looked and what he would be wearing, and Camellia sent a reply saying that she had booked a table under the name 'C' in the Park Lane Hotel coffee shop. She would try and get there first, so that he merely had to ask for the table to find her. If, by any chance, she was late, he should ask to be seated, and she would locate him in the same manner. She was, Stephen noted, an organized woman adept at making arrangements and managing situations. Perhaps, later – in Year 3, Semester 2 – she would enjoy managing him.

22

I arrived punctually at three thirty and was shown into the drab, basement coffee shop of the Park Lane Hotel.

It was almost empty, with only three tables occupied by Chinese women taking afternoon tea, English-style. I was nervous – more so than on previous occasions – but also excited. This was the first time I had met a woman knowing I would have sexual contact with her during our first encounter. I had never slept with a prostitute, and, even if I had done, there was a difference between paying someone to touch your body – for sex or a medical massage – and agreeing to physical intimacy at a first meeting with a person who was not a professional.

The coffee shop attendant indicated a corner table and left. A thin woman with medium length black hair, a sparse fringe and owlish spectacles stood up and held out a hand.

"Hi, I'm Amy – I mean Camellia."

She was nervous. Her hand trembled like a trapped mouse and was withdrawn before I had a chance to shake it. She sat back down and stared at her teacup.

"I'm Stephen," I replied, realising I must start my work as Senior Lecherer in Sexual Studies by putting the student at ease. "Good to meet you. May I sit down?"

"Of course," she replied abruptly. "What would you like to drink? Beer?"

"No," I said, as I lowered myself on to an upholstered chair covered in off-pink fabric and smelling of disinfectant. "I'm not a big drinker. What are you having?"

"Chamomile tea," she replied, still staring down at her cup.

"Ah! Chamomile for Camellia. Very good."

She laughed, for the first time, and glanced up. I smiled a reassuring smile and studied her face. It was a pleasant, plain face with pronounced cheekbones, thin lips and a small, well-proportioned nose. The eyes mixed wariness with curiosity and intelligence and reminded me of a pre-pubescent boy, a female Harry Potter. The thin-rimmed glasses, minimal makeup and flat chest added to this effect and made me wonder whether sexual abstinence influenced appearance, and whether sexual indulgence, at this late stage, would 'mature' her face and bring it to life. Because, along with the schoolboy, there was something of a Victorian porcelain doll in her looks – a cold, untouched feel to the pale translucent cheeks. This, I realised, was the almost blank sheet she had given me permission to work on, and I wondered, with a shiver of anticipation, what would happen to such a composed, innocent and asexual face when I began my first lesson in arousal.

"I'll have the same," I said to a waitress in a black dress and white apron, hovering by our table. "Chamomile tea."

We sat for half an hour sipping tea and exchanging pleasantries. She said she had taken the day off work, which was why she was wearing jeans and a shirt. Normally she wore a suit at the office. She was a departmental manager in charge of sales and had to meet clients from abroad, who also wore suits. She hoped I did not mind her dressing informally for our first meeting.

"Of course not," I exclaimed, pouring the last dregs from my willow-patterned teapot into the matching teacup. "I'm not a client from abroad trying to buy your software, am I?"

"No," she laughed.

"Though a skirt might be useful later on," I added, making my first allusion to the reason for our meeting. "More comfortable, less constricting."

I felt excited at the thought of putting my hand up her skirt. Fumbling with buttons on jeans or squeezing fingers inside her waistband was inelegant and less erotic.

"I can change," she said, a flush of embarrassment colouring her pale cheeks.

"Good," I replied. I studied her face for moment and then added: "You still want to go through with the session? Now you've seen me in the flesh?"

She nodded, avoiding my gaze, her hand trembling as she lifted an empty teacup to her lips.

"Are you sure?" I persisted. "I won't be offended if you pull out."

"I'm nervous," she whispered, "but sure. You are just like I imagined – a trustworthy English gentleman."

"Trustworthy and English, yes," I laughed. "Gentleman, perhaps."

She ignored my remark, or appeared to, but for the first time found the confidence to look me full in the eye. I caught a glimpse of nascent lust, or puppy love, or a pre-pubescent mix of the two.

"You remind me of a real life lecturer," she said, studying my face with her deep black eyes. "At Baptist's University, on my Communications course. He looked very much like you."

"Oh," I chuckled. "And was he handsome?"

"I had a crush on him," she replied. "At least, I think I did."

Her gaze reverted to the empty teacup now back on the table. She picked up a paper napkin and wiped the corner of her mouth.

"But, at that time, you didn't know what to do," I said with a smile.

"No," she said, glancing up again, momentarily disconcerted, worried I might be making fun of her. "No, it was a very – how do you say?"

"Platonic crush?"

"That's it. A platonic crush."

I drained my cup.

"Let's hope, after your studies with me, that the next crush on a middle-aged balding man will be very erotic indeed."

She laughed loudly at this and her face relaxed. It was time to start.

"Shall we go?" I said.

She nodded and signalled to the waitress for our bill. She waved away my proffered notes and settled it with a Bank of China credit card.

We stood up and she led the way out.

She had long slender legs and finely shaped hips, and, like many Chinese women, an almost flat behind. She was around five-foot eight inches in height and, with high heels on, would be as tall as me or taller, a useful attribute in Year Three. Her feet splayed outwards when she walked and her deportment was stiff and ungainly, perhaps because she had never presented herself to the outside world in an even mildly sexual manner. Most Chinese women – unlike their Western counterparts – knew how to combine elegance with sexiness; a potential inherent in Camellia's build, but not yet realized.

Gangly, I thought to myself, as she climbed into a taxi outside the Park Lane Hotel. *She's a gangly schoolgirl on the edge of womanhood.*

She lived at the eastern end of Hong Kong Island in Chai Wan, and we were soon out of the crowded streets of Causeway Bay and rattling along the urban freeway that runs on stilts beside Victoria Harbour. She pointed out where she worked in Fortress Hill and named each successive district as we sped by. This was a new part of the island for me and I was keen to put names to places.

After twenty minutes, we turned into a typical Hong Kong housing estate abutting on to the harbour. A dozen high-rise blocks situated at regulation intervals with concrete-covered 'green spaces' in between and the occasional windswept playground.

We drew up at block seven and Camellia paid off the taxi.

"My contribution to the negative equity mountain," she said, as we passed an ancient and nosy-looking female porter in the entrance hall. "I bought my flat at the height of the property boom in 1997. Now it's worth fifty per cent less."

I nodded, but made no comment. She did not pursue the subject and we made our ascent to the seventeenth floor in silence. Maybe she just wanted to let me know that she was not a tenant with a nearby landlord. We left the lift and walked down a bare concrete corridor to her flat. It had a steel grill outer door and an inner wooden door. She unlocked them both and led the way inside.

"I have some spare slippers," she said, reminding me that in China, as in most of Asia, removal of shoes on entering a house was expected.

"Thanks," I said, bending down to unlace my Clarks ankle boots, "I'll be fine in socks."

Her flat was a small bright space. Compact living room dominated by sofa, dining table and AV entertainment centre; tiny kitchen and bathroom; small bedroom, with a single bed to match her single celibate status, and a second, even smaller bedroom filled with a large, double register keyboard in hardwood veneer, a full set of organ foot pedals and a complex, digitalized control panel.

"Do you play?" I shouted to Camellia.

She was now in the kitchen preparing more tea.

"Not really. Ten years practice, but I still only play simple tunes. Do you?"

"Sort of. My own improvisations mostly."

"Wow!" she said. "You must show me."

"When you graduate," I laughed. "When you've passed Year Three."

I returned to the living room and found her already sitting on the sofa. A pot of tea and two cups had been neatly placed on the spotless glass-topped table in front of her.

"Do you want me to change?" she asked.

"Maybe slip on a skirt," I said, realizing we were already in class and that I was the teacher in charge. "The shirt's fine."

I had decided to combine Years One and Two into one session, with a break for refreshment in the middle. It seemed mean to exclude the possibility of orgasm on our first outing – particularly for Camellia, who had never experienced one – and a shame to stay fully clothed the whole afternoon. I explained this to her and she replied that, as I was the lecherer in charge, I should make the decision.

"Let's go for two years then, and review progress at the first break."

"Fine," she said, and went off to her bedroom to change.

I stood by the window, watching children play basketball on a 'green space' far below. A jet passed overhead and I glanced up. The sun glinted on silver wings and I thought of my flight to Japan, of Aioko in her red-tiled house, of how much I had loved her, still loved her. I wanted to be with her, up in the sun and blue sky, at the top of the cellar steps. But the plane disappeared, and the door to heaven closed. The children screamed, and I fell back through space with eyes closed and pain in my heart.

Back to mad reality.

When Camellia returned, she had on a loose pleated, mid-length navy blue skirt. Her thin silk shirt was unchanged – grey and long-sleeved, with the top button now undone. She asked if the skirt was acceptable, and I said it was fine. She sat down on the sofa and poured us jasmine tea. I sat down beside her and began to talk. I tried to explain what men were, how they functioned in the sexual context and why, in my experience, they differed from women. I said that no one knew for sure how much of a man's makeup was inborn and how much conditioned by upbringing and society. But one thing was clear: men were easy to exploit on the sexual front. Although most liked home comforts and the regularity of family life, almost all men spent considerable amounts of time thinking of the possibility of sex with women – or men if they were gay – other than their wife or partner. They were aroused by visual stimuli related to the female body whether in real life (a woman with a pronounced bottom walking along a street in tight trousers), or in reproduction (an advertisement showing the stocking-clad leg or bare midriff of a female, or a pornographic magazine or film showing the whole body). Gay men were similarly aroused by visual images of men, and the vast industry devoted to producing lingerie and other libido-rousing fashion items further confirmed the importance of visual stimulation. The traditionalists believed that this reflex male response to the female body was a vital link in the reproductive chain and that, without it, the human species would not have managed to go on reproducing itself. They argued that, even before clothing, the simple display of rounded breasts and bottoms had been enough to encourage the male to mate. Now, in modern 'civilized' society, the exploitation of that primal urge meant men – and women – were bombarded day and night with sexual images: images encouraging them to buy clothes, cars and food; images implying that these products would help them attract new people to have sex with, or improve an existing sex life. Feminists, in the late sixties and seventies, believed that this exploitation was itself the cause of male promiscuity, of the male tendency to regard women as objects and the satisfaction of male carnal desires as a God-given right. Remove the exploitation, feminists said, remove the images and men would cease to be philanderers, molesters and rapists. Later, this stance was modified and women began to make pornography for their own consumption. In these products, the sexual satisfaction of the females involved and the non-objectification of the female bodies displayed were of paramount importance...

I paused to take a sip of tea.

"I thought you said only men were visually stimulated?" Camellia commented. "Now you say women like pornography too."

She had been listening closely, glasses perched on the end of her nose, knees crossed and covered by the blue skirt with hands folded in her lap. I had assumed a sideways position to lecture, with my back supported by the high padded armrest of the sofa and my right leg and socked foot curled up on the sofa cushion.

I put down my teacup, wondering how much longer Semester One should last. In my own Institute, stress was put on combining theory and practice, on not having too much theory on its own; but in this curriculum it would be hard to return to lecturer – as opposed to lecherer – mode once the practicum had started.

I decided to talk for a further ten minutes.

In answer to her comment, I said that modern feminists believed their older sisters had been too prudish and censorious. The first generation had failed to see the importance of sex, and sexual stimulation of all sorts, for women. By concentrating on the 'badness' of men, and male exploitation of women, the seventies crowd had turned heterosexual sex into an unpleasant and exploitative activity simply because men were involved; many women had become lesbians as a result – or, at least, dabbled in the Sapphic Arts. Their younger sisters of the eighties and nineties – egged on, no doubt, by younger brothers, and led into battle by pop icons such as Madonna – proclaimed, 'Girls just wanna have fun!' ...and lots of sex with lots of men. But, ironically, much of the imagery that came out of this wave was still of women rather than men, and most women viewers seemed more interested in the females in a PC pornographic context than the men performing with them.

"The fact of the matter is," I said, staring at Camellia's legs emerging from the blue cotton of her pleated skirt, "that when

I, as a man, look at a woman's body, clothed or unclothed, I can, in a certain mood and in a certain context, be aroused by that visual stimulus alone. Some women enjoy watching men, and will compare men's bottoms just as their male counterparts compare female buttocks and breasts. But the same level of arousal is not usually attained, and the image – whether live or reproduced – of a naked man, or of a man in a posing pouch or leather pants, will not produce the same level of immediate stimulation in a heterosexual woman, as the image of a naked woman, or a woman in sexy lingerie or a rubber body suit, produces in a heterosexual man. Men also like to masturbate to such images, whereas women, on the whole, do not."

I took another sip of tea and stretched the toes on my right foot. They had heard my talk before and gone to sleep.

"I've never masturbated," Camellia said suddenly. "I know what the word means, I think. But I've never done it."

I repressed an exclamation of surprise and nodded wisely, a lecturer's look of infinite understanding on my face and a lecher's surge of excitement in my stomach. She really was virgin territory. Almost anything I did would be new and exciting for her. And, as I watched her innocent, middle-aged eyes prepare to hang on my next word, I realised she would not know the difference between 'normal' and 'deviant' sex. Perhaps I should issue her with advanced standing credits, and jump straight to the final year.

No. I had to be patient, play the conscientious mentor and pervert her step by step.

"Really?" I said. "Well, we might include masturbation in Year Three. It goes rather well with fantasies. But it's not a topic I want to go into in the first semester."

"No," said Camellia.

"Now, where was I?"

"Still on visual stimulation," said Camellia.

"Yes, image of woman excites man – image of man does not always excite woman."

Camellia nodded. I saw her eyes glance up and down the leg of my jeans, stop for a split second at my crotch, and then come to rest on my foot. She did not appear aroused by any of these sights, so I moved on to other forms of stimulation. I explained that touch, smell – perfume for example, but also sweat – and even aural stimuli played an important role. Whispering sweet nothings in the ear could arouse a woman, and a man might be turned on by overtly sexual expressions such as 'fuck me, you fucker' or 'stick your cock up my cunt.' This last example made Camellia giggle, because, she said, she had no idea what I was talking about. I gave a dictionary definition of 'cock' and 'cunt,' which appeared to arouse her more than my legs. I then went on to the importance of touch and the male tendency to want attention centred on the 'cock.' I explained that, like women, they had many erogenous zones – from nipple to toe – and that, stimulated in the right way, these could give great pleasure. Camellia knew the word erogenous, but wanted more details of the female zones.

"Perhaps," I said, sitting up and easing down the sofa, "this might be a good moment to move on to Semester Two."

"Semester Two?" she said, reddening, uncrossing her knees and knotting her hands in her lap. "Have we finished Semester One already?"

"Well," I said, placing a hand on her knee. "Too much theory might make you think sex is all very dry and boring, when, in fact," – and, at this point, I leant across and began to lick her ear – "it is very wet and exciting."

She shivered and giggled, but kept her hands tightly clenched in her lap.

"Is that nice?" I asked.

"Mmm!" she replied. "More please, Lecherer."

I continued to lick and tongue her left ear, whilst bringing my left hand up from her knee to play with the lobe of her right ear.

"Yes," I whispered, "Year One, Semester Two: 'Kissing and Body Stroking with Clothes On.'"

"Do I have to do anything?" she asked, her voice quavering with excitement.

"No, not yet," I cooed. "Just sit back and enjoy."

Virgin territory. Almost every move I made with my mouth along her neck and cheek and lips, and every touch I made with my hand and fingers along her arms and knees and waist, produced a sigh or giggle, or repressed shriek of excitement. I progressed slowly and methodically, but did not indulge in french kissing. I felt it was better to leave that to a later stage. It felt too intimate for the friendly, but strictly educational, activity I was undertaking with Camellia.

When she was rigid with excitement and her breath was coming in short gasps, I slowly unbuttoned her shirt and put two fingers inside the left cup of her black cotton bra. I placed them on either side of her already enlarged nipple and squeezed gently; at the same time, my other hand crept under her skirt and up the inside of her thigh until it reached her panties. I cupped my palm over her vagina and pressed my forefinger softly into her crease, which was already damp. Her legs clamped together over my hand, but she did not try to remove it. I squeezed the nipple and pressed my finger in the crease. She gave out a high-pitched, half-swallowed squeal of pleasure, unlike anything I had heard before. Her unused nipple enlarged under my fingers, until it stuck out from her breast like a small penis; her crease became wetter and wetter, until I could feel the outline of a swelling clitoris beneath the cotton of her panties.

"Oh my God!" she cried.

"This is called heavy petting," I whispered, nibbling her ear again.

"Oh my God!" she repeated, as I switched to the right-hand nipple and increased the intensity of finger movement between her legs.

And then, before I could stop her, she was having an orgasm, spluttering and shrieking and jamming her legs together over my left hand.

"Oh my God! Oh my God! Oh my God!" she kept repeating in a kind of muted scream. "Oh my God!"

I removed both hands and sat with my right arm around her shoulder. She was shaking like a leaf and staring straight ahead at the blank television screen. I stroked her hair and explained that what she had experienced was quite normal and just the beginning. After a minute or two, she calmed down and leant forward to take a sip of tea.

"Wow!" she said. "You are a good teacher, Lecherer Stephen!"

"Actually," I replied. "I probably went a bit fast. Orgasms come in Year Two. After the break."

"Was that an orgasm?" she exclaimed, a look of amazement in her eyes.

"I should say so," I laughed. "Though only you can tell for sure."

"How can I tell?" she asked, her eyes alive with a new light, a light that had been waiting to shine for twenty years or more.

" If it happens again. When I do things, when I touch you like that."

"Really?" she glowed.

I nodded and suggested a pause before going on to the remaining element of Year Two: Undressing and More Intimate Touching (*Oral Sex or Not*).

"Haven't we done enough for one day?" she asked.

"You want to stop?" I said.

"Oh, no. But you must be tired."

There was a note of concern in her voice, along with an undisguised wish to continue the journey of discovery as soon as possible and for as long as possible.

"I'm fine," I laughed. "A lecherer is always happy to help a keen student."

She giggled and stood up.

"I have tuna sandwiches in the fridge. I thought we might get hungry, so I bought some in from Maxim's. Shall I get them?"

"Please," I said. "And some strong black tea, if you have any."

"I do," she beamed with her newfound radiance. "Milk and sugar?"

"Just milk. Please."

And so we sat for ten minutes, sipping English tea and munching sandwiches made of fresh tuna, mayonnaise and tomato on white bread with the crusts cut off.

We did not talk much. I asked a few polite questions about the flat — how long she had had it, how much it had cost — and she asked me what I taught at City University. She also asked me how long I had been with my current partner. I said five years. It seemed a good round number and long enough to qualify as more than a passing affair. Camellia did not press for details and seemed anxious to return to her studies. I downed a last corner of sandwich and drained my teacup. Camellia whisked the dishes to the kitchen and then sat, once more, at the end of the sofa, hands in her lap.

"What now Lecherer?" she asked, with a grin of nervous anticipation.

Her glasses were perched on the end of her nose as they had been in the previous session. She had the air of a serious student, who's just discovered the meaning of fun.

"Undressing," I murmured, "yes…"

I debated, within my head, the option of us both undressing, of exploring our bodies in their nude state, but then decided against such a simple, and potentially didactic, approach. It was too reminiscent of a school biology class. Instead, I eased along the sofa again and started to unbutton Camellia's grey silk shirt.

"Undressing a woman," I explained, as I opened the buttons one by one, "or watching a woman undress is very arousing for a man. The gradual revelation of flesh leads to increased visual stimulation and the prospect of more intimate and comprehensive touching."

She shivered. I placed my hand on her back, leant her forward, removed the shirt one arm at a time and put it to one side. I then stroked and kissed her shoulders, while passing my hand across the flat of her stomach. She trembled and moaned. I moved my left hand round her back and unhooked the clasp of her bra. I slipped the straps down her arms, leaving her bare-breasted on the sofa beside me. She tried to cover herself, but I held her hands in her lap. Su-yin once told me that Chinese women considered revealing breasts to a man to be more shameful than revealing any other part of the body, and that, if caught naked, they would cover their chest before their vagina.

Camellia's breasts were small and firm with pronounced, dark brown nipples. I lowered myself to the floor and knelt in front of her to observe them better.

"Beautiful!" I said. "Sexy nipples."

She stared into her lap. Her face reddened.

"This feels strange," she said. "Me sitting. You staring."

"Yes," I replied, after a pause, in which I continued to stare. "Men like to stare, but many women do not like being stared at. That is why there are paid strippers."

"I could never take off my clothes in front of a room full of men."

"No," I said, continuing to watch her breasts. Every now and then they quivered as an involuntary shiver or shudder passed through her mind and into her body. "Understandable. Though some women enjoy it, and men too. The exhibitionists."

"What's that?"

"People who get excited by showing off their bodies in public."

She nodded and started to cover her breasts again. Then she remembered and returned her hands to her side. She was visibly shaking now, but whether from pleasure or embarrassment I could not tell. I moved forward and leant across her lap, until my lips touched her right nipple. I licked the small button of flesh with my tongue and then enclosed it with my lips and sucked. She squealed, and the nipple grew in my mouth. I did the same to the left nipple with the same result – squeal and growth. Then I sat back on my haunches to observe. I was amazed at the length of the two protuberances now protruding from their dark black areolas. I reached out my hands and took hold of them. I squeezed and rotated the nipples between thumb and forefinger and then pulled them towards me until the flesh of the breasts was drawn away from the body and suspended in mid-air. Camellia flushed a deeper red and began to breathe heavily. I let them fall back and slid my hands down across her stomach and around her waist, until I found the fastening of her skirt. I undid it and eased the blue pleated cotton down over her hips and thighs, until it was lying around her ankles.

Now she sat on the sofa naked apart from a pair of thin black cotton panties. Her legs were clamped together and refused to relax or open, even when I stroked them. I returned to my squatting position in front of her.

"Do you want me to stop?" I asked.

"No," she whispered, sitting bolt upright and staring straight ahead. "Just nervous."

"Do you want me to take my shirt and trousers off?" I suggested. "So, we're more equal?"

"Yes," she whispered.

"Perhaps you could help," I said.

After a moment's hesitation, she leant forward and began, with shaking fingers, to unbutton my black silk shirt. When she had removed it, I stood up and pointed to my belt. She loosened the bronze buckle and then stopped.

"And now the button and zip," I instructed.

"I'm too shy," she said.

"Shall I do it?"

She nodded, and watched intently as I undid the top metal button, lowered the zip and let my jeans fall to the floor. Now I was wearing just a white T-shirt and black underpants. She looked me up and down, covered her mouth and giggled.

"Not too exciting?" I asked

She shook her head and giggled again.

"Hairy legs. Like my father."

"And a hairy chest," I laughed, pulling off my T-shirt.

I knelt down in front of her and placed her fingers on my nipples.

"Squeeze them," I whispered.

"Like you did mine?" she asked.

I nodded. She hesitated and then, reaching out her hands and brushing aside a few wisps of greying chest hair, she took hold of the nipples and squeezed them between her thumbs and forefingers.

"Mm!" I said. "That's nice."

"They're very small," she laughed. "Difficult to keep hold of."

"Squeeze them harder then," I said, beginning to feel aroused by her inexpert but eager touch.

"Like this?" she asked, pinching them gleefully with her nails.

"Ow!" I laughed.

"Sorry," she giggled.

"A bit softer," I sighed. "That's it."

I felt a bulge appear in my pants. But she was too intent on nipple manipulation – brow furrowed, lips clenched, eyes lit up like a child playing with a new toy – to notice.

"Not all men have sensitive nipples," I explained, lowering her hands and placing them on the sofa either side of her hips. "I'm lucky."

"Do you want me to touch anything else?" she asked innocently.

I thought of teaching her how to make me come with her hand, but decided against it. She needed, and deserved, to experience more pleasure herself first. I could wait for Year Three and a more complex scenario to make my orgasmic debut.

"Not at the moment," I said with a smile. "Lean back again."

She did as I asked. I lowered my face to her legs and kissed her thighs from the knee up to the hip, gradually approaching the damp centre of her panties. Her legs remained closed, but her breath came faster and her repressed squeals intensified. I pulled her towards me, cupped her bottom in my hands, squeezed it and then buried my head between her legs. This time she parted them for me and squealed with a new urgency. I opened my mouth and sucked at the damp cotton over her vagina, feeling for the clitoris with my tongue. As with my finger the first time, I had only licked and nibbled for a few seconds when she began to shriek and gurgle, like a trapped goose. A moment later, a strangled scream issued from her mouth, her legs clamped round my face in spasm and she came again, shuddering for a minute or more with my head jammed in the vice of her thighs and pinned down from above by her hands.

"Oh my God!" she repeated as before. "Oh my God! Oh my God!"

At last her hold relaxed and I was released. I took a gulp of fresh air. We had, I decided, done enough to cover Years One and Two. I was tired and Camellia might expect extracurricular orgasms late into the night, if I prolonged the tutorial any further.

"Well done, Camellia," I said, rising from the floor and slumping on to the sofa beside her. "Two orgasms completed, so you're ready to progress to Year Three."

"Already?" she squeaked, still out of breath, a hint of disappointment in her voice.

"Yup!" I confirmed, putting my arm round her shoulder and giving her a lecturer-like squeeze. "All done for today."

"Was that oral sex?" she asked, after we had sat in silence for a moment.

"Sort of," I said. "Mouth to genital contact with a millimetre of cloth in between."

"What about you?" she asked, glancing down at my crotch. "I didn't make you have an orgasm. Hadn't we better do that? Wasn't that in Year Two?"

I nodded and reached out for the bottled water she had placed on the table earlier.

"Let's fit 'Making Him Come' into Year Three," I said, taking a swig.

"Intercourse?" she exclaimed. "I thought that was ruled out."

"No, not intercourse. 'Fantasies and Games People Play.'"

23

Half an hour later, Stephen left in good spirits, feeling he had performed a useful service. Camellia was a different woman from the one he had met three hours earlier and, on the way to the MTR station, expressed genuine gratitude for his concern and conscientiousness as a sexual mentor.

On reaching home, however, the blue sky of well-being gave way to dark clouds of depression and loneliness. He showered, collapsed naked into bed and wrapped himself in the familiar smell of his duvet. He wanted Aioko to be lying there beside him, sneezing and snuggling into his shoulder, a real partner with whom he had a real bond. He had felt nothing for Camellia, nothing except a kind of benevolence and curiosity. How could he have done? They had only met four hours ago. And yet, he suspected, she was already in love with him. After her second orgasm, and before dressing, she asked him to lie on top of her and hold her. It would make her feel secure, she said, a fitting end to Year Two. He did as she asked – she flat on her back along the sofa in nothing but her panties, he on top in nothing but his underpants. She had hugged him for a minute or two and sighed repeatedly. They had not kissed, but in the eye nearest to his there had been a romantic glint in the jet-black pupil. Warning to all staff: Lecherers and students are advised not to start relationships!

Stephen chuckled, rolled over and ran through scenarios for Camellia to act out in Year Three. There was feeling after all, a feeling of lust for her, for the situation. She was exciting because she was not exciting, because she was so plain and inexperienced. Everything was new to her, everything untried. She could be converted to his perversions, become a partner in his investigation.

Roman Catholics claimed that a soul caught in a child was a soul caught for life, and, sexually speaking, Camellia was still a child. He just had to ensure that the fantasy he prepared truly excited her, excited her to a greater extent than the simple fumbling, licking and sucking of Years One and Two.

And judging by her reaction to the story he sent a week later, it did. After an exchange of emails, in which they agreed how enjoyable the first session had been and set a date for Year Three on Wednesday, Stephen asked Camellia to describe any fantasy element she would like included in the Year Three practicum. She replied that her only wish was for someone to kiss her on the lips and say he loved her. This was a challenge to Stephen – the romantic heroine she wanted to be was not the character he had in mind for her to play – but, after a rewrite of the ending, he incorporated the required element and sent the story, entitled *Mademoiselle Camille*, with the following covering note:

Dear Student Camellingerie,

Mm! Just writing that makes me feel sexy and reminds me of stroking your panty-covered bottom last time. I hope you enjoy the attached story and do not find it too strange. It is an erotic piece of writing with elements of pornography and a line or two in the language you are learning for your summer trip, *le français*. I have drawn on my imagination (the male character is half my age but you deserve a younger hero, at least in the story!) and, as intercourse is ruled out, I have incorporated other areas of fantasy. If you don't like it, or it doesn't turn you on, please let me know and I'll try again. But I think and hope it will! Heterosexual male fantasies tend to take two forms: dominating or being dominated by women. Anything in between is considered too ordinary and belongs in the marriage bed! Read the story and you will see which of the two I have chosen. If you feel the urge to experience the other type (i.e. the one I have not chosen) you are free to ask me to act in that way in the second half of our session (see attached notes).

Lecherer Stephen

At the end of the story, he included the following 'Lecherer's Notes':

CHARACTER NOTES:

CAMILLE CHAN: Just forty. A secondary school French teacher who takes pleasure in mentally disciplining her pupils. Her out-of-school hobby is inviting home vulnerable young men from her adult evening classes to play with in a similar, but more grown-up and physical manner. She presents a disdainful exterior to the world and this both disturbs and attracts men. In her own way, she manages to satisfy the carnal desires that course through her body, but has never found love or, perhaps, has never allowed love to find her. She stays in control of affairs, expects total obedience from male visitors and keeps emotion at bay. But tonight, after a session that is harsher and more intense than usual, something changes. Inside Mademoiselle Camille, a woman ready to love rises up at last.

STEFAN ZWEIG: Around twenty-five. A sensitive young man from Austria, who becomes infatuated with Mademoiselle Camille, his teacher at French evening classes. He goes home with her because she makes it a precondition for having a drink and because he is curious and more than a little in love with her. He is both shocked and excited by what she asks him to do. It is something he has never experienced before. He discovers he likes the feeling of being dominated, likes the hard aura of controlled lust that comes from her, likes the fact she enjoys it – though he is frightened of what she might do next. He is a man looking for love, too, and, as the night progresses, his attempts to satisfy the demands she makes of him become more than just physical. Emotions get involved, both his and hers.

STAGING AND 'ACTING' NOTES:

For this to work, it is important for us to stay in role once we have begun – at least in the first, scripted part. I suggest you change into your costume once you have got home from picking me up at the MTR (as in the script, in fact). Then, when you come back into the room, you are in character! You do not need to stick to every detail of the story (particularly at the end, after I am on the bed!), but should try and follow it fairly closely so that we both know where we're going. Lines of dialogue can be improvised if not remembered, and should, in any case, be kept minimal. The most important thing is to enjoy it, and to know that I will enjoy it if you do! If you want to add bits in the early stages, please do so; I shall be at your mercy and you can play with me in whatever way you want. You can make me wait longer, touch and be touched in extra ways, smack me more than once etc., as long as you keep the key physical events in place. Costumes we have discussed and props are minimal. I will bring my silk dressing gown cord to act as 'the cord'! And do not worry, nothing I have described is dangerous to me physically; I have tested it (as writers do when writing) and am sure it will cause more pleasure than pain. Whatever happens, you should stay in role as the hard, lustful Mistress. Do not be tentative in your toughness and do not think of it as acting. Connect to a part of yourself that enjoys what Camille enjoys in the story. We have many sides and they are all, more or less, repressed. So, stay yourself, but draw on your hard side in Part One. And, at the end of the scripted 'story,' I will take my lead from you. Your fantasy begins then. So, continue to be yourself and connect to whatever side of your personality you want to. I will, as requested, act at being in love with you, as long as you won't be upset afterwards when the acting stops. I will try to be true to myself in that role, too, and will not present an over-the-top romantic hero. So, if we are lucky, both mild masochism and loving romance will be in the air, and if you want to try out anything else in the second half (e.g. me being the sadist), just ask. It is your chance to taste forbidden fruits. Good luck!

Camellia responded the next morning in a note that reconfirmed her practicality, as well as her sexual ignorance:

Dear Lecherer Stephen,
    Jesus Christ! I never imagined anything like your story! It made me feel like a slut – and that was just reading it! It's very erotic and I felt aroused, but it's acceptable. The thought of trying it out makes me excited – the repressed part of me, no doubt. But some clarifications: (a) I dominate in the first half (the written out story), while you take the lead in the second half (the improvisation), right? (b) Need another lecture on biology: in the story Mademoiselle Camille has to squeeze your – sorry, the young man's! – balls. Where are they? (c) As you have to lie on the floor, do I need to cover it with something? So that it won't be too cold or hard for you? (d) How do I ensure I do not hurt (really harm) you with the cord? (e) When you lie on the floor, and I stand above you in skirt and stockings, will your hand be able to reach my thighs, if I am in high heels? (f) On costumes and props: I will buy the loose skirt you mentioned and use stockings from the starter pack; long gloves I can borrow from my sister – though they may not be leather; high heels, I have. You're very imaginative! It will be the thrill of a lifetime for me, an experience I'll never forget as long as I live!
Student Mistress Camellia,

The 'starter pack' refers to a pair of pantyhose Stephen had given Camellia at the first session. He called it her 'Bachelor of Sexual Arts Student Starter Pack.' The pantyhose were open around the crotch and thighs, allowing the man to glimpse flesh, as he might do with real stockings, at the same time as sparing the woman the discomfort of wearing a garter belt.

Dear Student Mistress Camellia,
    I am glad you enjoyed and were aroused by the story. This does NOT mean you are a slut, but someone discovering a healthy and varied sexual appetite. Answers to queries and

worries: (a) Yes, you will be totally dominant in the first half –
until the end of the written story. Then I can dominate
and take the lead, if that is what you would like. Is it? One
advantage, if I am in charge, is that you will not have to
remember script details. I will try and combine 'romantic
love' with some surprise elements of mild domination – IF
you think you might enjoy that. Would you? Or do you just
want soft romantic loving? (b) The balls are just below the
penis (between the penis and the anus) and should not be
squeezed too hard! (c) A cover on the floor would be nice,
thank you for thinking of that. Though if you want to make
me lie naked on the cold hard kitchen tiles, that is your right
as Mademoiselle Camille! (d) I think my hand will reach your
thighs, even with heels on – I have long arms and fingers. (e) If
anything hurts to the point where I am not enjoying it, I shall
simply say, 'Please stop, Mademoiselle!' So, do what turns you
on and, unless I say that phrase, assume it is turning me on too.
I will NOT let you 'really harm' me, but you must be tough
(with the cord, or smacking, for example) in order to make it
'real.' (f) Costume sounds like it is in hand. So, with one soft
and respectful kiss between your silk-pantied legs, I remain,

Obediently your servant,
Stephen

Camellia, in a last mail before the session, responded in brief and
raised Stephen's hopes of a full conversion to perversion.

Dear Lecherer Stephen,

The last sentence in your mail was killing me! I'm not
good at acting, but I'll try to be a tough person. I think there's
a part of me like that somewhere inside. When you take over
in part two, I don't know what kind of mild domination
you'll undertake. But I think it's OK and you don't need to
tell me now. I like surprises. If I don't like it, I'll tell you!

Student Mistress Camellingerie.

★

On Wednesday afternoon, Camellia met me at her local MTR.

As agreed, she was wearing her everyday clothes of long-sleeved shirt and blue jeans. We walked back to her block chatting in a normal manner, ascended in the lift and entered her flat through the double doors. Then, after I had visited the bathroom and changed into a clean T-shirt, she asked me to sit on the sofa while she prepared herself in the bedroom. I felt relaxed and ready to enjoy myself. I was acting out a story in someone else's home, and, despite being the author of the piece, I was not – as I had been with Christine – responsible for setting and direction. There was also the fact of Camellia's innocence, which I wanted her to lose in the most pleasurable manner possible. For me, pleasing a woman was as important as pleasing myself – if she was not enjoying the action, then nor was I. That, I reflected, had been the problem with earlier women in my life. Sexual contact was old hat to them and – even dressed up in new ribbons, as it had been with Aioko – sharing bodies a familiar ritual that had palled with the passing years. Camellia was different. She was enthusiastic, longing to be touched and aroused, and, most important of all, totally ignorant of what to expect from a man – or, indeed, from her own mind and body.

And I was not disappointed.

From the moment she came in, dressed in her white blouse, long black skirt and black high heels, to the moment – three hours later, right at the end, when, wearing nothing but her stocking panty hose, she made and witnessed a man achieve orgasm for the first time in her life – she was fully involved, continuously aroused and never going through the motions for my sake. Even if she had not confirmed this in person afterwards, and in a mail the next day, I would have known it to be true. It was written all over her face, it shone in her eyes, it shivered and quivered round her body, and exploded into a climax on at least five occasions during the course of our activities that afternoon.

For me, for the first time, the reality was more exciting than either the writing or reading of the story and, contrary to Lacan's theory of fantasy, better than the imagined event. The presence of real bodies – of my body and her body – did not get in the way of mental stimulation, did not pall beside those imagined situations and imagined actions – carried out by the reader's mind on the back of the writer's words – but rather complemented and intensified them as it was supposed to do.

The sight of her staring at me when she asked me, right at the start, to stand up and remove my clothes – her face hard and strict, her eyes glued to my lower body – aroused me instantly and visibly. The point where she made me lie on the floor and stood over me, so that I was gazing up her skirt along stockinged legs to the roundness of her bottom far above, produced exactly the right mix of pleasure and humiliation in my mind and body – sensations intensified by her grunts of unfeigned lust as I stroked her legs, and by the abruptness with which she pushed my hands away and flicked my erect penis with the toe of her shoe when the time for a new torment came. The moment when she lowered her buttocks to within an inch of my tongue, and I had, at her command, to stretch it out and lick her panties at the tautest, wettest point between her legs, was almost perfect and synchronized to within a frame or two of my imagination.

It was mutual pleasure with no pretence. She played the role of mistress with enjoyment and enthusiasm, continually commanding me to touch her here, there and everywhere and smacking me or kicking me with her pointed toe if I was too slow or did not do it in the right way. And, at the same time, she was aware of my enjoyment. When, with silk cord tied tight around my balls, she lead me to her bedroom on all fours, she made sure the order to 'sniff her bum like a dog' was enforced with a hard push of my face into her behind and a harsh tightening of the cord across my anus as indicated in the story. Once I was on the bed and bound to its head and foot with red velvet ribbons, she tormented me from top to toe with the callousness and curiosity of a teenage village girl inspecting, tweaking and squeezing some boy she has found in the barn and tied to a bale of hay for fun.

It was a first experience set in the context of female domination and 'do whatever turns you on,' rather than in the context of doe-eyed demureness and nervous submission to conventional intercourse – the normal lot of a woman on her first full-bodied sexual outing. Camellia, instructed to play the part, enjoyed herself as only a first-timer can, finally yanking off her panties, jamming her naked buttocks over my nose and cheeks and forcing me to lick and suck her swollen lips and newly burgeoned clitoris until my mouth was sore and my tongue tested to its very tip.

"Make me come!" she yelled, and I did.

And I played my other parts, too, when the time came.

In doing so, I may not have experienced the same intensity of enjoyment as in the first half of our session, but I still felt a high level of physical and mental satisfaction. After her first full-throated climax, she untied me and lay on the bed beside my much-abused body. I leant over and, as promised, kissed her on the lips and whispered, 'I love you.' Our tongues met as if we were hero and heroine falling in love in some second-rate – or even first-rate – film. I was acting, but so engrossed in the part that it would have been difficult to distinguish my feelings and physical tenderness from the real thing.

Camellia was overpowered again, but this time in her role as lonely maiden rescued by the long-awaited prince from the loveless world that had been her home since childhood. Her kiss was full and hungry, and she would not let me go. She sighed and moaned and sucked and probed, and, when I put my hand between her legs, it was wet once more. Indeed, as our tongues crossed and uncrossed, and our lips merged and unmerged, she came for the second time in ten minutes, arching up beneath me and grabbing my back so that the breath was squeezed from my lungs.

After the break, taken together sitting naked on the sofa in the living room, sipping tea and munching tuna sandwiches, I decided to try some mild male domination. It was not my forte, and I had never given much thought to the genre – except as part of the occasional fantasy where I, and a woman, were dominated and abused together, usually by other women. But I had developed an idea or two the night before and now instructed Camellia to put back on her stocking panty hose and nothing else, and sit on the bed and wait for me. I left her there for five minutes while I finished my tea, assuming anticipation would heighten her pleasure. I then pulled on my black Helmut Lang underpants and my black Giordano T-shirt and went through to the bedroom.

I blindfolded Camellia and told her to lie on her back. I then tied her arms and legs to the four corners of the bed so that her stocking-covered legs were splayed apart and she could not clench them together, as she had been doing in all our activities so far. I also put a gag across her mouth, checking that it was not too tight, that she had no problem breathing and that she could shout a muffled 'Stop!' if she did not like what I was doing.

I then began moving my hand around her body, stroking and caressing it, occasionally smacking a thigh or tweaking a nipple. She struggled but could not break free. After a while, I moved my hand between her thighs and found to my relief that it was as wet as before. I opened the lips and exposed the clitoris. She tried to close her legs but could not. I took the bobble of pink flesh between my thumb and forefinger and squeezed it. Camellia strained at her bonds and brought her knees as close together as she could, but did not ask me to stop. I then inserted two fingers of my free hand inside her vagina and massaged its front wall, squeezing and tweaking the clitoris as I did so. When she was approaching climax, I stopped, removed her blindfold and gag, took off my underpants and repositioned myself so that my balls hung down above her face. I took her two erect nipples and pulled them up as far as they would go, before squeezing them hard and releasing them, watching as the breasts fell back on to her chest and resettled like two jellies on a plate. I repeated this a couple of times and then leant forward over her stomach and began massaging her clitoris and vagina as before. As she approached climax, her legs desperate to close and her shrieks and squeals loud enough to summon the police, I told her to take my balls in her mouth and not make any sound. She did as I commanded and I felt her lips close over my scrotum and suck like a baby on its dummy. My fingers then squeezed and squashed the clitoris to its third climax of the day.

I climbed off and left her tied up on the bed, this time without a kiss or cuddle. I finished the one remaining tuna sandwich, lay for a further five minutes on the sofa reading a newspaper and then returned to the bedroom.

I untied Camellia and told her to kneel, still in her stocking pantyhose, on the floor against the bed with her face buried in the bedclothes. I then secured her arms to either end of the bed and, using longer scarves, tied her two knees to two metal casters at head and foot of the bed base. She now had her legs splayed out and compelled to stay open as before, but this time with her bottom exposed, its crease parted so that both anus and vagina were on view. I asked her if everything was all right and she replied, with a gasp, that it was. I then stroked her long black hair and, pulling her face to one side, kissed her hard on the lips, my tongue forcing its way into her mouth. I nibbled her ear, ran my fingers down her back and then raised my hand and smacked her hard on the behind. She winced and tried to get free but did not ask me to stop. I again kissed her and whispered in her ear that I loved her, before smacking her for a second time. I told her to bury her face in the mattress and not look up, or she would be punished.

I then climbed off the bed and knelt on the floor directly behind her. I felt my penis grow and for the first time that day imagined entering her. But intercourse was not on the agenda, an important rule that underpinned the success and intensity of the session. It would have changed the entire nature of the game, and the relationship between Camellia and myself, if we had copulated. Instead, I licked my left index finger and inserted it into her anus.

She gasped and pushed her face into the mattress.

"Are you all right?" I asked.

"Yes," she said in a muffled voice.

"Good," I said, and smacked her hard on the right buttock.

Then, with my finger still inside the anus, I used my free hand to alternately smack her and play with her clitoris, until, with a great commotion and straining at her bonds, she came for a fourth time.

My first time performance as a male dominator was finished and I was relieved. I had not felt comfortable in the role. My arousal had been accompanied by guilt, and, more importantly, by an intense desire to be the woman tied up on the bed. Her pleasure at being humiliated and mildly tormented had given me some satisfaction, as pleasing another always did, but I still wanted to be the smacked not the smacker. My preference had not changed with this brief exposure to the dominant role, though it had confirmed my obsession and fascination with unconventional contact and, in that sense, furthered my investigation. I untied the scarves, laid her out on the bed, lowered myself on to her body and held her tight, as she had asked me to do at the end of our session a week before.

"How do you feel?" I asked,

"Mmm! Very nice and very tired," she replied.

"What about the last bit," I said. "Did you enjoy being smacked?"

"Sort of," she murmured. "When you touch me, too. But I prefer smacking you!"

"Best of all?"

"No," she laughed. "Not best of all. Best of all, I like being kissed on the mouth and being told that you love me."

I nodded and smiled.

It was unlikely I would ever find a woman who did not make that her first choice. And maybe, with the right woman, with Aioko, it could be my first choice again, but not with Camellia. Camellia was a student and, like all students, she must move on, fade from my life and find her own way after graduation later that day. She had been a good student and I debated offering her a Masters, or even a practical PhD in sadomasochism. But she was already in love with teacher, and it would not be fair to take our partnership further.

I closed my eyes and rested a cheek on her shoulder. She stroked the back of my head and, for a while, we lay like that, content in each other's arms, playing the part of long-term lovers we would never be.

"Can I make you come now?" she suddenly whispered in my ear.

I opened my eyes and, for a moment, wondered where I was. Then Camellia's face came into focus and I saw beginner's lust burning in her eyes again.

"Yes," I said with a stifled yawn. "Why not? We haven't done that yet, have we?"

"What shall I do?" she asked eagerly.

"Probably best with the hand," I said, rolling off Camellia on to my back. "Unless you have a strong desire to try fellatio."

"Fellatio?" she enquired.

"Putting my cock in your mouth."

"Oh," she exclaimed, a look of mild disgust passing across her face. "I'd rather not. The balls were bad enough!"

"Fine by me," I said. "I prefer the hand. Have you any oil?"

"Oil?"

"Massage oil. Moisturizing cream. Something that lubricates."

She went to the bathroom and returned with a tube of intensive care cream.

"Will this do?" she asked.

"Fine," I said.

And so, for the next fifteen minutes, I instructed my charge on how best to hold my penis; how hard to squeeze; how best to move her hand up and down around the head and neck; when to take hold of the balls, or insert a finger up the anus; when, in my case, to reach up and tweak a nipple.

I explained the difference between circumcised and uncircumcised heads, taught her how to talk dirty, and admitted that what I really liked – along with a number of men, but not all – was to have a woman sit on my face and masturbate my penis with her hand. She learnt quickly, and complied willingly and effectively with all my instructions. And, despite a touch that remained rough at the edges, and an over-enthusiasm that had me crying out in pain once or twice, she managed to combine all the elements and bring me to orgasm with her bottom still clamped firmly on my face. In fact, the sight of my semen flying out of her clenched fist made her shriek and push her own clitoris even harder on to my mouth and tongue so that my first orgasm became her fifth of the day.

"What a lot!" she shrieked with excitement, squeezing the last drip out of the tip of my battered member and continuing to grind into my face. "My God!"

Satisfied client and satisfied lecturer, too. We showered, dressed and had another cup of tea. I played the keyboard and we sung Beatles' songs to celebrate her graduation. Finally, we danced around the living room, arm in arm, bodies close – the last waltz.

At six, I said it was time for me to leave.

"Wouldn't you like to go for a meal?" she asked, resignation already in her eyes.

"Better not," I said, kissing her on the cheek. "Now you have a Bachelor of Sexual Arts degree, there will be many dinner partners queuing up."

"Not like you," she sighed, putting her arms around my neck and hugging me. "I'll never forget my Lecherer. Never."

I removed her arms and we walked to the lift. When the doors opened, I stepped inside and turned to look at her one more time. She raised her hand and waved.

"Goodbye, Camellia," I whispered, as the doors closed. "Goodbye. And good luck."

24

On the face of it, a straightforward end to a straightforward *liaison érotique*, but the level of post-graduation gloom Stephen felt was far from straightforward. He fell into a pit of despondency in the darkest corner of the lecher's cellar and could not climb out again.

The day after his Year Three session, he sent, as a kind of antidote to this black mood and pervasive sense of depravity, a brief, upbeat mail to Camellia telling her how much he had enjoyed the afternoon and expressing the hope that it had been what she wanted and that she had not been too disappointed when it was all over. A responsible note from a responsible and conscientious teacher, to which Camellia responded:

Dear Lecherer Stephen,

Thank you so much for spending the afternoon with me. I enjoyed it very much, too. And, yes, this is what I had hoped for – sex and emotion, love and lust. While I liked the stroking, kissing, smacking and sucking very much, and found it all very exciting, it's the tender moments that I recall most vividly: sitting beside you while you played Beatles songs, dancing a silent waltz with you, sitting on the sofa naked holding hands and sipping tea, lying on the bed with your head on my shoulder and your breath on my cheek. Never before has anyone been so close to me, physically and emotionally. You have satisfied my yearning for love (albeit briefly) and my curiosity about lust. This has really been a very wonderful and fulfilling experience.

You also gave me confidence about myself and my body; I always thought men only liked women with big breasts and big bottoms. So, I will always remember this day in June 2001 with Lecherer Stephen and will have no regrets later in life, even if I never develop a long-term relationship or touch a man again. And, yes, there was a feeling of emptiness after you left. But then again this was expected at the beginning, and I did not feel too bad about it. After all, we are sensible people. Just one question though: if your current relationship were over some day, would you like to develop one with Camellia? Cheers.

Your first (and only?) BSA student

Satisfied customer, happy memories, life stretching out ahead in the real world as it did for all students after graduation day. On the face of it, Stephen had nothing to reproach himself for, nothing to feel guilty about, and no reason not to turn over a new page and continue the next part of his investigation with renewed vigour and enthusiasm. And perhaps he might have done, after wallowing in the shadow of remorse for a few days, if her reply had not again made him question the investigation itself.

He had, he realized, acted purely out of lecherous motives, and no amount of playing with words such as 'investigation' or 'sexual preference' or even 'social service' could change that. Her final question in the mail brought this simple truth home to him. It made him query the sanity of what he was doing and feel like a crazy guy. How could he have spent an afternoon kissing, smacking and sucking a woman's body, while telling her he loved her and pretending she was the most important person in his life, only to end the contact as abruptly as it had begun? What good did it do him, or her? Her letter was positive; she had been through a worthwhile learning experience, she said; she would never forget it, she said; but then, at the end, came the sting. The reminder of reality, the reminder that life was not a series of sketches acted out in some basement club; a reminder that life was there to be lived, not performed, however much one-act plays might protect a person from the long term reality of living in the world.

Her question was open and justifiable: there was no reason he should not develop a relationship with her. She had a well-paid job, owned her own flat, was eminently eligible in terms of age and education and probably happy to go on indulging in submissive-dominant role playing for the rest of her life, as long as there was the occasional kiss and cuddle in between. He could investigate his sexual preference to his heart's and penis's content. What more did Stephen want? What was it that eluded him? Was he bound forever to need new women – new women to prove his power with, to prove his power to please? Was it all done for the brief moment of pleasure that his own orgasm afforded, or as some kind of penance for an original sin – for an original act of debauchery, the nature of which he could not discover? Or was there, somewhere in his childhood, a moment when he had failed to do what was expected of him, failed to please in the way demanded – a failure he had been trying to compensate for ever since?

In his investigation so far, his efforts had gone into satisfying women, and one woman in particular, rather than himself. Perhaps because he still did not know what it was that would satisfy him, and because satisfying someone else seemed the easiest way of avoiding the conundrum of his own dissatisfaction. What had happened to him back in the darkness of time that had made him like this? Or what had he failed to learn, to comprehend about living, about being in close proximity with another human being? Was he investigating – seeking new experiences with new people – to avoid the truth, or to discover the truth? In the days after Camellia's graduation, he had no idea, and no sense of where he was going. He was in a pit of blackness with no light to show him the way out, no route back to the established pattern of monogamy, and no way forward, except the path of ever more extreme servitude. His only hope was that, somewhere on his tortuous crawl across the cellar, he would discover a truth, some absolute moment of satisfaction and catharsis. But even then there was no guarantee that this – the most total and illuminating experience imaginable – would offer more than temporary relief, more than a momentary spark of light in the darkness. There was no guarantee it would ignite a lasting flame to burn and guide him for the rest of his life.

Was this his destiny then: to wallow in the darkness outside the walls of real life, giving, and occasionally getting, physical satisfaction with unsuspecting spinsters and worn out wives? Was this a worthwhile investigation, a meaningful way to spend the sixth decade of his life?

His mood became so bleak he was forced to take another week off work. Although there was no physical illness present, he felt too exhausted to get up in the morning and too confused to concentrate on anything but the most mundane of tasks. And as he lay on his bed day after day, staring out at the bright June sunshine and the shimmering towers of Hong Kong offering their daily illusion of wealth and well-being, he could think of only one thing, the one thing that was not a way forward, the one thing that had already proved a dead end in the foothills of Mount Fuji.

He tried to push it from his mind, hired DVDs and watched old movies: the Alfred Hitchcock catalogue (including early silent films like *Manxman* and *Easy Virtue*), the Audrey Hepburn films with their frivolous plots and sugar-coated endings, the Marilyn Monroe classics. Of these, only Monroe's work offered solace. There was something about the peroxide blonde's combination of softness and sexiness that soothed his mind and body. Her stomach protruding in an unashamed manner to match the roundness of her behind, her eyes naughty and kind at the same time, her soft and sensual mouth, her breasts and lap offering warmth and security for an aching head. She was the good angel of sex and womanhood that had tried to protect him as a child, tried to teach him about the kindness and eroticism of women, tried to show him that there was no need for warmth and lust to be split, no need for him to fret and worry that he could never ever satisfy the mental and physical demands of a woman. These demands were not so outrageous and infinite as he imagined them to be, and his own demands – if only he would recognise their true nature and learn to express them in an open manner – could be met, too. Nothing was impossible to an open mind and body.

He felt like Laurence Olivier in *The Prince and the Showgirl*; a stiff unyielding man who had never been taught to love, who picked out women for his pleasure and then discarded them; a man who Marilyn had to turn back into a child before he could discover himself. A superficial film, a film that was nowhere in the pantheon of cinematic masterpieces, but, in his despondent state, a simple, straightforward film offering greater hope and insight than a Bergman, Kieslowski or Fassbinder. A film that returned him to the innocence of the fifties; to his own childhood, when women seemed larger, more mysterious, more all-powerful than they did now; to a time when the distant image of 'happy ever after' in his own future seemed as certain as the happy and fulfilled existence Prince Olivier and Showgirl Monroe would live out, in the audience's mind, in Transylvania, after the film ended. The catharsis of a happy ending, of an ending to the story, of any ending that promised peace and quiet; perhaps that was all he sought, perhaps that was the light at the end of the tunnel, the secret passageway out of the cellar.

But when the disc finished and the solace evaporated, she, the most impossible of women, returned to haunt his heart and thoughts. A woman with none of the all-knowing innocence and sensual softness of Monroe; a woman who, like him, was in a pit, but unable to share her pit with him, or consider joining forces to climb out of the pit's darkness and start living anew in light. And the longer he lay stretched out, staring into the blue heat and neon night, the more the impossible woman solidified on the bed beside him: Aioko-san, bad girl, curled up and sleeping as she had been all those weeks ago.

And so, on the fourth day of wallowing in the pit and searching in vain for the key to the cellar door, on the fourth day – after watching *The River of No Return* and letting the images of Mitchum and Monroe fade into the sunset – he climbed off his bed, sat down at his piano and wrote a song. A song that was simpler than his earlier poems, a direct plea, an open demand for understanding: *Wakarimasu ka* he sang *Wakarimasu ka watashi wa iitai koto*: 'Do you understand? Do you understand what I'm trying to say?' He sang the song, polished the tune, trimmed the text and wallowed in the yearning that filled his chest and voice and fingers as he caressed the keys.

Then, on Saturday, at the end of his second week off work, he took a number six bus to town at six in the evening, crept into his office and mailed the lyrics to Aioko. It was his first contact with her since returning from Japan and he added no message, no explanatory note, no response to her handwritten letter handed down in the shadow of Mount Fuji. But the act of mailing brought some sense of sanity back to his fractured world, and before leaving he decided to sift through the pile in his in-tray. Not to clear the backlog, but to see if there was anything of interest he might latch on to as an antidote to his catatonic state. He sifted through the missives: grade sheets, endless memos and, somewhere near the bottom, a list of forthcoming cultural events. He perused it and shook his head. Nothing new, the usual mix of old hat Western culture imported and consumed by Hong Kong's middle classes to make them appear more cosmopolitan and compensate for their inability to create and crow about their own cultural products, or even the products of their motherland. All part of the colonial schizophrenia Britain had inflicted on the city along with much of Asia and Africa; the damaging remnants of British class snobbery and its hierarchical paraphernalia internalised lock, stock and whisky barrel by the Hong Kong elite; a substitute set of values to replace the roots, and identity, of a people brainwashed from the top down by Whitehall mandarins…

Stephen grabbed a pen and started scribbling his thoughts on a piece of paper. Then he gave up, threw his pen across the office, and watched it bounce against the window and land on a pile of Dutch film magazines beneath. Who cared a fuck about all that, anyway?

He propped his elbows on the desk and sunk his face in his hands. He was due to give a talk in September – 'Colonial Schizophrenia and Cultural Confusion in Hong Kong' – but sitting there in mid-June, on a Saturday evening, the only topic he could think about was 'Sexual Schizophrenia and Confusion in the British Ex-pat Male.' Not a suitable subject for opening the academic year.

He rubbed his eyes and noticed a white envelope at the bottom of the in-tray. He picked it up and tore it open. Inside was a gold embossed invitation to the Institute's Gala Ball – an annual dinner and dance for Hong Kong's political and social glitterati. Stephen stared at the sloping letters of his name, carefully entered in black ink. Why had he been invited? And why, if he was on the guest list, had his invitation arrived so late? Then he remembered: the Chairperson of the Board of Governors – an immensely rich heiress by the name of Mrs Lau-Hughes – had decreed that Deans of the Institute be invited on a rotating basis. This year it was the Media Faculty's turn, but its laid back Californian Dean had accepted a last minute invitation to a conference in Los Angeles and Stephen had been delegated the task in a call from the Dean's office to his voicemail. At the time, he had been glued to *The Seven Year Itch*, waiting for Marilyn's skirt to be blown up around her waist by an air vent, too catatonic to fabricate a prior engagement of his own.

He stared at the invitation a moment longer, then chuckled. Perhaps this was just what the naturopath ordered, the diversion he needed. Perhaps he would meet some wild sadistic *tai-tai* with pots of money and a taste for latex and leather, some liposuctioned millionatrix keen to tie him to her gold-plated bedstead and pay him to lick open her zip-up underwear while she beat him with her Gucci handbag. He laughed out loud. He might be in the pit, floundering in darkness and covered by a black cloud of lecher's self-loathing, but his imagination was still alive and anything that fuelled his imagination was worth its weight in abandoned principles. He would accept, attend and observe, and then expose the whole privileged shenanigan to the outside world.

He left the office in a lighter mood, rang Connor from reception and arranged to meet his friend for a drink in Lan Kwai Fong. He was back in the land of the living, but henceforth everything would be seen from the perspective of the pit and filtered through the fetid half-light of the lecher's cellar.

25

A week ago, on my first day back at work, I received a new response to the online advertisement. It was from a Chinese woman in Shenzhen, Hong Kong's twin boomtown just across the border in mainland China. It was the most overtly sexual response I had received. The English was good and indicated that the writer enjoyed 'tying men up and tormenting them!' This language alone would have made me respond, given the nature of my investigation, but an extra inducement came in the form of four colour photographs of a thirty-year old Chinese woman dressed, for the most part, in very little. She had a full bottom, trim waist and breasts that were larger than those of most Chinese women. In one picture she was dressed in black-trimmed red satin panties, kneeling on all fours and staring back at the camera in a suggestive manner. In another, taken and lit from below, she wore stockings, suspender belt, high heels and a biker's leather jacket. In a third she sat astride a sofa arm clad in long, stiletto-heeled PVC boots and a black spandex swimming costume. The fourth was more demure. In this, she had on a suit with white blouse and sensible shoes and was seated on a park bench with an older woman, who, according to the accompanying mail, was her mother. Perhaps this photograph was included to give an air of respectability to her solicitation, to imply that her other photographs, despite their raunchiness, had prior parental approval.

But what attracted me most was the face. I had been long enough in a Chinese environment to distinguish between different social types and was now able to deduce character and background from facial features that many Westerners still referred to as 'inscrutable.'

My e-correspondent's face was neither the whitened blank sheet of the Hong Kong middle-class female, nor the weather-beaten brown of the rural peasant girl. It was a face full of backstreet mischief and working class naughtiness – not a glamorous, pretty or elegant face, but a down-to-earth, sexy, factory-girl face made up in a tart-like manner for a night on the town. It was the Chinese equivalent of nanny Sally's face, round and rough and rosy, with a hint of Muriel's mean streak thrown in to darken the picture. An ordinary, common face that exuded sensuality; not in some artificial, made-up way, but in a straightforward projection of the inner self that was healthy, earthy, dark and dirty all at the same time. It was a face that made me excited, for reasons I could not fully understand – a face that promised fulfilment in a way that the more sophisticated, fashion-magazine faces never could.

I am by nature a trusting man, but it did occur to me that this Shenzhen siren might be a professional using the web to attract clients. And so, over the next couple of days, I plied her with questions. I asked about her background, her motivation for wishing to dominate men, her reasons for wanting to meet a partner on the *South China Post*'s Meeting Point. Then, along with this 'security-check,' I asked her what she would like to do to me, what she would wear and where we should meet. Her responses mixed dirty talk with indignation: 'If you think I'm a prostitute, may be better not come see respectable and strict Chinese lady,' she wrote in one mail. In another: 'What Hong Kong papers say about Shenzhen women is lie. We do not all drug visitors and steal wallets! Some of us are one hundred per cent genuine dirty-minded women.' How she reconciled her roles as respectable lady and dirty-minded woman was not clear, but her use of such expressions, inflated with English from advertising slogans, made me laugh and convinced me she was a genuine seeker of lust and pleasure, and not a paid sex worker.

Her interest in luring a man across the border did, however, have one economic string attached – a shopping list. In each mail, a new item was added for me to buy and bring to our, as yet, undecided mainland meeting point. Some requests, she assured me, were for use in our 'games' – five quality silk scarves, two pairs of black stockings, a garter belt and a pair of open crotch panties – but others were for her personal use and 'beautification.' These included Max Factor creams and lotions, a specific brand of nail varnish, hair curlers, a handbag and any 'sexy clothes' catalogues I could find. Uncovering a source of non-functional underwear proved difficult. After scouring Hong Kong's top boutiques, I ended up at Fetish Fashion, a black-painted den in poky premises off the Mid Levels escalator. There, with the aid of a dour-faced assistant, I managed to buy the undergarments, along with a catalogue of very constricting clothing. The creams and curlers I found at Watson's and the silk scarves at the Chinese Arts and Craft Centre. The handbag I crossed off my list, but I was still five thousand dollars down: Max Factor creams at four hundred a pot, open crotch panties at seven fifty and scarves, of Shanghai silk, at three hundred apiece. Perhaps not a prostitute in search of a client, but definitely a sugar in search of a daddy, I decided, after tracking down the nail varnish in a beauty salon on Hollywood Road. Finally she asked me to buy sex toys online. I told her I did not buy online, but would bring a switch my son had once bought for riding.

Agreeing on a meeting place proved harder than shopping. She favoured a hotel in Shenzhen. I preferred the Nanhai in Shekou. I had stayed there with Su-yin and its proximity to a ferry offered an easy escape route. Stories of mainland women 'ripping off' tourists from Hong Kong were persistent and confirmed by Connor. When, under the pretext of research, I asked him if he had ever been with a woman across the border, he replied, 'Not bloody likely, mate!' adding that, apart from the risk of Aids, there was no way of knowing whose side the police were on. They might be in cahoots with the woman and, unless you offered a bigger cut than her, you'd end up in jail for immoral activities. When I asked about Shekou, he backtracked and acknowledged that, according to a friend who 'played the world woman wise,' Shekou was a better bet than Shenzhen proper. This recommendation confirmed me in my resolve to use the Nanhai, and my preference prevailed in return for a promise of taxi fare reimbursement.

I was becoming more professional in my approach and, despite her refusal to say what she planned to do with me, I felt our meeting would break new ground. I printed out her pictures and placed them by my bed: nanny Sally and naughty Muriel, forbidden bodies from my youth, reincarnated and rolled into one Chinese Yu-lin – or, as she called herself in English, Ellen.

But before Ellen, there was the Institute's Gala Ball to attend.

On Friday afternoon, I went to my barber in Queen's Road East. Then, with fluff removed, I crossed to the Hopewell Centre and picked up my dinner jacket from the dry cleaners. I showered and shaved at seven and was dressed to kill by seven forty-five. At eight, I ordered a taxi and, at eight thirty, was in the foyer of the Institute, clutching my invitation. It was my first time at a Hong Kong Ball, but I felt at home. At age eleven, I had been sent to Pony Club Balls, in my teens promoted to Hunt Balls, and, at the age of twenty, been feted at the Coming Out Balls of debutantes. True, at twenty-one, I had foresworn dinner jackets and become a revolutionary, but Balls were in my blood, unforgotten like bicycle riding, and I was not about to fall off.

I nodded at a few Hong Kong Chinese society women. They peered at me. Was I someone they knew? Someone important? Or both? Most gave me the benefit of the doubt and smiled with the constrained smile of made-up lips and face-lifted skin. Their dresses varied from traditional, floor-length ball gowns, to more modern, higher-at-one-side-than-the-other creations 'run up' for them at astronomical cost by Vivienne Westwood, Donna Karen or, perhaps these days, Stella McCartney. And off the throats and ears and wrists and ankles of these nipped and tucked human clothes hangers dripped the jewels – the silverware, the diamonds galore – of in-kind investment; on display to out-dazzle the competition and jingle in a refined manner when the dancing began.

Chinese and Caucasian men, anonymous and identical in black, also gave me nods of recognition presuming, perhaps, that I was old so-and-so from the pre-Handover Civil Service, now retired and almost forgotten, but still with some residual credibility. I have that English type of face – high cheekbones, long nose, thin lips – that could belong to anyone between fifty and seventy, who might once have been someone, or still was; someone who no longer appeared on the social circuit, but probably still cut ice. In other words: worthy of a nod, to be on the safe side, but not worth wasting words or time on.

I crossed to the entrance of the Institute's largest auditorium – the Melody Theatre – and approached one of the ushers. She asked for my invitation and matched it to a table.

"Please enter theatre and follow corridor," she said. "Your table at back on right."

Following the corridor was not difficult. It was three feet across and walled in with silk. When I reached the stage, I realized the organizers had, at great expense, built this tunnel to block any glimpse of the ballroom area as it was approached. The effect on emerging was impressive. Dry ice wafted in the air and chandeliers hung from the gods alongside gel-covered theatre lights, creating a strong sense of theatrical anticipation.

I found my table and introduced myself to the occupants: a famous gay chef, who shook hands and then ignored me; a rotund Swiss entrepreneur with a claret-coloured bowtie who wanted to bring a circus to town; his Chinese wife, in a cheongsam with diamond clasp, who shook my hand and asked whether we had met before; and an austere Japanese lady in her forties with backcombed hair, black lipstick and a green chiffon dress.

She introduced herself as Chieko Fukuda, seemed unimpressed by my Japanese, but perked up, in English, when I said I worked at the Institute. Perhaps I knew a student who could make a video for her.

"What about?" I asked.

But just then her partner, an American banker, arrived. He had rabbit teeth and a baldhead that barely came up to her chin. She introduced him as: 'Harold, my friend for tonight.' Later, after several glasses of champagne, she leant across and whispered that he was 'stinking rich, excruciatingly boring and *totemo* impotent.' '*Yappari!*' was my raised eyebrow response – and, this time, my linguistic efforts were rewarded with a smile.

Suddenly, a Filipino band burst into life with Chuck Berry's 'Johnny B. Goode' rearranged to match the requirements of a *paso doble*. The middle-aged ladies, to whom I had nodded in the foyer, took to the floor, but instead of dinner-suited husbands as consorts, the matrons were partnered by dashing young men. These Adonises weaved and ducked, scissored and quick-quick-slowed without putting a foot wrong, and whilst the *tai-tais* gazed longingly into their adolescent eyes, the firm-buttocked young men stared into space disdaining all eye contact with their face-lifted females.

I leant across to Chieko, with whom I was now on good whispering terms, and asked the obvious question.

"Why are all the men so young?"

"Paid dance partners," was the hissed reply. "Husbands can't or won't dance, so wives pay professional boys to do business."

I watched with fascination. Not only was the dancing more like a ballroom dancing competition than a debutante's ball, but the dancers were also competing with each other for real. Competing for best dancer award, for best dancing partner award, for best-dressed award, for best-dressed dancing partner award. Competing to see who had spent the most money in the most noticeable way. There was none of the camaraderie and pride in self-sewn costumes that pervaded a dance palace in provincial England, none of the confident amateurishness of a hunt ball in Yorkshire. This was money competing with money, and the bought in partners made the charade not only ridiculous but tragic.

"Do they have affairs?" I whispered to Chieko.

"The boys and the grandmas?" She shook her head. "But with each other, yes."

"Each other? What do you mean?"

"Boys with boys," she hissed. "All queer as coots. Can't you see?"

I glanced back at the dance floor.

One or two of the men were exchanging winks, co-conspirators in pulling wool over the eyes of the gold-fleeced sheep they were herding around the floor.

"Once," whispered Chieko, putting her lips so close to my ear I could feel the warmth of her Japanese breath, "once, a *tai-tai* did persuade her partner to 'do it.' Then she fell in love with him. Would not let him out of her sight. Had him followed by a private eye. Found him with another woman, or man – I'm not sure which, but wrinkle-free – and, at next dance lesson, took out knife and stabbed him to death."

"No," I said. "I don't believe it."

"It's true," said Chieko, sitting upright in her chair and pushing away the dwarf banker's hand, which had wandered to her thigh. "It's true."

"Did she go to prison?"

"Of course not," laughed Chieko. "All covered up: cooking meal, practicing *paso doble* in kitchen, knife slips, an accident. Rich people do not commit crimes, they have accidents and somebody else clears up. Unless, of course, person in trouble has broken rules, then" – she mimed a knife slitting her throat – "then they are thrown to wolves."

"Rules?" I asked.

"Another time. Now, I must dance with the dwarf. I need something from him."

She turned to her right and held out a hand. The banker's face lit up and he allowed himself to be led on to the floor. Chieko towered above him and swept his body round and round like a rag doll. As they passed our table, she winked and I waved back.

After five minutes, they returned – the American out of breath and sweating, Chieko with every backcombed hair in place.

"Get what you want?" I whispered, after the banker had gone to the 'bathroom.'

"Not yet," she said. "He wants favour first."

"Most people do."

"But I do not know if I want to give," she sighed.

"Depends on the favour, I suppose."

"He wants me to dress him up in women's clothing and whip his *oshiri*."

She turned to gauge my reaction and burst out laughing.

"Just joking. He is American. Only English like to be whipped, I believe?"

I smiled and nodded.

"Get a taste for it at school."

"So I heard. Very strange – Englishmen."

"Yes," I echoed.

She stared at me, and then bent her head to my ear once more.

"Do you know how Japanese say 'to whip'?"

"No. No, I don't."

"*Muchiutsu*," she whispered with a hissing tone. "*Muchiutsu!* *Muchiutsu!*"

"Yes," I nodded, as her breath chastised my body. "Good word. Very good word."

She took my hand and, before I knew it, I was on the dance floor.

The band started a quickstep. I took her in my arms and closed my eyes. Were the dance steps there, waiting to be summoned back from all those years ago? Or would the bicycle buckle beneath my feet? I led with my left and followed with my right, and then took two smaller steps to my left and a half-turn to the right. She followed my lead and I repeated the mantra 'slow, slow, quick, quick, slow,' praying for forward motion, not on the spot rotation. My prayer was answered, the pedals turned, I did not fall.

We progressed round the floor, and, when I opened my eyes, she was staring at me. I smiled, but her lips did not respond. Only the pupils of her painted eyes appeared to twinkle, and maybe even that was just a reflection of the lights. We slid along in silence, brushing shoulders with the professionals.

"They don't like amateurs," hissed Chieko. "They say we spoil the show."

"We do a bit."

"Nonsense," scoffed Chieko. "We are real. They are plastic."

"You don't like *tai-tai*'s?" I asked.

"They don't like me," she replied with a wry smile. "I steal their husbands."

"Do you?" I said, as a tall Caucasian man with a carefully curled quiff and too-feminine features swirled his doting sheep across our path and glared at me. "What for?"

"For money. That's how I survive. Dinner and a discreet service or two."

I nodded and we danced on, our bodies in tune with each other and the music.

When the last chord had faded, a Chinese man with a familiar face approached us. He nodded at me, put his arm around Chieko's shoulder and led her off to another table, leaving me to my own devices. One of the husbands, I assumed, and then remembered why the face was so familiar. It belonged to the Assistant Chief Secretary

210

of the Hong Kong government. Her services must be discreet, and pricey, if she moved in his circles, and why, if she had the cream of high society to choose from, had she bothered with me?

I returned to my table and pondered this conundrum while the Swiss entrepreneur's Chinese wife told me about her horses in England. When Chieko returned, twenty minutes later, her hair was mussed on one side and her lipstick smeared – a discreet service no doubt.

"About that video you want making?" I whispered in a confidential tone.

"Yes," said Chieko, perking up. "You know someone?"

"Well," I replied, keeping my voice low. "I could do it for you."

She gazed at me for a moment and then, putting out a hand, patted my shoulder.

"How sweet of you. When we were dancing, I wondered if you would do."

"You mean, if I would do it for you," I corrected.

"Yes, if you could do it," she mused, withdrawing her hand.

"And?" I asked, after a moment's silence.

"I decided," she said, spotting her lips with a napkin, "that you were too old."

"Too old?" I exclaimed with a laugh. "Too old to make a video?"

"My video, yes," she replied, her face now cold and composed. "Too old. Sorry."

And with that she took her dwarf's hand, whispered in his ear and departed.

I felt disappointed and rejected. I was too old. Too old for what did not matter. I staggered outside, took a gulp of humid air and hailed a taxi.

I fell in and fell asleep.

When I awoke, we had reached Stubbs Road and the taxi driver was tapping my shoulder. I glanced at my watch. It was one o'clock. Not late for a young man, but late for an old man – very late for a tired old man like me.

I paid the fare and watched as the taxi disappeared.

Where was it headed? I wondered, mesmerized by the red taillights. Where was I headed, for that matter? Where the hell *was* I headed – apart from hell itself?

26

The next day, Saturday, I awoke at ten o'clock with no ill effects from my two glasses of champagne. I was a light drinker and abstinence had paid off. I glanced at the photos of Shenzhen Ellen by my bed. The short black hair, firm body and everyday face still seemed inviting and exciting, even to a man who had not yet drunk his early morning tea.

I dialled her number. She had asked me to ring on the morning of my visit – 'As soon as you wake!' – to confirm everything was in order.

After three bleeps, a female voice answered. It was deep and loud.

"Hello? Ellen here. Good morning."

"Good morning, Ellen. It's Stephen."

"I know. That is why I speak English."

"Right."

"Still coming, yes?"

Her voice was insistent.

"Of course," I replied. "But you asked me to ring…"

"Yes. Have you shaved yet?"

"No," I replied, feeling the stubble on my chin.

"Well, do not!" she ordered, and then softened her tone and dropped the volume. "I like my men with stubble. Rough and ready!"

"But…" I protested.

"Stephen!" she barked down the line.

"Yes?"

"Do as I say!"

"Of course."

She laughed and I compared the laugh with the photo by my bed. It seemed to fit.

"And you have the things I ask for?" she continued.

"Most of them."

"Punishment for missing items," she said. "You understand?"

I glanced at the photo of her in long PVC boots and nodded.

"I understand."

"Good. Ring me from hotel – when you arrive. Goodbye."

Before I could reply, she had turned off her phone. I raised my eyebrows, shook my head and went to shower.

After breakfast, I packed a case with a change of clothing and the items I had bought for Ellen: catalogues, five silk scarves, two sets of black stockings, a PVC garter belt, open crotch panties, nail varnish, two tubs of Max Factor skin cream and a set of hair curlers. I checked my wallet for cash and credit cards, reset my answer machine and was about to leave the flat when I remembered my son's riding switch. I had promised to bring it and punishment for failing to do so would be less interesting without it.

I found it in a cupboard. It was thin and springy, three feet in length and had a leather thong at one end and a wrist loop at the other. It was also brand new. The only way to fit it in to my case was to bend the body in half and jam it inside the concave hollow of the case's lid. It lay there like a spring-loaded trap or tranquillised snake, and I prayed that my luggage would not be opened by customs.

I took a taxi to the Macau Ferry terminal and bought a ticket for Shekou. The journey took forty-five minutes. Under the Lantau suspension bridge, past the Gold Coast – a cluster of high rises and condominiums crowded on to a narrow strip of land between sea and mountains – round a headland at the north western tip of the New Territories and into the mudflat-flecked inlet that separated the mainland from Hong Kong. As the boat approached its landing stage, I could see the Nanhai Hotel off to the right, its concrete and glass curves standing out from an ill-kempt customs house in the foreground. I was glad I had picked it. I had only stayed there twice, but it offered a friendly and familiar face, as I prepared to enter the People's Republic of China for real.

There was no luggage check, and I passed through passport control without delay. In the arrivals hall, a cluster of hands pointed at waiting cars and tried to grab my bag. I ignored them, marched outside, surveyed the sun-drenched square full of rusting bicycles and outdated vehicles and set off to walk the hundred or so yards to the hotel.

I checked in and was told, with much pride, that I had been upgraded to a business suite. This entitled me to use of the eighth floor cocktail bar, breakfast in the eighth floor restaurant and a complementary drink in any of the hotel's bars before eight in the evening. Unfortunately, due to renovations, the suite itself was not on the eighth floor. So, after a guided tour of the penthouse facilities and a ceremonial signing in to the Executive Club, I was herded back down to the second floor and into my 'recently redecorated' business suite – opposite the laundry room. It was a tunnel-like affair with an entrance hall, a windowless lounge-cum-kitchen, a basic bathroom and a medium-sized bedroom with balcony and view over hotel garden, mudflats and Hong Kong hills.

I tipped my guide, waited for her to leave and inspected the bedroom. It had a pea-green carpet, turquoise curtains, luminous white walls, a pine-framed double bed with matching tables and a wardrobe in imitation teak. Scandinavian cool meets Chinese tradition and creates the worst of both worlds. But it would have to do. I opened the left-hand door of the wardrobe and felt the hinges give. I closed it and opened the right hand one. On the floor, beside a shoe rack, I found a small safe with a digital lock. I deposited my passport and wallet and tapped in my birth date as code. I then unpacked my clothes and slipped them into a drawer. Ellen's items, individually wrapped, I arranged on a table beside the television and covered with a towel. I wanted them to be a surprise.

I surveyed my handiwork, picked up the phone and dialled her number.

"Hello?"

Again the deep voice, the immediate use of English.

"It's Stephen," I said.

"I know."

"I've arrived," I added, somehow expecting congratulations.

There was silence at the other end.

"I'm at the Nanhai. Room 215."

"Good," she said. Her voice sounded distracted, her mind elsewhere. I heard someone call out in the background, perhaps the mother. "I'll be there in thirty minutes."

Again the phone cut off before I could say goodbye.

I ordered scrambled eggs and toast from room service. It arrived with a glass of water and a wilting flower. I ate at a small table in the windowless living room. I did not want breadcrumbs on the pristine sheets and day-glo carpet in the bedroom. When I had finished, I called room service again and asked them to fetch the tray. Then I went to the bathroom, spruced myself up, and lay down on the bed to wait. I was nervous.

Forty minutes later, the phone went. It was Ellen at the reception desk.

"Tell this idiot to let me up," she shouted down the phone.

"What's happened?" I asked.

"Nothing. They won't let me up, that's all. New security rules!"

She handed the phone to a receptionist and I explained that the guest in question was expected and should be allowed to proceed to my room. Ellen came back on the line.

"Listen!" she said, lowering her voice to a whisper. "I'll be up in three minutes. I want you to leave the door unlocked. Take one of the silk scarves, blindfold yourself so that you really can't see, sit on a chair and wait."

"But..." I began.

"Understood?" she hissed. "No looking. This is very important."

"all right," I said, after a moment's hesitation. "I'll do as you ask."

"Good."

The line went dead.

I sat staring at the receiver in my hand. Was I going mad? Letting a strange woman, in a strange land, into my room and promising to blindfold myself beforehand – was that the act of a sane man? She could creep in, grab my belongings and be halfway to Beijing before I knew it. Then I smiled, shook my head and went over to unlock the door. There was nothing to steal except the presents. My valuables were in the safe and she was welcome to a clean change of male underwear. Worth the risk, I thought, as I opened one end of a package and pulled out a blue-patterned square of pure silk. It had set me back three hundred dollars and felt cool and smooth as I tied it round my head. Even if her photographic image was familiar, the idea of not seeing the person who was about to arrive appealed to me. I wanted the blindfold to be effective, I did not want to cheat and, by the time I had finished adjusting the material over my eyes, I could see nothing.

I felt my way back to the bed and propped up all four pillows against the bed head. I wondered if I should remove any clothes, but decided not to. There had been no instruction. I lowered myself on to the bedcover and then remembered she had asked me to sit in a chair. I climbed off the bed and felt my way to a small armchair by the window. I sat down and waited. I could not see, only sense the dense blue light that filtered through the scarf.

After a short wait, I heard the door close and someone move softly into the room.

"Where are my presents?" the deep voice from the phone said.

"By the television," I replied.

"Can you see me?" she asked.

"No," I said. "Though I can imagine you."

"From the photos?"

"Yes."

She chuckled and went silent.

I heard her unwrapping the gifts one by one. She was pleased with the garter belt, the panties and the scarves, but disappointed there was no handbag.

"I'm sorry," I said.

"You will be," she retorted.

I heard her remove the clothes she had arrived in and go to the bathroom to shower. Two minutes later I heard her return and unzip a case.

Without vision, hearing is more acute, more intelligent, and feeds the imagination in a way the eyes can never do. I heard stockings slip on, the clip of suspenders on the new garter belt. I heard the click of studs – pop, pop, pop – on a bra, or some other unimagined item. Then, grinch–grunch as two more zips were closed, one after the other.

"Know what that is?" she asked.

"Leather boots," I guessed.

"Correct," she replied. "Sure you can't see?"

"Positive."

"Good."

I felt her approach and stand close. I could smell her scent: Calvin Klein or Chanel, one of the two.

"I shall touch you," she said. "But you must not touch me. Understand?"

I nodded and my body tingled in anticipation.

Her hands unbuttoned my shirt and yanked up the vest beneath, exposing my chest and nipples. I tensed, both nervous and excited. Her hands cupped my unshaven chin and pulled it up, so that my neck was bent back at right angles.

"Good. You obeyed my order."

Her hands moved down my throat and across my chest.

"Mmm! I like men with hair."

Then, without warning, she squeezed my left nipple and slapped my right cheek.

"That's one for the handbag!" she said. "More later."

Not a strong blow, but it shocked me. A woman had never hit me on the face – at least not in my adult life. I felt my cheek redden. She laughed, squeezed my right nipple and slapped my left cheek, harder this time. I shuddered despite myself. I wanted to take off the blindfold and reach out. Seek forgiveness, reconciliation.

She read my mind.

"No touching!" she barked. "And no looking! Stand up!"

I stood up and felt, for the first time since starting my investigation, fully at the mercy of a mistress – like a child in the hands of his nursemaid. No prepared script, no certainty of who was touching me, just an agreement she would command and I obey.

She pulled off my shirt and vest and again squeezed my nipples. I moaned.

"You like that?" she asked.

I nodded.

She kept hold of the nipples between thumb and forefinger and gently rolled the bobbles of flesh back and forth, back and forth, back and forth. They became hard and tender, disseminating arousal around my body. I sighed and opened my mouth to be kissed. She chuckled her low, malicious chuckle, and then, without warning, dug a fingernail into the right nipple, grunting with satisfaction as she did so.

I yelped.

"And you don't like that!"

I bit my lip and tried to sit down, but she held me up by the chin and dug a nail in to the left nipple.

I yelped again.

"Should have bought me the handbag, eh?"

"Sorry, I'm very sorry," I whispered, putting my hands up to cover my breasts.

"OK. We forget it now."

She stroked my cheek for a while and then continued to undress me.

She unbuckled my belt and lowered my jeans, making me step out of them like a sleepy child. I felt a mixture of pride and shame at the bulge between my legs. She passed a hand over my crotch, grabbed the back of my underpants and yanked them down to my knees. I felt my penis grow, my face go deeper red. I wanted her to touch me there, but I also wanted to touch her, to share my vulnerability, to show some sign of affection.

She moved away, leaving me alone, in silence, with my pants around my ankles. I heard her open a bottle of wine and pour herself a glass. Then, after a minute or two, she returned and stood in front of me. I imagined her eyes travelling up and down my body.

"Where's the whip?" she asked, after a minute's silent inspection.

I had forgotten the black switch, the coiled snake in my case. Given the pain already inflicted, I regretted bringing it. Perhaps I should lie. Say it had been confiscated by customs. No rules of disengagement had been set, and I could not be sure she would use it in moderation. I hesitated, uncertain what to do, and then heard the sound of another zip, followed by the swish of a switch being passed through the air at speed.

"Trying to hide it?

"No," I said.

"Mm! Good one. Where'd you get it?"

"A sports shop. It's for riding."

"Can I keep it?" I heard it swish through the air again close to my ear. "Leather whip instead of leather handbag?"

"Maybe."

She chuckled and I heard her hit the bed as hard as she could, three times in a row. I winced with each blow.

"Go and shower," she ordered. "You may remove the blindfold in the bathroom, but put it back on when you come out."

I relaxed. Her singsong Mandarin accent soothed me.

I shuffled towards the bathroom. When I bumped into the bed, she smacked my behind, but then took my elbow and guided me, like a blind man, to the bathroom door. Once inside, I removed the blindfold and inspected my nipples for damage. No blood drawn. I showered, wrapped a towel round my waist and replaced the blindfold. I had no desire to cheat. I had a photographic image of the woman beyond the door, of the woman with my body at her command, and the element of surprise, the literal loss of foresight, excited rather than frightened me. I was liberated from the tyranny of seeing with room to expand and heighten the sensitivity of my other senses. Like a radio play, but with added elements of touch and smell; unlike a film, where all is seen and nothing imagined. Suspended between fantasy and fact, visualizing mentally what occurs in reality.

When I emerged from the bathroom, she was waiting outside the door. She lifted the towel and cursorily sniffed my behind. Then, like a nanny who has just changed her charge's nappies, she grunted with approval and ripped the towel away. She grasped my right wrist, pulled me to the bed and pushed me face downwards on to the covers. She forced my hands behind my lower back and tied them together with a silk scarf.

"Can you get free?"

I tried, but could not. I shook my head.

"Good."

She splayed my legs and, with two further scarves, tied each ankle to the pine frame at the foot of the bed.

Then, with me trussed and exposed, she paused.

I heard her take a sip of wine and pick up the phone. She dialled a number and held a short conversation in Mandarin. Anxiety returned. Was she calling her accomplice? A brute of a man, who would force me to reveal the safe's code and then make off with the loot, or, worse still, send her to an ATM whilst he tortured out my pin codes and helped himself, and her, to all my hard-earned ex-pat cash? I was just another sucker, letting sexual predilections cancel common sense. I strained at my bonds but they held. Ellen sensed my discomfort. She sat down on the bed and stroked my head.

"It's all right, little man," she cooed. "Just calling my mother. She looks after dogs today. Checking they've had their walk. Woof, woof."

She stood up. I let my body go limp.

Imagination is one thing, too much imagination quite another. I was letting my mind run wild with speculation, putting my body on red alert for no good reason. She did not sound like a criminal – a little crazy, maybe, but not criminal.

I smiled and closed my eyes behind the blindfold.

I felt her fingers walk down my spine and stop at the top of my splayed crease. I shivered in anticipation. Then, without warning, and with only the briefest of aural indicators, the switch hissed through the air and cut into my left buttock. I yelped like a dog and buried my head in the bedcover.

"Not bad," she cooed. "Not like whip I use before. But not bad!"

Hiss! She stung me again on the right buttock and I bit the covers, but this time the fingers of her free hand caressed the wound, and, when the pain was soothed, slipped down between my legs and played with my balls, cupping and squeezing them. I moaned and tried to close my legs, but the scarves held firm.

Again the switch hit my behind, followed this time by a rubber-gloved finger circling my anus. I felt warm breath close to my ear.

"You won't know whether I'm going to punish or pleasure you," she whispered, as an exploratory finger pushed into my anus. "Does that excite you?"

I nodded, and then wished I had not.

Two fingers were thrust up hard inside me, as far as they could go, touching my prostate and almost making me come. I gasped and pushed my groin into the bed, but the rubber fingers remained inside, wiggling back and forth, whilst the other hand, soft-skinned and gentle, caressed my balls and stroked the inside of my thigh.

"Pleasure – and pain!" she repeated. "Pleasure – and pain!"

She continued her alternate games for a while and then withdrew her fingers, squeezed my balls and whipped me once more, as hard as she could, across both buttocks.

I winced and lay still.

The rubber glove was unpeeled and thrown into a metal waste bin. Wine or water was poured and a number was dialled.

"I call room service for tea," she said. "Anything you want?"

I shook my head, and then imagined the waiter coming in and seeing me tied up.

"Hadn't we better wait?" I said.

She laughed.

"Embarrassed?"

I nodded.

"Good."

I struggled to slip my bonds, but to no avail.

"Ellen, please," I said, with authority and volume this time. "I don't think…"

But before I could finish the sentence, she had yanked my neck round to the left, forced open my mouth and jammed a pair of damp nylon panties inside. They smelt and tasted of sweat and female excitement.

"My dirty laundry," she laughed. "Please enjoy."

I tried to spit them out, but could not.

I imagined the woman from the photos staring down at me with a grin, or even a sneer, on her face: standing there in her thigh-high boots, black stockings and garter belt; in her see-through panties and bra with studs that made popping sounds when closed. And, despite myself, despite the ignominy of the situation, I again felt aroused. Above all by the face, the face I had not seen in the flesh, but fixed in my mind from the photos. The fresh but sensual working class face that had sat by my bed for a week, now taking pleasure in controlling its Western victim and forcing him to submit. The Chinese Sally-and-Muriel face – on top of a firm, rounded but not-too-fat body – flushed and aroused by my discomfort. I shook my head and smiled. I was perverted beyond redemption.

The doorbell rang and I returned with a shock to reality.

"Please, don't let him in!" I spluttered into the panties. "Please!"

But my words came out as a gurgle and she ignored them.

I heard her put on a bathrobe, walk to the door and open it. She said something in Mandarin and then repeated the sentence in English, for my benefit.

"In the bedroom, please. By the bed!"

"*Tse tse!*" a male voice replied.

I froze and tried to bury my head under a pillow. At least that way my face would not be seen. But it was too late. I heard the tea tray land on the table beside my bed, followed by a sentence in Mandarin from Ellen and, again, the English translation. "Please, pour two cups. Thank you."

I felt her sit on the bed beside me and stroke my cheek.

"Do you take sugar?" she asked.

I shook my head. My face was burning, crimson with embarrassment, but there was nothing I could do.

I felt her hand move down my back, caress my bottom, push between my legs and squeeze my balls. I heard the tea being poured into cups.

Was he watching? Was he embarrassed too?

After what seemed an age, I heard him say something in Mandarin, followed by the chink of coins as she tipped him and gave some final instruction.

Then he was gone, closing the door behind him.

"Did you enjoy that?"

I shook my head.

"Neither did he," she laughed. "His hand shook so much, he almost dropped the pot."

I heard her take a sip of tea and return the cup to its saucer.

She stood up, untied my feet and rolled me on to my back. I debated jumping up and calling a halt to the proceedings, but my hands were bound and I could not see or speak. I let her refasten the ankles, untie my hands and retie them behind my head. She then took the cord of her bathrobe and bound the tied wrists to my neck so that I was almost throttled. She removed the panties from my mouth and, before I could speak, forced two fingers between my lips and took hold of my tongue. Her fingers tasted of wine and I sucked on them like a baby. Her other hand played with my nipples, alternately caressing and pinching them, and then slid across my stomach, took hold of my penis and squeezed the semi-erect flesh with a pumping motion, inflating it like a balloon.

The fingers in my mouth slipped in and out, the hand below slid up and down.

I was about to come when the doorbell rang again. I tensed and shrunk. I was even more exposed than before.

"Please," I begged. "Please cover me with a towel."

But she ignored my request and went to the door. There was a short exchange with, judging by the voice, the same bellboy, but this time he did not come in. I gave a sigh of relief and my penis grew again in anticipation.

Ellen returned to the bedside and put something down on the tea tray. He must have forgotten the sugar or the milk – or maybe she preferred lemon.

"You like iced tea?"

I nodded and, as I did so, she grabbed my cock in one hand and with the other smothered my balls in ice cubes. I screamed in shock. She jammed one up my anus and I screamed again.

"Ice, but no tea," she said, grinding the cubes into my groin and up the shaft of my penis. "Like it?"

I shook my head. It was too cold. She persisted until tears came to my eyes, and then stopped.

She cupped my head and bound hands in her arm, lifted me to a sitting position and made me drink some wine – cheap, Chinese Red Bull wine. Was it poisoned? Drugged? I sipped a little and then closed my mouth. Perhaps the room service attendant was in on the game, perhaps I was to be kidnapped and held to ransom. But who would pay up? Tom? Irene? Connor? The Institute? No. The Institute would terminate my contract and have me expelled from Hong Kong. Messing with madams on the mainland was not only not an approved activity, but, in the words of my contract, an activity 'likely to bring the Institute into disrepute.' I would be left to the mercy of Ellen and her accomplices – a man beyond the pale, who had dug his own grave and must lie in it.

I was lowered back on to the bed and left to wait in silence.

Then I felt two feet on either side of my head. I smelt the leather of boots but had no hand or eye to help me understand what she was doing.

Something hovered above my face, also smelling of leather.

"Want to lick?" she called from far above.

I put out my tongue and touched leather, but it was not the leather of boots. I withdrew my tongue in confusion. What was she doing?

"Want to lick my leather panties?"

I nodded but, when I strained my tongue to touch her, I felt the weight of her behind push my head back on to the bed and her hand smack my erect penis.

"Changed my mind!" she barked. "Not licking. Smelling."

She lifted her behind, until it hovered just above my nose. I sniffed and smelt leather, this time mixed with Ellen's excitement.

"Smells good!" I said.

"That's because sitting on a man makes me wet!"

Again my tongue came out, again she smacked my penis; but this time it grew.

"Mm!" she groaned. "I'm getting wetter."

I felt her climb off my face and reposition herself by my side – though what part of her body was where, I could not tell. She unbound the cord fastening my wrists to my neck and untied the scarves around my ankles. Then, as one of her hands played with my penis, the other guided my right forefinger to her body. Without warning, it was enclosed in the wetness of a mouth, lips folding around its tip. It touched a cheek, a jaw and a tiny, slippery tongue that swelled. But it found no teeth. This was not a mouth.

"Play with me," she ordered, a new thickness in her voice. "Now!"

I did as she commanded and, after a minute or two, she came with the loudest screams and yells I had ever heard. They must have been audible throughout the hotel, but, when I tried to calm her down, she pushed me away and screamed louder.

224

I lay and listened to her caterwauling until it ceased.

Then she laughed and rolled over to the far side of the bed.

"Want to take your blindfold off?"

"Can I?"

"Sure."

Her voice was still deep and loud, but now more relaxed and normal in tone. Perhaps the orgasm, the intensity of the orgasm, had mollified her dominant side and she was ready to treat me as an equal – at least for a while.

I put my hands behind my head to untie the knot. It was tied tightly and it took me a minute to undo. But eventually the blue silk fell from my eyes. I blinked and waited for my retinas to adjust to the bright sunlight streaming in through the balcony door.

Then, slowly, my partner of the last hour came into focus.

27

It was all I could do not to scream.

Instead of the fresh complexion and firm rounded figure from the photographs, I found myself staring at an obese mountain of flesh. Enormous thighs, rolls of fat around the waist, large hanging breasts and an overfed face covered in blotches that might once, with a great stretch of the imagination, have been the face in the photographs.

It was so far removed from my imagined image, from the photographic images, that the shock to my system verged on the traumatic. But instead of exclaiming my disgust out loud, instead of expelling the foundation-shaking shock in a shriek, I took a deep breath and counted to ten. I was, for all my faults and perversities, a kind-hearted man and would never knowingly hurt another person's feelings. Some men might have bodily thrown her out, or called room service and had her removed – along with the tea tray. Others would have evacuated the hotel themselves, at speed, tails between their legs.

I allowed my eyes to get used to her, to accept the mounds of flesh as part of another human being. I instructed my mind to erase the imagined image, based on real but no longer true-to-life photographs. The person I had been with up to a few moments ago flickered before my eyes, a retinal detainee in the process of disintegration, and disappeared.

"Like the clothes?" she said, either not aware of the discrepancy between her present self and the photos, or ignoring it.

I nodded as my eyes roamed wildly across the cheap, calf-length, winter walking-boots, the overstretched, already laddered stockings, the delicate garter belt that had been squeezed round an enormous waist and was now hidden, for the most part, in folds of fat.

"Very sexy," I said.

"So are you," she replied with a smile. "Very good fingers."

"Thank you."

"Will you do it again?" she asked, no longer ordering, but still, I sensed, regarding me as her plaything.

Perhaps she felt it was she who was doing the favour, not vice versa. Despite her weight, she looked no more than thirty. I was a balding man in the second half of middle age.

"Maybe," I said, turning to the bedside table for a glass of water. The taste of her panties was in my mouth, but no longer aroused me.

I propped myself up on a pillow, smiled at her and sipped the water. Why on earth had I decided to stay the night? And suggest, in an early mail, she stay over with me? I should have said I had to get back the same evening, insist that our liaison begin and end in the afternoon. Perhaps I still could: plead urgent business, emergency at home. But she would smell a rat, know why I was leaving, curse her weight and take offence.

And so I stayed, and she stayed, and over the next few hours I gave her three more orgasms – all as loud as the first one, all with my tongue – but refused her plea to have intercourse. During the oral interaction I tried to imagine Ellen from the photos, but it did not work. The thick thighs around my ears and the fleshiness of the caterwauling features above were too powerful. The fresh-faced, working class, socialist girl from China – svelte, seductive and seeking adventure – had been erased and replaced by an Americanised monster fed on McDonald's and KFC and hungry for Western goods and ways. She said the photographs were from a year or two back, and maybe that was true. China had changed so much over the past few years, why not Ellen with it.

In the evening she took me to a restaurant on the far side of Shekou, owned by a friend. She said we could walk, but it took an hour, along dusty, traffic-filled, half-built streets full of migrant workers in search of wealth. By the time we arrived, I was covered in sweat and feeling like a fool. Ellen insisted on a private dining room, perhaps in the hope of inducing me to order more. She wanted to show off to her friend, provide her friend with a little extra income or perhaps even get a cut of the evening's take herself. But I dug my heels in and ordered one fish dish and some rice. The half-dozen attendants hovering round our table in the small and claustrophobic 'executive' room were disappointed and drifted away one by one, until only a child of ten remained to pour the tea. And, despite the meagreness of the meal, I still did not have enough cash with me to settle up. Ellen had to pay the bill and no doubt answer for my meanness later.

We returned to the Nanhai in a taxi with protective metal grills around the driver's seat. Trust in China, along with other socialist values, was disappearing fast. Ellen wanted to sing karaoke in the basement – an extra 1000 dollars on the bill – or crawl the bars in Shekou's 'red light' district. I insisted on bed.

Once under the sheets, she again begged me to put my penis inside her. When I refused, she opened her considerable legs and settled for a fourth oral orgasm. She seemed to be permanently wet, almost insatiable and always noisy.

After her final climax of the day, she sat on the balcony naked, sipping wine in the night air. I told her to come in and put a dressing gown on. She laughed – we were paying the bill, so could do as we wished. Capitalist values, I suppose. After ten minutes of parading her nudity to the night, and a vocal local child in the garden below, she returned to bed and masturbated me with her hand. Then she took my greying head, laid it on her bosom and went to sleep. She snored, and dreamt no doubt of consumption still to come. I lay awake, feeling my life slip away. Part of me wanted to hold on to it, but did not know how. Part of me no longer cared.

The next morning, we had breakfast in the eighth floor restaurant. Ellen ate enough bacon, eggs, hash browns and beans to last a Hunan peasant a lifetime. I sipped Chinese red tea and played with a croissant. She suggested meeting again and said that, next time, I should book into her friend's new hotel in Shenzhen. She could get discounts on the karaoke, coffee shop and mini-golf, and all the rooms had cable. I said I would think about it. She expressed an interest in becoming my regular mainland mistress, and hoped I would continue to bring her gifts. I said I would think about that, too.

I packed and asked her to go down and wait in the lobby. I then removed my wallet from the safe in privacy. I paid the bill, avoiding eye contact with the hotel staff, who must have heard the bellboy's tale a hundred times by now, and let Ellen walk me to the ferry terminal. We stood on the pavement outside the arrivals hall, shook hands and then kissed each other on the cheek. She was wearing a baggy T-shirt and long shorts, a person as far removed from my original image, my original fantasy, as anyone could be. But I had got to know her – another human being amongst the billions – and, I hoped, treated her well. Like all the women in my life, she had taken on a real form and refused to stay the sneering, distant, mocking will o' the wisp that my imagination fed and demanded I follow and find.

I walked off into the terminal and turned once more to wave goodbye.

"Don't forget the handbag next time!" she called.

I nodded and watched as she raised her hand and trotted off across the crowded square towards a dilapidated bus on the far side, a bus that would take her back to mother and dogs. I think she still thought she was beautiful, or at least sexy and attractive to men, and perhaps this opinion of herself was more important than my opinion of her. I was on the way out, she was on the way in – the West and China changing places. We had overindulged ourselves for decades, now it was their turn.

28

For a week after his return to Hong Kong, Stephen felt better. His expansion of the investigation into more dangerous territory gave him a sense of pride, and he congratulated himself on surviving the adventure unscathed. His readiness to take risks was, he decided, a sign of progress and not, as he had felt earlier, a sign of insanity. He mailed Ellen to thank her for the weekend, politely declined her services as a mainland mistress and wished her well. She replied with no hard feelings, and said she had enjoyed herself and hoped he would find what he was looking for.

It was the last week of term and he worked hard: Monday and Tuesday, year-end grading meetings; Wednesday and Thursday, graduation shows; Friday and Saturday, degree and diploma ceremonies with their endless congratulations, good-luck-for-the-future conversations and long goodbyes. He worked hard, bathed in the glow of his students' gratitude and forgot Aioko – or, at least, removed her from the forefront of his mind. He had checked his Hotmail account on Monday, ten days after sending the song, found no message and renewed his vow to let the fickle letterbox die a natural death.

On Sunday, he walked in Sai Kung Country Park with his erstwhile partner, Su-yin. She was back in Hong Kong for a few days, on leave from her current posting in Beijing. She had found a new *amour* – a sixty-year-old German banker working for the Dresdner in China – and was returning to Germany with him at the end of July. She was aglow with the warmth of the loved and loving, and made Stephen promise to fly over for the wedding in October. He said he would.

In the evening he phoned his son. Tom and Cheryl were off to the US and Canada for a working holiday. They planned to hire a Winnebago in LA and tour around, checking out possible locations for Tom's Fodder on the West Coast. They might be incommunicado for a while, Tom said, as they had scheduled a 'total switch off and chill out' for at least part of the trip – probably in Mount Washington National Park. Stephen felt a pang of nostalgia for the time when Tom still enjoyed his father's company; for summers spent in Paris or Brussels or Rome, exploring, chatting, sleeping – deconstructing Europe by train and boat and car. Now it was more than six years since they had shared a holiday, six years since he had felt the pride and contentment of having a son by his side, of watching a son sleep in the silence of the night, as he had watched that first night of Tom's life. But Stephen was not a possessive man – at least, not with regard to his son – and after a brief bout of melancholia, he put on a CD of Mozart's oboe concerto and wrote a letter to his sister.

Irene preferred old-fashioned post to phone calls or email and, despite the illegibility of his handwriting, liked Stephen to use a pen rather than a keyboard. So, as Mozart played, he scrawled down indecipherable words about work and the weather, about his conversation with Tom and the news of Su-yin's wedding in the autumn. He said he would remain in Hong Kong over the summer. He had writing to do and did not want the twin distractions of jetlag and cultural re-orientation to reduce the time available. He knew Irene worried about him losing touch with friends 'back home,' so he promised to return at Christmas and make a tour of 'all and sundry,' or perhaps invite his circle of friends and relations to spend Christmas in Edinburgh. In a PS, he asked Irene to check the family photo albums for pictures of Sally and him when he was little. He was writing an autobiographical piece, he explained, and needed the pictures for research purposes. If she did not want to send the originals, she could have them scanned on to a disk at a photo shop. He read the letter through, crossed a few 't's and dotted a few 'i's to increase legibility, affixed a stamp and walked down to the post box on Stubbs Road.

He heard the comforting plop as his letter hit the bottom of the formerly Royal Mail red, now lurid green, post box and wished that email had never been invented. Perhaps he and Aioko would not have imploded with pen and paper – then again, perhaps they would never have met. He stared up at the scrub-covered hills behind his flat and yawned with something approaching contentment. Despite the strangeness of the previous weekend, it had been a normal week: work, family and friends – the stuff of real life. It gave him a momentary sense of release, of having left the cellar's darkness and rediscovered daylight within the open prison walls of normal living.

But it was a passing shaft of sunlight, an illusory sense of well-being. For what he could not know, as he turned and walked up the hill towards his home on that warm Sunday evening in late June, was that this had been the last normal week of his life.

A six-week summer vacation began on the Monday and Stephen decided to spend a few days in the office sorting through creative projects pushed to one side by the drip-drip distraction of an academic year. Students and most staff were gone, and peace had descended on the Institute. During his first term of service in Hong Kong, he had jumped on a plane to Europe the minute vacation began. This year, he planned to stay put and immerse himself in his own company and that of best friend Connor, who was staying over to choreograph a dance project. They would walk, talk and eat, and, in between, Stephen would write and pursue the investigation as and when the mood took him.

On arrival at his office, he sat down and prepared to make a 'summer timetable.' But he had barely typed out a heading, 'Creative Schedule July/August,' when the phone rang. It was Connor. He was in a state and needed to meet Stephen for a cup of coffee.

They settled on a new Starbucks in the Wanchai Lawcourts Tower on Gloucester Road, and Connor was already seated at a corner table in a high-backed armchair when Stephen arrived. They ordered cappuccinos and Connor came straight to the point. His eighty-year-old mother had died from a heart attack, leaving his bed-ridden father alone. Stephen reached across and held Connor's arm. Was there anything he could do? Connor shook his head. He had not asked Stephen over for help, though he was grateful for the offer. There was another bit of sad news. Because of his mother's death, he was leaving the Institute and returning to Australia to fill a vacancy at Edith Cowan University in Perth, where his father lived. He had been headhunted a few weeks earlier and turned the post down, but would now have to take it. Less pay, less power and fewer resources, but he had no choice. "What about notice?" Stephen asked, already uneasy at the thought of his close friend and confidante upping sticks. "No worries there," Connor said. The Institute's Principal, whom he had been to see earlier that morning, had waved the three-month rule and released him with immediate effect. When would he leave? This afternoon. Stephen's face fell, and this time it was Connor who put an arm around his friend. "Real shame, mate," he said. He'd looked forward to some 'good beanos' over the summer, but life was a bastard and no one knew 'how cookies are going to crumble.' Stephen nodded, took a deep breath and again offered condolences. Connor glanced at his watch. He must go. He had to pack, get a removals firm sorted and clear his utility and tax bills.

They stood, embraced and then Connor was gone.

Stephen returned to his office.

He could no longer generate enthusiasm for his Creative Schedule. Connor had not sat at its centre, but formed an important element. Without his occasional company, evenings – and weekends, in particular – would be harder to fill. There would be no one for background support, no one at the end of a telephone, no one he could trust to be available, if darkness descended. The summer would be less sunny, less serene, and after the summer, what then? What about next year? Stephen looked forward to seeing Connor at the start of each autumn semester, exchanging news, moaning about the year ahead. Connor was a stabilizing factor in his life, a number to ring for common sense – a colleague down the corridor who talked real life, not just curriculum and overwork.

'Goodbye Connor,' he wrote on his computer screen, and then enlarged it to point size seventy-two, until it burst off the page in meaningless bytes of black and white.

He sat for a while trying to postpone what he knew he would do, what he could not avoid doing. In the end, he could wait no longer.

He turned his gaze from the green swell of Victoria Harbour and clicked the blue Internet icon. He waited for the Institute's home page to settle and punched up www.hotmail.com. He hesitated, and then typed in the email address that he had reserved for Aioko followed by the password, '*ninniku*.'

He waited, in trepidation, as the screen went white and then re-formed into the familiar blue format of a Hotmail account opening page – New Messages: 0.

He shook his head and was about to sign out when a thought occurred to him. Suppose she was waiting for another sign from him – a sign of forgiveness, an offer of reconciliation? Given the adamant tone of her last communication, she would be too ashamed, too proud, to take the initiative – even if, for some reason, she had changed her mind. He must offer her one more chance, send one more mail into the ether; reach out one last hand across the virtual sea. It was, he reasoned, the equivalent of a message in a bottle tossed by a child into the waves of an endless ocean; a child with no playmate to share his summer and only the hope of future happiness, somewhere beyond the wind-whipped seas, to keep him from entering the surf himself and never coming back.

He opened the inbox and reopened Aioko's second to last message.

It was the one asking him to meet her at the Marriott for 'important' news. News in a shampoo bottle, a shampoo bottle with green shampoo that could never be emptied to the black line by an almost bald-headed man – well, not for a long, long time, not until he had forgotten her and she had forgotten him.

But he had not forgotten. He had let her memory, her ever-changing face rest for a week, but given permission to return it re-formed in his mind's eye like a gently agitated sheet of photographic paper in a developing tray:

A FACE FOR ALL SEASONS
It must be a sign that you really like someone
When you like their face in all its forms
Not just the seductive sun of summer smiles
But also the rainy sadness of winter storms

It is a sign you accept it for what it is
As you do your child's which laughs but also cries
Melancholy mouth when it wakes to meet the day
As dear to you as mischief in its eyes

The sleeping face you sometimes see at rest in soft repose
The face you watch as fire flares from somewhere down below
The face that feels dear to you come snow come rain come shine
The face that flutters in your hands when tears begin to flow
The office-suited formal face with lipstick-painted lips
The early morning muted face with makeup washed away
The fevered face, the tear-stained face all one face to you
A face you'll like as much as now when it is old and grey

Some faces hide behind a mask and stare and make you scared
Some faces smile brightly but have eyes with nothing there
Some faces promise sweetness but hide bitterness below
Her face is true in all its forms
The mirror of her soul

He tapped out the words and sent them – message in a bottle, hand across the sea.

But he received no reply the next day, the day after or the day after that, and by Friday he gave up and for the third time in a month vowed to never open his account again. He also gave up planning his summer. He would live from day to day and lose himself in the bars of the expatriate sub-culture, a demi-monde he abhorred and had, up until now, ignored. He had not smoked or drunk heavily for ten years. Now he determined to do both, despite having lungs prone to bronchitis and an allergy to liquor.

On the Saturday after Connor's departure, he wandered into Wanchai. He roamed along Lockhart Street, Jaffe Street and Luard Road, watching bars fill with paunchy *gweilos* and raunchy girls, and then settled at a corner table in Joe Banana's, with a low window open to the pavement. The Chinese barman was naked to the waist and the Chinese waitress wore leather boots, a beige mini skirt and a sleeveless low cut blouse.

He ordered a Beck's and drank it. He ordered a second and drank that too.

He felt self-conscious – aware of starting a process he might not be able to stop. He was sitting at the top of a slide, edging away from the safety of the platform, away from the ladder that led to terra firma. He did not know where the slide would end, he only knew it headed downwards and that once descent began – once contact had been made with the slippery, downward-tilting metal surface – the trip was fast and irreversible. He tried, with a third Beck's, to reassure himself he was in control, merely glancing down the polished slope with no plans to try it out. But reassurance ran away.

Every now and then, girls smiled or winked. The more daring parted wet lips and asked him if he was 'looking for company.' He shook his head and said he was waiting for a friend. The girls said that they had friends, too, and what about a foursome for the disco.

Stephen shook his head and longed for a mobile phone.

He was the last of the mobile-less men, an antediluvian who normally dismissed this ubiquitous means of communication as an unnecessary and annoying accoutrement of modern life, only good for unnecessary and annoying conversations with unnecessary and annoying people in unnecessary and annoying places. But now he saw its usefulness for lonely souls in public spaces. A mask to hide behind, a pretence of company, an image of being wanted, a warning to others to keep their distance or wait their turn. And maybe, if he had owned a phone – to keep his fingers busy and his mind at bay – he would not have started smoking again. But his hands were empty and his mouth in need of succour. And so, with the fourth beer of that first night, he ordered a pack of Marlboro. He had forgotten the brand names, but the image of the cowboy in Marlboro Country, the cowboy killed by cancer as he smoked his way into the sunset, had not gone away.

The tobacco loosened his tongue, and, as he lit up a third cigarette, Stephen began a drunken conversation with an Australian on a visit to a toy fair at the Convention Centre down the road.

This ageing toy boy came to Hong Kong once a year, set up deals, sold and bought, bought and sold, got drunk and got laid – either for money or for free – and then went home to wife and kids, hoping the condom had done its work both ways.

When two Indonesian sisters, barely out of their teens, came and propped up the windowsill beside the table, the Australian patted his considerable stomach and said: "We're on, mate!" In fact, they were off – off to three discos in a row, each one noisier and smokier than the last. First the Laguna, a block to the West of Joe Banana's, with a postage stamp dance floor and a bevy of bare midriffs, bouncing bottoms and come-on eyes. The oldest of the young Indonesians attached herself to Stephen, perhaps because he was slim and did not try and grab at her body in the way toy man grabbed at her sister and anyone else within grabbing distance. Then they drifted out of the Laguna, on past the pungent scent of beer and vomit from the neighbouring Wanch pub, and along Jaffe Street to the Baracay, a dark hole across the road from Joe Banana's. This was even fuller, considerably louder and dominated by Filipino women and handsome Nepalese and Indian men with charming smiles and sinewy bodies. Stephen said he felt faint, so they surfaced to the street once more, though no longer with the same two girls. Toy man gave him a nudge and a wink and said, "Not to worry, cobber – they're all good in the sack," and then led the reformed quartet on to Fenwick's.

This third club was more up-market and featured clusters of well-to-do white women dancing in protective corrals around their husbands and boyfriends, or around one another. Stephen's new partner was an older Thai woman. She bumped and ground her thighs into his and offered to get even closer for a small consideration of five hundred dollars negotiable downwards. Stephen wanted out. His lungs were hurting, his head spinning and his dance movements – minimal from the start – non-existent. He disentangled himself from Thighland, pushed past a colonial outpost of pale-faced wives doing synchronized shimmies to an old Cher hit and made it to the exit. He met the Australian coming back in with a third partner and, fearful of being returned to the melee, said he had to call his stockbroker. The toy man tried to keep him 'on the razzle' but Stephen was not 'up for the' – rib-breaking nudge, bleary eyed wink – 'main course,' having been well and truly floored by the starters.

Above ground, and back on the street, he bumped into the Indonesian sister, her arm round an Indian man. She waved. Stephen felt a pang of regret, of loss. Perhaps she had the sought-for solution hidden in her sparkling eyes and smooth skin. But it a was a momentary pang, and as he staggered up a narrow Wanchai Street with closed market stalls and rusting balconies, as he lurched on through the humid heat, determined to walk off the poison he had fed his body, he knew one thing for sure: he was not like other men, not like men who sought their sexual solace in the nubile girls of the Hong Kong night and returned business class, and business done, to the safety of home and hearth. His investigation was darker and did not lead to 'humpy-dumpy' on a lumpy hotel bed. There was something in the cellar that was his alone, and, until he found it, he would not rest.

So, for the next four nights, he went to Joe Banana's at six and stayed until after eleven, drinking, smoking and trying to sort out the demons in his mind. He took advantage of Happy Hour discounts, engaged in conversation with salesmen and other lonely souls from the ex-pat community, but avoided discos and the siren call of goodtime girls. He drank and smoked and observed, and went to bed drunk with only a vague idea of where, or who, he was. It was the kind of life he had lived in his twenties, when the tail-end time of being young had given him an excuse for a last binge. Then he had known he would give it up, turn over a new leaf and concentrate on the serious side of living. Then it had been a swansong of youth on the threshold of adulthood, a devil-may-care attitude justified by inexperience, a rite of passage on the way in. Now he was nearer the end of life and there was nothing left to sacrifice his rediscovered crutches of nicotine and alcohol for, nothing that presumed and required a clear head and healthy body. Like many of the ageing ex-pat figures dotted around the bars, Stephen was overindulging as a form of euthanasia, a way to forget failure and the reality of growing old – an anaesthetic for the over-sensitive soul, a final fling for the raddled old fart, a rite of passage on the way out.

On Thursday, his routine was disrupted by the arrival of American sailors on R&R shore leave. Their aircraft carrier had parked up in Victoria harbour and disgorged its inmates to spend dollars and get laid. Stephen could not understand why the Chinese allowed the ships to call. Did it not offend Beijing's sense of sovereignty to have the new SAR swarmed over by overweight, overpaid Yanks? He knew that, on occasions, the Americans had been told they were not welcome: a spy plane incident, the 1999 bombing of the Chinese Embassy in Belgrade, a difference of opinion over Taiwan. But on occasions only; otherwise, dollars and diplomacy spoke louder than lost dignity and the hamburger-heavy hoards were let in to roam at will where PLA soldiers feared to tread. So, on the Friday, the second night of being hemmed in on all sides by 'US Navy Personnel,' he retreated to his flat with a six-pack and twenty Marlboros and wrote his penultimate – perhaps most atypical – sexual tale, *The Terrorists*.

29

On Saturday morning a second source of inspiration arrived – by post, not aircraft carrier, this time.

On the one hand, a source of inspiration that led him to write his final story and come within a hairsbreadth of discovering the cellar's secret; on the other, a source of desperation that sent him plunging down the slide. The alcohol and tobacco, the despair at losing Aioko, the loneliness of Hong Kong with his friend Connor gone – as well as the endless ups and downs of his investigation – had already brought him to a low ebb. It was not going to take much to tip him over the edge. But as is often the case in such situations, he was the last person to recognize where that edge lay until it was too late.

Certainly, when he opened a letter from his sister and some black and white photographs fell out, he felt no sense of foreboding, rather a surge of energy and a sense of being on the right path again.

*

Irene had sent six photographs: four were of Sally with me, aged two to five; one was of Sally alone; and one was of neither Sally nor me, but enclosed by Irene 'in connection with our little chat in May.'

This sixth picture depicted two young women on horseback – one with blonde hair tied in a bun under a black bowler hat, the other with a long black ponytail emerging from a traditional velveteen riding cap. They were dressed in dark ladies' hunting jackets, pale riding breeches and calf-length black riding boots with metal spurs attached. The blonde-haired woman, the plumper of the two, was situated in front of her companion smiling at the camera; the black-haired woman, who was older and more mature in appearance, was staring at the blonde-haired woman – from a position to the rear – her gaze focused not on the head, but on the round behind of her companion.

I stared at the picture for a while and then turned it over.

On the back, Irene had written: 'Muriel and me setting off to the gymkhana, 1963 – on a horse, at Mum's command!' I would not have recognized my sister without this information. She must have been seventeen at that time, Muriel around twenty-two or twenty-three. But in smart riding gear and with hats well down over their faces, they both seemed older. Or perhaps I had always seen my sister as older than she was. When we were children, she had existed on a different plane to me, always one step ahead. At the time of the photograph, I would have regarded her as an adult, Muriel as ancient, and both of them as inhabitants of a world I knew nothing of and cared little about. I stared at the picture and shivered. A mixture of anxiety and excitement passed through my body and rattled my mind. I sensed the image contained some secret, some piece of information crucial to my investigation – some clue as to what I was trying to discover.

I had asked Irene for pictures of Sally in order to check my adult reaction to her image, to see if there was anything unusual or suspect in her demeanour. But in the four black and white photographs of nursemaid and charge there was only the same kind, protective face I had known and loved as a little boy. No hidden message or dark secret in her round, smiling features; no spark of pre-pubertal attraction reignited in my brain by her soft, sepia-tinted eyes. I had always felt she was a good woman and the pictures confirmed my childhood judgement. The rumour of her affair with Muriel had surprised me, but seen from my present perspective there was nothing wrong, or even sinister, in her having had sexual contact with another woman. It was just hard to imagine my Sally being intimate with someone as loose, lecherous and 'bad' as Muriel. After Father's death, Mother could not afford a proper nanny, as she had done for Irene, and Sally was plucked off the village street, still an innocent and naïve country girl of sixteen. So why would she have fallen prey to Muriel's games, once safe within the walls of our substantial mansion? Why would she have wanted to? Or had no village girl, not even Sally, been as innocent as I liked to imagine? Maybe scrabbling up each other's skirts and in between each other's legs was normal behaviour, no different from that of the rutting, chewing, licking, sniffing farm animals in the surrounding fields. Perhaps, it was only my kind – the protected middle-class, and especially the protected male middle-class – who developed fears and anxieties, fixations and fetishes, with regard to bodily contact.

I put the pictures of Sally in a desk drawer and concentrated my attention on Muriel and Irene.

Had Irene been involved with Muriel more than she let on? It was hard to tell from the photograph. Muriel had always carried an 'up to no good' leer on her face and that was why, from an early age, I had found her both attractive and frightening. One school holiday, when I was fifteen and still a virgin, she used to walk up and down the village street beneath my bedroom window every night. I would sit with curtains open, lights off. She would glance up, as if she knew I was watching. I am sure, if I had let her, she would have shown me anything and everything there was to know about sex. But I was too cautious, too concerned with love and longing, too caught up with the soft side of girls and of myself. I knew she was not a soft girl, not a stroke-your-cheek and gently-kiss-your-lips type of girl, not a girl to lie in the hay and stare at the stars with, and so I let her pass on by. She was a corruptor; she liked her victims to be innocent and untouched, unaware of the pleasure and pain that sex could bring; she wanted to be the one to initiate them and turn them into addicts of perversion, force them to become co-conspirators in her dark world, partners in crime and fellow corruptors of innocent souls.

Perhaps her glances on those hot summer evenings had done their work on me without my knowing. Perhaps she had sown some slow-growing, salacious seed – implanted some deep-seated desire for a dark-sided mistress that was only now coming to fruition, forty years on. But would she have managed to ensnare

Irene? I doubted it. Irene had always been her own mistress and did not fall easily under another's sway. She was too independent, too self-willed and stable to become a slave to anything as transient and superficial as sex. She was also honest and open, and, having told me part of the story on that walk in May, having revealed the opening scene in the loft, she would have told me the rest had there been any rest to tell. So the lascivious look on Muriel's face, as she stared at Irene's behind, had probably never been more than that – a look. She had made her pitch in the loft and lost, and, after that, was forced to follow – occasional older village riding-companion to an educated young lady of means: look but don't touch, Muriel, Miss Mason is well beyond your reach.

Except in fantasy, of course.

In Muriel's fantasy, in my fantasy, everything was possible, and as I stared at the two faces and compared the open softness of my sister with the secretive hardness of her companion – back and forth, back and forth, soft and hard, hard and soft – the kernel of a new story, perhaps the definitive story, took shape in my head.

I had noticed with Ellen how much I enjoyed the alternation of pain and pleasure, the administration of punishment followed by a touch of healing and concern. But what if these two elements were combined, what if hardness and softness were applied simultaneously? The thought of this fusion of opposites brought a glow to my mind and body. It seemed to bridge the gap between two warring elements in myself and connect their outlying corners and disparate demands in a way I had not experienced before. One woman was not enough, not because she did not have enough hands or lips or orifices, but because she could not be in two moods at once, could not express two sets of feelings at the same time. The extra limbs would be useful, of course, but were not what excited me. I wanted to be punished and soothed at the same time – body protected while being exposed; soul abused while being consoled. Hardness and softness were the keys, not good and evil or right and wrong; opposites that met in me, a synthesis of saint and Satan.

Could it be achieved? Well, I think my latest story, *The Riders*, which I completed last night, comes close. No story has ever excited or satisfied me more. It is a strange, amoral and pornographic tale, but true to me – to the me that has never been released, to the me that has always been imprisoned. I am sure the scene I describe never happened in real life. Humans can repress many things, but a sixteen-year-old boy would not have forgotten such a scene, unless it had induced a bout of total amnesia or he had died, and I am still alive and in possession of all my faculties. And nor do I think I would have wanted it to happen – at least, not with my own kith and kin – at that time in my life. But now I am curious to try it out with two women playing polar opposites and fleshing out the female characters of my fantasy, and me, the male protagonist, bringing them together in reality, not just imagination.

In fact, I am more than curious. I have to try it out.

If my re-enactment of *Mademoiselle Camille* worked, then something more ambitious may work, too – and take me to the highest (or, perhaps, lowest) level that my investigator's obsession now demands. In fact, it must take me there. Because with this story, I feel I have found the key to my submissive side, and if, when I try it in the lock – the lock of life, as it is lived and experienced by my mind and body – if, then, it still does not fit, I am doomed. Doomed, because I will be alone with a secret, with an obsession that cannot be released. A secret that prevents me being either one-night superman or long-term-partner man; a secret that makes me baulk at straight-on sex; a secret that makes me start the monogamous mating dance time after time, knowing it will end in failure, with me on my own again and something waiting in the dark to claim me back.

It must work. The key must fit. I must be released from fear of life, and feel at home within the prison walls that life sets round us. Or, I shall have no choice but darkness and the final void.

★

This may sound a melodramatic conclusion from Stephen. It may seem odd that a man with a good job, a son, a sister, friends – at least in England – and no physical illness should have been brought to such a pass by what, in some ways, appears to be no more than a form of sexual frustration.

But that is what makes his case so tragic. For Stephen, the search for mental and physical wholeness had become, without warning, a case of all or nothing. For thirty years, he had survived by muddling through: starting new relationships and using the excitement of newness to give a semblance of success and satisfaction in sex; accepting his own need to please and be approved of as a stand-in for real love. But each time, when the novelty wore off, and the demands for warmth and closeness that he had awoken in his partner became too much for him to handle, he ran and hid. This time, after breaking a five-year bond with sensible and loving Su-yin, he had set out on his investigation, and, in the course of that investigation, he had met Aioko and experienced the trauma and fascination of love combined with jealousy and impotence. This combination had somehow called his bluff and left him no alternative but to break the repetitive pattern of serial monogamy and finally solve what had remained unsolved for so long.

What did he want from women? What was the sexual need that remained so elusive, so hard to fulfil? What was the emotion that was missing in his make-up? What was the anxiety that made the closeness of another cloy and claw away his sense of self? Was their some trauma somewhere in his childhood? Or was he just a man, like every man, in search of sex and solace in the same person? Certainly most men, in the end, settle for compromise, as women do in their search, too. They accept that the ultimate sexual experience is a will 'o the wisp not worth following; that love is built on time and familiarity and shared experience, not on novelty, desire and obsession. For them, trust and security outrun the youthful urges of curiosity and competition, and age brings reconciliation with the self, not resignation and regret.

But Stephen had missed the path, not learnt the lesson, and was now like an ageing novice who no longer has the time to learn, but also cannot live with ignorance. He saw himself as a *grensverlegger*, a pusher-back of borders; but the borders to be crossed were running out and only the edge of life itself remained. Perhaps, if he had not been quite so alone in Hong Kong in those summer months, if he had made some effort to talk to friends back home, or let Irene know the state that he was in, he might have saved himself and lived out life within the safety of his self's own borders – borders set by nurture and the semen and the egg. But then again, perhaps his fate was sealed in the cellar of his childhood – on a summer afternoon, so long ago, he could not now distinguish what it was that cast its shadow on his soul and refused to go away.

Certainly the desire to try once more to unlock his personal Pandora's box was strong and drove him forward with a new determination, a new urgency and a new sense of controlled desperation. He was no longer prepared to wait until women came to him, no longer content to let his advertisement do the work. Now he took the initiative and, as with all services required in a hurry, threw, for the first time, real money at the problem – and, some might say, all caution to the wind.

★

I have made contact with an English woman called Kelly. I found her number in *Hong Kong Magazine* under 'Services Offered.' She described herself as a domme who did twosomes and seemed to be a suitable candidate for the story I wanted acting out.

I had never rung a sex worker before and felt nervous.

"Hello?" I said, my voice coming out higher than usual.

"Hello," replied a female voice with a North Country burr.

"I'm ringing in response to your advertisement in *Hong Kong Magazine*."

"Yes?" the woman said warily, perhaps wondering if I was from the police.

"Umm!" I muttered, uncertain how to proceed. "How do you work exactly?'

"What do you mean? How much do I charge?"

"Yes," I said, grasping at the straw she offered. "How much do you charge?"

"Two-and-a-half grand HK for sixty minutes. Cash."

"And what do you do?"

I heard a laugh, and then a clearing of the throat.

"Anything you like, love. I've me own equipment. Just tell us what you want."

"I see," I said again. "Well… Thank you."

"First time, is it?" she asked, sensing I was about to hang up. Her tone was kind, not condescending.

"Yes. Maybe I'm not ready yet."

"Well, when you are, give us a call."

"The thing is…" I began again, and then hesitated.

"Yes?" I heard a call come in on another line. "Bear with me a minute, love, I'll be right back."

The line hissed. This was important for me; I wanted to do it and I had to do it. I took a deep breath and hung on. After a minute, she came back on the line.

"Sorry about that. Another client."

"I have a story," I burst out. "A story I want acted out."

"Helps if you know what you want."

"You mean you'd read it?"

"Is it long?"

"About twelve pages," I replied, gaining confidence. She was taking me seriously, not treating me like a freak. "The thing is I need two people."

"Twice the charge – five grand HK. Cash."

"You'd both need to be British," I added.

If I were to pay that sort of money, the re-enactment had to be right. In fact, I did not want to do it unless it was right. The sexual contact and release were secondary to the emotional dynamic I wanted to generate, and *that* required good casting and good acting.

"You'd have to wait a bit," she said, after a moment's reflection. "Chinese I could do now, even Russian, but a born and bred Brit…"

"She has to be British," I insisted. "With a British voice and accent."

"And British boobs and bottom, eh?" She laughed and then, reverting to her serious tone, added, "I've a colleague over from England next week. She's coming for a rest. But she might do it – if I twist her tits. Blonde, full figure, twenty-something."

"A northerner like you?" I asked.

"No. She's posh. Boarding school and a plum up her bum. Is that a problem?"

"No. That's fine," I said, trying not to sound too excited.

"She's top drawer. Works the CEO circuit in London. Might want a bit more."

"How much?" I asked.

This was my first contact with a prostitute and I had no idea how to bargain.

"Depends on what you want. She's not a domme like me. More into fancy frills and flirting. Let's 'em spank her, too. But that costs."

"How much?" I repeated.

I did not want to spank her, but wanted to get some idea of the scale of charges.

"Another grand at least."

"I see," I said. "And if you spanked her?"

"The same. Though she'd enjoy it more."

Were these normal charges? Or was she pulling figures out of the air?

"If I send you the story, could you cost it?"

"Plumber's estimate?" she said with a chuckle. "Sure, love. I'll do that for you."

"Where should I send it?"

"Mistresskelly@yahoo.com. Send it as a Word attachment."

I sensed she had been through this before, and that made me feel better. As with the experienced plumber, she would know how to deal with the situation in a professional and expert manner. A beginner would be cheaper, but the job might be botched.

"Thank you," I said. "You've been most helpful."

"My pleasure, love. Goodbye. Hope to hear from you soon."

"Goodbye."

I sent her the story the next day, which was a Monday. I highlighted the parts to be acted out in our session, but emphasized the importance of reading the whole piece and understanding the context – both psychological and physical – of the characters.

Two days later, I received a reply. She said it was a complicated commission requiring 'in-depth femdom role-playing,' mouth-to-mouth kissing – normally forbidden – and complex equipment and costuming. However, she had discussed it with her friend in London and, together, they would do it for an all-in fee of ten thousand HK or just under one thousand pounds sterling. This seemed a large sum, so I mailed back asking Mistress Kelly if she were confident of their abilities to portray the two characters – one soft and loving, one hard and lustful – in a realistic and convincing manner. I also asked about costumes and props, hair colour and location. She told me not to worry. They would take care of everything in the costume, props and makeup departments, including provision of suitable clothing for me. Her friend was a natural blonde and would be playing the 'nice girl;' she herself would ensure her own hair was suitably dark and severe for the 'rotten apple.' As far as location went, that was up to me. I could use my own home, book a hotel room or – for an extra two thousand HK, inclusive of props and set dressing – engage her to organize a discreet rendezvous. And, she added, in answer to my first question, as both she and her colleague were professional role-players there was no need to worry about authenticity or acting ability. Performances would be as true-to-life – or true-to-story – as humanly possible. In fact, the only thing I should worry about was the soreness of my backside!

I smiled. Despite the levity of this final remark, I now felt sure Mistress Kelly would do her best to put on a serious and convincing performance.

I went for a walk along Bowen Road – almost deserted in the mid-summer heat – and passed a Caucasian woman, who looked very much like I imagined Kelly to be. On my return to the flat, I drank one more deliberative cup of organic tea and decided to accept the offer.

We made a date for three o'clock on Wednesday 20th July – tomorrow, as I write this report – and agreed that Kelly should find and dress the location. I will receive instructions on where to proceed by telephone tomorrow morning, and am expected to bring the fee in cash. I have also sent my waist, chest and inside leg measurements. I am feeling nervous, but quietly confident. It is a new departure for me on two counts: it is my first paid sex, and my first sexual experience with more than one partner. Two people is a gamble, but paying will, I hope, remove any lingering guilt and allow me to focus fully on my role. Not that I plan to act much. I am hoping that the exposure of my mind and body to the powerful polar opposites portrayed in the story will reveal, and connect to, something deep within myself without me having to act at all. I have told Mistress Kelly the session is important to me, but have not attempted to explain the full nature of my investigation. Although I have read that some prostitutes like to play the amateur social worker and psychologist, I think it is better, in this case, for Kelly and her colleague to work from the story and not from my analysis of the story.

I have not eaten much over the last couple of days and have, at times, felt like praying. If God exists, I do not think that he or she is a prude. I also imagine that discovery of self is a God-approved task, regardless of the path taken to achieve it. I do, however, feel very alone and would appreciate some inner confirmation that what I am doing is acceptable in God's sight. This means – for an atheist like me – that I want my own blessing on the project.

So I will now meditate, in the same way that I have for the past twenty-five years, and seek the strength and wisdom to accept whatever truth is revealed to me tomorrow afternoon. I wish I could have Aioko's blessing, too; that she was here to hold my hand, as a mother might hold a child's hand before some painful operation. But I have made a vow to let her mailbox die and will not check again for a message that is not there. I must do this alone and be content with the image of her face, her sleeping face, beside me on the bed that afternoon so many weeks ago. '*Baka na igirisu-jin!*' she called me sometimes: 'Crazy Englishman!'

We will see.

30

To understand what Stephen imagined was going to happen, readers may, as before, wish to read the story he was about to enact. Alternatively, they may prefer to wait until Stephen's real-life tale is done. This time there is not a single account of what happened at the session. Afterwards, Stephen was in no fit state to write more than a few lines and, a day later, he disappeared. There is, however, enough information from various sources – including Stephen's jottings and an account received by the police from Kelly – to piece together a third person narrative of events.

He arrived on time at a top floor flat in Blue Pool Road, Happy Valley. This was Kelly's residence, though she did not tell him that at the time.

He was greeted by an elderly Filipino maid, dressed in worn jeans and a T-shirt, and asked to sit in a small hallway. He was given a cup of tea and the money was taken away to be counted: ten thousand plus an additional two thousand for the flat, making a total of twelve thousand Hong Kong dollars, or just over one thousand pounds sterling. The maid then returned with some khaki shorts, a pair of long grey socks, a pair of tight rubber underpants with holes for cock and balls – 'professional gear' contributed by Kelly to 'improve stimulation' – and a Ralph Lauren open-necked sports shirt as a stand-in for the nineteen-fifties Aertex shirt described in the story.

He was shown to a bathroom to change and told to wait in the hallway again when he was ready. To help him 'get in the mood' Kelly had provided a copy of *Wuthering Heights* by Emily Brontë, the book his character was reading in the story. In a handwritten note, stuck inside the front cover, she explained that the hallway was to act as the hayloft and would be where the two returning riders discovered him. Otherwise, as his was a passive role, he merely had to do what he was told. She would stick to the script as far as possible, though might introduce the occasional improvisation for space reasons, or erotic enhancement. 'And, of course', she joked, 'there are no horses!'

Stephen folded the note and put it in his pocket. Then he sat and waited.

He tried to imagine himself as a teenager, a sixteen-year-old boy with no sexual experience and a penchant for peace, quiet and Victorian literature. He picked up the book and tried to bury himself in the dense prose. Why had he picked this tale? Was Heathcliffe a role model? No, it was the common connection to Scarborough that made the Brontës feel like kindred spirits. Scarborough, the seaside town that Bronwyn, Emily, Anne and Charlotte visited with their parson father and to which Sally would take Stephen in the summer on a green bus caught at the top of a steep hill on the A64 near Castle Howard, or, for a treat, on the little steam train with its two carriages and tank engine that stopped near their village on its way from York. He heard the whistle, smelt the smoke and saw the steam. Scarborough, Brontë, Yorkshire and Sally emerged from memory and merged in his conscious mind to recreate the world of childhood. And when he heard female giggling in the adjoining room, and the creak of a door as it slowly opened to cast a beam of sunlight across his face, he was as apprehensive and alert as any introspective male teenager might be when girls are about to enter his private space.

The two women squeezed into the hallway, dressed in a very rough approximation of the riding gear described in the story. They had on brightly coloured, jockey-style caps instead of proper riding hats; white blouses with ties; white pants made of cotton with jodhpur wings at the thighs; and calf-length high-heeled boots that no self-respecting rider would have worn. They had done their best, but it was not a movie with high production values and the budget was as tight as the blouses.

Stephen was seeing the women for the first time and, as they took up positions for their opening lines – one by his chair and one by the door – his eyes travelled from top to toe and back again, twice. Kelly was the taller and slimmer of the two – over six feet in her boots. She had combed her black hair into a ponytail and used a dark lipstick and nail varnish for lips and fingers. She had also darkened her eyebrows and eyelids and appeared suitably mean and cruel. She was carrying a bone-handled riding whip. The plum-up-the-bum cast as Stephen's sister had a fuller figure and was shorter – a little less than six feet in her five-inch heels. She had blonde hair tied in a bun and was made up with skin-tone lipstick, a hint of rouge and pale blue mascara.

Posh took up a provocative pose – not in the original script – and pouted her lips at Stephen. Kelly unravelled the whip and dangled the lash in front of Stephen's face.

"Little brother hiding in t'loft, eh?" she said in a broad Yorkshire accent, following the script word for word.

She grabbed Stephen and, followed by Posh, led him into a room with a rubber sheet on the floor, a massage table to one side and a see-through toilet-like contraption against the far wall. Beyond the room he could hear clattering in the kitchen, but after a moment or two an outside door slammed and there was silence. Around the room a variety of flails, masks, handcuffs and harnesses dangled from the walls. A twenty-first century torture chamber furnished from the S&M equivalent of an IKEA catalogue, not a nineteen-sixties village saddle room smelling of saddle soap. But it did smell of leather and, for some reason, reminded Stephen of his childhood, so he did not complain.

They went through the scripted parts first: Stephen in his non-scripted but highly stimulating rubber pants forced to try and mount his blackmailed sister as she knelt on all fours with her breeches round her knees; Stephen whipped for failing to do so and made to lick his sister's cunt while she cried and stroked his hair; Stephen tied to the saddle horse (massage table) as Kelly inserted a turnip (half-peeled cucumber) up his anus and big sister consoled him with french kissing and soft caressing of the face. As the action progressed, lines that had been carefully composed in the original were often reduced to 'Take that, you bastard!' or 'Like being fucked up t'arse, lad?' But the soft-hard dynamic was adhered to, and the two women did their best to stay in role and provide him with the dual sensations of tenderness and terror that he hoped would unlock the cellar door and release him back into life.

Indeed, in his subsequent jottings, Stephen admits that, up until the unscripted denouement, he was in a permanent state of arousal, but that the arousal was purely physical and without that sense of soul-touching, self-revealing fulfilment he had hoped for. He seems to have acted rather than experienced the part, and been more concerned about giving the two women a sense of professional pride than giving himself a good time. The missing element was emotion. The plum-up-the-bum role-player did her best as Stephen's sister, but kissing a man she had met half an hour before was a physical act devoid of feeling – and devoid of the frisson kissing your naked brother under duress should engender. In the same way, Kelly, a professional domme and dab hand at delivering pain in an erotic manner, could not be meaningfully involved in the mental and emotional dynamics of the situation. Stephen knew that, from the way she switched off when she thought he wasn't looking. Both women were acting out roles, but were not trained actors. Their business was sex, not Stanislavski, stimulation of human bodies, not the intricacies of method acting and, in the end, Stephen had to role-play, too.

When, however, the women went a step too far, he could play his role no more. The denouement described in his story was theatrical rather than erotic and did not involve sexual release. But since sexual release was assumed to be the client's goal – and the best way of ensuring he got value for money and returned for more – the women had decided they should give Stephen a surprise bonus to round things off. So, after completion of the cucumber sequence, the see-through contraption was positioned on a rubber sheet in the centre of the room. Kelly, whip at ready, ordered Stephen to lie with his head inside the Perspex box and told her colleague – still playing the unwilling sister – to sit on the oval-shaped hole on top. Kelly then positioned herself between Stephen's legs, took hold of his cock and told the sister to urinate on her brother while she made 'little bugger come.' The sister pretended to protest, but, before Stephen could protest for real, she obeyed the command and aimed a stream of warm urine straight on to his face.

Stephen accepted the bonus in silence, but, after a squeeze or two at her end, Kelly knew something was wrong. Instead of the expected surge of arousal, Stephen's member went limp in her hands and did not revive. Inside the Perspex box, a pool of urine formed around his head. He lay quite still, quite silent, staring up at the naked behind of his 'sister,' until, one by one, tears formed in his eyes and flowed down his cheeks to join the urine. He was in an almost catatonic state, and made no response to Kelly's 'You all right love?' She signalled to her colleague to climb off the box and together they eased Stephen out of the urine and rested his head on the rubber sheeting. Kelly fetched a flannel and towel, washed his face and neck, and then wrapped the towel around his head. Her colleague offered him a slug of whisky from a silver flask.

"Thank you," Stephen whispered. "Thank you, ladies. You did your best."

"I'm sorry, love," Kelly began. "We thought…"

"Don't worry," Stephen interrupted. "I'll be fine. It'll be fine."

Stephen closed his eyes. Kelly glanced at her colleague and shrugged her shoulders. She had seen all manner of clients, but this was an atypical reaction.

"Want to go on, love?" she asked. "Jill's good with her mouth. Aren't you, Jill? And you've twenty minutes on the clock."

Stephen shook his head.

"No need," he whispered. "That's not what I came for."

"You're a rare one then," Kelly chuckled. "But so long as you're happy."

"I'll be fine, it'll be fine," Stephen repeated and then, raising himself on his elbows, added, "Do you think I might take a shower? My hair…"

"Of course," said Kelly. "Here, I'll help you out of these. Give us a hand, Jill."

Together, the two women rolled the now lacerated rubber pants down Stephen's legs and off over his feet.

Stephen felt like he was in a hospital or a morgue. A dead mind and dying body that had failed to connect back to life. The whole thing had been a fiasco, and he felt ashamed and defeated. His investigation was at an end because there was no way of completing it. He could not recreate what he had imagined, and what he did recreate was not how he had imagined it would be. He was caught between imagination and reality, unable to connect to both at the same time, and now at risk of not connecting to either. Warm urine falling on his face had been the sign that his fragile world was doomed; his cold, lonely world of pure hope and endless horizons – of future promise and past pleasure, but never present life. The warm urine had washed away the pretence that he could thrive, or even survive, in the here and now; washed away the last remnant of his self and left a shadow on autopilot – a shadow that would soon crash into the sea, erasing his existence once and for all.

"Thank you," he repeated, as they helped him up. "I'll be fine. It'll be fine."

He let the shower wash away the waste of Jill's body and wished it could wash him away, too. Flush him down the drain to join the sea and be at one with the Earth. He was detached from himself, from the world, and wanted to return to the peace, quiet and certainty of childhood – or, perhaps, of a time before childhood. He dried off and pulled on his jeans and shirt. He looked in the mirror and saw the shadow still functioning, the respectable outer image of a middle-aged man – no sign of the turmoil within, no sign he had just been pissed on by a prostitute with a plum up her arse.

He found Kelly and Jill, now dressed in 'civvies,' waiting for him in the hall.

"Feeling better?" Kelly asked.

Stephen nodded.

"Yes, thank you."

"If you want another go," Kelly said, handing him a name card with a small embossed emblem of a whip in the top left hand corner, "just give us a call."

"Or if you're in London," Jill added, handing him her own plain white card. "I have a friend who's the spitting image of Kelly."

Stephen smiled and put out a hand to the two women in turn.

"Thank you, Kelly. Thank you, Jill."

"Our pleasure," the two women crowed in unison.

"Goodbye."

"Goodbye, love."

Kelly held open the door and Stephen stepped out into the evening sun, no wiser and much weaker in mind and spirit than when he had entered. He hailed a taxi, collapsed inside and, for a moment, could not think where to go. He thought of saying 'home' and seeing where the driver took him, but in the end mumbled 'Stubbs Road' and a number.

The taxi driver smelt of sweat. Or was it urine?

Stephen was no longer sure.

PART THREE
BEYOND THE CELLAR

31

I do not believe in God, but, now, I must believe in miracles.
When I returned a few minutes ago, I found the green light flashing on my answer machine. I pressed it and heard my sister's voice say she was off to Norway, on a trekking tour. She would be up above the Arctic Circle, somewhere in the frozen North, and mobile phones were banned. She wished me a happy and productive summer and promised to call me in September. Her message did not surprise me. I did not expect anyone to know how much I was in need of help, of support, because I never let on. Even if I had been there to answer her call, I would have said I was fine, told her to have a good trek and kept my chaos to myself.

Perhaps that is the same for all people, when they are near the end of their tethers. They do not ask the trusted goatherd to untie the rope or move the stake to fresher grazing grounds; instead they strain and twist and eventually strangle themselves without having uttered as much as a bleat. Or else they pretend to graze happily on ground where there is no longer grass, where the land is barren, until they collapse in stoic silence from starvation. Keeping up appearances is just that: maintaining the act, pretending everything is fine, not burdening anyone else with your problems; letting difficulties and disorder slowly crush you to death like so many boulders in a landslide, like so much ice cold snow – disturbed by the insane rumblings of your mind – descending from above and encasing you in a numbing, suffocating avalanche of dislocated, unsolved thought.

I wanted to collapse there and then and let myself be buried, but, as I reached my finger out to turn the voicemail off, a second message started. First, just silence, just a crackle in the air, and then a tiny, tiny voice, so weak and small it was almost swamped by the hiss of static.

"*Moshi-moshi,*" it said. "*Moshi-moshi.* Aioko *desu.*"

There was a pause. I sat bolt upright, my senses alert and fully functioning again.

"*Kibun wa hontoni warui desu* – Aioko ill, Writer-san. Can you come? *Onegai shimasu.*"

And then the line went dead.

I have tried to ring her mobile, but it is disconnected. I have rung her work, too, but they say she has been off sick for four weeks. Now I must go to find her, to save her – to Japan again, if necessary. Her voice has washed away the smell of urine from my face. I was a fool to think that salvation lay beneath a woman's thighs, a woman's buttocks or in a woman's whipping hand; it lies within a woman's soul, within herself – within a voice that summons, within a voice you have no choice but to obey. To serve is to love and to love is to serve, and I am such a willing servant of Aioko-san. Now I will find her again and we will seek salvation in my willingness to serve and her desire to command. I do not believe in God, but I must now believe in miracles. Or else I would not be sitting here writing this, as I wait for Japan Airlines to ring me back.

★

So keen was Stephen to find and console Aioko, he almost did fly to Japan, forgetting that his mistress would probably not have summoned him if she were there. But, as chance would have it, he had left his passport at the Institute, and when he took a taxi into town to retrieve it, he found the building closed. In his frustration and still disturbed state he hurried across Harcourt Gardens to Pacific Place and on up the escalator to the British Consulate for an emergency passport. But it was six o'clock and the guard refused to let him in, threatening to call the police if 'Sir' would not stop banging on the door.

He gave up, walked along to Hong Kong Park, climbed the steps to the relative peace and quiet of the Tai Chi garden and slumped on a bench. He closed his eyes and, exhausted by the session with Kelly, would have slept if a German tourist had not asked him the way to the Peak Tram. Stephen, keeping up appearances to the last, politely led the man to the end of the Tai Chi gardens and pointed to the tram station below.

He then turned to gaze across the harbour.

His eyes alighted on the Outlying Islands Ferry Terminal, just visible between the triangular glass panes of the China Bank building and the inside-out drainpipes of Norman Foster's Hong Kong Bank headquarters. For a moment he did not register its significance. Then, one by one, the names of islands defined as outlying trickled through his mind: Lantau, Lamma, Peng Chau, Cheung Chau. Cheung Chau! Aioko's home!

Now he was running down the steep hill that leads out of the park; across the six lane artery of Garden Road, where it cuts up in a steep curve from Central to the Mid Levels; past St John's Cathedral, down Battery Path, into the air-conditioned iciness of the arcade that leads from Queen's Road through to the Mandarin Hotel; out on to Des Voeux Rd, across the pedestrian bridge, down the escalator three steps at a time and along the canopied promontory to the Cheung Chau ferry. Breathless, he slammed his Octopus travelcard on to the automatic barrier entry point, felt the turnstile give and sprinted the last few metres to the gates just as they were closing for a ferry's departure. He dived through, jumped on board, sank into a seat in the front row and fell asleep.

When the boat reached Cheung Chau, a deckhand had to shake his shoulder to wake him. He blinked, stood up, thanked the man and stumbled off down the wooden gangplank. He emerged on to the main harbour-front thoroughfare and paused. Which way should he go? Could he remember where Aioko lived? It was now almost dark and he had only been here once. Then, she had led the way – at a distance, 'in case of spying neighbours' – her fragile figure beckoning him on like a will o' the wisp.

He smiled at the memory, took his bearings and turned to the left.

After a hundred yards, he tried a lane to the right. It smelt of fish and felt wrong. He returned to the harbour and continued by the water for another block. Again he stopped and peered into a dark alleyway. This time the configuration of balconied houses crammed into the cobbled street struck a chord. He walked up the gentle incline, casting a glance at doorbells as he passed, remembering how her silhouetted figure had paused at the end of an alley, pointed to a door and disappeared.

He approached the last few houses and read the name cards with more care. Most were in Chinese or illegible, and he was about to give up when he noticed a bell on the last house with no card at all, just a space where the card should be. That would be like Aioko, he thought, not wishing to advertise her presence, keen to preserve her privacy and her good name as a married woman. He glanced up at the windows above – her flat had been on the first floor, he remembered. But there was darkness, no sign of life, not even a flickering candle. He hesitated and then rang the bell.

Silence.

He rang again and heard a window open above his head. Someone peered down, beckoned and disappeared. A moment later, a buzzer released the lock on the door. He pushed it open, closed it and crept up the stairs. At the top, he saw a tiny figure wrapped in a blanket standing in a doorway.

It was Aioko, his Aioko-san.

★

"Please remove shoes, Writer-san."

That was the first thing she said to me after six weeks. A simple command and I obeyed. She was so thin, so frail. I wanted to take her in my arms and hold her, but once inside the flat she started coughing and lay down on a day bed at the end of the living room. I followed her and knelt on a sheepskin rug spread out beside the bed.

"I know you will come," she said, putting out a hand and stroking my face. "Writer-san *wa ichiban no tomodachi desu ka*. Best friend. Best friend."

"*Mochiron*," I whispered. "Of course."

I clasped her hand and held it to my lips.

"Aioko not well," she continued, lying back on the three pillows behind her head.

"'Macau' not well or 'Tahiti' not well?" I asked.

"Hawaii, Tahiti and beyond," she sighed.

"Then I take you to Hawaii and Tahiti and beyond," I said, laying her hand back on the bedclothes. "Until you are better."

"Aioko will not be better," she continued, after a short silence. "You remember I saw doctor before going to Japan?"

I nodded.

"He said first test wrong. Second test wrong. Need another test. More blood. More playing with Aioko's *omanko*, more whispering and shaking of heads. In Japan, I hear result. Very bad. Aioko very ill. Aioko dying. Aioko so alone…"

Tears streamed down her face and she shook her head back and forth like a disbelieving child. I reached out and took both hands in mine. She had cried like this before, in Dan Ryan's, and then it had been a false alarm, perhaps even a trick to get my sympathy, to make me take her home to Writerworld. This time, I believed her.

"Now I am here," I whispered. "And I will not leave you. Ever."

She squeezed my hands and we sat in silence, until she had recovered enough to continue with her story.

"Mother wanted me in Japan. But Japan no longer home. So I come back to Hong Kong, to little home. And to husband, but husband has gone. To America, his mother says, no word to me, nothing, and I do not know how to reach him. Now, I am alone…"

I waited for her to continue, but she fell silent again.

"And Superman?" – the word slipped out – "Your American friend?"

She smiled and stroked my cheek again.

"The man who made my Writer-san so jealous? So crazy that he cried and cried and cried for his Aioko?"

I nodded and she gave a chuckle. I noticed the old fire and petulance in her eyes. She had made me suffer, and she had been flattered – perhaps even aroused – by that suffering, but I did not mind. She had the right to pick and choose, and I had followed her finger when it fell on me. Followed of my own free will, and suffered of my own free will when the finger moved elsewhere.

I was her servant, because I loved her. I was her servant, because she was the only good thing to have come out of my investigation, because she was all that was left of my investigation. I was her servant, because she was my mistress and I wanted and needed no other.

"Superman has flown away. I will not see him again. Flew back to wife and home. Did not care for Aioko. Only cared for Aioko's body and body no good now."

Again, tears flowed down her cheeks. This time I wiped them away with a tissue.

"Should you not be in hospital?" I asked.

She shook her head,

"They cannot cure me. I have cancer in cervix, and cancer in blood, and maybe cancer in brain as well. They can only make me live a little longer."

"Well?" I said. "That is better than nothing."

"No," she replied, shaking her head again. "Nothing is better. Pills and x-rays make hair fall out, insides sick, mind empty. I prefer to feel, Writer-san."

"But if there is pain," I protested, though I knew what she was talking about.

"If there is pain, I will end it," she sighed. Then she took my hand again and held it to her cheek. "And Writer-san will help me."

"I will do whatever you want, whatever helps Aioko-san. I promise."

I kissed her fingers and felt them flutter like a butterfly against my lips.

"Did you get my mails?" I added after a pause.

She nodded.

"Yesterday. I go to Cheung Chau Library. Very weak, but I walk, stopping each minute for breath. Wait for computer to come free, so cold in ice-cold air-con air. Then computer free, and I find song and poem, and know Writer-san is still my friend. My only friend, my real friend. A friend who will not mind a sickly face because he likes my face 'in all its forms.'" She paused, short of breath, and then added: "That is why I ring you."

She coughed and closed her eyes.

I felt overwhelmed by her fragility, by the fragility of human existence, the coincidence of human contact and the odds against like-minded souls meeting. I felt overwhelmed with relief that I had sent the mails; that I had not given up, despite the harshness of her letter; that I had written the poem. I had shown my faith in her, in my feelings for her, and now she had put her faith in me and I would not let her down.

I laid my head on the bedspread and allowed my own tears to flow; tears of happiness, tears of remorse, tears of sorrow, tears of terror that what I had found again would so soon disappear. She stroked my head and whispered "*Oyasumi nasai. Oyasumi nasai,*" like a mother to her child, like a mistress to her servant, like a slowly drowning soul to its soul mate in the night. Soon, I heard her snoring, 'sneezing.' I climbed up on to the small bed and lay down beside her.

Outside, the sky was dark and clouds covered the moon. Inside, bad girl slept with bad boy and dreamt her bad girl dreams, as, within their sleeping bodies, two souls prepared to die.

32

That was the last piece of coherent narrative Stephen wrote before he disappeared, or, at least, the last piece found in Hong Kong. It is known from neighbours, however, that he moved in with Aioko the next day. He crept out of her house at dawn, went to his flat and returned at lunchtime with a suitcase on wheels and several bags of shopping. For the next week, he seems to have done all the household tasks: fetched daily groceries, cleaned the flat, washed laundry and hung it out on the balcony. Some days he went to a nearby Watson's drugstore and bought the strongest painkillers available, a few at a time: perhaps because he was rationing her – perhaps because she was rationing herself.

Once, and once only, they emerged together. She was wafer-thin and white as a sheet, wearing sunglasses and dressed in a long white nightgown. He was in navy blue shorts and a black T-shirt and had an old fashioned, straw sunhat on his head. He carried her in his arms, stopping at intervals to get his breath back and rest his muscles. They walked over the crest of the hill at the top of the street where Aioko lived, and down the other side to the small semi-circular beach that is so popular with visitors at the weekend. He set her on the sand, opened a red umbrella to protect her from the sun, and sat down beside her. They did not talk, but stared out across the sea to the distant high-rise blocks of Pok-fulam glinting at the western end of Hong Kong Island. Occasionally they would kiss each other lightly on the lips, or hold hands, or touch feet, but mostly they sat quite still. After half an hour, he stood up, closed the umbrella, picked up his charge and, step by step – with rest stops as before – carried her home.

They were not seen again outside the flat that week, or the
next; and when the landlady, who had promised to have the air-con
fixed, received no reply on three consecutive days despite repeated
knockings, the police were called. After some debate and a discussion
with headquarters by radio, two officers made a forcible entry. There
was no one inside. Just a neatly ordered, recently cleaned flat, with
an empty fridge and bedclothes folded on the mattress. Indicating –
or so the police said – that the occupants were not planning to
return for some time. On the walls, the mirrors that Aioko had
decorated with her beach-combed shells were displayed, as if on
show in an art gallery, in symmetrical rows. The police counted one
hundred and fifty mirrors in all. On the table was a note written in
the precise, childlike hand of Aioko: 'We have gone to Hawaii and
Tahiti and beyond. No need to look for us, we will find ourselves.'

All flights to both destinations, direct and indirect, were checked,
but Aioko's name did not show up. The police were unable to say
who her male companion had been, as there was no evidence of
his identity anywhere in the flat. They found neither ID card nor
passport for Aioko, which led them to believe that the 'parties
concerned' had probably settled for the third destination on the
note: 'beyond.' This, they pointed out, could mean anywhere in
the world, as one of Asia's biggest international airports was only a
thirty-minute taxi ride from the flat. What they did not point out,
at least in public, was that it could also mean anywhere beyond this
world.

Those writing up the 'Mystery of Missing Couple' story for
newspapers knew only too well that it could, and so descended
on the infamous Cheung Chau hotel, where couples were known
to go to commit double-suicide by sealing off their rooms and
burning charcoal. They found two teenagers, whose charcoal had
failed to ignite, but no sign of Aioko and her mystery man. The
owner further dampened speculation by saying he had never had a
couple over thirty 'try it on,' and that 'foreigners' avoided the place
'like the plague.'

Pictures of Aioko and a man with a question mark for a face
were posted in police stations and circulated to airports and ferry
terminals; but no one came forward with information and, after a

week or two, the story disappeared from the papers and the police moved on to more important matters. The mystery couple had vanished into thin air, and even the subsequent replacement of the question mark with a picture of Stephen – after Irene had flown out and found his diary – produced no new lead. In fact, it was not until Christmas that the mystery was solved and, by that time, it was of interest only to family and friends and no longer a matter of public concern, or worthy of more than a line or two in the newspaper.

★

We are at the Westin Resort Hotel on Coloane Island in Macau, just twenty miles across the sea from Aioko's Cheung Chau home.

If we cannot go to Hawaii or Tahiti, Macau is better than nothing. Macau is the place I promised to take her to, if she were not ill, so, maybe now we're here, she won't be. Either way, I am happy to be at her side. Nothing else seems important or relevant – or even possible. Last night, I asked why she did not return to Japan. She said she preferred a home created by her to one created by her father. Later, she added that if she were in Japan she would want to go and lie down in the wood at the foot of Mount Fuji and sleep forever, but as this would upset her mother – 'daughter's body found near family home, not good' – it was better to be here. She misses her mountain more than her mother, I think. The spirit of Mount Fuji is very powerful and soothing to dead souls, she says, and she is not sure if such a spirit is present on our little island by the sea. I tell her not to think such thoughts and say that I will make her better. She does not believe me, and sometimes nor do I. Today she read an article about the Goddess Ma, whose name is in Macau. She is a goddess of the sea and her statue stands high on a hill above our hotel. Aioko wants to climb up there and feel the spirit of the Goddess – 'to make her acquaintance.' How she will do that, I do not know. So far she has not moved from the room, and it is already our third day. She sits on the balcony beneath a parasol and stares at the sea. I order room service and feed her like a baby, as she is too weak to feed herself. She does not eat much, mostly miso soup with extra garlic and a spoonful or two of rice. Otherwise she sips green tea and bottled water through a straw, and stares at the sea and sky and the ships passing on the horizon. Sometimes I sit on the balcony with her. Sometimes I lie on one of the two large double beds in our airy room, with its soft ochre walls, flower patterned curtains and wooden Chinese cabinet to hide the mini-bar. It is peaceful, soothing and timeless, and I cannot imagine returning to normal life. It is as if we are in a waiting room, but what we are waiting for I am not quite sure. I have been down to the beach once or twice – Hac Sa Beach, Black Sand Beach – and walked across to the village where Portuguese Fernando has his restaurant, and where I once imagined Aioko and me eating a moonlit meal. She is too ill to do that now and prefers not to be seen in public. At night we sleep in separate beds, but sometimes she wakes and calls out, "Writer-san! Writer-san!" Then I go and lie beside her and hold the tiny body in my arms, and she rests her head on my shoulder and returns to fitful dreaming. One time, when she was feeling better and a little bored, she said that I should make some Writer's Cream for her, and I obeyed. She watched and smiled, and told me to shower when I had finished. But, otherwise, sex is not part of our daily existence and that feels right. We are somehow beyond such superficial sensations; they are no longer relevant and offer neither solace nor solutions in our current situation. We are soul mates in our waiting room and touching souls is not like touching bodies; it does not lead to some dramatic climax, to arousal and release. Thoughts and feelings coalesce in the air, billow against each other and then recede, just as our flower-patterned curtains rise up in the evening breeze, touch the bed and then fall back. Mingling and dissolving into one another, and yet still part of separate bodies. Mistress Soul and Servant Soul, I like to think, and, when I tell her this, she cries and says that I am her *henna no hito*, her strange, strange man. And then we hold each other, our tears mingle and we sleep as one:

Aioko-san don't leave me for another world,
Or, if you must, then let me come as well
The mystery of my life has now unfurled
And nothing more remains on earth but hell

★

These were probably the last words Stephen wrote. They were found much later, signed, dated and hidden behind the Chinese cabinet in his hotel room. The evening after writing them, on the first of August, he carried Aioko down to the foyer, sat her on one of two large sofas opposite the entrance door and asked the Filipino woman at the reception desk to order him a taxi. When it arrived at seven forty-five, he picked Aioko up, carried her down the broad marble steps, said thank you to the man, also a Filipino, who held the door open for him, and placed his charge gently in the back seat of the waiting vehicle. He told the driver to go to the statue of Ma, and when the driver did not understand, Stephen pointed a finger at the white floodlit figure standing aloof and alone on a wooded hill above them.

The driver nodded and chugged away into the night. He wound his way round and up the hobbit hills, until he reached the highest part beneath the outstretched marble hands of Ma. He asked if he should wait but was told not to, and when Aioko had been lifted from his car, he drove away, wondering how this strange unlikely pair would make it back again.

But it was not his problem, and so he left them: two figures in the shadow of the Goddess Ma, one carrying the other like some sacrifice of love to the floodlit marble face. How long they stayed there is not known, but at some point they must have decided to descend by foot to the hotel. Even in daylight, the crumbling paths, with their rough-hewn steps of rock and unmarked edges thick with summer undergrowth, are treacherous and not the safest place to walk. That Stephen – carrying Aioko, and with a loaded rucksack on his back – managed to get as far as he did is almost unbelievable. But he did.

Their bodies were found four months later at the bottom of a reservoir above Hac Sa Beach. The reservoir was being drained for maintenance and their remains were revealed, caught in an outflow grill at the base of the inside wall of the reservoir's dam. The dam is just above the road that runs along the south side of the island to Hac Sa village. It is no more than five minutes' walk from the hotel. Police said Stephen must have slipped when carrying his charge along the walkway that traverses the dam. The weight of mini-bar bottles in his rucksack meant the bodies would have sunk faster than usual and a wound to Stephen's head indicated he might have been knocked unconscious by the concrete lip of the dam. The only strange circumstance, mentioned in the Portuguese coroner's report, was the fact that they had their arms around one another and seemed to have been making no attempt to disentangle their bodies or remove the dead-weight of the rucksack before drowning. In addition, Stephen's right hand was clamped to one of the iron bars of the outlet grill, as if trying to prevent himself from floating to the surface. But the verdict was accidental death and, after separation, the bodies were sanitized, bagged and sent back to their respective countries, Japan and England, for burial. Whether their souls were separated in a similar manner, by whoever it is that controls the universe, we shall never know, until we too leave this world. We can only hope that, somewhere in the great beyond, a Mistress Soul and Servant Soul – Aioko-san and Stephen-san – now rest in peace and perfect equilibrium, side by side for ever.

Epilogue

When I had finished writing my account, there were many questions left unanswered, not least of which was whether the deaths had been accidental or intentional. But the answer to that question, along with many others, died with Stephen and the truth will never be known for sure. Indeed, perhaps Stephen himself did not know, at that last moment of slipping over the dam's edge. He had written of imminent death, but what we write down and indicate as our intent is not always what we end up doing, or, if we do carry through an imagined intent, it is not always in the way that we originally intended. All that can be assumed is that, in the case of death, the gap between fiction and reality, between imagination and physical performance, is closed in a way that Stephen could not achieve – or even have imagined – in life.

There was, however, one question, which, if not totally answerable, might be open to further investigation, and this question haunted me for many weeks after the main body of my work was complete. Stephen's use of the cellar metaphor in the latter part of his writing may have resulted from Irene's remarks on the way to the airport in March. She had mentioned then the possibility of Sally and Muriel having an adolescent lesbian relationship and joked about them kissing in the cellar while Stephen played outside.

I decided to try and find out the truth of her surmise and ascertain whether such an episode, if it did occur, could have had an effect on Stephen's subsequent behaviour and predilections. I am not a great believer in the single traumatic event that explains all, or in the notion that releasing such a trauma will restore a person to so called normality, but I do believe we are the product of nature and nurture in equal parts, and I was curious to know whether he had been aware of, or even witness to, his nanny's activities.

His sister Irene was not helpful, at least not to start with. She said she regretted having given me access to Stephen's papers, and, despite my assurances that all names had been changed, she said she now wished the matter to be left alone. But, two months after my letter asking if she knew the whereabouts of Sally, I received a second reply. I had, she said, ended up making her curious too, and she had done some research on my behalf. Sally was alive and well and living in Scarborough with her husband of forty years, a retired gardener and odd-job man. She had not herself made contact with the former nanny, but she gave me Sally's address and telephone number with the proviso that, if I did 'make a call,' I should be discreet and considerate, and bear in mind that not all elderly people liked 'raking over the coals.'

I rang Sally and got her husband on the line. Sally was away on a Women's Institute coach trip to Scotland, but would be back on Saturday. He added that if I was from social security could I please sort out their 'special needs' payment as soon as possible. Then he said goodbye and put the phone down. Sally rang on the Sunday at lunchtime, announcing herself as Mrs Hibbins. She said she had traced my number by ringing the 1571 service on her return from Scotland. They did not get many phone calls and she was concerned her husband might have missed something important. I explained who I was and the research I was involved in. I said I was studying the life of village women in the nineteen fifties, with particular reference to childcare, and that I had been given her name by Irene Mason.

She was silent for a moment and then asked if I meant Stephen Mason's sister. I said yes, hoping she would give me some indication as to whether she knew of Stephen's death. But, after a further silence, she merely asked how she could help and what it would involve. I said that I would like to come and interview her and that, prior to doing so, I would send her some questions to consider. I stressed that her name would not be used or published and added that I would be happy to pay her a small fee for any assistance given.

That clinched the deal and we settled on December 10th – a Friday, when her husband would be away in Hull – for our meeting.

I drove up on the Thursday and stayed the night in a village on the edge of the North York Moors. Irene refused to tell me which village she and Stephen had been brought up in, so I picked one at random, hoping to get some idea of how life might have been for Sally fifty years earlier. But the village I chose was now a dormitory for commuters to York and Leeds, and even the smallest cottage had been spruced up and painted over.

The next morning, beneath a pale winter sun in a cold blue sky, I drove across the moors to Scarborough – vaguely wondering if it was the same route the Brontë sisters had taken in their father's carriage, and preparing my approach to Sally.

As it turned out, preparations were not needed. Sally was a warm and welcoming woman in her mid-seventies, who took me under her wing as if I were her long lost brother. She lived above the steep, crumbly cliffs of North Bay in a street dominated by Victorian guesthouses with 'Vacancy' signs in net-curtained windows. Hers was a more modest affair, a two-storey semi-detached from the nineteen fifties with stucco walls, front garden and a neatly trimmed hedge. She took my coat and sat me down in the 'front parlour,' a small living room with television, three armchairs and a tiled fireplace covered in photographs of children and grandchildren. She returned with two cups of tea and a sheet of paper on which she had written answers to my questions.

She sat down and smiled at me.

"It's about Stephen, isn't it, love?"

I nodded.

"Irene rang me," she continued. "Told me about him dying. Terrible business."

I nodded again, and saw a tear come to her eye.

"Such a sweet, loving lad. No trouble. Always keen to please."

She shook her head and surveyed the photographs on her mantelpiece.

"Like one of me own, he was. Little Stephen Mason."

She took out a handkerchief, which she had tucked up the sleeve of a grey cardigan, and dabbed her eyes.

"Irene's a naughty girl, though," she sighed. "Not telling me about the funeral. But I'll visit his grave. It's in the village, you know. Irene arranged that. He'll be at home."

And so our conversation began, without need for questionnaires or bogus research, and, after an hour, I had learned all there was to learn about Sally and Stephen.

After further coaxing, we turned to Muriel. She said that Muriel had been the village bad girl and interested in 'one thing only,' and it made no difference to 'that one' whether the person she was kissing was a 'lad or a lass.' Sally admitted she had fallen for Muriel – and that they had done a bit of canoodling – but it had not amounted to much.

When I asked if they had ever gone down into the cellar of the Mason's house to kiss, Sally had to stop and think.

"Yes, we may have done," she said finally. "It's a while back now, though."

I nodded, but felt she was hiding something and, despite Irene's warning, I pressed on. I said that, towards the end of his life, Stephen had been obsessed with the notion of a cellar, a cellar that held some secret for him. Did Sally have any idea why?

Again, Sally went silent.

After a while, she began shaking her head back and forth and up and down, as if debating with herself whether to reveal something.

Eventually, she spoke.

"There were this one time," she began. "This one time."

And then, after taking a deep breath, she went on to recount a tale of village life from fifty years before, a tale that, perhaps, throws light on Stephen's search – or not.

One summer afternoon, when he was three, Sally had put him out in the garden with an old enamel hipbath full of water. He was romping around in it naked when Muriel turned up. She had seen Mrs Mason drive off to York and knew there would only be Sally and Stephen at home, as Irene was away at boarding school and Mr Mason at work in Leeds. Stephen seemed happy splashing about, and the hipbath was too shallow for him to drown in, so Sally had allowed Muriel to take her down to the cellar. Once there, Muriel had opened a bottle of beer and begun kissing Sally.

She had removed Sally's blouse and bra and then taken off her own blouse and bra and begun 'fooling around more serious, like.' Without them noticing, Stephen must have opened the cellar door and come down the steps, because he suddenly called out that he needed a 'wee.'

"I looked round and there he was, staring up at two sets of naked boobs."

Sally covered her breasts, but Muriel leant back against the wall and stuck her tongue out at Stephen, who was shivering and, like most small boys in need of a wee, sporting an erection. Muriel joked that 'someone was pleased to see her' and grabbing a ribbon from Sally's hair bent down to tie it around Stephen's penis. Sally tried to stop her, but their struggle made Stephen more nervous and he urinated onto Sally's new sandals. Sally picked him up, put him over her lap and smacked him, telling him he was a 'Dirty little boy!' Muriel drained her beer bottle, ruffled Stephen's hair and offered him a tit to suck. Sally had then stopped smacking Stephen and started hitting Muriel. Stephen had wriggled onto the floor and run off up the cellar stairs. Muriel had shouted after him that he'd better not tell his mother or she'd come and bite his turnip off. And that was it.

By the end of the story, Sally had tears in her eyes, but she was laughing.

"Poor lad," she chuckled. "I wouldn't let Muriel near him after that. Nor me."

I smiled and waited for her to go on.

"Didn't do him no harm, though," she said, after a pause. "He were right as rain when I came up to garden. Splashing around in bath, right as rain. Not crying or upset, like. Not in the mopes cause he'd just been down in cellar with two loony lasses."

She laughed and took a handkerchief from her cardigan sleeve to blow her nose.

"Don't want to rush you, love. But I've a bring-and-buy starting in ten minutes."

I apologised for keeping her, offered some money, which she refused, and then, after thanking her for her help, left the house and drove off.

It had been a worthwhile trip and I wondered, as I headed south past neat Yorkshire villages bathed in winter sunlight, how one afternoon could resurface fifty years later and cause such consternation in an adult mind.

Or was there something deeper still within the cellar's darkness?

Had Sally held the key for all those years within her memory, or was the key still hidden in the darkness of the great beyond, in the endless time and space before birth and after life? Or was it lost forever in the infinite, now defunct recesses of Stephen's mind, that far-from-perfect entity which guides and misguides us while we live? Or was there not a key at all, the cellar just a place below within our common self; a space we cross at dawn of life and re-cross at its dusk, through open door, down slippery steps to death.

www.ingramcontent.com/pod-product-compliance
Lightning Source LLC
Jackson TN
JSHW020016141224
75386JS00025B/548